Beneath *the* Surface

MIRANDA RAE CARTER

Copyright © 2013 by Miranda Rae Carter
First Edition – August 2013

ISBN
978-1-4602-1977-5 (Hardcover)
978-1-4602-1978-2 (Paperback)
978-1-4602-1979-9 (eBook)

Age Category: Upper Young Adult and Adults aged 16+

Summary: After being rescued from a deadly car crash, Melissa "Liss" Lawrence is pursued by Rion, a young malion healer, who is wanted for murder.

Edited by Jessica Lowdon

Copy edited by Micheline Brodeur, Purple Pen Editing

Cover design by Kim Killion, The Killion Group

Produced by:
FriesenPress
Suite 300 – 852 Fort Street
Victoria, BC, Canada V8W 1H8

www.friesenpress.com

Distributed to the trade by The Ingram Book Company

Dedication

No one is more deserving of this than my editor, Jessica Lowdon, who believed I could craft a roaring bonfire from a tiny, fraught spark; and because a bazillion thank-you's would never be enough.

The heart has eyes which the brain knows nothing of.

Charles H. Perkhurst

Prologue

He was afraid it was too late, but he wouldn't give up until her soul absconded. With shaking hands, he hugged her frail, young body close to his chest. When he could finally compose himself enough to speak, he looked up at the cold, starry sky, and cried: "Return to me! Return to me!"

He met her vacant eyes once again, and a vast heat rose from his hands. But it was too late. She exhaled a last, trifling breath. He leaned over her, overcome with excruciating guilt.

But as he crouched there, holding her still body and surrounded by carnage, his eyes cleared, and his heart was lifted. He looked east to the rising sun and smiled, for he knew they would meet again. And he knew also that he would wait for her. That no matter the number of lifetimes they lived unknown to one another, when they finally met, they would be together. The next time, he would let no one separate them.

I

I'd managed to avoid talking about Jeff Philips' party all day, mostly thanks to the looming deadline of our chemistry presentation, which my best friend, Chelsea, and I were immersed in finishing. But, at the stroke of 3:03 p.m., we were done, and there wasn't much else to talk about. As we strolled out of class into the hall, our fellow grade twelves swapped details about the party with ear-splitting glee. Everyone I passed claimed to know something fresh-squeezed and juicy.

I knew Chelsea would want us to go for her birthday, but house parties were the kind of thing that took me thousands of kilometres beyond my comfort zone. However, when my best friend wanted something, she could be absolutely *tenacious*, so I wasn't surprised when she cornered me in front of our lockers before I had the chance to bolt home.

"So. Tonight's Jeff's party."

"Yeah…"

"Well, do you want to go? You haven't said a word about it all day."

"I dunno. I'd rather not."

"Oh come on, what else are you gonna do tonight?"

"Still…"

"Pleeeeeeaaaaaassse!" she begged, holding my clammy palm, her grey, inquisitive eyes locked on mine.

I spotted a poster across the hall out of the corner of my eye, and inspiration struck. "Why go to the party when we can see that really cool laser show at MacMillan Space Center? You love that kind of stuff. I'll take us out for sushi and then—"

"No way." She turned her nose up and shook her head. "I really want to go to Jeff's tonight. And it's my birthday weekend, so I get to choose!"

We were back to square one. She was puckering her lips with irritation, but I wasn't ready to wave my white flag yet, even though I was out of excuses and drained of ideas. I frowned and looked down at my seriously scuffed winter boots.

"What, Liss? *What?*" she demanded. "Why do you keep avoiding everything to do with grad? This is our last year of high school, and you never want to go anywhere except to the bookstore or the movies. You're totally missing out, you know."

I took a deep breath. "It's just not my thing, that's all."

"Why?"

I looked up at the ceiling, hoping that some divine courage would rise within me, but I felt nothing when I looked back into her eyes. I swallowed hard and answered, "I'm sorry Chelsea. I just can't."

"Is this about that Kyle guy who was mean to you at some party way back when?"

My heart leapt into my throat at the sound of his name. I hadn't heard it in months, and now I wish I'd never told her about him—even though what I'd revealed to her was mostly false. "I...I don't know."

She huffed, and tossed her backpack over her shoulder. "You know what, Liss? Forget about it. We've been friends for a year, and you're not even willing make an exception for one *little* time when something's important to me. So here's the deal: I'm going. With or without you."

I called her back as she walked away, but all I got was a grumble in return. She stormed out of the school, checking the door open with her hip as if it were one of her soccer opponents, and at that moment I had this sickening feeling that I'd finally managed to push my best friend away for good. Make that my only friend.

As I drove home, I realized that I should have feigned excitement the moment she asked me. I should have jumped up and down (okay, maybe not that enthusiastic), or cracked a smile instead of glowering. Chelsea hadn't balked at my birthday movie last December—even though I knew she hated it. So fair is fair. But the second she brought up Jeff's party, I'd shifted into survival mode again, even though it didn't work. With her, it never did. Since my first day at Gladstone Secondary just over a year ago, she always had a way of getting under my skin, but in a really good way. That is, until today.

I parked my car in front of my house, slipped through the front door, and closed it as quietly as I could. I could feel myself losing control as I thought about what I was going to have to do tonight, and I needed a moment to pull myself together before Mom discovered me. My stomach had been summersaulting on the drive home, and the scent of lemon Mr. Clean I now found myself suffocating in wasn't helping. I licked the salty sweat from my lip, and closed my eyes as I supported myself against the back of the door. My knees were shaking, threatening to buckle, but I willed myself to stay vertical.

I told myself to relax, clenching my teeth together and driving my nails into my palms to prevent the primal scream I felt building—the kind that's long and loud enough to ruin your vocal cords for a day or two afterward. I hated how weak I was at those moments.

I pulled the invitation to Jeff's party from my bag; it was a crumpled disaster. When I looked down at the sparkly plum cardstock, I wished again that I could have put Chelsea off with a convenient excuse, instead of waffling around, trying to avoid admitting the truth: I just didn't want to go.

I don't know why Chelsea's enthusiasm for her first party surprised me so much. After all, I had felt the same way, once upon a time. I remember what the evite looked like, and how light-headed I became as I skipped around the house getting myself primped and polished. I'd changed my outfit ten times before settling on a blue chemise with a little daffodil embroidered on the bottom, a jean skirt with navy blue tights, and my beige Toms.

I shuddered suddenly at the memory, and grasped my head tightly as I attempted to shove the memories of that night back into the darkest corner of my mind, where they belonged. Where I hoped they'd never surface again.

Though I knew they would. They always do.

I couldn't possibly let Chelsea go to Jeff's alone. Not a chance. I was going to have to show up, and even though I knew she'd probably shoot me dirty looks all night, I just needed to know she was safe. The last thing I wanted was Chelsea getting taken advantage of by one of Jeff's drunk 'roid monkey friends. Grade twelve boys here in Vancouver probably weren't all that different from grade twelve boys back in Edmonton.

I took a deep breath and looked at my watch. Three forty-five. I had just under three hours. Why does time always speed up when you're dreading something? Stupid Murphy's Law.

I thought about texting Chelsea, but as soon as I bent down to reach for my purse, the door opened behind me, knocking me to my knees. When I yelped, a voice barked back, "Why are you standing in the doorway? Get out of the way." It was my sister, Katherine. As I got up and turned around, the vanilla body spray she'd bathed herself in almost made me gag. She was holding her own purple invitation and fanning herself like she was just crowned Miss Teen Universe or something.

It looked like Katherine was going to the party, too. She saw the invitation in my hand and guffawed. "Where'd you get that?"

"Jeff gave it to me before first period."

Katherine rolled her eyes. "Awesome." She swiftly adjusted her purse onto her shoulder and marched past me. Her stiletto boots on

4

the laminate echoed throughout the house, shaking the floor with each *stomp.*

Having a sister who is almost a whole year older, but still shares the same grade is completely overrated. It freaking sucks—particularly when you don't get along. My stomach gurgled as she disappeared into the living room. It was time to get something to eat, because I certainly wouldn't be touching any food or drink at the party—especially if someone else was getting it for me.

One cucumber sandwich and three Tums later, I felt marginally better. I grabbed my bag and headed toward my room, but when I got to the foot of the stairs, there were six boxes stacked, labeled and ready for the neighbourhood garage sale next weekend.

Crap. I'd forgotten about agreeing to help Mom.

"Hi Mom!" I called up to the second floor.

She came out, her hair held back by a bright green bandana, sweating through her tank top under her boobs and armpits, but smiling. She loved organizing and was clearly in her glory with the fall cleanout in full swing. Even though Mom and I look exactly alike—chocolate eyes and thick red hair (though mine is miles shorter)—I highly doubt I'm going to be as much of a clean freak as her when I get to that age. In fact, I know I won't.

"Hi, Lissy!" She huffed and puffed to catch her breath. "How was your day?"

"Um…good." I made my way up the stairs and past the umpteen boxes stacked at the end of the hallway. How do you tell your mom you had a fight with your best friend, her other daughter needs a serious dose of happy pills, you have two hours of math homework, and the only words that came out of your mouth on the drive home had four letters? You don't. She didn't need to be burdened with my stupid problems, anyway. She had way more important things to think about, like keeping up with her medical bills. "I had a great day."

"Great, honey." She smiled at me. "Do you have a moment to help me with these boxes? My back is getting sore from all this lifting."

She began to pick up a box of books with her free arm, clearly straining to stand upright, so I quickly stepped in. "Let me take those, Mom. You shouldn't be doing all this by yourself. You know what the doctor said." I snatched the box from her arms and balanced it on top of my shoulder. "I can carry these, go sit down for a while."

"Thanks." She bent around to loosen up. "I wish your father was here to help me, I hate not having him around all the time—though he did phone and say that he'd be home for turkey dinner on Sunday…"

"Oh, good. I was going to ask him if he could help me with my calculus."

I lugged a few more boxes downstairs. Even though my stomach was still churning, it felt good to do something physical.

"I'm going to make some iced tea," Mom called to me from the kitchen. "Would you like some?"

"Sounds bang-a-rang." I headed back up to the next box, which hadn't been labelled yet.

When I got closer, I saw books from my childhood sticking out of the top. There waiting for me with *Go-Dog-Go*, *Wacky Wednesday* and my collection of Robert Munsch, was my childhood favourite, *Moonstone, Mae and Malion Tales*. Its red cover had faded slightly, but the title was still a shimmering gold, and I could see the black ribbon bookmark. It wasn't very heavy, and from cover to cover there were only five stories, but from the day Nan brought it back from Europe when I was four, it was the only bedtime storybook that had been read in my room. I flipped to the last story, which had always been my favourite: *Jared and the Malion*.

It had been Nan's favourite story, too. When she visited us, she would help me dress up like Princess Alysia, and read the story to me over and over again until I finally fell asleep at night. My favourite part had always been when Prince Jared came to rescue Princess Alysia from the beastly malion, who had kidnapped her and taken her deep into the Black Forest, and their ensuing fight to the death.

My eyes shot up to Katherine, who was standing in front of me with her arms crossed, wearing her two-hundred dollar jeans (thanks to her rich arse of a boyfriend), a dark grey cardigan, and more of that freaking vanilla spray (excuse me while I barf). Her short blond hair flipped out at the ends like she had purposely styled it that way, and her makeup was layers deep—and damn perfect.

"You're not going to sell that, are you?"

"I'd never sell this," I replied. "Nan gave it to me."

"No," she fired back. "She *actually* gave it to me. I let you *borrow* it because I didn't like the scary stories. But I'll have that back now."

"Oh, I—"

I started to hand it to her, but she snatched it away, adding, "And stay out of my room!"

"I didn't go in your room!" I stood up as she stormed away. "If I did, you'd know. I would have choked from the smell of that stupid spray and whatever's growing fur under your bed."

Katherine stopped suddenly and craned her neck around. She'd perfected her red carpet stance. "Why don't you shut the hell up!"

She banged her door shut, and I glued my arms to my side to stop myself from chucking something at it. I despised the relationship I had with Katherine. It hadn't always been like this between us; if I'd only stayed with her in the corn maze at that party two summers ago, things would have been very different between us today. Maybe we would have been making plans to go to Jeff's party together. Maybe she would've offered to do my makeup and lent me some of her nice clothes.

"Ready for some iced tea?"

I jumped. "Mom—you scared me!"

She looked down at the box of books and handed me a full glass. "I didn't mean to go into your closet, hon. I just wanted to bring it out so that you could decide whether you wanted to keep them or not."

7

"That's okay." I shrugged.

"Well, I'll be downstairs if you need help with anything else." She turned to go down the stairs. "Judy and I are meeting for coffee at six, and then we're going to see an early show together, so I'll be home around ten thirty. Don't forget to feed Duke—and bring him in before six tonight, it's starting to get cold earlier now."

"'kay." I was listening, but didn't make eye contact with her. I was still thinking about Katherine and how much she despised me. Then I realized Mom was still standing beside me. I could feel her eyes searching me.

"Is everything okay, Liss?"

I quickly looked up and smiled my best fake smile. "Perfectly fine, Mom—couldn't be better."

"What are you up to tonight?"

I sighed. "Well, I was thinking about going to this guy Jeff's house. He's having some people over, and he invited Chelsea and me."

Mom raised an eyebrow. "Is this the same party that Katherine is going to?"

I circled my toe on the carpet. "Yeah, I guess it is."

"Well, that's fine. But stick together, please. I don't know who this Jeff guy is, but I know that you're responsible enough to look out for yourselves. Just keep your cell phone on, no drinking, and home by eleven—okay?"

I nodded.

She gave me a gentle squeeze, and I leaned into her as she pecked the top of my head. She smelled like her water lily and lavender deodorant. I loved that scent. And I loved her little hugs; the warmth of her skin always seemed to linger with me afterwards. "I'll see you in a while, have fun tonight."

"I will."

She made her way downstairs, and I moped back to my room, only to find myself staring at my phone. I really needed to text Chelsea and apologize. I slumped down on my bed and opened up a new message, but my phone rang before I could finish. It was Chelsea.

I was surprised she wasn't texting me; it had to be important if she was calling. Maybe she wanted to give me another piece of her mind. Maybe she wanted to get rid of all my stuff at her house. I took a deep breath and answered.

"Don't hang up, Liss," she cried. "Please don't hang up."

"I won't Chelsea, I won't."

"I know you're upset, Liss. And I just wanted to call you, and tell you that I'm sorry about today. I had no right to ask you about Kyle. He was a jerk to you, and I know you hate talking about it. Crap, Liss. I can't believe what I did. I must be getting my period or something. I'm so sorry…I don't know what got into me today!"

"Don't worry about it, Chelsea. I'm sorry, too. I just…I don't know…I just think that house parties are overrated."

There was a little pause. "You know what, Liss? If you don't want to go to the party, then I don't want to go, either."

"What do you mean?"

"I'm serious, Liss, you're right. There are so many better things to do in Vancouver this weekend. I looked up that laser show, and it sounds awesome, so we should totally go. And besides, Jeff's just wouldn't be fun unless we went together. I mean, I just know that if I went by myself, I'd be sitting in a corner thinking about our fight all night, stuffing my face with chips and hot dogs, and regretting how awful I'd been to you—"

I closed my eyes. She always rambled when she was nervous. And to save our friendship, she'd reneged on her plans, putting my feelings before hers. But it didn't feel right to me; I knew how badly she wanted to go. So even though I knew I'd hate it, I gave in. This weekend was about her, not me. "Chelsea, let's just go."

"—you know….WHAT?"

"Really, Chelsea. I mean it. Let's go, okay? I'll pick you up and we'll go together."

She gasped. "Do you *seriously* mean that?"

"Yes." I gulped. I'd officially sentenced myself to a night of socializing with my intoxicated peers. "Let's go. We can drink a bunch of pop and laugh at all the drunkies if we get bored."

Chelsea giggled. "I'll pick up our sugar smorgasbord! We'll also need some salty things, because I know you like salty stuff, so bring a backpack and we'll stuff it full before we get there."

I smiled. "No way. This is your night. *I'll* pick up the goodies."

"Tell you what, pick up some gummy bears, too, and then we can lick them and chuck 'em at your sister when she's not looking!"

I burst out laughing as I opened up my closet and riffled through my sweaters. "So what time did you want to meet tonight?"

"Well, I have to stop by the gym at six and drop off my registration cheque for soccer, and then I was going to head straight there."

"Shouldn't we go in together? What if one of us gets lost?" She must have known I meant *her*, but I didn't want to make it obvious that she sucked at following directions.

"We won't, don't worry. Colin Mansfield left pretty clear directions on the back of my invitation at lunchtime. It's easy: right off the Sea-to-Sky Highway. Jeff changed the location to Colin's parent's vacation home in Oliver's Landing when he found out they were going away this afternoon, but it's supposed to be nice, so they're having a fire at Porteau Cove, just down the road. There's going to be signs up, too, in that same sparkly purple colour. You won't miss it."

I sighed out of frustration. It wasn't at Jeff's house, as I'd assumed. I hated going to places I'd never been to before. "Then text me when you get close and I'll come out to meet you."

"No, *you* can text *me*, because I'll beat you there!"

"You'd better!"

"And Liss?"

"Yeah?"

"If it becomes a big sex fest, can we just leave?"

"I'll already have the car warm, *sister*."

"You're the best, you know that?"

"Thanks, Chels. You're not so bad, yourself."

"And I wanted to tell you again that I love how you wrapped my locker this morning. No one else in the world knows how much I love rainbows."

I smiled. I'd splattered every single rainbow sticker, streamer and bow I could find at the dollar store onto purple and yellow wrapping paper, and covered her locker door, in true Gladstone tradition. It took me almost an hour to complete, but she was worth it.

We said goodbye and I changed into my brown sweater and a pair of stone washed jeggings. When six thirty came, I had the dishwasher unloaded, Duke fed and in the house, a bit of my math homework completed, and my purse in hand. Katherine had already taken off, so I locked the doors behind me.

When I sat down in my Civic, I took out the invitation and my map book (I know, I'm old-school). My nausea was back in full force, something I knew I wouldn't be able to avoid, regardless of the fact that things should be—*would* be—just fine. Hopefully, once I arrived at the cove and sat down with Chelsea for the night, it would disappear.

I rummaged around in my purse, because I felt as though I was missing something, but I didn't notice anything, so I headed toward the freeway after a quick stop at the gas station for a fill-up, candy, chips and gum.

When I arrived at the Sea-to-Sky Highway interchange, I rolled up my window and turned on the heat. The forecast said that it would be the coldest night in the Lower Mainland since the end of summer, and as I started twisting around the mountains, it didn't surprise me that it was starting to become foggy. I also realized that I hadn't turned on my cell phone. I hoped Chelsea hadn't been trying to text me.

Usually, I could locate my phone by keeping one hand on the wheel and one in my purse. But after a minute or two, when I still couldn't find it, I stopped the car and pulled over. It was becoming quite dark, so I had to put my interior light on to see inside my purse. I looked in and around the pockets, and unzipped every compartment. It wasn't there.

That's what I had forgotten.

It was seven fifteen when I pulled back on to the road, deciding to continue my search for the purple signs, but unfortunately, after another twenty minutes of twists and turns, I hadn't seen a damn thing except for a sign saying "Entering Furry Creek."

While I was trying to remember if my map book said Porteau Landing was before or after Oliver Cove or Furry whatever-the-names-were, my headlights illuminated another turn-off up ahead. There were no purple signs, but I was running late, and I began to wonder if maybe someone had just taken them down or if they had blown off in the wind. Whatever the case, I had a full tank of gas, so I turned right and headed up the hill to see if it could possibly be the one. The fog condensed as I drove, so I turned my lights down to see the road more clearly, just as I came to a fork. My first instinct was to get out and look for a fallen star, but I didn't want to chance being attacked by wildlife in the mountains, so I slowed to a stop and turned on my bright lights. Nothing.

I decided to continue for another few minutes. If I still hadn't found anything, I would go home to get my cell. I turned down my lights again, and turned to the left. At first, it was slightly wider than the road to the right, but as I continued, the road became narrow and dense with trees. The branches were so over-grown that they seemed to make an umbrella over the top of my car. And even though I had only been traveling at thirty kilometres per hour, I still couldn't see, so I shut off my headlights completely only to find the road had become a little slippery as well.

And then there were no more reflectors. It was time to go home. Safety was much more important to me than making it to the party on time. I looked around, but the shoulder on the other side of the road was too small to make a U-turn, and on my side a large ravine had opened up. I didn't want to stop, in case a car came up behind me, so I kept going, hoping that there would be a driveway or larger shoulder up ahead. I took a last look around—

SMASH.

12

Something collided with my car. Something huge. The impact spun my car around so fast that I couldn't steer it back in the other direction. I tried not to panic as it approached the ravine, but the brakes were useless. Before I could take another breath, the car flipped upside-down over the edge and started to tumble down the embankment. I heard a blood-curdling scream—my own.

My car rolled, and then again and again, tossing my body around like a towel in a dryer. I tried desperately to cling to something, but the violent rolls threw me against the roof and cracked the side of my head into the steering wheel on the next turn. The last *BANG—crunch* I heard wrenched my neck around. That's when I closed my eyes and stopped resisting…

II

A sharp burning tingle in my arm startled me, and I jerked into consciousness. I tried to move my head, but the strength it required from my neck was much more than I could handle. Every inch of my body throbbed, I couldn't feel my legs, my whole body felt heavy—pressed—and my skull pulsed in time with a beeping somewhere off in the background. The last thing I remembered was driving up a dark road; everything after that was a complete blur—not a good thing.

I summoned just enough energy to open my eyes, and though my vision was fuzzy, I immediately found the light in the room. It was a candle. Three wicks in the center flickered intermittently, releasing enough light that I could make out a few shadows here and there. I blinked a few times.

I had no idea where I was.

As I looked around, my stomach churned and I lost control of my breathing as my chest tightened. There was nothing in the room that I recognized. It even smelled different, like burning incense, pine, and rosemary.

I suddenly realized that I must be in some stranger's house. I couldn't form a coherent thought; I just kept running through the different sorts of people who keep incapacitated teens in their homes: serial killers, sociopathic psychos…and rapists.

"Are you in pain?"

I gasped, startled. The voice was deep, and cracked on the last word.

I tried to swallow so that I could speak, but my tongue stuck to the top of my mouth, and I realized why I felt so confined: I was on an enormous bed, covered by what felt like a hundred blankets. Things were not looking good. "Where..." I coughed and attempted to clear my dry throat.

"Do not try to speak," the voice whispered back. "Just rest, Melissa."

I coughed again. "No! I...I...where—" I tried to pick up my arms, but the blankets prevented me. "Get me..." I wriggled around. "I can't—"

"If you do not lie still, you will delay your healing. Now *rest*."

I swallowed again, finally able to work up a small amount of saliva. "Tell me where I am!"

"You are below the city."

"What?" I whispered. "How did—?"

"There will be time for questions when you have recovered."

I was more awake with every second that passed, as adrenaline powered my limbs. I wanted to sit up.

"I know you are scared," the voice continued in an almost whisper, "but I will not harm you."

"I want to know who you are." I tried to lift my chest up off the mattress. "And I want to know why I'm not at home."

"My name is Rion. Be still, Melissa. We will talk about home when you are more coherent. You have a serious concussion, and I fear that you will not understand or remember if we discuss this right now."

I felt as if I understood perfectly. "How do you know my name?" I asked with as much confidence as I could gather, trying to prevent my tongue from bonding to the roof of my mouth again.

"I found your identification in your purse when I pulled you out of your car."

"Pulled me out of my car?" I began to cough again.

15

"Your car spun out of control and flipped down a ravine."

I thought for a moment. I didn't remember any of that. "How did you find me?"

He exhaled hard. "I…I saw the entire thing."

I just stared at the ceiling with my mouth hanging open. I didn't know how to respond.

"I sense that you are still frightened, but—"

"Because this isn't a hospital!"

"No."

I gulped. I was shaking now. "How long have I been here?"

"Just a few days. We have a doctor who has been checking on you. It was better to bring you here than the hospital. You would not have made it that far, anyway."

I felt better when he said "doctor" and "we," but what I really wanted to know was *exactly* whom I was speaking with. That's right. I wanted a last name, an ID number, and anything else he was willing to offer. "Where—" I coughed and tried to turn my head around, ignoring the pain it caused me. "Where are you?"

"Over here, by the door."

I tried to turn my head in the direction of his voice, but it was behind me, and I couldn't turn my neck that far. "I can't see you."

"I know. And I will keep my distance, if you do not mind. This is a strange place for you, and I do not want to upset you by coming any closer."

That made me feel a little better; distance was good. And he could just *stay* over there. But I still had many more questions that I wanted answered. "How did I get here?"

"I carried you."

"*Carried* me?"

"You were unconscious when I found you in your car, so you would not have remembered. And…it was upside down. You would have died of exposure if I had left you."

"Oh my goodness." I felt goose-bumps develop on my arms. He saved my life. "I—"

A low growl abruptly stopped me.

16

"You would not have been in such a condition as *this*, had you been wearing a seatbelt!"

His sudden change of tone startled me. "But I just—" Then I heard something slide in the background, like a chair moving across the floor. "Rion?"

"I am going to leave for a few moments to contact the doctor now that you are awake. Do you need something? A cup of broth? Are you hungry?"

If he was upset that he had to bring me here, well that made two of us. I looked around again to see if I could get a glimpse of him, but he purposely stayed out of my line of vision. "I'm really thirsty, actually. I would really—"

"Very well, then." He was in a rush to leave.

"Thank y—" I coughed. A sharp pain suddenly pierced my chest, causing me to cry out. When I opened my eyes again, a giant black hood appeared above me and two large warm hands grasped my shoulders.

"Are you in pain?" the hood asked firmly.

I was frozen still as the mysterious hood above me waited for an answer, his hands moving slowly toward my neck. I wanted to scream, but I couldn't.

"Tell me if you are in pain!"

I winced, turned my head away from him, and began to shake uncontrollably. "P-p-please...I would just really like some w-w-water...please."

Rion took his hands off of my shoulders, stepping back as if I had shocked him.

"You are only making things worse for yourself by not telling me...and the swelling on the side of your head will worsen if your blood pressure surges." His heavy footsteps shook the bed. He was walking away. "If you are truly well at this moment, I will fetch you some water and return shortly." More stomping. Each foot hitting the floor rang like a grandfather clock going *BONG-BONG-BONG* inside my head.

"Rion?"

"Do not get out of bed. The doctor will be here shortly. I will answer your questions when your examination is complete."

I shook my head. "Do you have a phone that I could use? I would really like to call home and—"

"Not now."

I picked my head up off of the mattress—it hurt but I didn't care. "Please let me use the phone! Why can't I—!"

The door slammed shut.

"Wait!" I wanted to say more, but I was back into another hacking fit.

When I was finally able to catch my breath, thoughts began running through my mind: Would he really *not* hurt me? Did he lock the door behind him? Why did he hide behind that hood? What if he never let me go?

"Screw this." I didn't care about his warnings anymore. I was getting the hell out.

I lifted my head off the pillow. The pain in my neck surged, but I ignored it and pushed back on my elbows to prop myself up and almost blacked out from sitting up too quickly. It was clear that I couldn't stand, but as soon as I could, I was leaving.

I lay my head back down on the bed to rest for a moment, discovering that my eyes had finally adjusted to the room. I was frustrated that I was so weak, but there was very little I could do at the moment, so I slowly began to look around. There were piles of books, a desk, a laptop, and a clock showing six o'clock. The walls looked like they were made of stone, giving the room a rounded shape, almost as if it had been carved out like a cave. It was cold, but I had so many blankets on top of me, it was only my face and arms that sensed it. The bed was soft, and something furry underneath me softened it more.

I wondered how long Rion would be gone. I also thought about my parents and Chelsea; surely they were looking for me. And Duke, he must have thought he'd done something wrong when I didn't come back. I had run away once before, but certainly everyone knew this time was different. I hoped they weren't just waiting for me to come home, that someone had found my car and knew something was wrong.

Minutes later, the silence in the room was broken by muffled voices, though I couldn't understand what was being said. I figured the doctor must have arrived. Then the voices became louder, as if someone was yelling. A loud clang made me jump, and then a growl made the hair on my arms stand up.

My heart sank as I considered the implications of a visit from the doctor. What if the doctor wanted to sedate me again? I resolved to not let that happen; I was going home. It was time to try standing again.

I sat up, gritting my teeth through the pain, and pushed the blankets away. I was dizzy from the position change, but I could see well enough to know I was not wearing my own clothes. I was dressed in some kind of a cotton wrap. I touched the side of my head where it had been pounding away; it was so tender, it made me cringe just to brush my fingers across it.

I looked down and saw an IV in my left hand, and a catheter coming from my privates. I remembered having something similar when my appendix was removed, only this situation was much different, and—

Oh my God.

Someone had touched me. *There.*

It was probably that complete stranger of a doctor, who may not even *be* a doctor.

Or it could have been Rion.

I lost it. My heart began to hammer my ribcage and my whole body blazed. I needed to escape—fast. No more pain medications, no more *anything*. The first thing I needed to do was get rid of the tubes, then I could search for something to defend myself with on the way out. I reached down and gently removed the catheter (it wasn't the first time I was grateful for having an RN mother), and slowly began removing the tape from the needle in my hand, clenching my teeth when the little hairs were plucked one-by-one out of their follicles.

I looked around for something to put over the needle site before I took it out, but there was nothing within close range, so I stood up, intending to get a tissue from the desk nearby. But as soon as I put weight on my feet they gave out, and I landed on the bed sideways, crushing my arm and pushing the needle right into the bone. I screamed.

Rion ran in, clouds of steamy breath puffing from his hood. I could tell he was pissed.

Well, I thought, welcome to the club!

He dropped the tray he was holding, sending bowls of broth and food crashing to the floor, and rushed to my side, somehow still keeping his face concealed. "*Melissa*...I asked you *not* to get out of bed for a good reason. Just look what you have done!"

I pushed myself back up and glared at where I thought his eyes should be. Even though I was ready to pass out from the pain in my hand, I wanted to face him straight on. And I discovered he was a giant. He stood much taller than my six-foot father, and judging by the size of the cloak he wore, he was quite a bit wider, too. I was scared, but I also wasn't going to sit there and let anything else happen against my will. I held my stare and hissed, "Don't come near me...and...you...you get me a phone...right... *RIGHT NOW!*"

"You are in no condition to be arguing with me." He was scornful. "Now lie back down!"

"The hell..." I closed my eyes for a moment as my head spun, and when I opened them again, Rion was spinning, too. "The *hell* I will. Stay away from me!"

"Melissa...stop this right now," Rion retorted. "You are being ridiculous. Give me your hand, you are—" He reached out, but I leaned back.

"Don't touch me!" I could feel something warm trickling down my wrist, and when I looked down at my hand, my vein was gushing red syrup everywhere. The pain of the needle in my hand suddenly became overwhelming as I focussed on it; it was time to get the thing out before it did any more damage. I took the plastic hub between my fingers, and tried to rip the damn thing out, only my hand was too weak; I lost my grip and the lights in the room suddenly began to blur.

"Melissa? *Melissa!*"

Rion quickly scooped me into his arms, hesitated, and pulled the wrap down lower on my legs. I began punching and kicking with what little strength I had left. "Let *GO* of me!"

He laid me back down on the bed as I thrashed about and bucked beneath him. "Stop fighting me, *y'ebesha maen*," he griped, "*vi sectoni forez commu daren'ush bould*—you are making it worse!"

"GET OFF ME!"

I made a fist with my good hand, as I'd been instructed in self-defence class, and when the moment was right, I connected it with something solid under that freaking hood. He stopped for a moment and then shook it off, snarling at me. I screamed right back. He pinned me down with his chest, so I arched my back and tried to kick him away, but then, as he tried to stop me from struggling, he reached over and grabbed my bad hand, pushing the needle even farther in. I felt the needle pop out through my palm and screamed again, just as the room vanished.

III

Intense voices startled me back into consciousness. One I recognized as Rion's deep voice, the other wasn't familiar to me.

"I did not—!" Rion sounded desperate. "She was just—!" He growled and muttered a few sentences I didn't understand. He was speaking a completely different language. The other deep voice growled back in the same language. How many people were in the room?

The two deep voices argued viciously above me, but I was too weak to respond, and I felt myself drift away again.

§

The next time I came to was when a door slammed, but this time I heard what seemed like a female voice.

"She looks perfectly fine, Rion. Her respiration is naturally much faster than yours, because she's human. Just calm down, you're not helping her by getting worked up, *remember*? Her vitals have been completely normal, and she's had three transfusions already."

"Does she need more?"

That was definitely Rion. I thought I heard an edge of fear in his hard tone.

22

I tried to open my eyes, but they were so heavy I gave up my efforts, allowing myself to drift in and out of the conversation.

"...accepting it...no there isn't..."

"What if...?"

"She's just weak now, but she'll come around soon. It's just syncope..."

Rion muttered something I didn't understand, and the female voice replied, "You need to trust me, all right? I promise that I won't hurt her, just let me make sure you wrapped her hand properly...It's okay, Rion. You can watch everything that I'm doing... *nee neena chembeas porvoctious, y vensa...cha coombidean y'ebesha maen tormehtu yoon pen tivis...y vensa Rion.*" The woman's accent was very strong, but I couldn't place it because she spoke so softly, almost whispering, just as Rion had at first. I wanted to speak up for myself, but I was so weak, I couldn't form the words.

"Can we not sedate her? What if she tries to get up again? I do not want her to hurt herself."

"You can't sedate a concussion patient, Rion, it's very dangerous. You'll just have to keep her calm in the very best way you can. And if that means giving her *space*, you need to find the strength do that." There was a little pause and then a warm hand touched my shoulder. "Melissa ...Melissa can you hear my voice?" the woman asked softly. "How long has she been out, Rion?"

"At least an hour and a half," Rion grumbled. "But her eyes are fluttering. Maybe she can hear us speaking."

I shook my head and blinked a few times, but I couldn't focus.

"She's opening her eyes, Rion. Maybe you'd better leave us for a few moments."

"I am staying right here."

"She's probably frightened. Please don't make it more difficult for me. I also need to examine her, and you will *not* be in the room for that."

"I am not leaving until she is awake and settled. She is much stronger than you think, and I want to be here if you need me."

23

"Very well…Melissa, dear, can you open your eyes? You need to wake up. We need to ask you some questions." There was a shift on the bed, and then, "No Rion, *wait*—!"

Someone took my hand. Large, hard and calloused digits slipped between mine and squeezed tight. At the touch of that hand, what felt like the strongest static charge of my life shot through me. My eyes opened immediately and I gasped. "What…what was *that*?"

Two black eyes and one large smile greeted me. It was the woman who had been speaking. I was relieved to finally meet someone with a face, and someone female. I relaxed—a little.

"She's awake. Give her some space, Rion," the woman ordered. Then she looked back into my eyes. "Melissa, my name is Dr. Abeo Mubarak. I am here to help you."

She was wearing a St. Paul's Hospital tag with her photo on the front, and I recognized the name. Dr. Mubarak was one of the best trauma physicians in Vancouver, someone many other doctors wished they could be. Her name had been in the papers for saving lives in the most unlikely circumstances. Mom had spoken of her medical expertise on many occasions.

I hoped she had come to get me out.

"Something…just shocked me." There was a moment of silence where she and Mr. Hood looked at one another and then again at me. I looked back and forth between them, waiting for them to say something, but they just stared. "Would somebody please tell me what's going on?"

Dr. Mubarak took my bandaged hand, inspecting as she carefully unwrapped it. "Well done, Rion. Looks like it has healed well." Rion nodded.

"Excuse me, my other hand?" I interrupted, staring into Rion's hood. "What did you just do to it?"

"What's most important is that you are awake," Dr. Mubarak answered as she touched my forehead. "How does your head feel, dear?" She had the most beautiful black eyes, smooth dark skin, and when she smiled widely at me, I couldn't help but smile back.

"I'm okay, I guess. Thank you, Dr. Mubarak."

24

"Please call me Abby." She shone a light in both of my eyes. "You had quite a bit of swelling on the left side of your head, but it has come down in the last twenty-four hours, and your pupils are no longer dilated. The anti-inflammatories are doing their job."

"I want to go home, Abby."

"I know you do, Melissa. But it is a dangerous time to take you home. Please don't ask why, dear, I—"

"No, you don't understand!" I said as loud as I could. "I'm not staying here—I just—I can't—" I was breaking up and coughing.

Rion shot up to his feet, but Abby raised her hand to stop him. She turned back to me. "Melissa, please. I know you're upset, but I can't take you home right now. It is too dangerous at the moment, and there is a lot you need to know before that happens."

I shook my head. "What do you mean? I don't understand why you can't just call an ambulance or something!"

"Let's start with the basics, all right? Let's get you up and see if you can walk first. Then we'll talk about going home."

"All right." I felt slightly more relieved.

"Do not move too quickly, Melissa," Rion said.

I glared at him. He was sitting in the corner, and I could feel his eyes on me, though I couldn't see them. I was suddenly very irritated with him. I was irritated with this entire situation. And why wouldn't he show me his face?

"How about you take my arm and we'll sit you up first," Abby said. "If you feel like you want to stand, I'll assist you." She let me hold onto her arm while I pulled myself up. I was light-headed and sore everywhere, but it seemed to fade after a few deep breaths.

"Just give me a second." I was concentrating hard. "Then I'd like to stand."

"Very good. When you're ready, just hold onto my arm and we'll go slowly. Remember, you've been lying down for a few days, so your legs will tire easily."

"That's fine. I'd still like to try."

"Good."

I took hold of her arm again. She braced herself, looking prepared to catch me. My arms felt weak as I strained myself to stand, but together we lifted my pathetically frail frame until I was upright. It took a lot of effort for me, but I willed myself through it. I had climbed the Grouse Grind many times the past summer, so this shouldn't have been difficult, but it truly was. My legs were shaking from the weight of my body.

"Would you like to take a step or two? I'll keep my arm here for you to hold on to if you need."

"Sure." I smiled at her. "It feels so good to get up." I took a deep breath. As wobbly as I was, I took two steps with the help of her arm then another rocky one before I stopped.

"Have you had enough, Melissa?" She patted my hand gently. "Maybe we should sit you back down and try again later."

I could tell that she wanted me to quit, but I wanted to leave; this was my ticket out. "No, I think I'd like to try a few steps on my own this time."

"Okay," she said warily, letting go of my arm and stepping back to give me some room. "I'll be right here just in case you need me."

"Thanks."

I stood still for a second to balance myself. I knew that I could walk on my own, even if it wasn't very far. I took one more deep breath and raised my left leg slightly, but as soon as I transferred all of my weight to my right leg, it gave out and I fell backward. Abby was standing too far in front of me to catch the hand I reached out for her, and I squealed thinking about my head hitting the rock hard floor. But I didn't get that far; two giant arms were around my waist and legs instantly, lifting me before I could hit. I sucked in a breath, just as my face turned to the side, and my mouth dropped open—Rion's bright green, almond-shaped eyes were staring directly into mine.

We stood there for a moment, staring at one another, both in shock. He was like nothing I had seen, or known to exist outside of the movies. The closest face I had seen to his was constructed of latex and makeup. I wanted to reach out and touch him to see if he was real, because his features were distinctly catlike: his nose was broad and square, just like a cat's, and his upper lip was indented down the middle, like a cat's, although it wasn't split in two. His face was covered in golden peach fuzz, but the hair on his head was dark brown, long, and mane-like, hanging just past his shoulders. When I touched it with the tips of my fingers behind his back, it was soft and fine, not like a human's. I couldn't see his teeth, and wondered for a moment if they were sharp.

It was then that I noticed the scars. The tip of his left ear was missing, and there were two long lines that extended from the upper left corner of his forehead, to the lower right side of his bottom lip. I wondered who could have done such a thing.

He looked down as if he was ashamed of himself, and took a step toward the bed, whispering, "I will put you back on the bed now, you have had enough for today."

I couldn't speak. I was still in shock. This massive man seemed to be shying away in my presence, and the only thing I could do was swallow—hard. He turned around to leave. I was going to call him back, but he raised his arm and angrily swept a mug off the side of the desk as he stormed past it, and slammed the door behind him on the way out. I winced as the cup shattered into pieces on the stone floor.

"Melissa."

I recoiled. I'd completely forgotten Abby was still in the room.

"I think we should keep you off your feet for one more day. Please excuse me for a moment, I need to speak with Rion privately." She turned to leave. "We won't be far away if you need something."

She pulled the door open, but turned back and smiled at me; she had obviously known all about Rion and his home below the city.

"Abby?"

"Yes, Melissa?"

"Is Rion the reason it's not safe for me to go home?"

Abby nodded and smiled. "That's part of it."

"Is he human?"

"Partly, yes. I'll explain very soon Melissa, I promise you that."

"Do you think he'll still let me go, now that I've seen him?"

"I believe so. But he's struggling with the decision because you'll be in danger above."

The decision seemed obvious to me. I couldn't stay here. And I *could* take care of myself; I didn't need him. I didn't need anyone. However, there were people at home that needed *me*, especially Mom, with Dad gone all the time.

I sighed. "Thank you, Abby."

She raised her eyebrow, as if she was wary of my intentions, then answered, "You're welcome, Melissa."

"Are you coming back?"

"Yes."

I had more questions, but I knew she needed to leave, so I just smiled back as she softly shut the door behind her. As I lay there in that large room, I wondered if there were others like Rion, how many people there were like Dr. Mubarak, who else knew about this underground place, how would I ever tell my parents about this, and if I *would* ever be able to tell my parents about this. That could only happen if I managed to get out, and right then I didn't have a lot of confidence in Dr. Mubarak. She seemed in on it, whatever *it* was.

I sat up and looked down at my weak legs. They were going to walk for me. I was going to try again. And then I was going to find a way home.

IV

I hung my legs off the edge of the bed, wiggled my toes, and swung them up and down a few times.

"Now…you're going to walk," I told them. "Don't fail me this time, all right?"

I stared at the door. It was approximately twenty feet away. I took one deep breath, searching for the last bit of tattered courage that remained in my heart, but the piney incense smoke from the burner stung my nostrils and I sneezed right before I could plug my nose. I liked the smell, but it was so concentrated in here.

I *so* needed to get home and far, far away from this place.

I wrapped my hand around the corner of the nightstand and counted to three before pulling myself slowly onto the balls of my feet. The rock floor was ice cold, sending shivers up my spine. But that wasn't going to stop me, because when I felt sturdy enough, I was going to run. Running was going to warm me up when I got the hell out of this room. I transferred my weight on my right foot. Then my left foot. Before I knew it, I was half-way across the room. I was going to make it to the door without falling down.

When I reached the door, I leaned on the cold rock wall and rested a moment. I'd come this far, and my legs were actually letting me continue. The only thing that could stop me would be a locked door, and I didn't remember hearing the *click* of a lock when Abby left, so I placed my hand on the lever and it quietly *creeeeeaked* open.

I stopped for a moment to listen, then poked my head out to see if anyone was guarding the door. There was nothing but a small gust of icy air. I shivered. It was freezing, but most importantly, the coast was clear.

I pushed myself away from the wall and ever-so-slowly let the door *creak* a few more times until it was open wide enough for me to pass through.

And I was out.

I looked both ways once again, and closed my eyes. I hesitated, trying to decide if I should be going left or right.

Deciding to go left, I opened my eyes and held onto the wall, seeing nothing but blackness in front of me. I was nervous, but I had to overcome that fear if I wanted to find my way home—stalling and worrying gets you nowhere fast. Reaching out with one hand to avoid colliding with rocks or walls, I started my way into the dark passage with my other hand on the wall for support. The smell of the underground was mustier now and much colder, almost like my Nan's basement in winter. I trembled and pressed on, hoping that walking a little faster would warm me up.

But then I stepped in a puddle of water. I jerked back, biting my lip accidentally. The temperature pierced my toes, but I gritted my teeth and walked through it. When the water covered my feet entirely, I considered giving up and going back, to spare my throbbing feet, but I made fists and continued on, and within five more steps I was out of the puddle, shaking all over from the cold.

I couldn't help imagining freezing to death in a deserted passage, never to be found. But I pushed those thoughts away; I couldn't give up now. I was only fifty feet from where I started, and my legs were already tiring, yet I kept on. It was time to start moving faster or I was going to become a human popsicle.

Ten minutes later, my legs were numb from the cold, and I couldn't feel my fingertips. I'd felt one fork in the passage and turned right, only to hit another roundabout of some sort, choosing passage number three—and all in complete darkness. There still wasn't a single glimmer of light, and I suddenly began to wonder if there ever would be. I hated being cold, and I was mad at myself for not taking a blanket from Rion's room, at least then I could have had something to sit down on, or wrap myself in. As tired as I was, I had to keep moving; it was the only thing that would keep my blood flowing. I shuddered against the frigid temperature, taking another few steps, and I felt the floor pulsate. My heart began to flutter. Something was behind me—or above me. I heard muffled sounds from further down the passage.

Rion must have discovered I was missing. Feeling a swift burst of energy, I started jogging away from the sounds with my hands out in front of me. I wasn't going back to that room. I had no idea where I was in these passages, but something, eventually, I was sure, would lead me above and home.

I stopped for a moment to make sure no one was coming up behind me, and then I ran straight into something. And it wasn't a wall. It was hard enough, but it was very warm.

Rion.

Two glowing green eyes stared directly down at me.

"Ri—" I wanted to scream, but a giant hand covered my mouth first.

"Shhhhhhhh," he whispered. "I am not who you think I am."

I reached up and tried to pull his hand away, but he stopped me.

"I will not hurt you, and I will help you if you promise not to scream. He will hear us if you do."

This was not Rion. His voice was deep like Rion's, but much softer and sweeter. And when he took his hand away, I swallowed hard, composing myself enough to whisper back, "I-I-I want to go home." I was trembling; not because I was scared, but because I was almost hypothermic.

"I know. And if you take my hand, I will lead you in the right direction."

I couldn't see anything but his glowing green eyes. "Wh-Who are you? And how do I know I c-c-can trust you?"

31

With one spark, a lighter lit and suddenly I was faced with another creature that looked identical to Rion, only without the scars. He was stunningly handsome, though not as large as Rion, and offered a sincere smile.

"My name is Rasadian. And your name is Melissa. And you do not belong here. Humans—*especially* females—do not belong in these wretched tunnels."

Rion must have been talking about me, and I was sure that everyone down here knew my name by now, however many of them there were. "P-P-Please help me get home, Rasadian. I just want to g-g-go home."

"Of course you do." He reached out to me. "Come. Take my hand. I will even carry you, if you would do me the honour, but we must hurry, Melissa."

I raised my eyebrow, wanting to trust him so badly, but I'd seen in the movies how lost girls were easily persuaded by men they shouldn't be trusting. I hesitated. This was going one of two ways.

"Quickly now," Rasadian whispered, letting the lighter go out and returning us to darkness. "They are coming!"

I looked back, and met his glowing green eyes again. Just as I was about to slip my hand into his and ask him to carry me, something growled behind us.

I jumped back and Rasadian stepped around me, placing himself in front. He growled a return threat to whatever it was that had found us. He was protecting me. I was relieved to have one of *them* on my side.

The other creature snarled, and it seemed as though they were arguing—in that same strange language. I couldn't understand anything, but from their tones, it was clearly a heated exchange.

"Step away from her, Rasadian," the other creature answered firmly in English. "She is not yours to protect, and this is none of your business. Now leave us!"

I recognized the voice immediately. It was Rion. He'd found us.

Rasadian hissed, "Perhaps you should learn a few lessons from the other males about how to speak to a female, *Brother*. You have absolutely no sense of—"

"*YE VENCA KAMED Y'FORTOS JEM*! Get out of my way!"

That's when I stepped out from behind Rasadian. "You take me home right now, Rion!"

A torch bolted to the wall beside us suddenly lit, and both the passageway and the difference between Rasadian and his brother became clear: Rion was undoubtedly taller, in fact, he had to tilt his neck down to almost ninety degrees. I realized Rasadian was no match for his brother, and that I would have to deal with Rion myself.

"You are coming back to my chambers. Right now!" Rion snapped at me.

"I don't have to do anything!" I snapped back. "I'm not staying here any longer. I'm going home, and Rasadian is going to take me, right Rasadian?"

Rion growled, and Rasadian laughed, adding, "Feisty one, is she not? Good luck, *Krighven*."

I looked between them as they exchanged a few more words in their own language.

"Could somebody please speak in *English*?" I demanded. "I don't appreciate being talked around."

"I was just warning my brother, Melissa," Rasadian said. "He knows very well that you cannot stay, but he seems to be struggling with the assembly's decision."

"What—"

"ENOUGH!" Rion silenced us and I jumped.

"Spectacular idea, Rion," Rasadian added sardonically. "Yell a *little* louder. She might not be as frightened."

"*Carsha TEN TENTAKAYS, RASADIAN*!"

"You know what? I'm tired of this." I pushed away from them.

"Melissa!" Rion barked.

"RION!" Rasadian scolded. He added a few more sentences in their language.

"Melissa," Rion spoke in a much softer tone. "Come back to my chambers."

Rasadian growled.

"*Pershav—*" Rion stopped himself, and then sighed. "You have not eaten, and I need to discuss your return home tonight. *Please* come." Then he gently touched my shoulder. I yanked it back but my heart leaped.

"I'm going *home?*"

"Yes," he muttered, "but there are things you need to understand before that happens, and I would like to speak with you—*in private*." He had come within a nose length of Rasadian when he spoke those last two words, but I knew very well he meant *me*.

I glared at him when his eyes returned to mine. "I want Rasadian to come with me."

Rasadian snorted and Rion bared his teeth at him. They *were* sharp.

"I will be waiting outside." Rasadian stared at Rion as he spoke. "If he does not keep to his word, there will be more than just myself helping him follow through. Is. That. Not. Right. *Brother*?"

Rion looked at me, and firmly replied, "You have my word, Melissa. I swear on the Creator that I will return you above this very night."

I took a deep breath, suddenly ready to fan myself from the heat wave I was experiencing from standing in between the two giant creatures. "Fine. Let's go."

"May I carry you, Melissa?" Rion asked. "Surely your legs will not be strong enough to—"

"NO THANK YOU!" Though I was unsteady on my feet, the last thing I wanted was to be any closer to him than I had to be.

When we reached Rion's chambers, he was huffing and sighing, infuriated because I refused his help each time that he offered. Rasadian kept to his promise and waited right outside, grinning from ear to ear.

"You should have let me carry you," Rion said, opening his door. "Your legs are not ready for such distance, and your muscles will not be kind if you strain them."

"I'm *fine*."

"Suit *yourself*." He growled under his breath.

I didn't bother to respond to his comment. Instead, I rolled my eyes, limped over to the bed, and slumped down. I was exhausted from all of the walking, but the only thing I was concerned about was this "discussion" of my return home.

"You must be hungry." He turned around and lifted something from his desk. When he faced me again, he had a tray of food, a large mug and a moist cloth. "I brought this for you, only you were not here when I came back. I hope it is not cold, but I will have it warmed if it is."

I looked at the tray of food when he placed it on the nightstand in front of me. There were strawberries, two bananas, grapes, various cheeses and a loaf of bread. Then I saw what was inside the mug and saliva surged into my mouth. White hot chocolate.

I hadn't had it in months. I looked up at Rion, and swallowed.

"Please." He gestured toward the tray with his hand.

I slowly reached out and took the mug, taking in the sweet scent. And when I took the first sip, it was everything I anticipated: rich, creamy—bang-a-rang.

"Take some food, Melissa. It may be a while before you eat again."

"I don't—"

"I am not taking you home until you have eaten something. Make your choice."

I scowled at him. Apparently I wasn't the only stubborn one here. "I'll never be able to eat all of this."

"Do not worry about that. I will eat what you do not."

I ignored the food and put the mug down on the tray. Rion smacked his hand on the chair beside him and looked up at the ceiling. "Please, just eat something. You look very pale, and your stomach has been growling since we have been back here."

Feeling embarrassed, I wrapped my arms around my stomach and eyed the plate.

"Go on," he encouraged again.

I picked up a strawberry as Rion sat on the floor. He buried his face in his hand and took a deep breath. I saw him rub his forehead, as if he, too, was exhausted. True, I hadn't been easy to deal with, but neither had he. Then I noticed a fresh cut above his eyebrow and remembered that I'd hit him. I must have scratched him in our little scuffle, too.

"I'm sorry about your eye."

He immediately looked up, astonished, before recovering his composure. "It is just a scratch. And I deserved it. I should not have come after you like that. I apologize, too."

"I just..." I trailed off. No sense saying why I hated people in my space.

"Is your hand all right?"

I looked down at my hand and rubbed it with the other; it was as if there had never been a wound there in the first place. "Yeah...I mean, what did you do to it?"

"Just wrapped it and washed it. The mark should be gone now, it was not significant. The needle just dislodged."

"Yeah, but it doesn't even hurt...like, at all."

"Good."

He wasn't giving me a straight answer. I could have sworn that the IV had gone through my hand or something, but I was also a little drugged, so it could have been my imagination. But that wasn't important. I glanced at Rion again, noticing his under-eyes were swollen and puffy, and I wondered if he'd slept at all since I'd been here.

I ate the strawberry; it was sweet and juicy, the taste lingering on my tongue and it felt so good to have something in my stomach, but I didn't take another. As much as I wanted to gorge myself, I needed more answers. "So when do I leave?"

Rion took a deep breath and shifted around on the floor in front of me as if he were trying to get comfortable. His chair was right behind him, but he chose the floor near me for some reason. "We have enemies, Melissa, and they walk among you. That is why we must take precautions when I bring you above tonight."

I shook my head. "I don't understand, Rion. What enemies?"

"They are *vykhars*...hunters, in English." His face hardened and he looked deep into my eyes. "They look like regular human beings. They are slightly larger and taller than average, but they also have special genetic advantages and gifts, like persuasion. Most humans do not realize when they are being persuaded, so it almost always goes unnoticed. They also have incredible strength and speed."

While I listened to him, I tried to remember if I'd ever known anyone who fit that description. I thought of my old neighborhood in Edmonton, with all the larger-than-average farm boys, but they just did a lot of chores at home, and they were by no means persuasive; if anything, they were hard-working, well-behaved gentlemen.

Except Kyle.

"Do you have special abilities too?"

"We are stronger and faster than the *vykhars*, but they have the benefit of living above. They can get whatever they need without hindrance. We do not have that luxury."

"Why doesn't anyone know that you exist?"

"That is a long story, Melissa, and not important for you to know."

"Well...what would happen if you were caught?"

"They would kill me."

I gasped. "Why?"

"Years of misunderstandings." He leaned back on his hands.

"All right," I sighed. "So you have enemies."

Rion held his finger up. "There is another issue that I need to discuss with you before we go any further."

"Okay." I took another strawberry. They were irresistible. "Shoot."

"Melissa," he swept off his hands and crossed them. "This is *serious*."

"I *know*."

"Then why are you smiling?" he growled. "Do you think this is *funny*?"

"No." I glared at him. "I was just enjoying this strawberry."

His mouth dropped. "Oh."

"Is that all right?"

"Yes. Yes it is." Then he looked down at the ground and blinked a bunch of times, almost as if he was trying to hide a smile.

"All right then." I swallowed. It really was delicious. "What were you about to say?"

"I do not want to upset you, but it is necessary for you to understand."

"Don't worry, you won't." There wasn't anything I couldn't handle; I'd been through the wringer this weekend, and I thought I managed pretty well.

"I want you to know that you can still change your mind about going home. You are safe here with me, and no one would ever find you if you decided that you would rather stay."

I shook my head. "Completely out of the question."

"Very well," he replied in a huff. He ground his teeth together again, but quickly stopped when he realized I was grimacing, adding, "I will tell you."

He had this horrible look of dread on his face, and my heart overreacted in response; all of a sudden, I wasn't sure I wanted to hear what he had to say.

"If the *vykhars* ever found out that you had contact with us, they would simply hunt you down and persuade you for information about me. You would be powerless against it, telling them exactly what they wanted to hear, and then they would have everything they needed to find my people." Then he rolled forward and came closer to me. "And *then*…they would kill all of us—and your family."

I gulped. The thought of anything endangering my family *was* serious, but I couldn't possibly stay here and let them think something horrible had happened to me. I loved my life back home, and so many things would be turned upside-down if I didn't return—I could never put everyone I loved through something like that.

"So you see the risk we are taking by letting you return home *unguarded*."

"Yes." My mouth became dry again. "But they'll never suspect anything. I'm a good liar. It won't be an issue. You don't have to worry."

Rion rubbed his hand across his forehead and shook his head.

"What?"

"I do not want you to leave, Melissa. You must know that by now. I am sick to death about it. I have never had to battle with a decision so much in my life. I do not want anything to happen to you..." Then he came closer to me and I moved back as he whispered, "I still do not know how I am going to let you out of this room, because it feels wrong. I am scared that the *vykhars* will discover you have been with me. The news issued a missing persons report on you an hour and a half ago."

"Rion...." I tried a gentler tone, hoping to reach him that way instead. "I don't belong here. Wouldn't it be easier if we just left right now?"

He shook his head. "It is too light to go out now, and it is not safe. Just a few more hours, and then it will be dark enough to camouflage me. But when you return, the hunters might be suspicious. They follow up on all missing people who just *magically* return out of nowhere."

"They'll never find out," I assured him. "I'll never talk to anyone about this, *ever*. You can trust me."

"Thank you, Melissa. That means a great deal to us. But it is *them* I do not trust."

I rested my head on the pillow. "What am I going to tell my family? I can't say I've been here."

"No. Dr. Mubarak has constructed a story that you *must* adhere to. No one can find out about your being here, nor can you ever come back—or attempt to find us." Then he turned away from me, and it sounded like he was grinding his teeth again. "*I must not exist to you after tonight.*"

That was harsh. I almost asked him if he really meant it, but changed my mind. "I...I understand."

A few silent moments passed. I couldn't stand the uncomfortable silence in the room any longer, so I decided to change the subject. "What are you, Rion? If I'm never going to see you again after tonight, will you tell me who you are and why you're here?"

"No." His hand hit the floor, startling me. "It is bad *enough* that you know *this* much about us!" He massaged his temples, heaving a sigh, before adding, "Please just eat, Melissa."

Well, there was something else that I needed to do now besides eat, but I didn't know how to ask. My bladder felt like it was about to explode. "Um, Rion. Do you think that I could, um...do you have a bathroom?"

His eyes shot up to mine. "Oh, yes, of course...you must want to...would you like to, uh...*freshen up* before we leave?" He began to wander aimlessly around the room, putting stuff this way and that. "The clothes you were wearing when I brought you here have been cleaned and folded in another room, I guess...so, uh, that would be good timing."

"Thank you." I sat myself up and smiled; typical guy, uncomfortable with girly-stuff. I guess he had more human male similarities than I originally thought.

"When you are finished, I am sure it will be close to the time that we need to prepare to leave."

"How do I get there?"

Rion stood up immediately. "May I carry you? It would probably be, you know—"

"Faster." We spoke at the same time.

"Yes, *please*." I just hoped it wasn't too far away. I sat up and he lifted me into his arms.

It was weird to be so close to him. *Uncomfortable* was a better word; I hadn't been this close to guy in forever (while conscious, that is). But it was also kind of neat. I was so high up. So... sheltered.

We left his room, travelling through a branching tunnel that forked many times. The air was chilly, but I was warm as Rion cradled me. Every twenty feet or so a torch would light the passage then it would be dark for a moment until the next torch shone through. The tunnels looked hand-carved. I counted four left turns and a right turn into different passages—I think—then finally we stopped.

"Our lavatory is just through there, Melissa." He set me down and pointed to another dark passage. "I will be waiting just around the corner. This will help you see." He touched his finger to the tip of the torch, and it burst into flame.

My mouth fell open, and he—I had to look twice—smiled at me. I smiled back, as a wave of heat washed over me. "Thank you," I finally managed to say.

"Take as much time as you need."

The bathroom was small and it smelled of lavender (just like home. I missed home!), coming from the incense that burned on the ledge of the carved stone sink. After I'd relieved myself, I had my first chance to look in the mirror since my accident, and I looked hideous: my face was bruised and swollen, and when I brushed it with my fingers I shuddered, it was so sensitive. My mascara was either smudged around my eyes or they were just black.

When I came out, Rion carried me back to his room.

"I will leave so that you can change into your clothes. I set them on the bed for you."

Rion promptly left. Everything was happening so fast; in moments I would never see this place again. But despite his warnings, I didn't want to forget that he, and this place, ever existed—I couldn't, it just wasn't possible after everything that had happened to me here. I changed quickly and sat back down on the bed, when there was a knock at the door.

"Ready!" I called back.

Rion walked in and examined me with his eyes from head to toe, and his lip curled. I pushed myself to the edge of the bed and decided to return the same scowl, though inside, I was worried about his hardened face. "What?"

"You should not be in those clothes—I had not even thought of it. My scent is all over them, and if they catch wind of you before you get home, those *manakackos* will know!" Then he growled something in his own language and turned around like he was looking for something to throw.

"Rion...I—"

"*Do not*," he interrupted, still with his back to me, hand raised. "I am about to change my mind, slam that *fenyeka dom* and keep you in here forever. So do not say another word."

"Rion please..."

"You have no idea what you have put me through in these last few days, and now you are...you are...!"

I didn't understand what came out of his mouth next, but it was nothing remotely positive. Then he leaned both arms on the door-frame, looking down at the ground. There was no getting through to him; not with words, that is. I'd seen it time and again in Dad when my parents argued, which was pretty often lately. And though it seemed crazy, something forced me to limp over to him. Mom had this magic touch with Dad, and I wondered if, somehow, it would work with Rion. I desperately wanted to go home, and at that point, I was willing to try just about anything to keep him from changing his mind.

I snuck up behind him, and noticed that he was shaking. I held my breath, then ever so gently touched his back with my fingertips.

Instantly, he spun around, astounded. I flinched and stepped back, gaping at him. "Do you think it's dark enough yet?" I managed to spit out.

He shifted away from me and looked at his watch, defeated. "Dr. Mubarak and I agreed on six thirty. We are a few minutes early, but I will take you above now. She will drive you the rest of the way home."

Not wanting to waste any more time, I replied, "Let's go then."

He huffed then picked me up in one quick motion. I wasn't sure where to put my hands or rest my head, and I had no idea how long it would take to get above from where we were, so I just sat still and hugged my arms around my waist. His irritation made things awkward again. Maybe I shouldn't have touched him.

"Close your eyes, Melissa. It is best if you do not know where the entrance is. I will tell you when to open them again."

I did just as he instructed, deciding to rest my head against his shoulder when he wrapped his thick wool cloak around me.

Twenty minutes went by then a burst of frigid cold stung my nose. We'd finally reached the outdoors, and I was dying to see where we were, but still I kept my eyes shut as he instructed. While he jogged, I thought about my parents, and what Dr. Mubarak was going to tell me. I was a good liar for small things, but this lie was *mammoth*; I hoped I could tell the story believably. Failure was not an option now.

"Open your eyes, Melissa."

His weary tone surprised me; I had thought that he was upset with me, but now I wasn't quite sure, so I didn't look up at him. We were at the edge of a forest, standing on the tiny shoulder of a country road. A black SUV was parked across the street and Dr. Mubarak was waiting in the driver's seat. She had seen us and smiled. It was almost dark and there were no streetlights, just the interior light from her car; the sun, which had almost set, gave just enough light for us to see one another. He set me down.

"This is it, I guess." I hated goodbyes. And how do you say it to the person who saved your life? I actually felt sick to my stomach.

"I should never have brought you below, Melissa. I should have taken you to the hospital, like everyone said and…I am…I am sorry."

My dad told me once that only a real man admits his own faults, so Rion's words elicited new respect, regardless of his mood swings—which were something I was likely responsible for.

"Rion…" I honestly didn't know what to say next, but then he reached into his pocket and pulled out a piece of paper.

"I know what I said before…"

He ran his hand over the top of his head and squeezed his hair. I had a moment of panic. Was he changing his mind? I took half a step back.

"…And…"

He swallowed like there was a humongous lump in his throat.

"…If you ever feel like you are in a situation that you cannot get out of, you can call this number. This is a human friend of mine, and he will bring you to me. But if you decide to come back, know that you will not be able to return to your family next time. We cannot risk exposure like this again."

With a sigh of relief, I nodded and took the paper from his hand, only he didn't let go of me right away. His thumb stroked my palm, and I felt that same heat from his hand, which made my skin tingle. This was the same hand that had shocked me into consciousness when I'd fainted in his room, and I was suddenly worried that he might not let go. I had to end this.

"Thank you," I swiftly drew my hand back.

He looked down at the ground. "Dr. Mubarak is waiting and I cannot stay here any longer. *Go*."

His words sent an imaginary stake into my chest—especially the last one. It physically hurt. I was suddenly unsure what to do, and briefly considered hugging him, but in the end I just stepped back. As I turned toward Abby's SUV, I found myself fighting back tears; not because I was sad to leave, but because walking away was suddenly much harder than I thought it would be.

When I came to the faded gold line in the middle of the road, I stopped and looked back. Rion stood there, watching me with unwavering eyes. A few awkward seconds passed where we both just stared at one another, while I snapped mental photos of him.

Despite his mandate that I erase him from my memory, I knew it wasn't possible. He'd saved my life.

My trance was broken when he grabbed a thick branch beside him, almost as if he needed to restrain himself—or brace himself. Then he nodded, encouraging me to continue across the road. I didn't want him to change his mind, so I hurried into the car.

Abby greeted me with a friendly smile. She must have known how I was feeling when I sat down, because she took my hand and gave it a gentle squeeze. I took one last look at the forest, searching the darkness, hoping I could see him just one more time, but he was already gone. I whispered goodbye to the empty bramble and trees.

Abby put the car in drive and I closed my eyes. I was never going to be the same.

Ever again.

V

Dr. Mubarak drove down the forested highway without saying a word, until the blanket of green and black above us became a haze of purple, pink, and yellow city lights under the starry sky. The closer we came to town, the more restless I became. Not even the chamber music she was playing could distract me.

"Melissa," Abby finally said, turning the volume down. "Listen to me very carefully, and follow each detail *exactly*. If you don't, you'll be endangering not only the two of us, but Rion and his family as well."

"I'm listening, Dr. Mubarak."

"Abby, please," she softly corrected.

"Abby."

"I'm taking you to St. Paul's Hospital, where I've been working for ten years. I'm going to carry you into Emergency and tell everyone that I picked you up on the side of the road. You were waving your hands for help and I was the first person who stopped, recognizing you immediately from the missing persons report I saw on TV this afternoon. I quickly examined you, and brought you straight here. You are experiencing some temporary amnesia, directly related to the trauma on the side of your head and the resulting concussion, so you do not remember anything about the

46

last few days. All you remember is waking up in your car, climbing out, and managing to find your way to the highway."

"That sounds very straightforward. I can definitely follow that." My palms were moist and warm, and my heart hadn't slowed. I wanted to go home and start putting the past behind me, and she made it sound so easy. But I knew nothing was going to be easy from now on.

"The police will be called when we arrive," Abby continued, "but I'd like to do an ultrasound and a few x-rays before anyone speaks to you. I'd like your parents to be there as well."

"Thank you, I'd really like to see them."

"They'll be a good defense for us. I'll inform the police that questions should wait, and having your parents present, I believe, will help to ensure that. I don't want you interrogated tonight. It's much too early."

Would the police actually believe me? I sighed and rested my head on my hand. I couldn't think about it any longer tonight, I was too exhausted.

"Melissa, you don't know how imperative it is that you don't answer any questions that could possibly incriminate us. You need to say, 'I don't remember,' if there is anything you're unsure of. The less detail you recall, the easier it will be for all of us. Let me take care of everything else."

"Abby, how long have you known about Rion and his family living below the city?"

"A very long time."

"How long is a long time?"

"Rion's father saved me from freezing to death years ago, when he found me in an alleyway, starving."

"How did you get below without anyone suspecting?"

"I didn't have any friends or family." She turned onto the freeway. "No one even knew that I'd left."

"Were you there for a long time?"

"I spent ten years with them, until I was ready to attend medical school. Ramses, Rion's father, has made a few friends over the years, and one of them helped me through the process of becoming a Canadian citizen. I owe Ramses my life, so when I can help him, or anyone in his family, I do—no matter how dangerous it is."

"That is truly wonderful, Abby."

"I think so too, my dear. They are the most wonderful people."

I ran my hands through my hair, and realized that I was beginning to sweat. My stomach was still churning, so I rolled down the window, letting the night air freshen my face.

"Melissa, are you all right? Are you still in pain? You haven't taken any medication tonight, and I was going to wait until we arrived at the hospital before giving you some more anti-inflammatories. That is, unless you need something right now."

I shook my head. Come to think of it, I didn't remember having much more than a mild headache all day; I'd been so distracted with leaving. "I'm just nervous, that's all. I've waited all weekend to go home, and now, I'm scared to be alone with this—this *secret*! I mean, what if—"

"Just pretend you don't remember anything." She turned off the highway. "You need to relax, Melissa. No one will expect you to come home and act normally. Post-traumatic stress is a common side-effect with accident victims—but don't over-do it." Then she patted my leg. "We'll be there soon. Take some deep breaths okay?"

I rolled up the window and inhaled a few times as Abby instructed. The leathery scent of the SUV's interior made me think of Dad's new Infinity—anything was better than that woodsy pine and rosemary smell that reminded me of *him*; trying to forget was going to be troublesome. Then a thought occurred to me as I glanced at Abby: I had one ally. "You're staying with me, right?"

She turned to me and smiled. "As long as I can, dear. But I can't make any promises. You—"

Abby's phone beeped a few times. She picked it up, muttered something I didn't understand, pulled over onto the shoulder, and began texting.

"What is it?"

Abby sighed. "We need to go back for your purse. Could you hand me that green notebook by your foot?"

Crap. My entire life was in that purse: driver's license, bank card, pictures of my friends, book and clothing club cards. Abby put on her blinker and began looking for the best place to get back on the highway. "There's a turnaround lane just up ahead we—"

"No Abby! Let's just go!"

Her ebony eyes hardened. "Are you sure?"

"I…It will just be too hard to see him," I lied. "I can't go back now." The truth was, I didn't trust him to let me go a second time.

Abby was analyzing me; she seemed to suspect that I was hesitating for other reasons, but she didn't press the issue. "Do you still need this notebook?" I motioned to the fluorescent green book at my feet.

"Not unless we're going back."

"Oh—no then."

We drove the rest of the way to the hospital in silence, and I started making a mental list of all the to-do's I had once I got home. It was getting pretty long, especially now that I had to get my ID's ordered again. Abby took a few short-cuts to avoid the busy traffic lights, and before long, we were in the hospital parking lot. And the mayhem began.

Abby carried me in through the front entrance yelling at the top of her lungs that she believed she had picked up "the missing girl from the news" on her way back from Whistler, and I pretended to be slightly incoherent. X-rays, four different monitoring devices and two ultrasounds came next. I was transferred from one exam room to another, and they all smelled the same: disinfectant and stale air. I hated hospitals. But that wasn't the worst part. What bothered me was that I was no longer Melissa Jayne Lawrence. I was "That Girl from the News," "Her," or "118-56303," the number on my hospital bracelet. I felt like a herded cow as I waited my turn for each assessment, among the gawking eyes and murmurs from nurses, doctors and technicians. I kept my head down as Abby—thank goodness—remained at my side, ensuring my comfort for the entire duration, propelling away unnecessary queries. And there were no needles or blood samples; she had the authority to override those tests. I was grateful for that.

Two hours later, I was finally given a private room and some peace and quiet. My parents had been contacted and were waiting impatiently for the go-ahead to see me. I was just as anxious to see them. It felt like the longest two hours ever. I couldn't stand the thought of them worrying about me any longer, and I couldn't wait to get home.

"Rest now," Abby said as she helped me into the hospital bed. "Your test results are all normal, but there is a badly bruised area on your head from the concussion, and I would like you to rest for at least another week or two." She turned to leave. "I'm going to speak with your parents now."

"You're coming back, right?"

"I'm sorry, Melissa. I have some personal business that requires my attention, so I'm leaving after that."

"When will I see you again, Abby? Can I call you if I need something?" I was trying not to sound desperate, but the thought of being without her, the only *human* who knew exactly what I was holding inside, was a frightening thought.

She hesitated as if she was looking for the right answer and then replied, "If you must. I'll be sure to give my office number to your parents."

All I was looking for was a simple "yes". Maybe I was just over-reacting, but what good was her office number? What about a cell number? For the last few hours she'd been so warm and caring, and now she was doing her best to distance herself from me. I didn't understand it.

"And before I forget, you need to discard that bag of clothes when you get home. It's not wise to keep them."

"But I—"

Abby's face was firm. "Please don't argue with me. It is for *all* of our safety."

I crossed my fingers underneath the sheets. That brown sweater was my very favourite. No way in hell was I getting rid of it. And those jeans were the only ones that didn't have a tattered hem. I was keeping them. Even if I had to wash them twenty times. "Okay."

"Melissa, if I have to throw them out before I leave, I will."

"I know," I glanced over at the bag on the floor. "I'll throw them out as soon as I get home."

"*Please* keep yourself safe." She gave me the same wide-as-a-coat-hanger smile before opening the door.

"I will, Abby. Thank you, for everything."

"You are most welcome," she answered, and promptly left.

I lay back on the pillow and decided it was a good time to try to rest, but it was short-lived. Rion's face appeared in my mind the second I closed my eyes. The angry expression he'd worn when I last saw him standing on the side of the road was now disheartened, and his eyes looked hollow and drained of life. In the mirror of his bathroom, I had looked the same.

How was I ever going to forget him?

The door slid open, and my thoughts were abruptly interrupted.

"Melissa! My beautiful little girl." Dad ran to my side. He had tears in his eyes.

"Dad!"

"Lissy, dear, are you all right?" Mom pushed herself in front of Dad. "We thought we would never see you again, I was worried sick! Thank goodness you're all right." She kissed my forehead and gently hugged me. "Mubarak deserves a medal! Are you sore? Are you all right?" She was inspecting every inch of me, and trying not to let me make contact with her puffy and swollen eyes.

"I'm better, now that you guys are here. Where's Katherine?"

"She's staying at the house to take care of the phone calls," Mom answered. "It's been ringing off the hook this weekend."

"You must be tired and sore, hey honey?" Dad asked.

I nodded. "I just wanna go home."

"Of course you do," Mom said. "Mubarak said that you need to take this week off school, and she wants you to finish the anti-inflammatories. You are on strict orders to rest and relax—no visitors, and no questions. I have already left a message at school, and I'll be talking to the principal tomorrow."

"Thanks."

"We are so happy to have you back," Dad added. "When the police—"

"Let's not talk about that now, Ronald." Mom hadn't made eye contact with him once, she just rolled her eyes in my direction before adding, "Let's get you home and into bed."

When we drove up to the house, it seemed like forever since I'd been there. Dad lifted me from the car, and carried me upstairs to my bed. It was obvious how much of an effort it was for him, but he didn't complain. I knew he wanted to do it.

"How about a good ol' fashioned tuck-in for my baby girl?"

"Sure Dad, that would be great." I chuckled to myself.

He pecked me on the forehead, tucked me in and smiled before he left the room. Mom was busy returning calls downstairs, telling everyone that I had been brought home safely, and it wouldn't be long before the news reports updated my situation—not exactly the kind of attention I wanted, but at this point I didn't have a choice.

It felt great to be in my own bed and in some clean pajamas. I had to admit, my bed wasn't as comfortable as Rion's double king-size, extra-soft mattress, but I loved my little daybed too; it was just my size. Before I closed my eyes, I heard Duke whining outside my room.

"Someone else missed you too!" Dad opened my door.

"Come here boy!" I called to him, patting the bed.

He jumped onto my quilt, sniffed and licked my face, and cuddled right up to me. He couldn't get himself close enough, but I didn't mind, I'd missed him, too.

"Hey!" Dad scolded when he saw me wince. Duke had leaned on my leg the wrong way. "Careful Dukester! Get *down*—"

"He can stay, Dad." I moved over to give him some more room. "It's okay."

"Are you sure?"

"Totally."

"Okay then, Mom will be up in a moment to check on you."

"Thanks, Dad."

"My pleasure, Lissy." He closed the door behind him.

I gave Duke a big hug, and he pushed his head into me, demanding I scratch his ears.

Knock, knock.

It was Katherine. "Come in."

She came around the corner and glared at me. Her contempt caught me off guard. "What's wrong?"

She wiped a tear from her eye and looked at her fingers, realizing she'd just smudged her mascara onto her cheek. "DAMMIT!"

"Want a tissue?" I reached over to the box on my nightstand. I wasn't sure what else to say to her, she hadn't cried over something that involved me in years.

"No." When she looked up again, her eyes were bloodshot, glossy and black from her makeup. I actually felt sorry for her because I was the one who had made her feel this way.

She sniffed and wiped her nose. "I've never been so worried in my entire life…"

Oh my, a glint of the sister I used to know had returned.

"…I've never been so mad at you, either."

My mouth dropped. "What? Why?"

She walked toward me. "You always find a way to ruin things for me, you know that?"

I pushed myself up straight. "*What*? What are you talking about?"

She swallowed and shook her head. "Maybe I should remind you, since you seem to have such a *selective* memory."

I crossed my arms. I knew the me, me, mes were about to begin.

"You *knew* I was dating Kyle Peterson, yet you moved right in on him the moment he said *boo* to you at our going away party and—"

"Oh, *seriously!*" I interjected. "I can't believe you're bringing this up again. I've apologized a hundred times, and you know I didn't—"

She rolled her teary eyes and shook her head. "Really, Liss? Really? You *still* won't admit that you remember being all over him in his car—I saw the whole thing!"

I honestly remembered nothing of that. What I did recall, I pushed swiftly out of my mind.

"Then you put up a big stink and wouldn't come home because you didn't want to leave for Vancouver! You had to be the center of attention—you had to make everything about YOU!" She kicked a book across the room, and Duke growled at her. "And then...oh forget it, you don't even care!"

"Katherine..."

She held up a finger to interrupt me. "I get that you were in an accident, Liss, and I feel awful that all this has happened, I really do...but Friday night was supposed to be *my* night with *my* friends. You weren't even supposed to be invited, until Jeff saw you sulking around school and felt sorry for you!"

I wished that he hadn't.

"I know that my grades aren't as good as yours, that I don't like all that outside stuff like you and Mom, and that you're Dad's *favourite*, but when are you going to stop interfering in my life?"

I sat back against the railing of my bed, and put my face into my free hand. "Katherine, listen to me, you're *wrong*..."

"I'm not asking for excuses, Liss. Right now, now that you're back, I'm telling you: stay out of my business and stay out of my life. You've done enough."

She slammed my door, bawling as she stomped down the hall, and I was out of breath. This was, by far, the worst thing she'd ever said to me, and I began to wonder if coming home was really worth it. I shook my head. For Mom's sake, it was.

My eyes began to burn out of frustration, but Mom walked in and I temporarily curbed my stormy emotional state.

"Is Katherine okay? She hasn't been talking to anyone, and she made a big stink about having to stay home and answer phone calls tonight. I know it's been a stressful weekend, but she's been Mrs. Moody since we moved here. I know it wasn't easy on her, leaving her friends and all…but sometimes I wish she'd just talk to me about it."

"She'll be all right, Mom." I stroked Duke's head as he rested it back on my lap. "She told me she's just having a hard time with everything that's been going on: me, Landon, school—the usual. Maybe she just needs to get out of the house for a while."

"You're right. I'll go ask her if she wants to go out tonight. I feel bad for making her stay in the house the past couple of days, but I really needed her help."

"I'm sure she'd appreciate that." I knew I would.

Mom left and I decided to call Abby and see if there was any way to get my purse back. Now that I was home, I wanted to save the expense of having to replace all of my ID's.

"Hey, Mom?" I called downstairs.

"Yes, honey?"

"Do you have Dr. Mubarak's number? I think I forgot my purse…uh—in her car."

"She's gone out of the country, Liss."

"WHAT?"

"Yes." Mom walked up the stairs with a fresh load of folded laundry. "She told Dad and me that she had a plane to catch. Did you know that her father is really sick?"

I slumped down on my bed. "No."

Mom's eyes widened. "Honey, are you okay?"

I was staring right past her. "Did she say when she was coming back?"

"She said that she didn't know. But she did leave her office number. Maybe she'll see your purse and leave it there for us. I can phone in the…" She rushed to my side, saying something, but I couldn't hear it, because the only person I could have ever talked openly to was gone. I was alone.

Mom started shaking my shoulders when I didn't answer her.

It all made sense. I must have put Abby in danger, too. How could I have done so much, to so many people? I knew why: I'd only been thinking about *myself*. Katherine was right: I *was* selfish.

I pulled my knees up to my chest and forced myself to tune into Mom.

"Liss! Liss! Please say something! It's just a purse. We'll get it back, okay?" She wrapped her arms around me in a bear hug. I swallowed hard as she turned me to face her.

"Liss," she stared intensely into my eyes, "did something happen that you're not telling me about?"

I shook my head.

"If you did something, or if someone hurt you, you can tell me, honey. I won't tell anyone, and I won't think any different of you. Are you sure that your car just skidded off the road?" She paused for a moment to give me a chance to answer. I didn't. "You didn't do it on purpose because you were in trouble, did you?"

The last thing I wanted was a trip to the psych ward because Mom thought I was suicidal. I closed my eyes for a second, and when I opened them again, they were looking directly at the bag holding the clothes I'd worn on the weekend.

"No," I finally answered. "I just… I just wanted to stay in contact with Abby, that's all. She…she saved me."

Mom smiled. "She is the most sought-after doctor in the province, Liss. You're not the only one who feels the exact same way." Then she hugged me again and rubbed my arms. "She'll come back. She loves her job."

What would I do if she didn't?

"Liss, I'm just going to make us all a late-night snack. I didn't get a chance to do up a turkey with everything going on. Are you hungry at all?"

After everything that I'd put her through, she actually felt guilty for not cooking turkey dinner as well. I'd completely lost my appetite now. I didn't want her to lift a finger for me. She'd done more than enough. Everyone had.

All because I decided to go to that stupid party.

"Don't worry about me, Mom. I ate at the hospital," I lied, wearing my best fake smile.

"Well, I'm going to head downstairs. Do you need anything before I go?"

"I'm good," I rested back down on my bed. "I think I'd just like to get some sleep."

"Absolutely." Then she kissed me on the forehead. "Dad's leaving early tomorrow morning, so I'll send him up to say good-night, if you want."

"He's not staying home?"

Mom smiled, but I knew she was just as disappointed as I was. "He's already taken an extra day off, and he has a big presentation in Toronto on Wednesday that he needs to prepare for. It could mean a huge bonus for him if they like what he has to say."

"Oh—right." I wanted to say something totally different, something that involved me hoping that he'd stay a little longer. But it wasn't about *me* anymore. He'd already lost a day's pay, and in our house, that was significant.

She winked at me. "G'night, hon."

"G'night."

As my door closed, I rolled onto my side and looked at the bag on the floor again. Rion had put himself, his entire family, and Abby, at risk for me, a complete stranger, and instead of feeling glad to be home, I felt horrible.

I took a deep breath and pushed myself up to sitting. It took every bristle of strength I had to get up to walk over to that bag of clothes; not just because of my sore muscles, but because they reminded me of *him*, and the problems I'd created when I insisted that he let me go.

I poured them onto the carpet, sat down beside them, and hugged them as tight as I could. I hadn't even taken a second to think about what I was doing, it was automatic. I think I was craving some sort of comfort after everything that had happened this weekend, and holding those clothes was like holding onto the part of me I'd left behind. I pulled the clothes closer to my face, and took a deep breath in—they still smelled of *him*.

My heart began to pound.

Pine, leather, and that musty underground smell of his world had me roiling inside. It was so strong. I inhaled again, recalling the moment Rion had smiled at me. It wasn't forced, we had actually connected, and when he carried me in his arms, I felt awkward, but safe…and so warm. I desperately wanted to feel that way again; I wanted to know everything was going to be all right again. And then I heard something crinkle.

I ripped open the pile of clothes and found the paper in the pocket of my jeans, and though the letters were difficult to decipher at first, I managed to read his messy, all-capitals chicken-scratch.

YOU WILL BE WATCHED CLOSELY. IF I SENSE
ANY DANGER, I AM COMING FOR YOU.

778-995-8884

♣

I sat there staring at the words, confused, because he said that we couldn't have any further contact. I read the note again and realized it was the *vykhars* he was warning me about.

I shoved everything back into the plastic bag and opened my closet door. Rion's scent was all over the clothes, and I needed to find a safe place to store them. In a few months, when everything settled down, I'd put them into a donation bin.

I took out an old backpack, shoved the bag in and threw it to the back of my closet. When they were securely covered by three layers of last summer's wardrobe, and I felt satisfied that they were hidden well enough, I slumped down on my bed. Even though I was completely exhausted, I couldn't shut my mind off.

When I thought about Mom, I had no doubt that coming home was the right decision, but I had no idea how messed up my life would become. Everyone's life had been put on hold this weekend because of me: my parents missed work and I'd worried them sick, Katherine cut all ties with me, I had driven the best doctor in B.C. into hiding, I still hadn't faced police questioning, I was apparently going to be watched closely by these *vykhars*, and, oh yes, I still had to go back to school and face my peers.

VI

I woke up Saturday morning to the chirping sound of the phone ringing downstairs. When I looked at the clock, it read 10:04. I'd slept a lot over the course of the week, but I was still exhausted. I would toss and turn for an hour and then sleep for two hours before the high pitched noise in my ears, a headache, or flashes of hot would wake me up again—thank goodness I'd stayed home. I'd drag myself around my bedroom every morning, attempt to get a bit of homework done, sit silently in my greenhouse and stare at the dirt-filled buckets, then find myself sleeping again in the afternoon. But I couldn't completely relax; I literally felt *wired*, as if every one of my senses had been amplified since the accident. Mom had mentioned that severe concussions could make a person irritable for a while, and since this was my first one, I assumed that was the cause.

I heard Mom coming up the stairs. The phone must have been for me, and I expected it to be Chelsea. She'd been over every day since Tuesday—sometimes twice; yesterday was the first day that she hadn't asked me if I was mad at her. I didn't blame Chelsea at all, it was my choice to go to the party, and when I didn't show up, she immediately got everyone's attention. The evening became a search party instead of a celebration. Only a best friend would do something like that.

She told me the police wouldn't issue a missing persons report until twenty-four hours had passed, because of my age. But that didn't matter to her, because everyone who was anyone at the party was out searching the streets of Porteau Cove, Furry Creek and the surrounding areas of Squamish. I was totally flattered, even more so when she told me how Jeff and his three friends seemed to be the *most* concerned—they were the four most popular grade twelve guys at Gladstone.

Mom opened my door a crack and smiled when she realized I was awake. "Phone," she whispered. "Do you want me to take a message?"

I sighed. "Tell Chelsea I'll call her after my shower. I was going to take her out for sushi tonight for her birthday."

She shook her head. "It's not Chelsea, hon, it's someone named Colin."

I sat up. I was no longer half asleep. "Colin?"

"Yes. Colin Mansfield. He's phoned twice already this morning."

I thought about it for a moment. Why would Colin Mansfield be calling my house? How did he get my number?

"I've got the cordless downstairs. Do you want me to tell him you're still sleeping?"

"No." I rubbed my eyes. "That's okay, I'll take it. Would you mind just telling him I'll be a minute?"

"Sure, love." She winked at me. "I made you some eggs for breakfast. If you're not hungry, I can put them in the fridge for later."

"That sounds great, Mom, thanks—I actually don't have much of an appetite yet."

When she left to head back downstairs, I stood up, stretched and ran my hands through my tangled hair, massaging my temples with my fingers. Fortunately, my headache hadn't affected my vision at all. Come to think of it, I hadn't used my glasses for reading at all this week. Maybe the concussion had knocked my eyes into seeing properly.

"Liss, its Colin Mansfield," he said when I answered the phone.

His voice was smooth and deep over the phone, as if he'd prac-ticed his greeting a million times. Most girls went completely *gaga* for Colin, but his popularity and the fact that he could be on the cover of a magazine with his arms around a beautiful model never fazed me. I'd been there before with a cowboy and been deep fried. However, his effort last weekend to find me had earned him at least one brownie point. "Hi, Colin. What's up?"

"How are you feeling? Chelsea told me that you've been having a hard time walking."

"I'm getting better," I replied politely, pulling open my closet and searching for my stretchy pants. "I'm coming back to school on Monday—I think."

"That's great, Liss. I can't tell you how worried we all were when Chelsea said you hadn't shown. I'm sorry my directions on the invitation weren't clear enough. I feel awful about it."

He was charming, but he didn't need to get all sappy about it. "That's okay, Colin. I think I must have just turned down the wrong road. But it's over now, and I'm trying to put it all behind me."

"For sure," he said as I grabbed my favourite grey hoodie and sat back down on the bed. "But if you don't mind, I'd really like to make it up to you somehow."

"You don't need to, Colin. I was actually just going to eat something and get started on my homework. Can I talk to you on Monday?" I wasn't interested in any more sympathy favours; I'd already ruined the party, and besides, Chelsea had done more than enough with magazines, candy, and visits in the past week.

"Well, I haven't eaten yet either...and if you'd like to get out of the house for a little while, I'd love to take you out for breakfast. Consider it an apology gesture—my treat."

"That's okay." I rolled my eyes. "I haven't even had a shower yet."

"Neither have I. But there's this great little restaurant in town that makes the best Mexican brunch. It's all homemade and I go there almost every Saturday morning before lacrosse. Are you sure you won't join me?"

My mouth began to water just thinking about fresh guacamole, hot salsa, warm tortillas and cheddar cheese—I could smell it and my stomach began this begging grumble. I hadn't eaten Mexican in months. It was one of my favourite ethnic foods and I couldn't resist. Maybe a full stomach would be my ticket to a good sleep.

"Well...all right," I finally agreed. "Can you give me half an hour? I just need to get myself ready."

"I'm ten minutes away. Call me when you're ready. And take your time, lacrosse doesn't start 'til after noon."

"Okay, I'll call you in a bit."

I jumped off the bed and made my way to the bathroom to clean myself up properly. A glance in the mirror showed me that my face and arms were still bruised, but they had faded to a dull yellow now that everything was beginning to heal. It was lovely. Even my back was covered in welts that made me wince every time I brushed up against something the wrong way.

I climbed into the shower, anticipating the warm, soothing water. But the instant the spray from the showerhead contacted my shoulders, I jerked forward. It was like a blistering hot needle attack on my skin. I assumed the temperature was too high, so I turned it down, but the lukewarm temperature barely made a difference; my shower was a sixty-second torture session rather than the soothing downpour of rain I normally looked forward to. I hated this concussion business, and I hated being so over-sensitive everywhere. It looked like taking hot baths to relax my muscles was no longer an option, either.

At 10:48, I called Colin, and exactly nine minutes later I heard the diesel engine from his Dodge pickup rumbling in front of the house. I let Mom answer the door while I gathered my things and put on a jacket, but I could still hear them crystal clear downstairs.

"Good morning, Mrs. Lawrence." He was so charismatic when he spoke, almost too confident—and a little annoying.

"Hello Colin, it's nice to finally put a face to a voice," Mom replied. "Thank you for taking Liss out today, she really needs it and Chelsea hasn't had much success."

It was true, but in my defence, Chelsea never pulled the *Mexican* card.

"Mrs. Lawrence, I just want to take a minute and personally apologize for what happened to Liss. I feel totally at fault for not giving her clearer directions to the party. I can't express to you how very sorry I am."

"Colin, that's really not necessary. We are just glad to have her safe at home. And don't be too long, we have a few things to take care of this afternoon."

She hadn't mentioned anything to me, but I would be there to help without question, whatever it was.

"No Ma'am. I'll just take her for brunch. I'll bring her straight home so that she can…be…*present*."

"Thank you, Colin."

Colin and Mom seemed to know something I didn't, and I suddenly had a funny feeling about the whole thing. That was my cue to get downstairs and find out.

"Hi, honey!" She smiled from ear to ear when she saw me— probably because I was out of my pyjamas for once.

Then I turned toward Colin and stopped dead in my descent. I looked like a train wreck compared to him. He was wearing designer denim jeans, a leather jacket and steel-toed boots. His black shaggy hair was slicked wet with gel and messy, and from the top of the stairs, the sweet peppery scent of his aftershave overpowered Mom's aromatherapy burner in the kitchen (as well as our school halls on a regular basis) and seared my nostrils when I inhaled. He looked way too over-dressed and out of place standing in the foyer our forty-year-old, two-story bungalow. I was wearing tights, runners, and my grey hoodie with half my hair tied back in a clip, looking more like his kid sister, save for the freckles and carrot top.

"Melissa…" Colin watched me carefully.

"Hey." I was totally uncomfortable from how his sea-blue eyes widened as he inspected me; I must have looked horrible enough that he couldn't even finish what he was going to say.

"Melissa—"

"Just call me Liss," I corrected him, without trying to sound snobby.

"You look—really good."

I didn't believe him. I stood there awkwardly when I reached the landing, and we just stared at one another for a moment. He'd already managed to make me nervous, so I turned to Mom to break the ice that was forming around us.

"What are we doing this afternoon? I thought we were having a garage sale."

She glanced at Colin, and back to me. "Well, I'm going to hold off on that until spring, honey. Don't worry yourself about it. Go and have a nice brunch. You've been in the house too long."

"All right," I said warily. She was hiding something from me, I could tell. I put my hand on my hip. "Are you trying to get me out of the house for something?"

She shook her head and half-smiled. "Honey, I don't want to worry you, but we have an alarm company coming to the house this morning. I think it's time that we have some more security around here besides Duke when your father is away." Then she came over and hugged me. "I didn't think you wanted to be here while they went through the house installing it and banging around. You just need to be back before they leave so we can learn how it works, together."

I sighed dramatically. "Thanks, Mom."

"No problem."

"Can I help you to my truck in any way?" Colin asked.

"No, that's okay. I can walk." I looked at Mom. "We'll be back in a while. I've got my cell in my bag."

Mom nodded and winked at us, but something was wrong with her expression. She had this nervous look on her face, and I hesitated for a moment because it was the same look she'd given me when she first came into my room at the hospital. I wondered if there was something else going on that she wasn't telling me about.

"Are you okay, Mom?"

She quickly nodded. "I'm great honey. Just have a nice time. And don't be too long, all right? I don't want to keep them waiting once they're finished."

"Sure thing, Mrs. Lawrence," Colin replied for me when I didn't answer. "We'll be back in an hour or so."

Something was off. I thought about staying home and telling Colin I'd take a rain-check, but he whisked me out of the door, and up into his truck before I could say otherwise.

We made our way to Chico's Mexican Restaurant, and Colin ordered the most expensive breakfast on the menu for both of us: a skillet of eggs, peppers and cheese, sausages (he ate mine), tortillas, fried potatoes and salsa.

Colin ate like it was his last meal on the planet, and talked casually about completing his graduation credits early in January, but I'd left my appetite at home. I pushed my favourite food around my plate after a few bites, while my insides lurched and swirled, and I only caught half of what Colin said about searching for me on the weekend. I wanted to know if there was something else Mom was hiding from me, and it took all of my energy just to sit still and wait for Colin to stop stuffing his face.

When we got the bill, I offered to pay for my barely touched brunch, but Colin refused, snatching the paper from the waiter's hand before I could see, and I thanked him profusely. On the way home, I was silent. Colin turned some music on and tried to make light conversation, but I gave him only one-word answers. And then when we turned the corner to my house, there were no alarm company vehicles to speak of. Instead, three shiny black SUVs surrounded my house, and two of my neighbours were peering out of their windows suspiciously.

The *vykhars* had come.

I knew instinctively that the SUVs weren't there by coincidence, and there were no emblems or company logos to speak of, so they didn't belong to the alarm company. Police would have come in cruisers or marked SUVs. I grabbed the handle on the side of Colin's truck door and squeezed hard. This was not the time to be afraid, but I could feel my hands sweating already.

"Looks like you've still got company, eh?" Colin joked, nudging me in the side with his elbow.

I tried to slow my breathing, but it was almost impossible with my heart hammering against my chest, and it took me a few moments before I could answer him.

"Colin," I finally said, swallowing hard.

"Yeah?"

I thought about asking him to get me the hell out of there, but it had *guilt* written all over it. Running away wasn't going to help me escape the inevitable. I would have to talk to them at some point, but I wished that I'd had more time to prepare. Then I felt anger surge through me as I saw Mom open the front door. She'd lied to me. She had no right.

"Thanks for breakfast," I said to Colin in a low monotone. I was busy glaring at my mother.

"Hey, no problem—that food keeps pretty well if you keep it cool, maybe you'll be hungry for it later." He handed me the take-out box and I slowly made my way out of his truck, slamming the door as hard as I could, hoping that Mom would take the hint.

She waved a "thank-you" at Colin and he beeped back his "you're welcome."

I limped up toward the door, trying not to think about them conspiring.

"Hi, honey," Mom said humbly. "You're just in time."

I shook my head at her. "Why didn't you tell me the…police… were coming? Why did you lie to me?"

"I didn't lie to you, Liss." She put her hand on my arm. "We do have a new alarm system, but the company that installed it also investigates cold-case disappearances in North America, and they want to talk to you briefly about last weekend. They've come in place of the police."

"But I don't know anything about any disappearances!" I argued, hoping to turn her words into a get-out-of-questioning-free card.

67

"I know, hon, but one of them is one of Dad's top clients, here as a friend, and he's come with some information for you. He just has some concerns about your accident."

"Mom, *please* don't make me talk to them." I began repeating Abby's instructions in my head just in case, and I realized that Mom was still talking to me.

"...things, nothing major, okay? They promised not to over-whelm you. This will be the only time, hon, and then you can forget all about it."

I stared blankly into the house while a technician holding a ladder passed by heading out the door. I'd had absolutely no time to mentally prepare myself for this. I dreaded walking into the house. I felt as though the ground was swaying, but it was just me.

"Come on, honey. You'll be fine."

Mom put her arm around me and helped me inside. When we crossed into the entranceway, I saw three large men sitting in the living room. Each of them was dressed exactly alike: black suits, grey shirts and matching ties. The oldest one, who looked to be in his fifties, had ear-length, slicked-back black hair and a diamond encrusted clip on his tie. He stood up and greeted me.

"Melissa, my name is Caine. I'm a friend of your father's." He held out his manicured hand and I reluctantly shook it as his eyes examined me from head to toe. Then he introduced his partners: "This is Agent...and this is..."

I lost track of the names the moment Caine introduced them; one had auburn hair and one was Asian. I was too busy rehearsing the lies I'd be feeding them.

"It's nice to meet you," I managed to say, making brief eye contact with each of them as I tried to stay composed.

Caine walked over to Mom. "Eleanor, would you mind leaving us for a few moments?" He took her arm gently and they exchanged a few whispered words in the foyer.

"Please don't leave, Mom," I pleaded to her turned back. "I really want you to stay."

Caine looked up and smiled at me. "She'll just be in the other, room. She's not going anywhere."

"I need to talk to your father on the phone, Liss," she replied. "He's coming in next week and Caine needs a few things ordered before cut-off on Tuesday." She looked a little spacey, staring at me, but it was almost impossible to get her to change her mind at the best of times, so I painstakingly turned around and faced the agents, hiding my terror. If I was going to do this alone, I had to remain calm—or fake a crying session if things got hairy—that was the only way. And I would tell them in one hundred different ways if I had to, that I didn't remember *anything*.

"Please sit," the auburn-haired agent said, gesturing toward the chair. Caine winked at me.

"This will just take a few moments, Melissa," Caine began, "and then we'll be out of your way so that you can rest."

I nodded, and Caine brought out a few files from his briefcase. They all had the Jaredsons Securities golden spider symbol on the front. My mouth dropped open. The *vykhars* were Jaredsons?

Jaredsons Securities was the largest private investigation group in North America. They were bigger than the RCMP. Bigger than the US Secret Service—everyone knew that. Jaredsons Securities had their hands in just about everything: cold cases, alarm systems, law firms, anti-virus programs, private security, body-guard services and customs brokering, to name a few. They operated worldwide on a contract basis with governments, mostly. And judging by the vehicles outside, they were damn expensive, too. I remember Dad telling me that it was originally a family-based business that skyrocketed in the early seventies, and when you had Jaredsons working for you, you were driving down a one-way street—*their* street.

All of a sudden I felt like an ant in a room with three elephants.

"Just relax, Melissa. We don't want to intimidate you; we just want to talk to you." He looked into my eyes, his blue irises oscillating, and I felt light-headed for a moment. I started to tingle everywhere. I had to blink a few times to bring myself around.

"Are you all right, Melissa?" Caine asked. The Asian agent began taking notes.

"Yes." I rubbed my eyes. "I just haven't slept very much in the past week."

"Is there something bothering you that you'd like to talk about?"

"My head's just not been in the right place. My mom said it's from the concussion."

"Well, if you don't mind, I'd like to ask you a few questions about last weekend."

I glowered at my hands, preparing for the worst.

"Why don't you tell us what you remember of the night of your accident?" Caine caught my eye the moment I looked up, and I felt that same fuzziness again, but I couldn't look away; eye contact with him was key if I wanted to be believable.

I shook my head. "To be honest, Mr. Caine, I don't remember much of anything. I was trying to find a party when I left my house, and the last thing I recall is turning down the wrong road. It's all a big blank after that, and then I remember waking upside-down in my car."

"You don't remember anything at all?"

"No, I'm sorry. Everyone keeps asking me, and I wish I did, but I just…don't."

He continued to stare at me, and I sat there, waiting for him to say something. I wondered when he'd try to persuade me. I was half expecting him to start waving his fingers in front of my face or pull out a pocket watch and tell me I must be feeling sleepy, very sleepy. It was awkward. Finally, he spoke again. "The reason we're so interested in your accident is because of its location. My brothers were viciously attacked and killed not far from where we found your car."

"Oh my—!" I exclaimed. "I'm so sorry."

"Thank you, you are most kind." He took a large drink of water from his glass. Then he looked directly at me again. "I'm hoping you can help me *find* the ones who did it. You see, I already *know* who murdered them."

70

My eyebrows furrowed. "I'm sorry Mr. Caine, but I don't understand how I can help with that."

"Melissa, there is not one person on this earth who could have survived three nights outside in that below-freezing temperature last weekend in Porteau Cove."

"I still don't know where you are going with this." I looked between them all, putting on my best confounded face, but I was very close to breaking down.

"We're trying to figure out if the same suspect had something to do with your survival, or possibly your accident. And we want to know if there's anything you can remember besides getting out of your car and making your way to the highway."

"I told you already, I don't remember."

There was another awkward pause where all three of them exchanged peculiar looks then Caine turned back to me.

"Have you ever seen a monster?"

"I don't know what you mean, Mr.—I mean, Agent—"

He cut me off. "The suspect's not human, Melissa. But it's not entirely animal either."

"What do you mean?" My voice cracked as I leaned back on the sofa.

"The suspect is a malion." Caine was clearly disgusted, speaking through clenched teeth. "Have you heard the term before?"

"Well...yes," I replied anxiously, "I mean...if a fairy-tale counts."

"*Moonstone, Mae and Malion Tales*, right?" Caine's smile made me uneasy, and I could feel myself becoming a little warm.

"Yeah, that's the one. Yeah...um...my nan brought me back a copy from Europe when I was four. It's always been my very favourite storybook."

He clapped his hands together. "Well Melissa, those tales *are real*, and so are the creatures within them."

"Are you serious?"

"I am only aware of the existence of malions at this time; the pegasi, selkies and mermaids, I am certain, are long since extinct."

Then he took another sip of water before continuing. "Malions were the only mystical creatures that posed a threat to humans back then, and they still do today. The stories in *Moonstone, Mae and Malion Tales* were originally passed down to warn people about malions. You see, we believed all those creatures were extinct, so the tales changed over time and became a collection of fairy tales for children. But a few years ago we discovered two malions up north."

"So you're telling me the story about Princess Alysia being captured by a malion—that's a true story?" I snorted.

Caine seemed to be saddened by my question, and answered me in an almost whisper. "She wasn't the only one the malions tried to kidnap. But it was her place in society, and her royal bloodline, that made her capture and rescue so historic. I don't know one person who *hasn't* heard her story. But let's not get off track here. I'd like to show you a few photos of the suspect. He's extremely dangerous, Melissa, and we want to bring him down before anyone else gets hurt."

I nodded and took off my hoodie, squinting at the thermostat in the corner of the room because it felt like Mom had turned up the heat too much again. I could feel my face starting to flush. I looked back at Caine as he opened the file and placed three eight by ten photos in front of me.

A part of me was expecting it, but I still gasped when I saw Rion's face on every photo. And what I was looking at made me feel sick. Rion's facial scars and ear wounds were bloody and fresh, and part of his cheekbone was exposed. He was unconscious, and his eyes had rolled back into his head. Another picture of his torso showed large deep cuts across his back from a side profile, and he was so much younger-looking and thinner than what I remembered. He must have been at least a hundred pounds lighter at the time of the photo, and in so much pain.

The longer I stared at the photos, the more nauseated I became, and then a wave of intense warmth washed over me and I involuntarily heaved. I put my head between my knees and heaved again. If I didn't get out of there fast, I was going to be sick all over them. Caine's wingmen just sat there watching me; Caine looked satisfied.

"If it's too much, Melissa, we'll take them away."

"I just need a second." I stood up. Keeping my mouth covered with my hand, I tottered over to the bathroom. When I got to the sink, I took a few deep breaths and drank some water, but I still felt sick and uncomfortably warm—not to mention that a million thoughts were running through my head.

I didn't think Rion was capable of murder, and Abby had said so many wonderful things about him and his father, but what reason did Caine have to lie?

I splashed my face with water. Those horrific images of Rion were etched permanently in my mind now, and I knew I would see them as soon as I closed my eyes again. Instead, I just stared at myself in the mirror and wiped sweat off my hairline.

Only Caine was there when I returned. "Are you all right?" he asked.

I wiped a few more beads of sweat from my forehead. "I think so. I…" I swallowed some of the sour taste in my mouth. "I just can't look at those photos anymore. I have a weak stomach, that's all."

"I know this is difficult for you Melissa, but this *thing* is very dangerous, and we need to know if you have any recollection of this creature—any memory whatsoever."

I shook my head, holding my stomach, while Caine observed me. All I could think about was what Rion had said about the *vykhars*. His voice was crystal clear in my head: *They will kill us all.* I willed myself to calm down, but I was struggling. My head spun; we were in danger unless I could get myself out of this situation fast. But not too fast.

"May I continue?" He was impatient.

"Sure…just don't bring out those photos again…please."

"Well, we captured him and one other in the Rocky Mountains a week before those were taken. There had been some reports of

73

livestock going missing in the area by a local farmer, and when we went to investigate, we found them. When we brought him to our security center, we ran a few tests, and the results were astounding, Melissa. Not only do they hunt and kill savagely, they also carry disease. We wanted to euthanize the male, he was extremely violent. But he escaped before we were able to, and killed my two brothers in the process. The crime scene was more horrible than I can say. He had literally ripped them apart."

I stopped breathing when I heard *disease*, and then *ripped apart*. "Oh my—"

He was staring at me intently, like a snake ready to bite. I stepped back involuntarily when he moved towards me. He opened his mouth to speak, but I cut him off before he could corner me into giving what I knew away.

"I need a bit of space, Mr. Caine," I searched for the right words. "I'm...I think I had some bad Mexican food this morning. I need my mom."

Caine reached for me and squeezed my elbow. "How about you come out to my vehicle, and I'll talk to your mom. We have our own medical staff at my office, you can lie down and the nurses there will take good care of you."

At that moment I began to full-on panic. He was going to take me, and I would never be able to fight him off.

All of a sudden, my body felt like it was on fire.

"No! I really...oh...!" The contents in my stomach came up so fast I was unable to control it. I vomited all over his jacket and pants.

He screamed out a curse and Mom came running in the moment she heard it.

"Liss, oh my word! Are you all right?"

Caine cut in before I could answer. "Would you just get me a cloth or some damn thing Eleanor, can't you see it's all over me!"

"Just a moment, Caine. Let me just get Liss to the washroom in case she goes again."

"Just hurry," he grunted. "These are brand-new pants I've got on here, and I didn't bring a change of clothes...ah for the love of...DAMMIT ALL TO HELL!"

Mom looked at me and rolled her eyes as she helped me to the upstairs bathroom.

"Please just tell him I'll call if I think of anything, Mom. I can't do this anymore."

She gently hugged me and kissed the top of my head. "You got it, hon. Let's get you into the tub, you're really burning up."

She gave me a fresh facecloth and began running me a cool bath. I don't know what I would have done to get out of going with him if I hadn't gotten sick, but I was safe. For now. When I turned off the water, I could hear Caine and Mom talking quietly downstairs.

"I'll have some of my men watching over the house for the next week while Ronald is away."

"Thank you so much, Caine," Mom replied graciously, "that would make me feel so much better. The news has been here a bunch of times, too, and I just don't want to deal with them. I need to focus on my girls right now."

"Well, if you notice anything suspicious, or if your daughter mentions anything, call us right away."

"Yes, of course I will."

Caine said a brief goodbye, and as the door closed, it hit me.

Rion couldn't possibly have infected me with something. We would have to have had some type of physical contact. He'd barely even *touched* me, other than carrying me once or twice. Everything going on in my body right now was a direct result of my concussion, just as Mom had said. And now that I'd foolishly put Caine and his *vykhars* on high alert, would Rion be coming for me? I didn't want to think about it.

Without warning, the images of his battered face and body reappeared in my mind's eye and my stomach rolled over once more as I remembered the brutality he'd suffered in the hands of the *vykhars*; for a moment, I swore I could almost *feel* the pain he endured, and a few hairs stood up on my neck. He must have been so scared.

Caine wouldn't be merciful with Rion the next time around. No, they'd do more than tear him apart. And what would they do to *us* if they found out I'd held back? Caine didn't strike me as a very understanding man.

I shuddered as that foul taste crept up into my throat again. With only a moment's notice, I stood up in the tub to head towards the toilet, but I had only one foot on the cold tile when I vomited again, all over the floor.

VII

I sat in my bed, wide awake, just before midnight, staring at
Moonstone, Mae and Malion Tales; I'd secretly stolen it from
Katherine's room, because I just needed to see it again. I'd read
Jared and the Malion forty times over the course of the last ten
days, and no matter how hard I tried, I couldn't drive my thoughts
away from Rion. Deep down, I felt he was an honest person, but
clearly he was no saint, either. A murder is a murder is a murder,
and two families were left without a father, husband and brother.

Not surprisingly, ever since my interview with Caine and his
associates, I'd vacillated between two nagging fears: of being
snatched by Rion for my own protection and separated from my
family, and of being abducted by the *vykhars* and possibly tor-
tured. I wasn't sure which would be worse. They circled our house
every hour, on the hour, from nine at night until six in the morning,
and though their vehicles were quiet, they still disconcerted me.
Whenever I heard one passing, I would wait, tense until it rounded
the corner, wondering if they were going to stop suddenly, burst
in and haul me off like a criminal. And it wasn't just that. Every
squeak, bump, peep and knock in the night would startle me. It
was nearly impossible to relax.

Caine called Mom daily to check how I was feeling and I
knew she texted him and Dad when I'd made it home safely from

school. That didn't bother me. In fact, I felt better knowing they were keeping watch from a distance; it meant they were satisfied with my story—but that was during the day. At night, I felt vulnerable. I didn't believe the Jaredsons high-tech alarm system would be able to stop a six-foot-whatever, two hundred and fifty pound malion from breaking and entering, and there was no way for me to express my fears without betraying Rion and his people altogether. I was going to keep my promise to Rion and never reveal to anyone where I'd been that weekend, but under no circumstance would I allow him to take me away without a fight. I was staying right here. I could never leave Mom, who was having a hard enough time keeping the house in some kind of order with her arthritis and work schedule—*with* my help—while forever trying to please my high-maintenance sister, and smile for my father, who barely had time for us anymore. She had taken the very best care of all of us for so long, and for that, every day of my life, I would be there for her, just the same, whenever she needed me.

Yet I couldn't help thinking about Rion. Reliving my time underground seemed to take up every moment I wasn't contemplating abduction. I could hear his voice so clearly in my head, recall how his captivating green eyes had arrested me, and ruminate about the touch of his strong, calloused hand so gently around mine. Some nights, if I concentrated hard enough, I could remember, quite vividly, how alive I felt in his presence, and every inch of my body would swirl with energy. Sometimes I just tingled all over, like my blood had been given an octane injection—it was something I'd never felt before, and never expected to again.

Chelsea picked me up each morning for school, and once in a while she'd ask me why I was "staring off into space." But I wasn't staring off into space. I was looking for *him*. The days were becoming shorter as we inched closer to December, and that meant more opportunity for Rion to find me without risking exposure in the public eye. Leaving the house was becoming an issue because I didn't have a car, and I kept thinking he was going to jump out of some dark corner and abduct me when no one was around to hear me screaming.

I hated walking to the bus for work, and I hated bothering Mom or Chelsea for a ride home (Katherine selectively answered phone calls, and could have cared less that she basically worked the same hours up the street). I'd even phoned Colin once, and he gladly came right into Waves, the coffeehouse where I worked, and escorted me right to my front door without a single complaint. Come to think of it, Colin had become a great friend. Chelsea and Katherine made their opinions clear that he was troublemaker, and the last person I should befriend out of Jeff's quartet. But he'd never been anything but kind to me.

I glanced at the clock again, and it read 12:17. I got up and took one last survey of the neighbourhood from my window. The sky was a boundless black blanket with twinkling stars. The only difference tonight was the quiet. No drive-bys and no noise, for once—except for that stupid buzzing from our new alarm system. Feeling completely exhausted, I dove into bed and closed my eyes, wishing dreamland would finally find me.

No such luck. I was boiling hot again, the moment I closed my eyes. Those stupid hot flashes were getting on my last nerve. I threw the blankets off. I never thought that I would have to start sleeping naked like Mom, but at this point, I was ready to give it a try. Right after a nice cold glass of water.

I rubbed my eyes and made my way to the kitchen in the dark, not wanting to wake anyone by turning on a light, since I could see just fine anyway. Opening the cupboard as quietly as I could, and trying not to let the creaking of the old cabinetry disturb anyone, I grabbed a mug and turned toward the sink. I let the water run for a few moments, wet my hands and splashed my face twice, before filling my cup. Just as I took my first sip, something moved out of the corner of my eye. I whipped around and Duke was there, growling low.

Bewildered by his reaction, I whispered, "It's me, boy. C'mere."

He remained where he was, and I got a little worried. He didn't see as well as other dogs and walked into things once in a while, but he should have recognized my voice. Then he took a deep breath, and the warning rumble deepened. I could see he was stiff with hostility from his head to the stub of his tail, and the little hairs between his shoulders were raised slightly. He was also vibrating.

I swallowed. I had never felt an ounce of fear in the presence of my canine brother until that moment, and I knew he'd sensed it. He'd never bitten me before, but something stopped me from taking a step toward him. I wished Dad had been downstairs to speak some sense into him, or turn on the light, because I was nowhere near the switch.

Unsteadily, I knelt and whispered again, "*Dukie*...stop that, now. Get back on my bed!"

But instead of lightening up, he lowered his head an inch and stood his ground. He licked his lips and saliva dripped from his floppy jowls onto the linoleum, as his lip curled up exposing those jagged, white, razor-sharp molars of his—the ones that, not so long ago, ate right through our chain-link fence when—

Something was wrong.

I stood up, and Duke took a step towards me. Then I realized that he wasn't looking at me, he was looking *past* me—out the window. For a moment I couldn't breathe, and I began to tremble. He'd heard something out there, and in the past week, he'd only growled at one thing: *vykhars*.

A few shortened breaths were all I could manage as I reached back toward the knife drawer, searching for the largest wood handle my fingers could track down. I grasped it tightly, shaking uncontrollably and then glanced down at Duke and nodded. He maintained his position and stood ready to defend me as I slowly turned to face what was waiting for us.

I felt my mouth unhinge the moment I saw what Duke was staring at: in the backyard, standing adjacent to the shed, thirty feet from where I stood was an enormous cloaked figure.

Rion.

The streetlight next to our yard made it just light enough for me to see his eyes narrowed to slits, glaring at me; his fists were clenched and he bared his teeth as our eyes met. At that second, every other thought in my head vanished. One remained: he was here to take me back.

"NOOOOOOOOOOO!" I cried, as the shattering sound of ceramic on the floor sent Duke into full attack mode.

I turned around and ran as fast as I could toward the living room phone to call the police as Duke barrelled past me, standing on his hind legs against the counter, barking incessantly. Lights flew on and Dad came rushing down the stairs in a panic.

"LISS! WHAT'S GOING ON?"

"DAD! HELP! SOMEONE'S TRYING TO BREAK IN! SOMEONE'S IN THE BACK YARD!"

"Get upstairs, NOW! ELEANOR, GET CAINE ON THE PHONE!"

"Dad!" I called back, "don't—don't go out there, Dad." I fumbled for the right words. "He...he might have a gun or something!"

"I said get up stairs!" he retorted. "Eleanor!"

"I'm on it!" Mom called back.

I heard Dad press the alarm panic button, and all I could think about was Rion crashing through the door any second. I stood at the lower landing of the stairs and a whole minute went by.

Duke stopped barking. Another minute passed.

Katherine was in the hallway when I got to the top of the stairs.

"What the *hell* is going on?" she spat at me.

"I don't know." I was still shaking. "I thought I saw someone in the back yard."

"You *thought* you did, or you *did*?"

"Did you get a good look at whoever it was?" Dad called up from the living room.

"I—" I thought about it for a second. I couldn't possibly tell him or the *vykhars* the truth. It would implicate me immediately.

81

"He was standing right against the shed in the backyard. I didn't see too much of him, there wasn't enough light."

The phone rang. "I got it!" Dad hollered. It was Caine, and he called me down to add my two cents.

"What was it?" Caine inquired the moment I spoke into the phone.

"It was a man. A short, thin man wearing a hoodie," I lied. "Brush cut. He was definitely not a teenager, and it looked like he was wearing glasses—I think."

"Glasses or *sunglasses*," Caine pressed.

"Glasses."

I was relieved to be talking to Caine on the phone, rather than in person, because he had no way of persuading me or seeing my facial expression, which I was sure was pretty guilty.

"Well, I'm halfway across the world right now, and it'll take me a few moments, but I'll have an agent there within the next half an hour to look around. Does that sound reasonable?"

"Um, yes—thank you." I rolled my eyes. "That would make me feel so much better."

I hung up and told my parents about the agent coming over to inspect the backyard. As I finished, I heard Mom giggling in the kitchen. "What's so funny?"

Mom laughed again. "Honey."

"*What?*"

"I just bought a bunch of landscape ties yesterday," she said, kindly. "They're all wrapped up in black plastic, leaning against the shed. There's a whole big bundle of them out there for the garden." Then she held out her hand. "Come and see. It's nothing but your imagination running away with you. Ron, call Caine back and tell him it's nothing."

"I don't care, El," Dad fired back. "I still want someone to look around."

"I don't believe this!" Katherine said, getting up from the stair she was sitting on and storming back toward her room. "Of the stupid, idiotic things to get worked up about—I've got a freaking math exam this morning, and I'm losing sleep—for this!" Before she opened her door, she stopped and glared at me. "What the hell's gotten in to you, Liss?"

I hesitantly walked into the kitchen and looked toward the shed as Mom cleaned up the mess from the shattered mug. Indeed, I saw the wrapped up landscape ties, and it looked eerily similar to the image of Rion I'd seen, but I wasn't convinced I'd imagined him. And even after an agent had scoured the house and surrounding yard and come up blank, all I could do was shake my head.

I knew what I saw. It was him. Duke had heard him. And I had this sinking feeling he was going to come back.

At seven thirty the next morning, I sat stirring my cereal, carefully turning each flake over and over and over. I needed to find a ride to school. Mom had left for the hospital to help out with two emergency Caesarean sections, Dad was spending the morning on the computer with important business calls and emails, and Katherine was skipping first period to study for her math exam. I'd phoned Chelsea almost every single day for a ride to somewhere since my accident, and given her twenty bucks in gas money, but I hated the sigh on the phone each morning when I called. She lived on the other side of town, and it took her twenty minutes out of her way to pick me up, which made me feel horrible. I had to find an alternate ride for a few days; it just wasn't fair to call her every time. The only problem was that I had exactly one alternative: Colin Mansfield.

I picked up my cell and fired off a text:

> Hi Colin—Liss. Any chance I could hitch a ride this mornng?

Less than thirty seconds later, his reply came back:

> Was going 2 phone u this mrnng—need some notes from humanities when I missed 1st thurs. Jst at Timmy's. Latte? Canucks sprinkle donut? My treat.

I smiled and texted back:

        `Ur 2 nice. Thanks.`

One last text came back from him that he'd see me in fifteen minutes, so I gathered my things and waited impatiently in my room. One of the nice things about Colin was that he's a big guy, and if Rion was to show up, I felt better having someone closer to his size around.

Colin and I got to school a few minutes before the first bell, and he walked me right to my locker. But instead of a quick "see ya" before heading off to his first class, he stuck around and waited for me to retrieve my books. I'd enjoyed his company lately, and I felt better knowing that he was watching out for me, like an older brother.

"Are you all right, Liss?"

His question caught me off guard. Over the course of the last week, he'd avoided pestering me with questions, but now his indigo eyes waited benignly for my response. I so badly wanted to tell him the truth: I couldn't sleep and that I thought I was being stalked. But like every other time I'd been asked in the last week, my reply was a complete falsehood.

"Yeah, sure."

"Bull." He came uncomfortably close to me. "You're lying." His eyes narrowed. "Why are you lying to me?"

I swallowed and shook my head. "I don't want to talk about it, 'kay?"

He shook his head, knowing full-well I wasn't budging. "I know your sister's been giving you a hard time. Is *that* what it is?"

"The fact that she can't stand me is nothing new," I sighed, taking my chemistry binder under my arm. "And I don't think that will ever change."

"Yeah, well, she's a freaking snob—and no one *else* can stand her, either. But there's something else, isn't there? Is someone bothering you? Tell me right now and I'll knock them into next week."

I looked down at the ground as he spoke. When I came back to school, Colin and Chelsea had made doubly sure that no one so much as looked at me differently. Because of them, I evaded all questions or anything that involved me having to speak about my accident. I didn't deserve such kindness; I had brought this whole ordeal on myself. I was the one who agreed to go to the party. I was the one who chose to come back.

"I don't think the answer is buried in your nails, Liss."

I took a deep breath and looked him in the eye, feeling overwhelmed by the guilt that inundated me. He had his sword drawn and I was stealing away his chance to be chivalrous.

"Just *tell* me," he pleaded.

"Don't worry about me, Colin. I just don't think I'm ready—"

"I *know* you're not interested in having a boyfriend right now," he interrupted, "and I'm not trying to hit on you, so stop going there. All right?"

That wasn't what I was trying to say, but I let it go, because I had another question burning in my mind since he first called my house last Saturday morning.

"Colin," I whispered. "Would you tell me something?"

He winked at me. "Anything."

"Why do you want to be my friend? You didn't even know I existed before the...well...you know—my accident. Now you're keeping tabs on me all the time. What changed?"

He frowned and his shoulders dropped. My inquiry must have offended him.

"Let's get one thing straight." He put his hand firmly on my shoulder. "Not all my friends are guys. And...don't take this the wrong way...but there are a lot girls I call on a regular basis—that are just my friends."

"And?"

"And when I gave out those directions to Jeff's parent's cabin, I didn't realize how unclear they were until four of my friends showed up an hour late." Then he took his hand away and started doodling invisible lines up and down my locker door with his first finger. "When I heard about your accident, I felt completely responsible. If I hadn't given out shoddy directions, none of this would have happened. I guess this is my way of saying I'm sorry, Liss. I'm an *acts of service* kinda guy."

"So you're trying to be my friend because you feel guilty?" I snapped.

"For crying out loud, Liss," Colin barked back at me. "Can't you just appreciate something without analyzing the piss out of it?"

My eyebrows narrowed, and I wanted to say something really nasty at that moment, but the warning bell startled us both.

"Can I walk you to your class?" he queried, in a desperate attempt to redeem himself.

"No, that's okay. I'll see you around." I turned to make my way to chemistry, but he grabbed my hand before I could take my first step.

"I'm not trying to be a jerk, all right? You freaking girls drive me nuts the way you always think we're looking to get laid or something."

I rolled my eyes and decided to put an end to it. I didn't have the energy for this. "Just don't talk to me because you feel you need to make up for something. There was nothing to forgive. Leave it at that."

"Point taken." He smiled at me. "But I still want to be your friend, and—"

"And I need to get to class," I started walking away. "Save your speech for humanities."

I kept walking, even when I heard him curse and kick my locker—something he'd probably never get in trouble for. How in the hell did he always get away with so much at school?

I marched into chemistry, and Chelsea's eyes were as big as saucers when she saw me.

"How'd you get here? I figured you were staying home and—"

"I phoned Colin."

She rolled her bottom lip under her front teeth a few times, something she only did when she was irritated.

"I waited all morning for your call, Lissy. You could've *told* me or something!"

"He needed notes for humanities," I answered swiftly. "Don't get all bent out of shape about it."

She shook her head. "I don't like you hanging around with him, Liss. He's a jerk, he lies, and he acts like such a douchebag some-times—Jeff said so himself! You should tell him to take a hike."

"Colin's Colin. And besides, he knows better than to pull the wool over my eyes. I see right through him."

Chelsea raised her eyebrow. "I just don't want to see you get hurt...again."

She was always looking out for me. I couldn't get mad at her for that. "Thanks, Chels—I hear ya."

"You're my best friend, Liss. You're worth it." Then she leaned a little closer to me, giggling and whispering, "Looks like Mr. Sallenkirk's got another hickey this morning."

"Oh for the love of..." I exclaimed when he turned away from us, revealing one seriously large purple welt he'd been trying to hide with his shirt collar. "Mrs. Sallenkirk is a freakin' leech!"

Mrs. Sallenkirk also worked in the school—as a gym teacher.

"They must *totally* get it on at lunch time," Chelsea whispered back.

I put my finger into my mouth and pretended to gag. "I didn't think people in their sixties still slept in the same bedroom!"

Chelsea laughed. "My parents have never slept in the same bedroom—except for a couple times, I guess. They *so* need to get out of the fifties."

We both laughed. "Maybe you should give them the Sallenkirk's email; they could maybe give them a few pointers."

"Oh, gross, Liss. I don't even want that vision in my head!"

"Could you imagine?" I opened my notebook as Mr. Sallenkirk turned off the lights so that we could see the projector for notes, and I pretended to type on my desk. "Yes thank you for contacting us, Anita, we'd love for you to come over so we can show you and Roger some of our favourite positions!"

87

Chelsea and I burst out laughing as quietly as we could. But Chelsea snorted and we laughed even harder. For a few hours, I forgot about Rion. That afternoon, I thought more about what it would be like to have Chelsea as a sister, instead.

We were driving home from school when I began to shiver. Feeling cold had become foreign; I'd gotten used to the Indian summer going on inside me. I rolled up the window and Chelsea looked flabbergasted as soon as she saw that I was pulling on my jacket.

"What? You're cold now?"

"I'm sorry," I apologized, holding myself tightly. "I'm freezing! Can you turn on the heat?"

She grabbed my hand, and gasped. "Holy cow, you're an icicle, sister!" Then she shook her head. "One minute you're hot, now you're chilly. Don't tell me that you're turning into a vampire now, too!"

"Very funny, Chels. Just crank the heat."

When I walked in the house, the first thing I did was run up to the bathroom to run a warm tub.

I was just about to close the door when I saw Katherine standing in the doorway, and I jumped. Her eyes were casting daggers at me, arms crossed, and her body was one straight line held at almost military attention, obstructing the doorway.

"He's not your type, Liss."

I shook my head. "What are you talking about?"

"You know *exactly* who I'm talking about." She threw her hands on her hips.

I got it. "Colin is harmless, Katherine."

"Landon said he's crooked. And I think something's not right with him. We heard his dad's thinking about sending him away to boarding school or some sort of military training if he doesn't straighten up soon. He keeps rebelling at home and—"

"I'm not dating him," I replied firmly, holding the door so that if she didn't leave soon, I could close it on her face. "And since when do you care about anything that's happening with me?"

She huffed and her nostrils flared. "Just stay away from him, all right? He's a player...and he'll play you too."

"Did you get all this from Landon?" I wanted to dismiss her words as part of her feud with Colin, yet Chelsea had told me almost the same thing.

"Landon wouldn't lie to me," she answered softly. "We just both thought you should know."

The "we" sounded like something that came from my parents.

"Tell Landon I can take care of myself." I steadied myself against the queasiness her overwhelming stench of vanilla always brought on. "But thank your two-timer for his concern."

"He's only cheated once, Liss. And it wasn't even cheating; the other girl threw herself at him because she hated me. Landon loves me."

"Right." I raised my eyebrow. "That's why he's always flirting with every girl who walks past him in the parking lot when he picks you up from school."

She huffed. "You know what, Liss? Forget I said anything. *Date* Colin if you want to. You'll learn your lesson, but don't come crying to me about it after."

"You're the last person I'd come crying to."

"Whatever!"

She turned around and I watched her little ballet feet disappear into her room before she slammed the door.

I hated Landon. He acted like he owned Katherine and it pissed me off how she just obeyed everything he said, how she never argued back and how she just allowed him to run the show. It was so not like her to be that way, and the more time they spent together, the less I saw of the sister I used to know.

The one who used to sew and sketch in her room until all hours of the night. The one who wanted to design a clothing line. The one who had this incredibly funny and light-hearted personality before the Vancouver rain washed it away.

I know she hated my guts, and she was an incredible snob most of the time, but I still hoped we'd come to some sort of common ground one day. I missed having a sister.

When I was done my bath, I went downstairs and found Mom reading the mail in the kitchen, with a fresh cup of tea in her hand. Something about the smell of Earl Grey was soothing.

"Hi honey, how was your day?"

I was ready to say how great it was, but then I looked out toward the shed and felt like there was no such thing as a great day anymore. There were reminders of my danger everywhere. Of the person waiting to catch me in a lie. Of the person prowling the darkness who—I was sure—wanted me back. Of Mom, who could lose her job at any time because of her acute rheumatoid arthritis.

I'd have given anything to go back and relive that night. I'd have never gotten in my car.

"Still feeling off?" Mom asked.

"Yeah," I sighed. "But it's nothing major."

Looking at Mom was like looking at myself in twenty-five years. We'd had the same hairstyle for years, until I cut my matching hip-length hair ultra-short, just after we moved to Vancouver. We had the same freckled ivory skin and chocolate brown eyes; and though her crow's feet and smile lines aged her, people still mistook us for sisters on a regular basis, which I loved. We enjoyed the same casual-comfortable style, even shared clothes (because we were also the same size). And every time I looked at her, I saw the person I wanted to be—minus the OCD for cleaning.

"Oh, I forgot to tell you...." Mom added milk to her tea. "This came for you today. I didn't know you liked National Geographic." She took the magazine off the counter and placed it in front of me.

I was about to say, "I don't," but the post label had my name on it. With nothing else better to do, I picked it up and flipped past the table of contents, and an olive piece of paper fell out.

Mom was still turned toward the cupboards, so I grabbed the paper and unfolded the silly origami configuration; when I read the type-written message, I knew immediately that this magazine

90

had been sent to me on purpose. I felt a chill run up my spine, goose bumps rose on my arms, and my stomach plummeted to the ground.

It was from someone who knew all about *him*.

THEY KNOW EVERYTHING ABOUT YOU. YOU ARE BEING DECEIVED. IF THEY THREATEN YOU AGAIN, HE WILL RAISE HELL. DO NOT GIVE HIM A REASON TO. TOMORROW NIGHT SIX P.M. SHARP: HAWKSON'S ON MAIN. ASK FOR MANTIS. GO ALONE. YOUR SAFETY WILL DEPEND ON IT.

BURN THIS.

♣

VIII

When Katherine and I were younger, we'd gotten into a lot of trouble when we were caught teasing our friend's dad's bull. We'd taunted him, and he charged at us and broke through one of the electric fences. We'd been told many times not to go near him, but we went ahead anyway, and then the three of us had to climb a tree and wait for her parents to come home to rescue us. We could've been killed. I remember how angry my parents had been afterwards, and how expensive the fence had been to repair—it cost Katherine and me six months of allowance.

When Dad came home that night, I thought he was going to scream at us or punch the wall, but instead, he said something that I'll never *ever* forget.

"Some people will take risks because their friends are doing it. Some people will take risks because they love the adrenaline rush. And then there are the people who take risks, not because they don't know the danger involved, but because they believe something much more spectacular is waiting on the other side. Those people hear all the warnings, but they're not *listening*…they think they're invincible. And once they get hurt, or killed, it's too late. The damage is done."

Dad grabbed Katherine's and my hands, adding, "Second chances don't exist, girls—remember that!"

My first reaction to the note had been to tear it up. I thought Rion was trying to trick me; that he wanted to capture me and take me below when no one was around. That going to Hawkson's would be like climbing in with the bull again. But Rion had had plenty of opportunities to take me since the night I'd seen him outside. I was beginning to think he'd been there to tell me something, perhaps to warn me, but *not* to take me. It must have been important, too, because he'd put himself at extreme risk to do so. If he wanted to take me away, he would have barged right in and done it—no one could have stopped him. When I ran, Rion must have known how scared I was and left, assuming he'd never get close enough to talk to me again. Whatever it was, it must be important for him to keep trying to reach me.

I'd been starting to feel that I had gotten one past the *vykhars*, but what if I was wrong and we were in danger?

When I got up to my room, I locked the door behind me and started digging in my closet. It didn't take me long to locate the backpack where I'd stashed my clothes from the weekend of my accident. I found the crumpled note from Rion; it had the same gold shamrock symbol as the note from the National Geographic. I buried my face in my arms, thinking hard.

Caine made me question Rion's motives with his gruesome photographs, but I was tired of doubting, tired of worrying; my instincts told me Rion would *never* hurt me. When I considered it now, I believed in Rion, because he *cared*.

I had distrusted the *vykhars* immediately, and it was *Rion* who had warned me about them. Caine's voice creeped the heck out of me every time I heard it, and now I knew why: he had been lying. I was finally sure.

I had to know if we were in danger; if that meant having to meet this Mantis person at some tattoo shop in the middle of Vancouver's Skid Row, I was going to do it. Plus, I needed to get a message to Rion. I wanted to apologize, set things straight, and I wanted to hear what he had to say.

I took a deep breath and called downstairs, asking Mom to call in sick to work for me. When she asked me why, I complained of a headache and told her that I wanted to rest quietly and go to bed early—which was a lie, obviously. There was no way I'd be able to sleep.

I went to put the note back in the pocket of the pants when I suddenly caught his scent from the clothes.

It was the same pine, leather and must smell, and like the last time, it triggered a crystal clear memory of his face. It was a pleasant smell, and I only intended to take one more breath of it before putting the clothes back, but as I inhaled, I found myself clutching the clothes to my chest, digging my nails into the spaces of my ribs, holding on as tight as I could.

My heart was aching.

The last time I'd held those clothes, the smell had comforted me, but now a much more distinct feeling rose in me: a longing desire. Something about his scent created a yearning so strong, I knew contacting him wouldn't be adequate. No, I *had* to see him again.

§

Friday was a daze of notes and lectures and crap that passed in one ear and straight out the other. My math teacher called on me three times before I realized he was saying my name; I'd been too busy watching the second hand on the clock and thinking about how much time was left before six o'clock.

I didn't see Colin that day, but I did notice one of his pals, Andrew, staring at me whenever we passed in the hall. He gave me these frequent, disturbing once-overs, as if I didn't belong in the same space. I avoided his group of friends whenever I could, but even so, Andrew seemed to magically appear wherever I was—which totally pissed me off. So, when Chelsea told me she was leaving early from school for her soccer tournament in Chilliwack,

I willingly accepted the ride home before last period, which was only humanities, anyway.

At five fifteen, I was beginning to feel nervous about going downtown alone; however, the thought of getting the information I'd need to see Rion again got me out the door. If it wasn't for the irrepressible need to see him again, I never would have been able to peel myself from the couch—dark streets at night scared the hell out of me. I really wanted someone to go with me. And it wasn't until I walked outside to feed Duke and bring him in the house, that I realized the only *someone* I needed was standing right in front of me. Whoever this Mantis was, he wouldn't care that I'd brought my *dog*.

"Dukester...." I held his spiked collar, patting his ribs and watching his little brown eyes spark up with the notion of a walk. "Tonight, you're going on your first bus ride!" I'd been taking transit so often in the last couple of weeks, the bus driver and I were now on a first name basis. And lucky me, it was almost empty, so he looked the other way as I boarded with Duke. The only other passenger was a girl at the back listening to her iPod, sipping a hot drink.

My saliva glands tightened and gushed from the sight of the cup. That was exactly what I needed to settle my stomach. I decided to take a small detour and stop in at work before heading to Main Street. I couldn't just pass it up now, and if Brenda was there, I could personally apologize for playing hooky last night.

§

Only two people were working when I walked up to the front counter. I didn't recognize either of them. I only worked one or two short shifts a week, so I never got a chance to meet the people who worked on my days off. The girl at the front looked a little older than me. Her jet-black hair was shaved off on the right side, revealing a small shamrock tattoo (was it just me, or were shamrocks the new fad?) and she had a long dark purple fringe, covering her left eye. Her makeup was perfectly shaded and penciled around her light blue eyes and her lips were bright red. She looked like a flawless work of art, and when I took a step closer, I could smell the lilac fragrance of her hair products. Then she flipped her hair back slightly with her hand, and I realized that her face had been scarred from burns where it was hidden by the fringe. I didn't stare; I just pretended that I didn't see it.

"Is Brenda here?" I asked her.

"No, she's gone home for the day. Did you need to speak with her? I can leave her a message if you like." She picked up a pen.

"No." I played with the back of my hair. "Can you just tell her I stopped by and I'll call her tomorrow? I'm Liss."

Her eyebrows rose, and she stood, goggling at me for a few seconds like I had three heads.

I looked down at myself and brushed off my jeans. I wondered if maybe I'd spilled something on my shirt. "Is something wrong?"

"I'm sorry…no…not at all. I just…I've just heard a lot about you—*at work*."

"I didn't know I was that popular," I chuckled, trying my best to lighten the awkward situation. "I hope it was all good stuff."

She nodded. "Everything *I* heard was."

Neither of us could think of anything to say, which was totally painful. I began to organize the gift cards—which did not need organizing. I looked at my watch: 5:50. I had ten minutes to get to Hawkson's. "Well, I better get going," I sighed. "I'm getting a, uh, tattoo consultation in a few minutes."

The girl stared oddly at me again, as Duke barked at me from outside. Evidently, I was taking too long.

"Did you want something before you go?"

"Yeah, thanks. How about a…" It was going to be cold tonight, but my nerves had kept my body in a persistent heat wave, so I decided to order something cold. "…a rooibos shaken iced tea?"

"Oh…sure," the girl answered. "Any flavouring in it?"

"Blackberry, please."

"Coming right up."

I stood for a moment while she poured my drink, wondering if she would be comfortable with me asking about her tattoo. I wanted the low-down on this whole shamrock thing, assuming there had to be some meaning behind it, like the Chinese characters and fairies everyone seemed to copy from one another.

"Um, excuse me?" I asked her.

"Yes?"

"I'm curious about your tattoo. Does it mean something?"

"Oh, this one?" she pointed to the side of her head, when she saw me staring at it.

"Yeah."

"My ancestors are Irish," she replied confidently, handing me my iced tea.

"Thanks...mine are, too." I put the lid over top of my cup. "That's a nice way of honouring them."

She looked at me, puzzled for a moment, then shook her head and said, "I think so too...and I hope your meeting goes well."

"Yeah, I'd better go. See you around."

"For sure." Her phone beeped. I watched her take it out, glance at me, and then start texting voraciously. If Brenda, our manager, caught her, she'd be in huge trouble, but I wasn't a tattle-tale, so I just smiled back and headed out, wondering what could possibly be so important that it couldn't wait until her break.

I walked the last few blocks up Main Street, tossing back my drink while Duke trotted vigilantly beside me. At this time of night, the less fortunate people of Vancouver were making their beds on the sidewalks, streetwalkers were out in full force, and groups of young adults loitered at every corner. I paid little attention to them, but everyone stared at Duke, who was 150 pounds of solid American Bulldog muscle. He gave each person that walked past us the don't-come-any-closer glare. I patted him, and he looked back at me for a second, as if to say, "No problem." I love him so much!

When I got to Hawkson's, the barred door was locked and the blinds were pulled on the window. It reeked of pee and rancid food outside, and part of me thought about forgetting the whole thing, turning around and bolting home before I got accosted by a pimp for standing on the wrong cement square, but Rion popped into my thoughts again, and my heart begged me to stay for another moment, so I decided to knock. Just once. A single light flashed on in the back somewhere a second later, and a tall, gothic-dressed man with a mohawk and sleeves of ink from his neck to the tips of his fingers came skulking toward the door. He took a moment and inspected me with his black-penciled eyes, looked at Duke, who stared right back at him, and opened a sliding slot near his face so that I'd be able to hear him.

"Whaddaya want?"

I gulped and cleared my throat, turning up toward the slot. He looked like he was sizing me up to be dinner on his plate, and I didn't want to know the size of the knife blade that was probably hiding in his back pocket. "I'm here to see...um...Mantis."

His black eyes seared right into mine and I felt a little worried that I'd said something wrong, but then he replied, "Show me your left hand."

I was about to protest his request, but if I was getting any information tonight, I had to cooperate, so held my very shaky hand out for him to see.

"Palm up!"

I jumped, but Duke just stood there, controlled, with his nose up.

I turned my left palm up, realizing that he'd been looking for my birthmark, a brown patch that made its home on my thumb.

"It *is* you." His tone was much friendlier. Then his face lightened, and he almost smiled. "It worked. You came."

I kept my face straight. "I want to know how to contact Rion."

He shook his head slightly. "Are you alone?"

I looked at Duke, back up at him, and took a step closer to the door. "Tell me where he is. I need to speak with him in person."

"That's not possible. Rasadian told me he's left the area, and I was to—"

"What do you mean? Where did he go?"

"I wasn't informed of—"

"Was it Rasadian who wrote me the note?"

He nodded as his eyes looked past and around me, but then he waved his hand to stop me from speaking again and said, "We don't have time for this, and talking out here isn't safe." He methodically unlocked four latches and a deadbolt, ushered Duke and me through then stuck his head out and scoured the outside for possible followers, locking the door behind us when he was satisfied.

I took my own look around the shop. We were definitely alone. I pulled Duke closer to me as Mantis approached, but he walked right passed Duke and patted him on the head, without hesitation, saying, "Come this way." Normally, Duke would have bitten the hand off anyone who did that. He trusted no one he didn't know, but for some reason, he hadn't even growled; instead, he pulled me after Mantis. I warily allowed him to, holding tight to the pepper spray I'd stowed in my pocket.

The shop stank of bleach and paint. The walls were covered in painted dragons, spider-webs, and the Virgin Mary holding baby Jesus. One giant lion roaring in the midst of a dark forest took up an entire eight-foot wall. We followed Mantis through the hallway and into a sterilization area. The solutions and instruments made me uneasy; it reminded me of the hospital again. I stood by the door and Mantis stood on the inside. Duke picked up on my apprehension and parked his butt on my feet. I kept thinking someone was going to come up behind me.

"Pretty protective dog," Mantis said.

"You don't know the half. He's chewed through steel fencing."

"Good." He cleared the counter of sterile bagged trays. "Then keep him with you at all times. Extra protection is essential—especially now."

His answer caught me off guard. I'd wanted to scare him, not the other way around. "Is Rasadian here?"

"No. No one else is here."

"You *have* to tell me where Rion went," I cut in hastily. "I won't tell anyone, I just really need to talk to him!" I realized I sounded desperate.

"I've only been given directions to watch over you closely from now on. I don't have any other information."

"Do you know when he's coming back?"

"He's not," he replied slowly. "The malions are in the midst of rearranging their hierarchy, so even if he did, you'd never get in contact with him again. He's too high up."

I felt my shoulders drop. "But—"

"Hold on, Melissa," he interjected. "I need to know something first."

I shook my head. "Yes…*of course*…I'm sorry."

"You've talked to the *vykhars*, haven't you?"

"Yes…and—"

Mantis groused and pursed his lips together. "What did you tell them?"

"Nothing—I *swear*."

"Then why do they keep following you around? They're everywhere in Vancouver, and I received information yesterday that more are on the way—you must have told them something!"

"Mantis…please believe me," I begged. "I—"

"What the hell were you thinking, coming back above after the missing persons report was issued? You should have stayed below. None of this would be an issue if you'd just stayed! Do you know what kind of risk you're putting the malions in? Their new capital's not even half-completed, dammit!"

He was almost yelling, and I could feel my heart sink into my stomach. Things were much more serious than I had thought, but I didn't like his tone.

"I had to! I wasn't going leave my family!"

"What? I thought that was the whole point! Don't you realize Rion risked *everything* to get you back above safely? And then, when he tries to contact you, you called the *vykhars*!"

"I know—*that's* why I need to see him!"

"What made you think it was possible? You know how things work."

I closed my eyes against the tears that were forming, but Mantis saw.

"Or maybe you don't know…" he muttered, eyeing me. "Why'd you go below in the first place if you didn't want to stay?"

"It was an accident; Rion pulled me from my car…" I stared at the ground. I didn't know how to explain everything to him. I thought he would have all the answers.

"You mean, the accident wasn't a cover for your disappearance? I thought you were being—"

Something clicked, and I heard the faint sounds of a voice.

I looked up. It sounded like it had come from just above us. Mantis put his finger to his lips, and listened intently before slipping silently out of the sterilization area.

Duke began to whine at me.

"Mantis!" I called quietly. "Mantis, what is it?"

I heard the same sounds above us again. Duke froze, looking after Mantis. I saw the little hairs stand up on the back of his neck. I gulped, ready to run if I saw someone, when Mantis came rushing back around the corner.

"Get out of here, Liss," he hissed, grabbing my arm and hauling me to the back of the building. He let go of me when we passed a wall of lockers and nodded toward the unlit hallway in front of us. "Go out the back door and go straight home. I'll find a way to contact you in a few days!"

"Wait a second…What about the *vykhars*? What about—"

He grabbed my shoulders and looked sharply into my eyes; his black irises locked on mine with fierce determination. "You know the symbol, right? The one on the note."

I nodded quickly.

"Always look for the symbol, Melissa. Trust no one else, do you hear me?"

I nodded again.

"Now get out of here!" His hands were trembling. *"Now!"*

He shoved Duke and me out the door and pulled it shut. We were in a recessed doorway opening on the alley behind the shop. My heart was pounding and the winter cold scurried up my spine as I started to step out into the alley. I was saved by Duke, who froze. I followed his line of sight and saw two tall men in black suits blocking the exit from the alley on my left. *Vykhars*. I was too paralyzed by fright to notice they had their backs to me. Before I could catch my breath I heard an ear-piercing scream coming from inside.

Mantis' scream.

I shot away from the wall, covering my mouth and sinking my teeth into my finger to keep silent. I didn't care if they saw me, I had to get away. I ran to the right, away from the suits, and chanced a look over my shoulder. They were gone.

Mantis screamed again and the sound was so blood-curdling I covered my ears just as six gun shots were fired. I hesitated, desperate for any sign that Mantis might still be alive, that he'd come bursting out of a door somewhere and lead me to safety. But instead, I was thrown onto my back as a giant fireball exploded out of the door. The first floor was in flames from the explosion. The heat was so intense I could feel it scorching my exposed skin as I grabbed Duke's leash and got back to my feet. I started to run again, and didn't stop as I emerged from the alley onto Pender Street.

I was running much faster than I thought possible, and Duke kept time beside me as Chinatown passed away behind us. I couldn't look back; I didn't want to think about what had happened inside Hawkson's, or about Mantis. I took deep breaths, trying to stop my heart from punching against my chest. I could hear the howls of sirens behind me.

The *vykhars* were even more dangerous than I had realized. And now I had absolutely no one to turn to—again—as the only people who knew about the malions were Abby and Mantis. One was in hiding and the other was probably dead. It seemed like every time I began to feel as if I was finally coping with this whole predicament, something else set me back. I couldn't take much more.

Running away from my second near-death experience in as many weeks, something suddenly boiled up within me. The anger I'd been keeping in check for the past few weeks abruptly seized all sense of control and tossed it back toward the blazing building, where my momentary friend lay in a pile of his own blood and ashes. Anger roiled through my body like venom and I was unable to stop it. I had more than enough change in my wallet, but I didn't want to ride the bus home. I wanted to keep running. It was that, or go back to the burning building and do something I would truly regret, like wringing those black-suited bastards' necks with my bare hands.

"Come on, Duke." I picked up his leash, and started jogging.

We'd run half way home when Duke pulled me to a walk. I wasn't even out of breath; I was on my fourth, second wind and I could have run the rest of the way at full speed. Rage possessed me, and my nerves spiralled into a frenzy of adrenaline, asking for more, but I settled with Duke and together we walked the rest of the way home.

Power walked.

As we made our way back to the house, my frustration mounted, as images of what had just happened tangled with what Mantis had said. At the core of that frustration stood Rion, who was never coming back. I would never get a chance to apologize for propelling him away, or thank him again for everything he'd done to ensure my safety.

The house was still empty when Duke and I arrived. The clock in the kitchen read 7:20 and I knew that Katherine wouldn't be home until well after ten. Mom, who was on her night shift, would creep in around five thirty a.m. I put Duke into his kennel so that he could have some water then marched back into the house and upstairs to my bedroom, feeling as if I was about to explode. The route home hadn't been a successful diversion—not in the least.

I clenched my fists tight and stormed down the hallway. I could feel my face becoming flushed; the more I thought about how much of an idiot I'd been, the more I began to vibrate. My nails dug into my palms, and I so badly wanted to scream. I was tired of feeling like a burden to everyone. I was tired of not being able to trust anyone. I was tired of being afflicted with secrets. I was tired of worrying.

I was tired of being tired.

When I opened the door to my room, I knew I was going to burst. And that's exactly what happened.

I took my pillows and whipped them across the room. Then I took my quilts, ripped them back and backhanded my textbook, sending it smacking against the wall. Clothes went flying, a cardboard box hit my window and I punched a crack in a wood carving I'd created last year in art class. My clock hit the closet door, splitting the face open and setting the alarm off which made me pick it up and throw it again. The last thing within my reach was a plastic binder that I'd brought out yesterday to use at school; unfortunately, it, too, was hurled at my dresser and busted before I remembered I didn't have another one. Only I didn't care at that point. And after all that I'd done in my bedroom, I didn't feel any better. I wanted to break something else. I wanted to punch a hole right through the wall. I wanted my fists to bleed. I wanted to pull every hair out of my head.

I looked around, and when there was nothing more of my own to damage, I finally let it all come out. I screamed as loud as I could. I bent back and bellowed to the ceiling, three words that described exactly what I had been feeling: "I. AM. DONE."

Out of breath, I stood up straight again and panted, looking around for something else I could hurl because I was still enraged. The first object my eyes found was that damn book, *Moonstone, Mae and Malion Tales*.

It was lies. A bunch of stupid, stupid lies.

I was ripping out the pages and tearing them in half when the doorbell rang. I immediately stopped in the middle of my fit. I wasn't expecting anyone.

Ding-dong. Ding-dong.

My cell phone beeped. I dove across the hurricane of my room and snatched it from underneath my sheets. It was a text message from Colin.

```
Its me at the door. I know ur home and
I heard u scream. If you dont come to
the door in 1 min Im breaking it down.
```

I quickly text him back:

```
Im not in the mood Colin. Go
away. I dont want to talk.
```

Seconds later, I heard the front door pop open. I threw my phone down and rushed to the stairs, just as Colin was closing the door behind him.

"I said I'm not in the—hey! How did you get in my house?"

Colin glanced up at me. He was soaking wet and his flattened hair was dripping all over the carpet.

"It's called an unlocked door, Liss. Don't you have any concept of safety? This isn't the fifties, you know." Then he turned around to kick off his boots; his black leather jacket glistened with rain beads, and his jeans looked as if he'd just been puddle jumping. It was hailing outside now, the pieces of ice pounding against the skylight above me, echoing like a standing ovation in a stadium. I was pissed off that I had just missed the storm on my way home. Maybe *that* would have cooled me off.

"Lay off," I barked back. I'd been so upset when I got home, setting the alarm again had completely slipped from my mind. "And you can leave now. I want to be alone."

He crossed his arms. "I'm not leaving until you tell me why you were screaming." Then his eyes narrowed. "And don't lie about it this time."

I scowled back at him. "Why are you so wet? Did you walk here?"

He shook the water off of his head. "Yeah, so *what*? Quit trying to change the subject. What's gotten in to you? You sounded like you were yelling at someone. Are you all right?"

I bit my lip. "No."

"Then what the hell is it?" he demanded, taking off his jacket.

"I meant what I said, Colin. I want you to leave—get OUT!" One of my hands was the on the bannister, the other had found an empty planter on a stand beside me that I was going to hurl at him if he didn't do as I said.

And of course, he didn't. His facial expression changed as eyes regarded me slowly, then he started making his way up the stairs.

"Liss," he whispered from three steps down, "you're shaking. Please tell me what's wrong." He looked at the planter in my hand and then up at me again. "If you think throwing that at me is going to work, it's not. Something happened tonight, didn't it?"

I looked down at my hand, and it *was* vibrating uncontrollably. Then I looked back at Colin, and he was reaching out for me.

"Colin." I backed up a few steps. "I...I need....Please don't come any closer." It wasn't just tonight's events that had traumatized me; it was the fact that Colin and I were the only ones in the house. Being alone with a guy was something I was not okay with; it reminded me too much of the past. And I had only known Colin for a couple of weeks, which wasn't helping the situation.

"I'm sorry," he said softly, raising his hands and stepping backward down the rest of the stairs. "I just thought I could take that planter out of your hand before you crush the thing." He waited there for a few moments, and when I didn't answer him or hand it over, he asked, "Would you like something to drink? I make a mean cup of coffee. Or maybe tea would make you feel better. You don't have to move. Just sit right there and I'll find my way around the kitchen, okay?"

I swallowed and just stared at him. His face softened and he tried to smile, probably hoping that I would smile back, but I didn't.

"Okay," he finally said. "I'll be right back."

106

I heard cupboards open, dishes clang, and the kettle boiling on the stove. And all the while I just stood there like a zombie, until the scent of chamomile and citrus caught my nose. It was my favourite herbal tea, and all of a sudden, my mouth began to water when I realized how thirsty I was from running. I slowly made my way to the kitchen and peeked around the corner. Colin was looking into all the cupboards, and when he found the chocolate chip cookies, he put the bag in his mouth and turned around.

"Hey," he said around the cookies. "Why don't you sit down on the couch? I'll bring you a mug and some cookies in just a second. Is that okay?"

I nodded and headed into the living room.

Colin brought in a tray a few minutes later and made himself at home on the loveseat across from me. He poured us both a mug and sat back as far away from me as he could. By that time, I was curled up with my head against my hands; my legs were feeling weak and rubbery, and exhaustion was catching up with me from my combination marathon and destructo-frenzy.

A few more minutes went by, then Colin said, "You don't have to say anything if you don't want to, Liss. I didn't mean to snoop."

My eyes looked up and met his. I'd been staring at the curtains, thinking about what Mantis had told me about Rion, almost forgetting that Colin was still in the room.

"I came here tonight to see if you wanted to go bowling with a bunch of my friends. They have cosmic bowling downtown on Friday nights, and I thought you'd really like it. But when I got here, I heard you screaming and—"

"I'm sorry for snapping at you, Colin," I sat up and hugged my legs into my chest. "I just…I just had a bad night."

"I can tell." He leaned forward to set down his mug. "Did someone hurt you, Liss?"

"No," I finally answered. "*I'm* the one that hurt someone. Hurt their feelings, I mean."

"I'm sure you didn't mean to, did you?"

I thought about what I would say for a moment. I fingered the rim of my mug, ran my hands through my hair and looked at my overgrown nails trying to find the best way to talk to Colin about my problem without giving everything away. "Can I ask you something?" I gulped, hoping it would come out right.

He inched closer to me, though sustained his distance by staying on the loveseat. "Anything."

I took a deep breath, let my feet dangle down off of the couch, and looked up at him. "How far would you go to apologize to a person who meant a great deal to you? Say if you knew you were never going to see them again."

Colin didn't waver. "That kinda stuff eats me alive. I don't like knowing I'm at fault for something, and it's even worse when I know someone has been hurt because of it." Then he smiled. "If I really cared about the person, I would travel to the ends of the earth and back."

I frowned. "I wish it were that easy."

"Last summer, when I dated this girl," he fidgeted with the zipper on his jacket, "her dad didn't like that we were together, so he made her switch schools. She hated me for not standing up to him, and the last time I saw her was on the top of this lookout point, when she told me that she wished she'd never met me.

"She was the first girl I'd ever loved. I *still* love her. But I'll never see her again, and I'll never get a second chance to make things right between us. She changed her phone numbers, her email address, and un-friended me on Facebook. I *actually* cried for, like, frickin', a whole day after that. For all I know, she could've run away or something." Then he grabbed his mug and took a big, long drink.

"How did you get over her?"

Colin shook his head. "I didn't. Instead, I went back to that lookout point, to say what I had *wanted* to say to her."

"Alone?"

"Yup." He shrugged his shoulders. "Even though she wasn't there, I just closed my eyes and imagined she was. It was the only thing I could think of to help me move on."

I wanted to comment on what he had said. I wanted to tell him it was the most beautiful thing I'd ever heard a guy say, and that I had more respect for him for being so brutally honest with me. But I could sense he wasn't quite finished talking, and when someone opens up to you like that, you can completely stomp on their self-confidence by interrupting, so I remained silent, allowing him to continue.

He sniffed, wiped his nose, and flicked his zipper around a few more times before adding, "You know, I've never told anyone about that, so I'd appreciate it if you kept it to yourself. I don't openly tell people I've cried over a girl."

I nodded. "You have my word."

"You probably think I'm a big wuss now or something."

"I didn't say that." I grabbed a cookie. "But what I *was* going to say...was thank you. Thank you for trusting me with something so private." Trust and conviction was something I valued within a friendship, and Colin telling me something so personal made me feel like we'd bonded a little. It felt good.

"I can't say doing the same will work for you, if that's even the case...but it may be worth a try."

I smiled, for the first time that night, and replied, "I—" I instantly took a bite of my cookie to cut myself off. I almost said, "I don't think it would make any difference", only I knew that would hurt his feelings, so I took a sip of my tea then said, "I hope she comes back to you one day."

Colin sighed. "I wake up every day hoping so. Because every day that goes by and I don't see her or hear from her, I feel like a little piece of me dies inside."

We made eye contact right then, and only for a few brief seconds, but it was just long enough for me to see he was wiping his right eye with the back of his hand.

When I went to bed that night, I lay there in the dark, wondering if I'd left Rion feeling just like Colin felt when that girl left him: completely hopeless. I wondered if Colin had gone to her house, like Rion had come to mine. Or if that girl wished she could see Colin again, like I wanted to see Rion.

Even though it was against his will, eventually, Colin had found a way to move on. It was clear Rion had found a way, too, according to Mantis, and that was to leave. I needed to get over what had happened, too, but there was no way in hell I was going back to that accident scene. Standing there, apologizing to a figment of my imagination, wasn't something that would help me move on. No, it would make things tremendously worse. I sighed.

The only thing which had gone right today was my talk with Colin. Despite Chelsea and Katherine's warnings about him, I was glad to have him for a friend. And though I couldn't give him any details, it was nice to know there was someone out there who truly understood.

IX

"Heads up!"

I heard the voice from a distance, but I just stood there. My eyes were fixated on the empty spot in the student parking lot where Colin's truck was supposed to be parked. He'd been absent from school for almost a month, and everyone seemed to think it was hilarious how he could still pass with flying colours while *apparently* working for his dad's business out of town. I wasn't laughing.

The last night I'd seen him, he actually had me believing I could trust him enough to talk about my secrets. But he got an urgent text message and rushed off, telling me that he'd explain tomorrow. I didn't think much of it at the time, but tomorrow came. And then the next day. And then the next day. He never showed.

It was now December, and I was beginning to think he'd switched schools, too. Nice so-called friend. He didn't even have the decency to text me, though I'd texted him a bunch of times. There was only one word for how it made me feel: ditched. Well, *if* he ever decided to show his face again, he'd be getting more than a piece of my mind.

"LISS! LOOK *OUT!*"

I turned slightly to the side, just in time for a black and white sphere to come crashing into the side of my head, connecting directly with my left temple. It stunned me for a moment, but I didn't fall down.

"Holy crap, Liss! Are you all right?"

Chelsea and Mr. Faulkner were bolting toward me, while everyone else in my gym class stopped and stared and sniggered.

"Huh?" I still felt a little dazed.

"Melissa, look at me for a moment," Mr. Faulkner replied. "I want to check your eyes." He pulled out his pocket penlight, flashed it in both of my pupils, and turned to Chelsea, whose eyes resembled a pair of saucers. "Maybe you should take her to the First Aid room to lie down, Chelsea."

"Good *grief*, Liss," Chelsea bleated as she wrapped her arms around me, squeezing hard while I slouched against her. "I'm sooooo sorry…I slipped on the frost and kicked the ball right at you. I can't believe I just hit you in the head. I *knew* I should have worn my cleats today!"

"It's okay, Chels." I shrugged. "It was an accident." Mr. Faulkner called the class to attention and continued the soccer game, and Chelsea and I slowly walked toward the school.

When we got close to the side doors, Chelsea grabbed my shoulders and spun me toward her. "Liss."

"Yeah?"

Her eyes flitted back and forth between mine. "Something is really wrong with you."

"What do you mean?"

"Don't take this the wrong way, but you look like the walking dead. No. You look like that donkey, Eeyore, from *Winnie the Pooh* with your head hanging low, and you've been ghosting around school for the past few weeks, hardly talking to me." Her shoulders dropped and she let go of me. "You've got huge dark circles under your eyes, your jeans are baggier than what I remember, you've fallen asleep in chemistry almost every day this past two weeks, and whenever I've asked about it, you say, 'Nothing.' I know it's not *nothing*, so please tell me…I'm your best friend, I can't stand seeing you like this any longer!"

I hadn't realized my distraction was so noticeable. "I'm just...I don't know...I don't want to bother you with my problems."

Chelsea's mouth dropped. "Then what the HELL am I your best friend for? I want you to burden me! Can't you see I care about you?"

I sighed and looked down at the ground. "I just need some time, that's all."

"Well, I'm calling your bluff, Lissy. Katherine said—"

My eyes immediately met hers. "Since when did you two start talking?"

Chelsea swallowed. "I ask you how you're doing every morning on the way to school, and you always say, 'Fine'. I'm getting tired of seeing you on this downhill slide and not getting any answers, so I asked her if something happened to you at home. I thought maybe you two had a fight or something..." she trailed off when she saw my fists ball up.

My face became hot and I bit my lip as hard as I could. "And what did *she* say?"

"She said you two haven't spoken more than a couple words to one another in the past few weeks..." She held out her hand, and starting counting on her fingers what Katherine had told her. "...you quit jogging, you never eat more than one or two bites at dinner, you never come out of your room anymore—except to sit on the couch and stare out the window like a lost puppy—and at night you mutter to yourself about some *Ryan* guy."

I felt my eyes begin to tingle at the sound of his name. My nails dug hard into my palms; though I couldn't see my hands, I knew for sure that I must have broken the skin barrier. I had no idea I'd said anything out loud.

"Who the hell is *Ryan*?"

"No one important. Not anymore, that is."

"I know I've been super busy with soccer tournaments and I haven't been around very much with my new coaching job, but why didn't you tell me you were having guy problems? I can't believe you didn't tell me!"

My eyes found hers again. "Chelsea...I...." I wanted to tell her I didn't want to talk about it, but she'd already heard it too many times. "I'm just trying not to think about it." I opened the side door and continued towards the office. Chelsea caught up to me after a moment.

"Well, clearly *that* approach isn't working." She grabbed my arm and steered me to a bench in the hall. "Who is this guy? Where did you meet him? Do I know him? Is he hot?"

I couldn't help it, I smiled. "Well, he does have these amazing green eyes..."

"And..."

"And the most incredible physique..."

"Physique? Who says that? Just say he's ripped."

"Whatever. Anyway, please don't take me to the First Aid room. I think I'd rather just go home."

"Ten four—roger that. What do you need, Lissy? Something sweet? Did you want to stop and get something to eat on the way home? You look like you could use a Big Mac and a chocolate milkshake—and an *extra*-large fries. Food always makes you feel better—*that* I know. Whaddaya say?"

"I think I just need to lay down, Chels. Can I take a rain-check on McDonald's? Maybe this weekend?"

She scrutinized me, dissecting my facial expression. "If I find out tomorrow that you haven't eaten dinner tonight, I'm going to hold you down and force feed you tomorrow at lunch. Got it?"

"I promise I'll eat dinner." I wanted to reply sarcastically, but I was feeling too happy about getting the subject off Rion.

We grabbed our things from our lockers and headed home. Chelsea told the office that she was leaving school to take me home; thank goodness the secretary didn't ask questions when Chelsea said I was sick. As we walked, I felt strangely light. It might have been the soccer ball to the head, but I think telling Chelsea about Rion, even just that tiny nugget of information, lifted something off me.

A few minutes later we pulled up in front of my house. "Hey, did you get your licence and Care Card in the mail yet?"

"Yeah. But it doesn't do much good when you have to keep bumming a ride off your best friend all the time. I'm saving up for a car, I promise."

"Well, maybe we could go car shopping together. I like that kinda stuff."

"Sure." I shrugged.

"Are you doing anything for your birthday tomorrow? You *did* remember your own birthday…"

"Ummm…" I hadn't forgotten, but I was hoping *she* had.

"*Please* tell me you're not boycotting it again."

"I hadn't actually thought about it…see you tomorrow."

I got out quickly, but Chels rolled down the window and shouted out to me: "I will see you tomorrow, birthday girl—I'm still wrapping up your locker, *chicky-pie!*"

"Right," I grumbled as I watched her speed off, burning down the street in her little yellow Firefly. Stupid birthday.

Seventeen. I should have been excited. But I wasn't. Not in the least. I didn't like being the center of attention for anything. It was the one thing I completely despised. I preferred to just lie low in the background and cheer along with the crowd; that was my style. Chelsea, on the other hand, loved to make a big deal out of nothing. Well, I'd tried.

I opened the front door to find Katherine standing in the kitchen archway with her hands planted firmly on her hips, glaring fiercely. She looked madder than she'd ever been.

"That is MY sweater! Take it off!"

I stood for a moment, trying to process her words. "Wait, what? This sweater?" I fingered my top. "You told me I could have it last year when you were thinking about trashing it. You *hate* this sweater!"

"I do *not*. Give it back right now. It's *mine!*"

Then she came storming toward me, stiletto heels banging on the floor in perfect time with her wild, swinging arms. I shook my head at her and leaned forward. If she thought I was bowing down because she was yelling, she thought wrong. I didn't put up with her shoddy attitude like everyone else our age. "You want your stupid sweater? Fine! Take it!" I whipped it off and threw it on the ground in front of her. "If I'd have known you wanted it back, I wouldn't have put it in the dryer on perma-press the other day!"

Katherine sucked in a big breath and her jaw dropped. None of her clothes ever went in the dryer.

"You…You…BITCH!" She shrieked, and called me a few more choice names—none of which should ever be repeated—finishing with, "I HOPE YOU NEVER—!" She was within two feet of me with her hands stretched out to throttle me, when Mom opened the door of her bedroom, sending the techno music from her exercise CD blaring into the foyer.

"What on God's green *earth* is going on down there?"

"Go to HELL, Liss! Don't go in my room again!" Katherine interjected, marching toward the stairs.

"Liss, what's the matter?" Mom called down. "And why don't you have a shirt on?"

I was panting heavily with rage, so I took a deep breath to calm myself before answering, with my glare focussed on Katherine's back as she climbed the stairs, "It's nothing *remotely* important."

Mom frowned. "Please don't fight anymore, girls. I don't want your father to see you two like this when he gets home tomorrow."

I perked up. "He's coming home tomorrow?"

"YEAH!" Katherine shouted from the top of the stairs. "ISN'T THAT NICE OF HIM! HE COULDN'T HAVE THE DECENCY TO COME HOME FOR *MY* BIRTHDAY THIS YEAR, COULD HE?" Then her voice softened as she made her way down the hall toward her room, but I could still hear her muttering, "He doesn't give a crap about me."

It was so very clear all of a sudden; this little outburst of hers had absolutely nothing to do with the sweater.

"Please don't make any special plans, Mom." I turned up to her.

"I know, sweetheart. I just thought I'd make dinner at home for us, but I still want to sing to you, if that's okay."

I sighed. I would have told anyone else to forget it. But I'd never deny Mom that pleasure; she deserved to celebrate just as much as I did, after enduring my babyhood. I'd almost died twice as a premature baby.

Mom continued talking, but I only heard a quarter of what she'd said. My head twinged, reminding me why I'd come home early in the first place.

"Liss? Are you listening to me? I spoke to the lady at the nursery today and she said that the bulbs you ordered are ready to be picked up."

"Oh, good. Sorry, Mom, I just need to lie down for a few minutes. Chelsea kicked a ball at my head in gym." Mom gaped at me for a moment, so I clarified, "It was an accident."

"Oh…right. I'll let you know when dinner's ready." She made her way into the kitchen, and I went to my room. When I got there, I locked my door and went straight for my bed. My beautiful, wonderful bed. The only time I had peace of mind was when I was asleep. Then I didn't have to worry about *vykhars* or feel guilty about Rion—at least, when I wasn't dreaming about burning buildings and the sound of screams.

I toyed with the idea of getting my Rion-smelling clothes out again, something which had comforted me before, but in the end decided it was in my best interest to ignore them. I knew I should get them professionally cleaned, but I wasn't quite ready yet.

§

The next night, Dad was running late. He was due home at seven, but at quarter to eight he telephoned to say his flight had been delayed. Later, just as I'd stirred Mom's spaghetti sauce for the fortieth time, the doorbell rang.

"Dad!" I hollered.

"Oh, joy on a *stick*," Katherine snarled from the living room. I ignored her and flung the door open.

"Hiya, sweetheart! Happy birthday!"

"Hi, Dad!" I threw my arms around him. He kissed my forehead and gave me a little squeeze, which was pretty good for him, not being the hugging type. "How's my *girls*?"

He clearly made the expression plural, hoping that Katherine would be happy to see him, too, but when he peered around the corner to where she'd been sitting, she slapped her fashion magazine down on her lap and shot him a curdled smile. Dad got the hint. "Nice to see you, too, sourpuss."

Then I heard a musical car horn coming from down the street. "Oh! I wasn't expecting her to arrive so soon!"

"Who, Dad?"

"Why don't you see for yourself?"

I looked at him, confused, then stepped around him to look outside the door, feeling my jaw slowly unhinge the closer the car came to our house. "Oh my goodness—Dad!"

"Happy birthday, Liss!"

I couldn't contain myself. I ran outside, just in time to see Chelsea pulling up next to the house in a black Volkswagen Beetle. My dream car.

"We got you, didn't we!" Chelsea said, getting out and running toward me to give me a hug. "Welcome to Club Seventeen!"

I hugged her back and opened the passenger door. My new bug had leather seats, a sunroof and a CD player. I grinned at my parents, who were right behind me. "I don't deserve this!"

"Sure you do, honey. Your cousin's hand-me-down Civic was ready to give up the ghost, anyway. We bought Katherine her jeep, and we spent the same amount of money on your Beetle. It was only fair, and, just like Katherine, we bought you three months insurance to get you going."

"Thanks, you guys." I hugged both my parents and thanked them again.

"Chelsea helped me pick out the car, but your mom planned the whole thing," Dad replied, looking at Mom with doe eyes.

"I got the ladybug seat covers for you," Chelsea added when the hugs were finished, "and some of those Black Ice air-fresheners you love."

"*Chelsea*," I sighed. "You shouldn't have!"

She beamed. "I knew that you'd been looking for those seat covers for your last car, and I found these ones online a couple weeks ago when your mom called." I hugged her again and she said in my ear, "I'm glad you like them."

"How nice."

I spun around and Katherine was standing right there.

"Katherine," Dad warned, "if you haven't got anything nice to say then don't say it at all. This is your sister's day…the least you could do is wish her a good one."

"I'd rather eat sh—!"

"Katherine!" Mom scolded.

"GET INSIDE THE HOUSE RIGHT NOW, YOUNG LADY!" Dad pointed at the house. "DON'T EVER LET ME HEAR YOU TALK LIKE THAT AGAIN!"

In sync, Chelsea's, Mom's and my mouth formed o's. I had never heard Dad yell at any of us before. He was the one who walked away and took something we valued with him—like our freedom to go out with friends or whatever. Usually, Katherine would yell back at him, but this time, she shot her fists down, voiced her frustration with a loud and exaggerated growl and trudged back into the house.

"She can stay home tonight, El," Dad said to Mom. "It's time she had an attitude adjustment. I'm sick and tired of it."

Mom grinned.

"So it will just be the four of us for dinner tonight then." Dad looked at Chelsea. "What time's the reservation for?"

"Eight thirty, Mr. Lawrence."

"Well then, let's get going, shall we, loves?"

Loves? Since when was Dad so casual? I assumed things must be going really well at work. I was thankful for whatever it was, because he'd been in Mr. Workhorse for a while, and his new exuberance was contagious.

"Where are we going?" I asked them, cheerfully.

"SIP," Chelsea answered.

"SIP?" I exclaimed. "Really?"

It was *only* my favourite restaurant, and I hadn't been there in almost a year. I couldn't get enough of their beer-battered fries.

"Yup, and you're driving us!"

At the restaurant, we ate while my parents told Chelsea stories about the past seventeen years. Chelsea's mother—the most talented baker I've ever known—made me a cake with beautiful vines of spring flowers all in different pastel colors, and a little rainbow that ended in a fondant pot of chocolate gold coins. The inscription on the cake read: *Wishing you all the best in your next 17 years, Happy Birthday Lissy*. I gazed at the number 1 and 7 candles, while everyone waited for me to make a wish. I couldn't think of anything other than Rion. But wishing to see him again so that I could apologize properly and move on had no better chance of coming true than wishing for Katherine and me to find common ground, or solving the mystery behind the Bermuda Triangle, for that matter. As a child, I'd wished for Mom to have another baby for years—something she desperately wanted, too, and which never happened—so why bother now?

I blew out the candles without wishing at all. Everyone clapped and cheered, and I smiled accordingly.

We dropped Chelsea off and arrived home after ten o'clock. I thanked my parents and headed inside to avoid witnessing my parent's public display of necking—though it was really cute how Dad seemed extra cuddly with Mom for once.

I was still over the moon about my new car. I could come and go as I pleased without looking at a schedule, transfers, or phoning a friend. It felt good to have something to smile about again.

"Ah!" Katherine's voice came from upstairs. "Hah! Mother of—"

What the heck was she doing up there? The noises continued, and I had this terrible feeling in my stomach. We'd come home early, and I wondered if...oh for Pete's sake. Katherine was up there having sex with Landon. Loud sex.

"UH!...AH!"

Was she really that brain-dead? As disgusting as it was, I thought I'd give her the benefit of the doubt and warn her she was about to be locked in the attic for the rest of her life when our parents came in. I raced up the stairs, and halted as soon as I found my bedroom door open and my light on.

She was not having sex. She was in *my* room. I inhaled fiercely.

"Katherine!" I shrieked, breaking into a run. "Get out of my room!"

Everything in my room had been turned upside-down. My clothes were everywhere, my drawers had been torn apart, my desk had been ripped open, and in the center of it all stood my horrible sister—who was going to feel my wrath if she didn't leave.

"You go into my room, I go into yours!" she exclaimed breathlessly.

"For the bazillionth time, I haven't gone in your room! Why are you doing this?"

She stood up, panting. "You've got my scarves, my nail polish and my pyjamas you lying little THIEF! I knew you'd been in my room!"

"I *HAVE* NOT! You gave all those to me when we moved. You had a whole bag of things you didn't want and you said I could have them!"

"The HELL I did! And this is MY bag!"

I saw the backpack in her hand, and my stomach balled up. It was the one I'd kept the clothes in from my weekend with Rion. My whole body began to boil.

"Where are the clothes that were in that bag?" I demanded.

"For your *information*, those were *my* clothes, and they are now in the wash! They freaking stank, and you had no business—"

"Those were never yours!" I hit my fist against the doorway, and I could feel the vibration on the floor. "Those were *mine*…you stupid, ugly, FAT COW! GET OUT!"

She gave me the finger, and without thinking, I flew at her. I literally dove across the room and slammed her right into the wall. She grabbed my hair and pulled as hard as she could, then she scratched my arms. "GET OFF ME! I HATE YOU, LISS!"

When she proceeded to tell me just how *much* she hated me, in so many words, I did something I never, in a million years, thought I would do. I punched her right in the face.

X

When my parents saw what Katherine and I had done to each other, they grounded us for a week. Katherine's left eye went black and swelled shut, and she threatened to press charges if I ever came near her again. I didn't care.

In fact, I didn't care about the grounding, either. And I could have cared less that my new (to me) bug hadn't moved an inch since my birthday dinner. I didn't care that I'd told Katherine I no longer considered her my sister, and I didn't care that my parents gave me the silent treatment for the rest of the night.

So what was it that bothered me? Rion's scent was gone. It was replaced by the smell of Mom's lavender detergent and summer breeze fabric softener. The phone number Rion had given me was now shredded into a thousand pieces.

I began to ache inside again. I hadn't realized how important it was to me to have those clothes—his smell—around, even if I never took them out. That scent was the only thing I had left from the man who had saved my life, the one who sat diligently by my side and nursed me back to health, the one who had gone to great lengths to ensure my safety and security—the one who I so desperately did not want to forget. By washing those clothes, Katherine had pulled the plug on the sense of well-being I had slowly been rebuilding.

I tossed and turned all that night, unable to shut off my brain, wishing there was some way to stop myself from hurting any longer. How much easier my life would be, if I could only let go. How good it would feel to have a day go by where I could think about Rion and not get an uncomfortable tightening in my chest or trembling in my hands and knees.

When I walked into the cafeteria at lunchtime the next day and sat next to Chelsea, she rolled her eyes.

"What?"

"I heard."

I sighed. "About the grounding or the black eye?"

"Both. My mom saw your mom at Price Smart. Socked her one, did ya?"

"Yeah," I sighed. "I feel kinda bad about it. It got us both grounded. I don't know what got into me...I just totally lost it. I tried to apologize, but—"

"Oh, whatever. It's only a week. It's not the end of the world. Get over it."

"You know, Chelsea?" I slammed my hands on down on the table. "You have no idea what it's like to live with a sister that makes your life a living hell." I was so tired. The last thing I wanted to hear was her sarcasm, and it made me angry that she wasn't siding with me, like she always did when Katherine and I argued.

Chelsea's face soured. "For your information, I *did* have a sister. And not having her around *does* make my life a living hell, but I don't drag everyone else down with me—or maybe you've just been a little too self-absorbed lately to remember!"

My hand cupped my mouth shut, and I tried to redeem myself. "You *never* told me you had a sister....Oh my goodness, Chelsea, I had no idea!" I tried to backpedal, but it didn't work. She was pissed.

"And you know what else?" she exclaimed, leaning toward me. "I would give anything to have her alive today—even if we *did* hate one another. You and Katherine need to grow up!"

"*I* need to grow up?"

"Yes, you do! And I'm tired of you moping around all the time. I've done just about everything I can to try to cheer you up, I even helped your dad pick out your favourite car, and you're *still* acting like you've had a death in the family or something. You have absolutely no coping skills."

I gasped. She'd never insulted me like that. "You have no idea what I've been through, Chelsea."

"Because you won't tell me!"

"Chelsea…I—"

"It's about that Ryan guy, isn't it?"

"Well…it's more complicated than that…and—"

"And you think, because I haven't had a boyfriend, I wouldn't know how to help you. *Right*?"

"Just *listen* for a moment," I pleaded, hoping to reason with her before she lost it. I didn't want her feelings to get hurt, but I sensed that it was already too late.

"You know what? Don't bother!" She got up and began walking out of the cafeteria.

"Chelsea! Hold on a second!"

She turned around. "Maybe I *would* have been able to help. But you refuse to give me a chance." Then she held her hands up and yelled, "WHEN ARE YOU EVER GOING TO LET ME IN?"

I stood there in the center of the cafeteria while everyone stared at me, and I had to look around myself twice, because it felt like all of the walls had just come crashing over top of me.

I had a spare block after lunch. I wanted to go home, but I couldn't while my parents were there, so I decided to spend it in the library. I opened my math textbook to make it look like I was actually doing something, but I just buried my head in my arms and tried to think of ways to fix my life.

I heard the library door open, and looked up. It was Andrew, Mr. I-Show-Up-Wherever-Liss-Is had followed me. In fact, he was walking right over to my table. I quickly looked back down at my books; he never approached me. Before I had the chance to get up and walk away, his black shoes were standing right in front of my table. Thank goodness we weren't the only ones in the library, because Andrew made me nervous: creeped-out, goose-bumps, he's-probably-a-sadistic-psychopath nervous. Even his eyes gave me the willies when he looked at me from a distance. It was as if they could read every thought in my mind. I hated feeling so exposed, so I refused to acknowledge him.

"Melissa," he whispered. "Look at me."

I huffed. "I'm busy, Andrew. Go away and stop following me around all the time."

He ignored me and grabbed my shoulder. I jumped back in my chair and the terror in my face must have startled him, because he immediately let go. I found myself involuntarily looking into his eyes. He waited a moment before speaking again.

"Breathe, Melissa," he said firmly. "Get control of yourself, I don't have much time."

"What do you want?"

Without warning me, he softly wrapped one of his large hands around mine. I was so stunned that I didn't pull away; my hands seemed to be magically locked inside of his. I began to feel light-headed as he spoke again.

"It's not your fault, Melissa."

I almost melted right there in my chair as his eyes stayed locked on mine.

"It's not your fault. Okay?"

"It's *all* my fault, Andrew. Everything is." I spoke without thinking. The words just rolled off my tongue, and I was unable to stop them. I couldn't believe I was pouring myself out so carelessly to him. It was so *not* like me.

"You need to let go, Melissa. You need to stop thinking about the *past*, and start living your life again."

"I can't, Andrew. I can't do it. I've tried everything!"

"No you haven't. To move ahead, you must say goodbye to the past."

"I don't know how," I complained, letting my head fall back into my arm just as the bell rang for fourth period.

"I think you do," he whispered, from what seemed like very far away.

I looked up and the library was empty. I expected Andrew to be right beside me, but it was as if he had completely disappeared. I looked behind me and around the room, just in case he decided to sit at another table, but I couldn't see him anywhere. It was really strange.

I went over to the librarian's desk.

"Yes?"

"Did you see where that guy I was talking to went? Tall, Asian, built like a brick house?"

He looked confused, and shook his head. "I'm sorry, but you've been the only one here this block, and frankly, your snoring was rather disturbing."

All oxygen left my lungs and it took me a moment to stop staring. I thought about accusing him of lying, but when I failed to make the words come out of my mouth, he crinkled his nose and huffed, walking away.

I bolted out of library and decided to skip last period. I'd been skipping a lot of classes lately, but it was easy to get out of class without raising questions given my recent history, and because of the fact I had managed to maintain my 3.8 GPA all the way through. The ability to email—and text, in the case of math and chemistry—your teachers was a brilliant technological break-through, but what helped me the most in those situations was that I was on a first name basis with all of them.

Walking to my car in the student lot, I realized Andrew was right, dream or not. There was something I hadn't tried yet.

I stopped in front of my car. The frost had melted and she seemed sad, sitting there cold and wet. She was begging me to get in, as if she already knew exactly where I wanted to go.

I don't break Mom and Dad's rules. Ever. But this time, ignoring my grounding was the right thing to do. I was at the end of my rope. Each day, another thread frayed away while I dangled. I couldn't hold on much longer and neither would the rope. It was time to let go.

If this was truly going to work, I knew I would have to surrender a piece of my heart and hope I could survive without it. I was afraid—more afraid than I was when I woke up in Rion's chamber. And no matter how much it hurt afterwards, I was certain this would be the only way to move forward.

I looked around to see if anyone was watching, and when the coast was clear, I took a deep breath, got in my car and sped off.

My hands were unsteady, even when I gripped the steering wheel tightly. My stomach began to roll summersaults, and I could feel moisture collecting above my lips as I drove north. The freeway was busy, but not in the direction I was heading. The sun shone brightly through my windows and I squinted to see without my shades until the Upper Levels Highway became the Sea-to-Sky, and the mountains blocked any trace of light. At that point, I was no longer driving my car; she was driving me.

Half an hour later, I saw the side-road coming from a hundred yards away, flagging me down like an old friend saying, "*Remember me?*" There was no street sign, only the familiar shoulder with a hollow tree trunk lying across the ditch. When I got close enough to turn off, I almost chickened out and kept going; I wasn't sure if I was quite ready. In the end, I turned and accelerated up the road.

In the daylight, it looked much different than what I remembered, and this time, I took in the scenery, slowing the car to ten kilometres per hour. The fir trees were thick and stacked closely together, the bushes bare and leafless, their skinny, old fingers reaching out to stroke my car. The frost had not melted here. The further I drove, the darker it became. And the trees, just as I remembered, formed a canopy until I arrived at the fork in the road where the trees opened up again. This was the last place I recalled with complete clarity, but I knew I hadn't stopped here. I'd kept going and I knew which path I'd taken. The only direction I ever took whenever I was lost: lucky left.

In this case, lucky left appeared to be the road less travelled: the asphalt was old and pitted. I wondered how different my life would have been if I'd just gone right instead. My eyes burned and my heart was beating fast, battering against my ribcage. I wiped the sweat beading on my lip and stepped on the gas again before I could change my mind.

I had to be close. It had been eight weeks since the night of my accident, and I hoped there would still be some marks to show me where my car had driven off the road.

I rounded a corner and spotted them. My mouth went dry and pasty, while my breathing became shallow and my blood surged ferociously. Two black marks snaked across the road. I swallowed hard and pulled off to the side. There was no shoulder, only one lane wide enough for an oversized dump-truck to navigate. I just sat there for a moment, staring at them. I couldn't believe I hadn't turned around sooner that night.

I shook my head. I hadn't come here to second guess myself. I'd come for one reason: to say goodbye. I wanted to have some sort of closure; then I hoped I could pick up the pieces of my spirit and carry on.

With one long deep breath in, I found the courage to open the door. The cold air outside pricked my nostrils, but I could still smell the pine and cedar as the breeze softly swept my hair out of my eyes. When I was ready, I pushed myself away from the car and began walking toward the marks I'd made all those weeks ago. Each step closer made me feel like I was taking off a layer of clothing, to the point that when I was standing over them, I felt naked, raw and wide-open, unable to shroud my sorrow any longer. Then, as Colin had told me, I closed my eyes, placidly dropped to my knees, put my hands together in prayer and whispered to the sky above, "Rion...I'm so sorry."

At that moment, large tears formed in the corners of my eyes, but I didn't blink or wipe them away, I let them come. Seconds later, more tears formed. And for the first time in years, I allowed myself to cry. When I could no longer hold my head up, I lowered it to the frigid ground and wept uncontrollably, unlocking the gate on my emotion. Every thought, every word, every bit of love and hate and worry bled into the pavement where I knelt. I bawled and sobbed to the point that my whole body was trembling; I was unashamed of my outburst.

When I managed to gather myself off of the pavement, I turned around to face the void where my car had toppled into the ravine. I slowly strode over, holding myself ever so tight, as the sun cut through the trees, warming me. The heat was so intense that I no longer felt the need to wrap my arms around my waist.

I closed my eyes again, took one more deep breath, and finally…I was ready to make peace with my recent past.

"Rion," I began, allowing myself to break down again, "I should have trusted you, and I hope you can forgive me. I never meant to hurt you, and I didn't mean to push you away like I did." I kept my eyes closed, enjoying the warmth of the sun on my skin, and I began to imagine that Rion was standing right in front of me, that I was looking straight into his beautiful bright green eyes. I could almost smell him.

"You were right," I continued, in an almost whisper. "I know how dangerous the *vykhars* are now, but I'll manage—I think." I took one more deep breath and decided to finish off by saying, "I know that you're not coming back, but I want you to know that I will never forget you. Thank you so much…for everything."

Another tear made its way down my cheek, and then another, but I kept my eyes closed for just a few seconds longer. I needed this. The warmth from the sun comforted me while I took a moment to come to grips with what was happening in my life and where I was going from here. I needed something else to focus on now.

That's when I opened my eyes and saw it, as plain as a red tulip in a field full of dandelions: a single, large blue flower bud lying on its side just inches from my feet. I'd never seen it before in my life, though I'd studied flowers for years. Its bright aquamarine petals were swaddled tightly together, and I could already catch its potent, heavenly sweet fragrance, which was slightly familiar, although I couldn't place it. Only one thing was certain about this flower: it couldn't have survived a night in this weather.

Someone had placed it here. Not long ago.

I turned and scoured the area, but there was nothing except for the sound of the wind in my ears. I wiped my eyes, leaned down and picked it up, and the strangest sensation came over me. I felt a series of shocks, like tiny lightning strikes, and with each one a scene flashed through my mind.

Flash. In the dark, the edge of the ravine. A horn blaring.

Flash. Rion, kneeling with his arms outstretched, screaming. There is something in front of him. A hand or a foot...?

Flash. Me, battered, lying on a bed staring up with vacant eyes as my face is gently sponged by a large hand.

Flash. Rion's room. A disaster of broken glass, shredded clothing, and destroyed furniture.

Flash. Me, standing with my back to—

I gasped. My eyes shot open and I whisked around, dropping the flower bud. Someone was watching me, I was sure of it. Then I heard a little *shift-crack* in the bushes behind me, across the road. I stiffened, ready to run. *Rustle-rustle-plunk.*

I gulped, realizing that the distance to my car was greater than the distance between me and the noise. Much further. I tore off sprinting toward my car, which was a least a hundred feet away, and then I heard a low growl behind me.

Heavy footsteps thundered behind me, their pace quickening. I begged my legs to go faster, and screamed as loud as I could, when a pair of strong arms encircled me and a hand covered my mouth.

I bit the fingers and my attacker yelped, moving his hand. I swiftly freed my arm, drove my elbow back into something solid and kicked my heel up to connect with what I hoped was a set of balls. A loud groan confirmed my aim, and I was released. I turned around, ready to sprint, but what I saw was a large hooded figure bent double and moaning.

I almost fell over. I had to pinch myself to be sure that I wasn't just having another nightmare, but yes, I was definitely awake. It was Rion.

"RION!"

He slowly straightened. We were both out of breath.

He was exactly as I'd remembered him. There was only one word for someone a big as Rion: gigantic. His bangs now covered his green eyes, but his beautiful, unique, catlike features were unmistakeable. As were his scars. He stepped toward me, lip curled and canines exposed. But I didn't care, I was just as angry.

"Don't ever do that to me again!" I panted. "You scared the hell out of me! Why didn't you say something?"

"WHAT ARE YOU *DOING* HERE?"

The ear-piercing volume of his voice startled me and I jumped. "WHAT ARE *YOU* DOING HERE?" I fired back.

"Do you have any idea how much danger you are in?"

"What?" I dropped my shoulders. "What do you mean? With who? I haven't done anything!"

He snorted. "You need to get out of this area. Right now. I cannot believe…"

He trailed off and muttered something I didn't understand as he cupped his jewels again, leaning over.

"Don't talk around me!" I retorted.

His lips pursed and he gave me a scathing stare. "We are standing on *vykhar* property. You never should have come here!"

I stamped my foot. "For your information, I came here for…for *personal* reasons. So stop being such a jerk. If you're so worried about being here then leave. I can take care of myself!"

He said something again in his own language and I caught two familiar words: *y'ebesha nesfara*. Though I had no idea what they meant.

"Speak English! I don't understand you. I hate it when you do that!"

He scowled at me. "I *said*, if you would have just listened to me in the first place, none of this would have happened. I told you never to come back here, *female*!"

My eyes widened in resentment. "I *have* a name. And it's not *female*."

His eyes narrowed and his nostrils flared. "You make the most outrageous decisions. I cannot believe I—"

"You know what, Rion?" I quickly interrupted. "Don't do me any more favours. I'm obviously just an encumbrance to you."

"A *what*?"

"An *encumbrance*. A *burden*. A *nuisance*. Speak *English* much?"

He muttered something else in his language, and that's when I turned away from him to get in my car and go home.

"Do not turn your back on me," he grabbed my shoulder.

"I'll do whatever I want." I jerked away from him. "I'm going home. Get out of my way!"

He didn't answer.

I began tugging at my door handle, wondering why it wouldn't open. Then I saw the keys sitting right on the console; she had automatically locked and alarmed herself. I'd been so distracted driving here, I'd completely forgotten about taking the keys out with me.

I kicked the tire in exasperation, and began walking away. I just wanted to get the hell out of there, and I didn't care how.

"Where are you going?"

"Away. From. You!"

"*Melissa*," he moderated his tone. "Stop."

I stopped, stomping my foot on the ground. But I didn't turn around.

"Here. I will open it for you." I heard something pop and click. When I turned around, Rion was holding my door open for me. I marched back toward my car and got in. When my seatbelt was buckled, I started the car and sneered at him, reaching to close the door. But he held it open.

"What now?" I protested, throwing my hands down.

He sighed and he looked straight into my eyes. "Melissa, I...we should talk."

"Then send me a note," I replied impatiently, searching for a good radio station rather than making eye-contact with him.

"No," he whispered. "In person."

"Not going to happen."

I heard him growl again. "Why?"

I was still searching for a station. "I'm grounded right now, and frankly, I could really care less what you have to say. You've said enough."

"Melissa, *pershavi*—please..." He reached in and touched the tips of my fingers.

I stopped suddenly, glared at him and took my hand away from his. "No."

"Are you going home?"

"That's none of your business. Could you move out of the way, please?"

He growled low when I looked straight ahead again. "Are you always this *difficult*?"

I could feel my chest getting hot. "Goodbye, Rion...I'm sorry I ever troubled you."

I yanked the door closed and watched his hand trail along the car as I turned around and drove off. Our reunion hadn't gone at all the way I'd imagined it, but his attitude infuriated me, and it was obvious that I was just a burden to him. When he was out of sight, I began to cry again, and I cried all the way home, feeling worse than when I'd left.

When I got home, my parents were sitting on the couch and, by the looks on their faces, ready to tear my head off; but when they saw I'd been crying, which was a rarity, their expressions changed.

"Honey," Dad started, "where were you? We were worried sick when you didn't come home from school, and your car was missing."

I sniffed and wiped my nose. I had no reason to lie to them. "I went back to the scene of my accident."

"Oh, my word!" Mom exclaimed. "All the way up there?"

"Why?" Dad asked. "You should have called us or something. I could have come with you!"

"No." I felt my eyes tingle and burn again. "It was something I needed to do alone. I've just been having a difficult time trying to get past all this…"

Mom rushed over to me and wrapped her arms around me. I tried to hug her back, but it was hard because I was concentrating on not collapsing on the floor. What I really wanted was some time alone in my room.

"We heard about your argument with Chelsea," Dad said. "She's called here a few times since three."

"I don't want to talk to anyone right now." I shook my head. "I'm sorry for worrying you."

"We understand," Mom replied. "It's okay. Just tell us next time, all right?"

"I will." I let go of her. "I'm just going to lie down for a while."

That night, my hot flashes returned. In the dead of winter, I was sleeping on top of my quilt in a sports bra and shorts. I presumed it was just anxiety, because I had cried myself to sleep. I covered my face with my pillow so my parents wouldn't hear. How long I'd bawled, how many times I'd tossed and turned, or even when I'd fallen asleep, I had no idea.

On Sunday morning, when my puffy eyes were watered out, my parents took away our grounding. Two days stuck in the house with Katherine had made everyone miserable, so Dad decided that we'd have an eight o'clock curfew instead until the following Friday. My sister and I agreed.

That afternoon, when I'd finally made it out of my pyjamas, I decided to check in with Brenda about my hours, and see about changing my days. I wanted to work more hours. I wanted to be busy. I wanted to do anything that would distract me from thinking about Rion. Brenda was more than pleased when I phoned and arranged to meet her.

The street outside Waves Coffee House was congested with Christmas shoppers. Sunday afternoons on Commercial Drive were usually quieter, so normally it would be the perfect time for Brenda and me to talk without being disturbed by customers; however, today I would just have to make it quick. I opened the door and held it there for an elderly couple to walk through before entering the shop. When I got up to the counter, I spotted the girl who had served me the night I'd gone to see Mantis. It was difficult to miss her black and purple hair. She made a very clear effort to keep eye contact with me, nodding and implying that I should follow her. She turned and walked away but looked back at me, checking to see if I had understood. I figured it was something to do with work, so I followed her.

We walked into the restrooms. She walked in and tapped on a stall door, gesturing me to enter the one beside her. I went in and closed the door.

"Well?" I said.

"I heard you're getting promoted to trainer."

"Oh!"

"Brenda wants to discuss giving you some more hours, to train the new employees for the weekend shifts."

"That's very nice of her." It was difficult to contain my excitement. A promotion could mean a raise, too.

"You're *not* going to take the promotion. The hours are going to be too much for you to handle with your schoolwork and other *out of school commitments*. Do you understand?"

Who did she think she was? This was just what I wanted. "What are you talking about?"

She handed me a note under the stall wall. On the front it said:

Flush this note as soon as you've read it.

I heard her exit the stall. Then her nails started this *clickety-click-click-clicking* on the counter. She was waiting for me to read the note, so I quickly opened it. I was expecting it to translate our conversation, but it wasn't that at all, it was a note from

136

Rion. I looked up at her even though she couldn't see me. "How did you—?"

"Just hurry, okay?" she interrupted. "Then ask questions."

I turned back to the note. Just as before, his writing was difficult to make out, and the ink had smudged in some areas, but this is what I read:

IF I HAD BEEN LESS OF A JERK ON FRIDAY, YOU WOULD HAVE STAYED, AND THEN I COULD HAVE TOLD YOU THAT YOUR CAR WAS BUGGED. THEY HAVE BEEN FOLLOWING YOU EVERYWHERE FOR THE LAST MONTH. EVERYTHING YOU HAVE SEEN IS A SETUP. YOUR DAD WAS PERSUADED TO BUY THE CAR SO THE VYKHARS COULD BEGIN TRACKING YOUR WHEREABOUTS BY SATELLITE. I FOLLOWED YOU TODAY AND DEACTIVATED IT WHILE YOU WERE OUT OF YOUR CAR. THEN I SAW YOU CRYING SO I HAD TO STAY TO MAKE SURE YOU WERE ALL RIGHT, AND YES, I DESERVED THOSE HITS. THINGS ARE HEATING UP AND I AM TRYING TO STAY ON TOP OF THEIR NEXT MOVES. I HAVE SO MUCH MORE I NEED TO DISCUSS WITH YOU, AND THEREFORE, I NEED TO MEET WITH YOU TONIGHT. CHARLOTTE WILL TAKE YOU TO JOHN HENDRY PARK. ON THE SOUTH SIDE THERE ARE TWO GIANT GOLDEN WEEPING WILLOWS AND A CHILDREN'S PLAYGROUND. I WILL BE WAITING FOR YOU THERE AND I WILL BRING YOU BELOW. COME ALONE. I WILL SEE TO IT THAT YOU ARE SAFE, AND RETURN YOU JUST THE SAME.

R

♣

P.S. TRUST CHARLOTTE, SHE IS THE ONLY ONE WHO CAN BRING YOU TO ME NOW.

I crumpled the note and flushed it. When I came out of the stall, she was still waiting for me.

"I'm not going."

She seemed genuinely surprised. "What? Why not?"

"Well, he's a jerk, for one thing."

Charlotte sighed. "You don't know him."

I glared back at her. "I don't want to know someone like that."

She sighed again, looked into the mirror at her makeup and huffed, "He was right."

"What?"

"I *said,* he was right," she repeated, glancing at her nails. "You *are* stubborn."

I made for the bathroom door, but stopped when she continued. "You may be interested to learn that no one's ever sacked him so hard. I had to bring him ice."

"Well then he shouldn't have snuck up on me."

"That's what I said, too." She applied some new bright red lipstick, and blotted. "It's actually a good thing you can defend yourself, but I would get more practice in if I were you, since you'll probably be using those skills on a *vykhar* one day."

All the colour vanished from my face. She raised an eyebrow and met my eyes in the mirror. "The danger for you is real, and it's not over yet. So, are you meeting him, or am I going to have to send him to your house?"

I rolled my eyes. It was obvious I didn't have a choice in the matter. "Whatever. I'll go. But just answer me one thing…"

She smirked. "Sure."

"Do you speak their language?"

She nodded.

"Then maybe you can tell me what '*y'ebesha nesfara*' means."

She turned her head slightly, her eyebrows wrinkling together as she replied, "Where did you hear that?"

"Rion called me that."

"He *did?*"

"Yeah. And it really pisses me off because I don't know what it means. For all I know it could be his word for C-U-Next-Tuesday."

Charlotte laughed. "I don't think you have to worry about that."

"Why?"

"Because *ebesha* is their word for precious or...*treasured*, and *nesfara* is their translation for female..." She hesitated for a moment. "It's pretty much the most polite way you can address a female within their community."

My heart began to beat a little faster. I wasn't prepared to hear something like that, and I wasn't sure how to react. It actually made me feel a little embarrassed, and I could feel myself blushing. "Then why was he such a jerk the other day? I thought he was angry."

"I highly doubt that." She smiled and winked at me. "He's... let's just say this girl stuff is not his speciality."

"I noticed."

"Well, I've got some things to do." She turned and walked out of the bathroom. "Don't forget to see Brenda. She's still expecting you. I'll see you at six. Sharp!"

I called after her, "Don't you want to know where I live?" But, she'd already left. I rolled my eyes, thinking, why me?

XI

Charlotte picked me up at six, just in time to meet my mom. They totally hit it off, and Mom was delighted when Charlotte told her we were going out for coffee so she could "help me with math." Charlotte was two years older than me, employed at both Waves Coffee House and a high-end salon in West Van as a hair stylist, and was currently working on an arts degree at UBC—which really impressed Mom. Before we left, I assured her that I would be back in the house before my curfew, knowing she'd be sitting on the couch waiting for me at the stroke of eight.

When Charlotte and I arrived at the park, the parking lot was empty, and the only light came from a three-quarter moon in the sky. It was going to be freaking cold tonight. I wished I'd brought my toque and gloves.

"How long have you known about the malions?" I asked her as we pulled into a vacant space.

"Since I was five."

"How did you—"

"It's a long story," she interrupted. "I'll tell you sometime."

I noticed that she hadn't shut off the car or taken off her seatbelt, and she began to play with her strawberry air freshener. "Aren't you coming?"

"Nope."

"I can't go by myself!"

"My instructions were to drop you off. And if Rion's being his usual super-punctual self, he's probably been waiting at least an hour for you already." Then she put her little blue Acura back in first gear, hinting that I should get out, and turned up her grunge music. "I'll come with you another time, all right?"

I groaned and got out of the car. I didn't want to do this alone.

"Hey, Melissa," she said before I shut the door. "Just hear what he has to say, and he'll bring you right back. I promise."

"Thanks," I replied as cheerfully as I could, though I think it came out sounding derisive.

We exchanged phone numbers (which made my solo take-off marginally easier) then I waved goodbye, zipped up my winter parka and walked over to the children's playground. The golden weeping willows were right behind me, and when I scoured the area, no one was there. I decided to sit down on a swing. It had been years since I'd swung, and it reminded me of when Dad had given me under-ducks for one straight hour once when I was younger. I loved the flying sensation, but tonight, swinging wouldn't help settle my soured stomach, and I'd had about enough of it.

A crunch startled me, just as all the hairs stood on the back of my neck. I stopped and turned around. Nothing; though I swore I could sense every nerve in my body fire uncontrollably.

"Melissa."

I shot up. There he was, out of nowhere. I stopped breathing for five full seconds, tilting my head *way* back to look up at him, towering over me like a football player in full uniform. A thick navy hood and cloak covered his entire body and face, but I knew that it was Rion. Only Rion had that pine and musty leather smell that I'd enjoyed for the last two months.

Damn, it smelled good.

"Hey," I whispered.

"Hello," he whispered back.

I should have been mad. I should have stuck to my guns and not met with him after his spazz-out on Friday, but I could sense that he was anxious about this meeting tonight, too. There was no use dwelling on something that would only serve to ruin the night.

Rion's hood dipped down as he stood back from me. He was inspecting me, but not getting too close. He learned fast. "Did Charlotte leave?" he asked when I looked down and kicked the gravel.

"Yeah."

"Good. Are you ready?"

I swallowed, hoping that my heart would slow down soon. "I guess."

He held out his hand. "Well, let us go then."

When I looked up at his navy hood again, my skin tingled everywhere. I couldn't see his face yet, and I didn't take his hand right away. I didn't want him to know I was shaking.

"Are you all right?"

I nodded.

"I will not take up a lot of your time tonight, but if you have changed your mind about coming with me, I will phone Charlotte and have her come and pick you up…I just cannot be here very long, it is not safe."

"I know."

"Please come," he begged, shifting his weight around. Finally I could see his face. He was wearing a brooding, pouty frown. "I swear that I will bring you back the moment you ask."

I held his eye contact. "The *moment* I ask?"

He nodded again. "If it makes you feel more comfortable, Charlotte knows exactly where we are going. And if I do not bring you back, she knows how to contact every one of my family members, who all know we are meeting tonight. This is not a secret, Melissa. Please just give me a chance to explain things to you."

When I just stood there staring at the ground, unable to move, he dropped his hand and said, delicately, "I am sorry about Friday, okay? I did not mean to frighten you and get so upset. This whole situation just has me on edge, and…seeing you upset just…"

My eyes flashed toward him. "Did you hear what I said…I mean, before you—?"

"Every word…"

I cringed.

"…but I am the one who is at fault for all of this. Not you."

His apology took me by surprise. "Just stop sneaking up on me, please. You almost gave me a heart attack. Twice!"

"I know, I am sorry."

I took a deep breath and replied, "I'm sorry, too. About nailing you, in the…you know."

He chuckled and offered his hand once more, and this time I accepted it. As he gently wrapped his warm, calloused fingers around mine, there was only one thought in my mind: the moment I'd been wishing for was finally here. And after tonight, I would *finally* be able to move on with my life.

"This way," he whispered, tightening his grasp on my hand, ever so slightly.

We ran from the open playground, to the nearest covered area about a hundred meters away. He stopped in front of a large manhole, lifted the lid up and looked at me. "I will go first, and then I will catch you when you come through."

I looked down the black hole. I couldn't see the bottom. "Are you serious?"

"Yes," he whispered. "Do not be fooled by what you see on the outside. Come, I will show you." He took one step and disappeared down the hole, out of sight.

I took one last look around to see if anyone was watching us, but the park was empty.

"I am here…I will not let you fall." His voice rose up from the dark. "Quickly Melissa, we cannot let anyone see!"

I closed my eyes with my toes on the edge, and hesitated, remembering my last visit below. Was he really going to let me go again? I didn't know what felt right anymore. "You *promise* to bring me back?" I called down to him after more than a minute.

"I swear on the Creator, Melissa."

Well, whether he was telling the truth or not, I still wanted to hear his side of the story. And really, he'd never lied to me before. I looked up at the sky and bit my lip. Taking one last breath of the fresh air above, I stepped forward and dropped down into the black. After less than a second, I was in Rion's arms, looking straight into two exquisite green eyes. "Thanks."

He smiled and set me down. "Thank *you* for not changing your mind."

I half-smiled back at him. "Where are we going?"

"Let me just close the manhole first." He jumped up, holding onto the edge of the manhole with one hand and pulling the cover over with the other. He dropped elegantly back to my side as it slipped into place. "We will get further below, and then we can talk more comfortably." He brought out a flashlight and took my hand again. "This way."

We began power walking in the darkness with only his flash-light to guide us. His hand was large, dry, and very warm; I held it tightly with both of mine. It felt strange to be holding hands so casually, but I didn't want to trip on something and fall flat on my face—he wasn't letting go, either.

"Is this how you get around? Down here, I mean."

"Yes."

"But isn't there, like, sewage down here?"

"We have our own passages, and they connect to storm drains and utility tunnels. No sewers. We also have some more conspicuous entrances in remote areas where there are no people around to stumble on them. The passages we have in the city are used in emergencies only."

"Oh. So we're below a street right now? Is that why I hear cars?"

"Exactly."

"How do you know which manholes are yours? I mean, how can you tell the difference?"

"There are only three places in Vancouver where utility tunnels connect to our passages." He slowed down so that I could hear him. "So, they are easy to remember. But in order to reach *our* passages, you must be strong enough to open the entry door, which takes the strength of three male malions. We post three guards at each one, to operate them. And if you get past the entrance, you have to be cleared by another set of guards with identification that has been issued..."

I chuckled to myself.

"What is so funny?"

"Filter, Rion."

"Excuse me?"

"Filter, please," I repeated, giggling again. "You could have just told me you have guarded entrances. I'd have been okay without all the details."

"Oh. Right. Sorry. I get carried away sometimes."

"That's okay."

It was dark in the tunnels; the flashlight only allowed us to see what was directly in front. But with those green cat-eyes, I assumed Rion could see just fine, so I just kept hold of his hand and walked beside him. At first it was interesting to try to guess where we were; sometimes the cars sounded louder than other times, but after ten minutes, I was beginning to wonder how much further it was going to be.

"About fifty-five minutes," he replied when I asked. "At your pace, I mean."

"Oh," I sighed.

"Are you tired already?"

"Well, I just wanted to let you know I have to be back by eight."

Rion stopped. "Oh, right. Charlotte mentioned that. Why did you get grounded?" He let go of my hand.

"Punched my sister in the face."

Rion laughed out loud. "Did she deserve it?"

"No, I don't believe in violence. But I just...lost it."

He laughed again. "What time *is* it anyway?"

"Just after six." I checked my phone. "Maybe we should just meet another time. I'm only grounded for a week."

"No," he replied firmly. "I actually had another idea. That is, if you do not mind me carrying you."

"Y—*whoa!*"

He didn't even wait for me to answer. He put his arms around me and lifted me up. Waaaaaaaayy up. So fast my stomach leapt up into my throat. "That was a yes, right?"

"Um...sure...okay." His giant arms held me so gently and securely, and his thick cape shielded me from the cold. I could feel my heart thumping against my rib cage and my head was spinning from exhilaration. I was getting déjà-vu.

When Rion was sure that I didn't want to be put down, he said, "We need to move faster, okay?"

"How much faster?"

"Quite a bit faster."

"Okay, like how fast?"

"Like...*roller coaster* fast."

"You're that fast?"

"Do you like fast?"

"I like fast rides."

"All right, well, hang on to this." He handed me the flashlight. "Keep it pointed in front of us, and tell me right away if you want me to slow down."

"Don't worry," I tittered. "I rode a roller coaster ten times in a row once."

He looked at me for a moment, smirked a little and raised his eyebrows a few quick times and took off. Did he ever.

It was like riding the Quasar at the fair. The faster the ride spun, the higher up the little beds would rise, and the harder it was to raise your arms and legs. The speed pressed me hard against his body. Up close, I could really smell him, and it was heavenly. I wanted to drink it up while I had the chance.

Seconds later we stopped, and I was, once again, out of breath.

"That was amazing. I can't believe you can run so fast!" I exclaimed. "But where are the guards and the entrance gates?"

"Right in front of you."

I turned and three pairs of narrow glowing green eyes were staring right back at me. The flashlight dropped from my hand, crashing down on the rock floor, leaving us in complete darkness.

"*Teneck fi,*" one of them grumbled lowly. "Rion...*letcha nee neena nevala. Kay viya funkor deedenta shae—*"

"That will not be necessary," Rion said, then caught himself and repeated it in malion. One of the guards turned the flashlight back on and handed it to him.

A few more words were exchanged between Rion and the guards, and Rion seemed to become irritated.

"What's going on?" I asked him.

Rion exhaled hard. "They want to check you for wires."

I gulped. "But—"

"Just give me a minute," he grumbled.

Rion set me down and shepherded me behind him, away from the guards. A few more words were exchanged and then Rion turned back to me.

"We have to let them search you. Can you just take off your jacket?"

I swallowed. "What? Why?"

"They are not going to let us pass until they can see that you are not wired—it is my father's rule. I cannot do anything about it. My only other option is to take you back home."

I shook my head. "I'm not wearing any wires. Can't they just take my word for it?"

"No." He glared at the guards. "We could just leave, but at some point, we will have to talk. So we get this over with now, or in a few days."

My eyes began to sting. All I could think about were the hands of strangers touching me. My palms were already sweating.

"I will be right beside you. It will only take a second." One of the guards muttered something, and Rion barked back at him in malion.

"This is crazy." I looked up at him and he shrugged and rolled his eyes. I truly had no other option. My heart began to race as I unsteadily unzipped my coat. I lost the grip on my zipper twice as I pulled it down. When I'd managed to wriggle out of it, one of the guards grabbed my arm and yanked me toward him so hard I thought he was going to pull my arm out of my socket. Rion snarled at the guard. Two of them began to pat me down, one starting with my shoulders, and the other my ankles.

I was hot and panicky at that point, and I tried squirming away from their hands. Rion growled, and the third guard parked himself in front of Rion, whose fists were clenched as he stood there glaring. I kept squirming, I couldn't help it, and Rion seemed to be struggling to hold himself back. Then one of them brushed my breast.

"Hey!"

Rion roared and started to push by the third guard, as another hand went down the back of my shirt toward my belt.

The second set of hands began heading north on my legs. "Stop! Stop it!" Writhing around, I tried to kick out at one of them, but his hold was so strong I could barely twist. I began to panic. "Rion!"

I heard a loud crash then Rion blew past me. Hands disappeared from my body instantly. Rion slammed the two guards into the wall, which thundered from the impact. I stepped back as far as I could, just in case a full-fledged fight broke out. The exchange of growls continued until the third guard got in between them all and broke it up.

"*Nee neena ky'ella parns vor m'ebesha nesfara!*" Rion growled. "Enough!"

I sniffed, and Rion must have heard me because he rushed over. "Melissa…" He lifted me up into his arms. "Are you okay?"

"Please get me out of here." If the guards weren't satisfied with the results of their search, I was going to ask to be taken back home. I didn't want Rion to witness one of my breakdowns.

"We are going. Right. Now." He gave the guards a dare-you-to-stop-me glare. Unsurprisingly, they stepped out of the way, and we passed through the open doorway. We flew into the darkness again, much faster than before, and Rion held me just a little closer as I cuddled myself under his chin. The intensity of his speed crushed us together, and though it felt good to be back in the safety of his arms, it began to restrict my breathing, and a wave of claustrophobia struck me.

"Rion?" I gasped.

"Yeah?"

"I changed my mind."

Rion skidded to a stop and almost dropped me. "What do you mean? You...you want me to take you back now, after all that? I thought..."

I could feel his heart hammering against my arm as I sucked in a deep breath, savouring the abundance of oxygen filling my lungs once again. "No, I changed my mind about liking fast."

"Was that too fast?"

I let out a great sigh. "Yeah."

"Sorry." He resumed his run at a more moderate pace. "When you said, 'Get me out of here,' I took that as a sign to push the *turbo* button."

"Well, I appreciate the speed." I smiled and rested my head on his shoulder once again. "But second gear would have sufficed."

XII

After a few minutes, he nudged me and said, "When we get back to my chambers, I will make you something to drink okay?"

"Have you got any of that really great white hot chocolate?"

Rion slowed down and smiled at me. "For you, I have *oceans*."

My mouth watered, and I smiled involuntarily. Just as I was beginning to get bored, we stopped. Rion gently set me down and took the flashlight from my hands.

"Where are we?"

He turned the flashlight off and lit a candle behind me. "My chambers."

I turned around, and my mouth fell open. Here, right in front of me, was the same room I had stayed in for the weekend of my accident. Everything was exactly as I remembered it: the books in perfect order, the oak desk, nightstand, the shelving. It was the picture of order. It even smelled the same—like Rion.

And then I saw his bed. The place where I'd slept for two days straight. The place where I'd woken up and learned that my life would never be the same again.

Rion stood silently beside me while I took it all in, and after a few moments, he put his hand gently on my shoulder. I started and he pulled away.

"Are you not comfortable here?"

My eyes began to sting. Ever since my one big cry, everything seemed to set me off. "No, it's not that at all. I just feel like pinching myself to see if I'm actually awake, or if this is just a dream."

"Do you wish it just was a dream?"

I turned to face him as he removed his blue hood. His eyes were much puffier and he looked completely exhausted, much more so than when I'd first met him. I could sense that he was worried about my answer, but when I smiled, his shoulders relaxed.

"If it was, I think I'd try to stay asleep for a while," I finally said.

He smiled back at me, then walked over to his desk and pulled the chair out. "Would you like to sit down?"

I accepted his offer, and sat with my legs crossed, looking at the ceiling. "How far below the city are we?"

"About seventy feet. Have your ears popped?"

I shook my head. "Not yet. But I'm sure they will soon."

"Well...I am going to get your hot chocolate before we start. Be right back."

I smiled. "Thanks."

He walked out of the room, and to my surprise, he left the door slightly ajar. I took a deep breath and pinched myself. Yes, I was definitely here. And there in the corner was that same incense burner I noticed before, releasing the scent that Rion had always smelled of, the same smell that had consoled me at home. I walked over and waved the smoke into my face a few times, taking a few deep breaths in to savour the woodsy aroma, though my stomach had not completely settled. Then I began to look around again. It was much lighter in his chambers tonight and there wasn't a speck of dust that I could see anywhere. He was just the exact opposite of me. I was a little obsessive when it came to *where* my things were placed, but I could have cared less if it became a little cluttered or disorganized. Or a little dusty, for that matter.

Rion was back with my liquid pick-me-up and a tray of food a few seconds later. He'd taken off his cloak, and for the first time, I was able to see what he wore underneath, which wasn't anything exciting: black fitted jeans, black boots and a black long-sleeved sweater that zipped up at the front. I did, however, get a great view of the outline of his arms and shoulders, which was enough to intimidate anyone. He was huge; one solid block of muscle.

He handed me the mug, which I quickly wrapped my hands around, though I wasn't really cold. "You didn't have to do all this. Thank you very much."

"Your pleasure is mine." He shuffled a few things around on his desk to make room for the food tray. There was everything I loved: red grapes, strawberries, blueberries, coined banana, sliced apple, cashews, cubed cheeses, cranberries and a small stack of crepes.

"You brought too much for me. Will you eat some, too?" I took a few grapes from the tray.

"When you are full, I will eat what is left."

"Don't be silly, you don't have to wait for me."

"Females always eat first in the malion community."

"Why?" I grabbed another grape and popped it in my mouth.

His face softened. "The female sex of any species is key to its survival because they are the ones that have the ability to bear young. Malions take that very seriously. Therefore, females eat first."

"That's strange." I swallowed a bite of banana. "In my house, we like to eat together."

"I know. But I could never deprive you of nourishment."

"I still feel weird eating in front of you."

"Do not. I like to watch you eat what I have prepared for you, it makes me happy to see that you like what I have gathered."

I giggled. "Is there something you want me to save for you?"

"No."

"Come on," I teased. "There must be something?"

"Not at all. But I hope that you will eat more than three grapes and a piece of banana."

I smiled, finished a few strawberries, some cheese, a handful of cashews, one crepe and half of my spectacular white hot chocolate while Rion put away the rest of the papers on his desk.

"That was so good." I was sure that I couldn't fit one more bite in my stomach.

"Are you full?"

"Stuffed."

He smiled wide. "How was the hot chocolate?"

"Bang-a-rang."

"Excuse me?"

I giggled, remembering he'd probably never seen the movie *Hook*. "Awesome."

He nodded, and seemed genuinely happy that my stomach was now ready to burst out of my jeans. "Good."

"Don't you want some?"

"Later. Let us get started."

I made my way over to his bed. It was just as soft as I remembered, but when I pulled my legs up, I noticed his blanket was different. I had a vague memory of a fuzzy quilt with a lion on it, which had been replaced with a thin sheet and one green lap blanket.

"Where's that other blanket with the lion on it?" I circled my palm over the new covers.

"Oh." He seemed surprised I'd noticed. "I put that one away. Why?"

"It was just really warm and soft. I liked it."

He smirked. "When you left, it still smelled like you."

I glanced up at him and he immediately looked away. "It had to be washed anyway. I, um…spilled on it," he added crustily, still turned away from me. Then he cleared his throat, put his mug down and took a deep breath, facing me again. "Let us get on with this before we run out of time, okay?"

I nodded. "Right."

He went from friendly to all business in a matter of seconds. "Now I do not want to come across too harshly. Forgive me if I do."

"Umm…okay."

He straightened his back and leaned forward, crossing his legs. "I do not know how to explain to you what is happening without scaring you."

I closed my eyes and shook my head. "It's better that you give me the unedited version. Don't sugar-coat anything. I can handle it."

He sighed, and looked at his hands for a brief second before making eye contact with me again. "All right....The dark-haired man that came to your house..."

"Caine. He's a *vykhar*."

"You got that?"

"Yeah..."

Rion nodded and took a sip from his mug. "He is *head* of the *vykhars* in North America."

"If you're worried, I haven't told them anything...anything at all, I promise!"

"I know." He held his hand up to silence me. "His persuasion does not work on you, though I am sure you must have noticed."

"I didn't even know he was trying. How'd *you* know?"

He huffed. "Oh, he will *always* try. I am just relieved to know that he cannot, because we would be in a lot bigger trouble right now if he could."

I suddenly saw my interview in a different light. "I think it's very frustrating for him."

He was quiet for a moment then he began running his hands through his hair. "I am sorry but I do not know how to tell you this..."

"Just say it, Rion. You're driving me nuts by stalling."

"Melissa...they have your entire house bugged. They are also tracking your phone calls, your car, as well as any conversations you have. It is all being recorded."

"I read in your note about the car, but how is that possible?"

"I know about the day the alarm company came to your house. Think for a moment about who was there."

"So the Jaredsons agents bugged my house while they were installing the alarm system?"

"The alarm system is the bug. It was all a set up. They think you know something and now they are tracking your every move."

I put my hand on my head. "Holy crap…when did they bug my car? They haven't been back since I got it."

"We think your dad bought it from Caine. I am sure he has carefully cultivated his friendship with your father in the hopes of an opportunity arising."

"How come they didn't follow me to the park tonight?"

"You were in Charlotte's car; they used to track your location when you were in your car, but I have already deactivated that device. I hope they do not get suspicious. I wondered if they might have bugged your shoes, too, but I did not hear anything when we met. Their bugs emit this really irritating high-pitched buzzing noise, so I should be able to locate any they place on you."

"I *knew* I'd heard something funny in the house lately."

Rion's eyes widened. "You can hear them? I did not think they were audible to humans."

"Oh my goodness, yes!" I exclaimed. "It sounds like a bee that's been caught in a blind. No *wonder* I've been having trouble sleeping."

"Well that is a relief then," he sighed. "You will know if they have put a bug on you, and then you can just remove it and trash it."

Something horrible occurred to me. "Did they follow me to Mantis' tattoo shop?"

Rion closed his eyes and scowled, shifting his mouth to one side. "I do not think so, but that is a whole other issue that I am dealing with right now."

"Is that why you came back?"

He shot me an icy look. "How did you know I was gone?"

I shrugged. "Mantis told me."

"I did not want to leave you, Melissa, but it was for something I just could not get out of. When I heard about Mantis, I came back early. I was worried you had been hurt, or worse, that they had taken you..." He huffed and shook his head at the floor. "I have not been so angry in a very long time."

I remembered my run home and trashing my room. "That makes two of us."

"Yes, and that is something else we need to—"

"Sorry," I interrupted. "Can I just ask one more thing?"

He cleared his throat. "Of course."

"Who was Mantis? To you, I mean."

Rion sighed. "He was the liaison between us and our trusted friends above. He was the most honest, loyal, respectable human I have ever met."

"How many trusted friends do you have?"

"Thirt—twelve now. In this area."

"Do all of them have the same shamrock tattoo?"

"Yes. It was Mantis' idea to have our trusted friends marked. But now I am not so sure it was a very good idea. The permanence of it bothers me."

"Charlotte just told me her ancestors were Irish when I asked about it."

"That is what they say to cover themselves. It is a code for: Are you a trusted malion friend?"

"That's why she looked at me funny when I told her mine were, too."

"Yes. The whole thing was Mantis' idea....I still cannot believe he is gone. I do not know what I am going to do without him now. He was such a gift to us."

I winced. Mantis' screams were all of a sudden fresh in my memory. "I'm so sorry about Mantis, Rion."

"Do not be, Melissa," he sighed. "You did not ask to be brought into the middle of this. *I* was the one who made the decision to bring you below, and now I am going to do everything in my power to keep you safe....By the Creator, if anything had happened to you that night at the tattoo shop I do not know what I would have done."

"I'm not scared of them, Rion."

"You should be."

"Well I'm not. They'll *never* break me."

"You are brave, Melissa. That is a good trait in a female."

I took a sip of my hot chocolate and crossed my legs the other way. "So are all Jaredsons agents *vykhars*?"

"Yes. Jared was the name of the very first *vykhar*."

"Are the stories true?"

"What stories?"

"Caine said that the stories in my book, *Moonstone, Mae and Malion Tales*, were true."

"That garbage came from a publishing house the Jaredsons own. The original stories were passed from malion to *cubshen*—child— but the Jaredsons got a hold of a copy, changed the stories around and sold it to the public, making everyone afraid of us. Once upon a time, we were known as the Great Malion Healers. Now, we are known only in storybooks as murderous monsters."

"You've convinced *me* of the truth."

"Yes, one of a few *billion*."

"So what's the real story? Because in my book, it says that a malion kidnapped Princess Alysia and that Prince Jared rescued her and killed the malion in a vicious fight."

Rion huffed and growled again. "See what kind of trash that is?"

"I tore up the book at home when I found out you were a malion. I just couldn't believe anything it said after all you'd done for me."

"Good, because the real story is called *The King and the Malion Healer.*" Rion walked over to his desk, rustled around with some papers and a couple of drawers, and tossed a book on the bed beside me. It had a dark green cover, and a shamrock embellished at the top. I flipped it open and everything inside it was hand-written in black ink; the strange letters and symbols must have been their language.

"The real story dates back more than nine hundred years. King Jared assumed the throne when his father died, and he took a wife immediately, the *dreg manakacko*. Her name was Alysia, but the lying begins right after that: King Jared was a self-absorbed, abusive man. He kept his kingdom on the brink of starvation while he bathed in gold. Queen Alysia had to withstand unimaginable torture; he did not leave her alone until she finally became pregnant. They had a son, Prince Warren, but when the queen did not conceive again, the abuse resumed.

"One night, when King Jared was bedding one of Queen Alysia's ladies-in-waiting, she fled the castle and paid a peasant to take her to a malion healer, hoping he could cure her barrenness, as you may have read. But the malion, whose name was Ranion, refused to help her. Instead, he offered her a new life with him in his malion community, with all the safety and protection she would need."

"That part was never in the story."

"Just my point. He had heard of her suffering over the years, and fallen in love with her long before she ever began her search for him. When they finally met, he begged her not to return to the king. But the queen would not leave without her son, so she returned to the castle, only to find the king waiting for her, furious as a selkie on the war path. The king's persuasion ability was so strong that Queen Alysia was unable to avoid telling him that she had been to see a malion healer. King Jared was so angry with the queen he took out his blade, cut off her beautiful long hair, and dragged her into the forest to kill the malion. The castle guard followed the king to the forest, but they refused to go near Ranion, because they were worried about the curses malions were rumored to possess."

"Is that true?"

Rion rolled his eyes. "No! It is pegasus dung!"

I laughed. "Sorry for interrupting...go on."

"Okay, so...King Jared became furious at that point..."

I listened intently as Rion continued. He became passionate and enthusiastic in his telling; it was as if he himself had been the one in battle with Jared. If there was anything I loved more than a garden full of flowers, it was a good story. I jumped when he used sound effects, and gasped when he began acting out the battle between Jared and Ranion. He had me on the edge of my seat and wired with excitement in just a few phrases.

"...Jared took out his sword to stab Ranion in the heart, only Queen Alysia ran at King Jared, jumped on top of him and fought to get the sword out of his hands."

"She jumped in?"

"Yes!" he exclaimed, with eyes wider than I'd ever seen them. "She was not your typical twelfth century Lady. She *actually* sacrificed herself for Ranion. But King Jared was so strong that he ripped Queen Alysia from his back and slashed her throat..."

I gasped. "Oh Rion, that's an awful ending—how could you end a story like that?"

"It is a true story, Melissa. They do not all have happy endings."

"Well I don't know if I want to hear any more."

"Then you will not hear the best part."

"It better be good!"

"It *is*..." Excitement smouldered in his eyes. "Ranion's fury against the king was so great at that moment, the tore the king apart limb from limb, and—"

"—He became the greatest *leighdur* of all time, after the Creator told him that the he and Alysia would once again be reunited..."

I sensed movement, and looked up see Rasadian standing behind Rion. "Blah blah blah...*spare* us the rest."

"Oh, *Krighven*," Rion teased Rasadian. "You were never one for the story of Ranion."

"That is because I have to hear it *every* night. You forget that the *cubshen's* play chamber is right next to mine; I seriously believe you ought to find another story to tell them."

"It is their choice. They want to hear it, so I tell it."

"Whatever. Father wants a word with you, something about the guards..."

Rion's eyes narrowed into a scowl. "Tell him I will meet him at the table when the females have finished eating."

Rasadian glanced over at me.

"Hi, Rasadian," I said.

159

"So you came back, did you?"

"Yes, I guess I did."

Rasadian glared at me and then at Rion. "Will *she* be eating tonight?"

"I brought her a plate," Rion replied. "We have much to discuss, and little time."

"Very well." He turned and began walking toward the door.

"Has there been any word from Abby?" Rion asked him.

He turned back around with a disdainful glare. "Not yet. And she was due back three days ago."

"She's coming back?" The thought of Abby returning was so exciting. I couldn't wait to see her again.

"When she returns, have her come at once," Rion answered Rasadian without acknowledging me. "I have some questions about next month. Urgent matters."

"Indeed," Rasadian said, rolling his eyes and turning toward the door once more. "Bloody humans. No offense, Melissa."

I sighed. "None taken. *Bye,* Rasadian. Nice to see you again."

"And you."

When he left, I looked at Rion. "What's his problem? He's in a mood."

"He is actually like that all the time."

"Doesn't he like Abby?"

"Not particularly. He does not trust her, and he has a difficult time trusting new human allies."

"Why?"

"We have been betrayed before—a very long time ago. But that was mostly bad decision-making on my father's council's part. It will never happen again."

"I see." I took another sip from my mug. "So you tell stories to the malion children?"

"They are exhausting," he sighed. "My father no longer has the energy to do the story-telling, so I am standing in for now, but I have been so busy lately, I do not always get time. The *cubshens* like the stories, but most times it just turns into wrestling match.

They like to act out the fight scene—especially the little females. They all want to be like Alysia: brave and sacrificial."

I smiled. Rion was a really good storyteller, and I had to admit, it made sense that the kids liked to play fight with him. Rion didn't seem like the cuddle-up-on-the-couch type.

"So, tell me more about the *vykhars*. How did they become the Jaredsons?"

Rion sat back down on the floor in front of me. "When Warren, King Jared's son, grew up, he was stripped of his royal title. But he was able to locate a few of his bastard brothers, and they used their persuasion, strength and speed to further themselves in the world. They cheated people out of money, and gambled and stole everything they could, building an empire that they hoped would have the world bowing at their feet."

"They do now."

"I know," Rion grumbled. "Warren spread lies about the malions and hunted us to near extinction; he offered rich rewards for our heads and hands. When Ranion found out about the rewards, he took the remaining malions deep underground to safety, and that is where we live today—in secret. Except when we are accidentally spotted, that is. Then they start posting all that Sasquatch *shenka* on the news again and—"

I snickered. "Hold on. Malions are *sasquatches*? That's too funny. How do you let those crazy people film you?"

"Well those are mostly humans dressed up as us, but they will never be large enough to be credible. It is really quite irritating. Especially when they put it on the Internet."

"Oh, my goodness."

"Apparently we have a Facebook page, and a Twitter account. And the last program they aired on television had us coming in on UFOs and beaming down to earth, if you can actually believe that."

I was laughing out loud at that point; I couldn't contain myself. "Sorry, but that's hilarious."

"That is all right." He rolled his eyes. "We are used to it."

"How many malions are there? Do you keep track?"

"Very precisely. There are currently fifty-nine malions in the Pacific Third. Twenty-five are female, and thirty-four are male."

"What's the Pacific Third?"

"In the beginning, the Creator divided up the malion territory into thirds, for each of his three sons: the Pacific Third, the Asian Third, and the Eurafrican Third. The border lines are vertical from the north to the south poles.

"Who's the Creator?"

Rion stood up and showed me his chest. A malion's head had been tattooed over his right pec. "Our Creator, or *Lorkon*, as we say in malion, is the great immortal malion, who serves in the heavens, healing the souls of those who have passed through the gates, so they may be reincarnated in purity. He fathered three mortal sons when he gave his seed to three mortal human females, giving them each a third of the land and sea to watch over, to aid in the continuance of mankind and all species that lived there. Ranion was the great, great, great grandson of Rison, son of the Creator who was given the Pacific Third to lead."

"What's with all the R's?"

"It is tradition for the first born son of the *leighdur* in the Pacific Third."

"I see. Well, that's an incredible story about the Creator."

"It really is."

"So the malions have lived underground since Warren began his revenge?"

"Mostly, though we do have a few places where we can be above, which we try to do as much as possible. Being underground all the time is difficult."

I took the last gulp of my hot chocolate. "So how do you make it, living down here? How do you get by?"

He smiled, put his hair behind his ears, and replied, "We are healers, Melissa. We make herbal remedies for just about anything, and they get shipped all over the world. It is in our nature. It is why we exist. We were put on earth to help the world thrive."

"What kind of herbal remedies do you make?"

"Have you heard of Hesenxia?"

"*You* make Hesenxia?" I exclaimed. "That company is world-wide! My grandmother took the anti-virals for her cancer. She lived for *years* longer than the doctors predicted."

He smiled and nodded. "They are very effective, though they cannot cure cancer entirely. That is, not unless we use our hands."

"Hold on a second." I put up my hand. "What do you mean, use your hands?"

"Our hands have the ability to heal with heat and light radiation. It is what we were known for before we were driven underground. With his hands, a male malion can cure just about anything that is viral or bacterial, a wound, any broken bone or puncture, even re-start a heart, as long as the soul has not absconded."

"That's amazing." I sat up on the edge of the bed. "Why do you keep that from us humans? Think of all the people you could save!"

He raised an eyebrow. "It would never be that simple, Melissa, as wonderful as it sounds. And...it is not like flicking a switch. For one thing, healing is extremely exhausting for us. And secondly, it is incredibly intimate. It is part of what bonds a female and a male malion as a mated pair, and to their *cubshen*." He wasn't looking me in the eye anymore. "If we tried to cure everything, with our numbers, we would die of exhaustion after the first hundred. So, we prefer to heal humans in the traditional way, by manufacturing the best herbal medicines on earth."

"Do you have other abilities?"

"We have greater than normal speed and strength, too."

Too true, they had strength. I remembered the way he'd shoved those two malion guards into the wall. I found myself studying Rion. He was playing absentmindedly with the hair tucked behind his scarred ear.

"Was it Caine that...scarred you?"

He turned around and I watched a wave of anger wash over his face. "I was hoping we would get through the night *without* that question."

"I'm sorry, I didn't mean to. I just—"

He growled. "For your information, yes. Right after they locked me up for a month." Then he stormed toward me, opening his shirt and raising his voice, "Get a good look at everything, *all right*? You have been talking about how you are not scared of them, so *here*, here is a great reason. *And they will do much worse to you!*"

His intensity forced me backward until the frigid stone wall cursed my back. Rion towered over me, his liquorice breath hot on my face as I tried desperately not to look anywhere but his eyes, but it was impossible not to peek down, just for a second. What I saw was unimaginable and I recoiled involuntarily: his entire torso was striped and puckered by scars, like he'd been clawed.

He raised his hand up, gesturing around his stomach, and I kept myself from shying away. "Do you *see* now?" he hissed.

"Yes," I replied firmly, swallowing the vomit that had just come to the top of my throat. "Now step *back*."

"Does it scare you?"

"You being so close scares me. Back off!" But he leaned closer. I was so angry that he'd invaded my space again, knowing I hated it. Ignoring my death glare, he proceeded to completely surround me with his body, placing his hands on either side of my head. I had nowhere to go. Just as I was about to scream, Rion's right hand softly tucked my hair behind my ear, driving me to close my eyes as his face came closer. If he tried to kiss me, I'd aim low and central.

"Is that what you think?" he whispered.

I didn't answer. My fear was suddenly replaced by insatiable heat, and my body began to tingle. Everywhere. I swallowed. What was happening to me? I was *angry*. Why did his touch drive it away?

"After everything that I have done," he continued, "do you *really* think that I would hurt you, or do *anything* you did not want?"

I took a deep breath, kept my eyes closed, and bit my lips as I tried pull myself together. His giant fingers brushed my jaw then my collarbone, so tenderly. It was something I'd never felt before.

164

It set my whole body on fire. I suddenly didn't want him to back away—or stop.

"Well, I would never hurt you, *m'ebesha*." His lips moved to the edge of my ear. "I do not ever want to sense that you are afraid of me. What I *want* is to protect you. It is *they* who should be afraid… because what they did to me does not hold a torch to what I would do to them if they so much as grazed your flawless skin." He then looked me straight in the eyes, slowly stepping back to give me the space that I needed.

"I wasn't expecting that," I attempted to regulate my erratic breathing.

"I know." His face softened and his eyes sparkled. "I just wanted you to take me seriously."

My eyes narrowed and I glared at him. "*Warning,* next time."

"Well…I meant every word."

I liked how he'd touched me, but I couldn't bring myself to tell him. It had been so long since any guy had been *that* close to me. Normally, I would have lost it, ducked out and dashed around him, but Rion had this mysterious and sensual way about him that made me want to stand there and find out exactly what he was up to. I decided to change the subject before he noticed.

"You weren't killing those animals on the farm where you were caught, were you?"

Rion's face turned serious again. "Who told you about that?"

I gulped. "Caine."

He crossed his arms. "Do I look like someone who would eat or harm helpless, starving animals?"

My eyes narrowed, searching his expression for an answer, which came to me instantly: lifting livestock would have been a cinch for Rion. And he would have been fast. "Where did you take them?"

"The ones Sorvath and I managed to relocate live on our pastures up north. I healed a few horses myself, and kept them for my own use."

I smiled as wide as I've ever smiled, breathing a great sigh of relief. "I knew it."

Rion returned the gesture and then winked at me as he opened the door of his chamber. "It is almost quarter to eight, we had better go."

"Oh…right…yeah." I had a momentary fantasy of him rescuing animals—and the touch of his finger on my cheek again.

I took one last look at his chamber, and one deep breath. This was it. I wasn't coming back. My mind furiously snapped photos, so I would never forget.

"Ready?" He held out his arms for me to jump into again, for the last time.

I sighed. "Yeah."

We were back at the manhole less than ten minutes later. I tried my best to put the feeling of being in his arms in my long-term memory: warmth and safety.

He set me down delicately. "Thank you for coming tonight."

"Thank you for dinner, it was really good."

"You are welcome." He adjusted and straightened his cloak. "If there is anything else I can do for you…"

"All I want is for the *vykhars* to leave me alone. I'm tired of worrying all the time, and…"

"I am doing my very best, Melissa, but it is not going to happen overnight."

"Let me *finish*." I laughed to myself. He apologized, and I continued, "I also wanted to say that I appreciate all that you've done for me and my family. Thank you, for everything. I am truly going to miss you."

Rion stepped back, and his eyebrows creased together. "Are you going somewhere?"

"No."

"Then why did you say you were going to miss me?"

"Well, it's not as if we're going to see each other again, right?" I stepped back and wrapped my arms around my waist.

He un-hooded himself, took my hands in his and looked directly into my eyes, stepping closer. "I have already watched you walk out of my life once before…I cannot possibly go through that again."

I gulped. This was not the answer I was expecting, and I had to think about a response. "I don't want to endanger our families, Rion. At some point, one of us will get caught."

"I know what I said about the *vykhars*, but I *have* to see you again," he begged.

"I'm not like you, Rion. I don't belong down here."

He ignored my protests. "For eight weeks, I have tried *so hard* to move on, but I cannot. You are the one I want." Then he clutched my hands a little tighter. "Give me a chance to show you that this could work…"

At that point, a pitched battle between my heart and my conscience began, as the romantic part of me tried to convince the pragmatic part that this could work, and that I wasn't completely out of my mind.

"Please say that you want to, *m'ebesha*."

He twisted a strand of my hair around his finger before brushing my cheek and slowly pulling me close. He was so warm, his touch so incredibly soothing. I couldn't fight it any longer; I found myself involuntarily squeezing his hand back, leaning into him and breathing in that wonderful scent of his, as I replied, "I…I *want* to."

XIII

It was difficult to think of anything else but Rion on my way to school the next day. I was giddy and anxious, all at the same time. I kept replaying our last few moments together, wondering if agreeing to see him again had been the right decision. I second-guessed myself to the point of madness, but my heart always overcame any objections.

I arrived at school a little after eight o'clock and I wasn't surprised by the absence of Colin's truck for the hundredth time. This was going on the seventh week he hadn't been at school, and I assumed he was never coming back, no matter what his friends told me. I found I didn't really care anymore, because I had much more important things to think about: Rion things.

My phone beeped right before I got out of my car:

```
Hrrd!! U n him—yay!!
Txt me bck anytme.
      Char
```

I rolled my eyes and began texting her back:

```
Told him Id C him again. Not makng
promises but Im giving it a shot.
   Im new at this stuff. Well c.
```

She returned:

```
Call it whtevr u wnt. Jst tke 1 day
at a tme & c wht happns. Dont thnk
     ull regret it. Hes a lcky guy.
```

I half-smiled. I wasn't sure lucky was the right word. Imperilled seemed more fitting, but I was trying to look past that fact. I took a deep breath and pushed any thoughts of violence into the back closet of my mind. It was time to start thinking positive and stop dwelling on the *what ifs*. It helped that I now had Charlotte to talk to. What a relief to finally have someone with whom I could share my precious secret; on the other hand, it didn't make the daytime any easier, because Charlotte didn't go to my school, and I was still not on speaking terms with Chelsea, who had refused to return my texts.

When I walked into the school, I began thinking about what I would say to Chelsea when I saw her. I was nervous, I have to admit. She'd been my best friend for over a year, and we'd never fought like this. To be brutally honest, it bothered the hell out of me that I couldn't open up to her about everything in my life. I would have to think of a way to tell her just a *little* more, if our friendship was truly going to endure. But then she walked around the corner and I changed my mind.

Chelsea had her hair straightened and down, instead of her usual low ponytail, she was wearing what looked like a pound of foundation and eye makeup, and she was dressed in a short jean skirt with black tights and a red blouse. On top of it all, she was making a dreadful attempt to walk in high-heels, stiffly wobbling around and pausing once to catch her balance. Who she was trying to keep up with just made things ten thousand times worse: Katherine.

"Got a *problem?*" Katherine asked when they stopped in front of Chelsea's locker, which, unfortunately, was right beside mine.

"What did you do to her?" I turned toward Chelsea. "Chelsea, you look *ridiculous!*"

Chelsea turned to face me. "You're just jealous, that's all."

"Why don't you mind your own business, Liss," Katherine added. "Chelsea's learning what it's like to have a *real* friend. And a *real* friend wouldn't let her best friend walk around wearing the same pair of stretchy pants three days in a row!"

"I wasn't talking to you, Katherine!" I retorted. "Chelsea, *you* called *me*. Why didn't you return my phone calls?"

"Take a hint, Liss," Katherine butted in again.

"Shut up before I blacken your other eye," I warned her. "Chelsea—"

"Tell someone who cares, Liss," Chelsea interjected. "I'm done here…. And the reason I phoned you was because I wanted you to come and pick up your crap from my house before I put it in the garbage."

My shoulders dropped. I couldn't believe it.

"Oh for the love of—" Katherine complained, stomping her foot. "Let's get out of here, Chelsea. She's playing the waterworks card again." Then she turned and glared at me. "That might work with Mom and Dad, but it doesn't work with *us*."

"How could you do this to me?" I said to Katherine.

Katherine didn't reply. I watched her pull a one-two-turn-and-strut toward her next class, with Chelsea following awkwardly behind her.

"Chelsea, wait!" I exclaimed. "Please…I'm sorry!"

Chelsea turned back for a moment, and I swore her eyes looked a little red. But she didn't stop. Two salty tears trickled down my cheeks, and I wondered if it was possible that Charlotte had a bit of space for me in her group of friends, because I was now officially friendless at school. This was the most horrible start to a week I'd ever had at Gladstone, and when I got to the washroom, I realized I'd also started my period and forgot to bring tampons. Fantastic. I couldn't go home, so, embarrassingly, I had to ask the school secretary for an "emergency" feminine hygiene product (of course, I didn't have any change for the machine in the bathroom), and the only thing she could offer me was a super-plus, night-time, thick-as-a-damn-phonebook pad.

I power-walked (well, power-waddled, I guess) out of the washroom and almost ran into Andrew, who was still showing up wherever I was. He quickly turned away, keeping one watchful eye on me. I huffed and sped up. I didn't want him to notice I was walking differently. Just before I turned the corner, he asked, "Melissa, are you okay?"

I stopped dead in my tracks. Besides the freaky dream I'd had about him in the library, he'd *never* said a word to me. But it was his discomfited tone of voice that made me turn around to answer him. "Nothing you need to worry about."

He nodded, turned away and began texting on his phone, thank goodness. I didn't want to be rude, but I also didn't want to answer any more questions.

§

I kept to myself for the rest of the week. I sat at the back of all my classes and watched cholerically as my witch of a sister moved into my place as Chelsea's best friend, dressing her up like a freaking Barbie doll, which was something Chelsea'd always made fun of until now.

Instead of staying in the house after school, I winterized my greenhouse, planted bulbs (*way* late in the season, but whatever) and listened to heavy metal; I just didn't want to be anywhere near Katherine, and I began to look forward to the end of the week, when my grounding—early curfew—would be over. When I could finally see Rion again.

By Friday afternoon, I was itching to get out of the house. I ran through the door after school and up to my room to put my backpack away, feeling relieved that Katherine didn't beat me home. I couldn't stand to see her and Chelsea together for one more minute.

"Liss? Are you home?" Mom called from downstairs.

"Yeah!" I threw my binders on my nightstand and made my way downstairs. "What's up?"

"There's someone here to see you!"

I froze. I hadn't noticed any familiar cars outside when I walked in, and I wondered if Chelsea had come by with my things, because I hadn't had the courage to pick them up. I'd been trying to avoid the inevitable; I just wasn't ready to call it quits before we had a chance to talk about things first.

"Just a minute, Mom!"

My mouth felt pasty. I was debating how I could talk to Chelsea without hurting her feelings again, but I came up blank. She couldn't know about Rion, that was evident, so I resolved to let her do the talking and then I would respond as best I could.

I walked downstairs and looked around, but she wasn't in the living room.

"We're in here, honey!"

Here goes nothing…

I knew Mom would be leaving for work in the next hour, so I thought about taking things outside with Chelsea, assuming it might be easier with some fresh air. But when I walked into the kitchen, someone else was waiting for me.

"Charlotte!" I was smiling from ear to ear. "What are you doing here?"

"Nice to see you *too*, Melissa," she replied sarcastically. "I was just telling your mom about what good friends we'd become since we started working together at Waves." She was dressed in her best: immaculate alternative. She wore black tights and a leather skirt, with tall black stiletto lace-up boots that covered most of her legs. She wore a matching leather jacket, a dark purple blouse underneath, and a very small spiked collar around her neck. Her makeup was perfectly matched with dark purple eye shadow that extended slightly beyond the edges of her eyes. It made her light blue eyes stand out, and from here, she looked very attractive. The tattoo on the side of her head was less noticeable today, as she had parted her jet-black hair on the other side, revealing a new pink streak in her fringe and the burn scars. A work of art, like always, and stunningly beautiful.

"Yes, we have so *much* in common." I smiled back at her. She knew exactly what I meant, but Mom looked at her suspiciously.

"I got your *text message* about *tonight*." She looked intently at me. "So I thought I would just come over after school, to save you from having to pick me up."

"Oh, *right*. I almost forgot!" She must've spoken to Rion.

"What are you up to tonight?" Mom asked, looking at me.

"Melissa mentioned that she needed some help with research for her humanities class report," Charlotte answered her. "So I came over to give her a hand because I don't have class tonight."

She must have rehearsed the line because there was no hesitation in her voice. She was brilliant.

Mom winked at me, and her worry seemed to disappear. "What are you taking in school, Charlotte?"

"I'm starting my degree in history and minoring in creative writing."

"That's wonderful," Mom replied. "What will you do when you're done?"

"I'd like to teach. But right now I'm working at Waves and a hair salon in West Van to pay for it all."

"Good for you, Charlotte."

"Thanks, Mrs. Lawrence."

"How was your day, honey?" Mom asked me. "Would you like some tea?"

"That would be great, Mom." I chose not to reply about my day at school, as she poured me a cup, and looked at her watch.

"Well I'd better get going if I want to beat the traffic into work tonight. I'm so glad this is my last graveyard shift!"

"Have a good night."

"Thanks." She smiled. "Your father is home next weekend, and he phoned this afternoon to remind you that it's your Friday to have dinner together, okay?"

"I haven't forgotten."

Then she turned to Charlotte. "It was very nice to see you again."

"Thank you Mrs. Lawrence, it was nice to see you again, too."

"I'm going to run, Lissy. There are vegetarian enchiladas in the fridge for dinner."

"That sounds great Mom, thanks so much."

"Bye then, I'll see you tomorrow." She grabbed her purse, her backpack, and headed out the door.

"Vegetarian?" Charlotte asked me.

"Meat's just not my favourite. I *will* eat it, just as long as I know the entire animal was used in some form, and not wasted."

"Cool." She nodded her approval. "I completely understand that."

"So…what—"

She immediately shushed me with her finger and pointed to her ears. I understood right away: the *vykhars* could be listening.

"Want to grab a coffee first? I'm craving a gingerbread latte."

"Sure, that sounds great."

"Let's walk then. I'll just grab my bag."

We left through the back door, and she headed toward the alleyway at the back of my house. I expected to see her car, but when she made a beeline for the side of my garage, I put two and two together: there was a manhole on the far corner, which must connect to the malions' tunnels. Standing beside it, she looked around and pretended to lace up her boots, while knocking twice on the cover. It immediately opened.

Charlotte flashed a wink at me, and disappeared.

"Hurry up, Liss!" Her voice rose up from below. "We'll catch you!"

I didn't hesitate. I hugged my purse close to my chest and stepped down. It was less than a second later that I was in someone's arms, but it wasn't Rion's.

Rion had dark hair, and this malion's hair was much lighter. He was also quite a bit shorter than Rion, and leaner.

"Welcome back, Melissa," he said as he set me down.

Charlotte grabbed my shoulders. "Melissa, this is Jordon, Rion's cousin."

"Oh." I reached out to shake the hand he offered. "It's nice to meet you."

"The pleasure is mine," Jordon replied. And instead of a shake, he raised my hand above his head and nodded.

"How do you like your new entrance?" he asked me.

"Wasn't it here before?"

"No," Jordon replied. "It is brand new."

"Oh then—?" I looked between Jordon and Charlotte.

"It was all Rion's idea," Charlotte answered. "He wanted you to have an entrance that was closer than John Hendry Park, so Jordon pulled up the blueprints of the city, and lo and behold, one of the largest city tunnels was only a hundred and fifty feet from this easement. It couldn't have worked out any simpler."

"Thank you. That's very nice of you all to do that for me."

"It is more *Rion* wanting to have a closer entrance to your house, so that he can bring you right to your door. He goes all out with female security."

"I noticed," I replied sarcastically. Then I turned to Charlotte. "So what are we doing tonight?"

"You'll see!" she chirped, with a broad smile.

"Well, let us get out of here," Jordon added. "I told the guards fifteen minutes."

Jordon closed the cover while Charlotte and I started down the new tunnel. When he caught up to us, he held our hands through the pitch black, and all I could think about was getting past the guards without another trip to second-base.

"Where's Rion now?" I asked.

"He is going to meet us halfway," Jordon replied.

"Will he be with us when we pass the guards?"

"Definitely. I heard about what happened last time. They do not mean to be so callous…it is just a human thing. They do not take any chances. We have been burned before."

"I just wish that I'd had more warning last time."

"It happened to me, too, Liss," Charlotte added.

175

Jordon shook my hand. "Well, it will not happen again. We got some scanners from a techie friend of mine above. They will not so much as lay a hand on anyone again. Unless they have to, of course."

I smiled at him, relieved. The passage was dark, and I was glad to have Jordon as my guide. Occasional sunbeams filtered in through the manholes we passed along the way, but most of the time we were in complete darkness, and I needed to grab Jordon's sweater to make sure that I was walking in the right direction.

"How much further is it?" I asked Jordon.

"We are about halfway. But not in length. We are halfway in time. Pretty soon, we will get to the place Rion is waiting to meet us, and we will escort you *ebeshas* the rest of the way, at *our* pace."

"I see." I giggled.

We walked briskly for another ten minutes until we came to a large open area the size of a hockey rink that forked into six different new tunnels. The ceiling was quite high so we must have been quite a distance below the city. If I had been down here by myself, I would never have known which tunnel to take.

"Are we going?" I asked when Jordon and Charlotte stopped.

"No, we are waiting," Jordon replied.

"For how I—"

"*Tarsh!*" he exclaimed.

"That's an informal term for *cousin*," Charlotte whispered.

I turned to where Jordon was looking, and across the open space was Rion. He was un-hooding himself at the entrance of the second tunnel. No sooner had I broken a smile, than he was standing right in front of me. I was startled by his speed, but thrilled as I inhaled his individual scent; all of a sudden, I forgot about the past week's events. With him here, everything was simple.

"How are you?" He leisurely reached for my hand.

"Really good."

His hand enveloped mine, and we stared at one another for a moment; the weeklong void I'd been experiencing began filling itself once again.

"Are you ready?" Rion asked, looking at Charlotte and me.

I nodded and Charlotte said, "Absolutely."

Then Jordon turned to Rion and said, "*Lefencha sengas nay?*"

"Indeed," Rion replied. "Let us get going."

Rion held out his arms for me, and when I stepped forward, he scooped me up. Charlotte trotted toward Jordon as he did the same.

"Let me wrap this around you," Rion whispered to me, covering me with his cloak. "It is getting much colder below now."

"Thanks." I tucked my head into his warm neck.

He gently rubbed the side of his head against mine, then without hesitation we were tailing Jordon through the tunnels, coasting just like we had before. I relaxed while he ran, and his body warmed me from the inside out. At one point, I felt his fingers slide down my arm, which startled me, but then I realized it was only to intertwine them with mine.

We stopped fifteen minutes later, and I recognized a familiar torch-lit passage and Rion's door. The boys set us down and we brushed our clothing straight.

"So what's happening tonight?" I asked Rion. "Or is it still a secret."

"Well, I thought you would like to join me for dinner with my family."

I smiled at him, and gulped. "Sure."

He seemed to sense the tautness behind my words. "Do not worry, Melissa. They have all been looking very forward to meeting you. I have been keeping you hidden from them for too long."

"You'll stay, right? Even though females are supposed to eat first..."

"Of course." He took my hand once more. "Dinner will be served in half an hour, so that will give us time for introductions."

"Come on." Charlotte tugged at my other hand. "You can sit next to me."

We walked into a very large dining hall, crowded with malions speaking animatedly. The ceiling was vaulted so no one had to duck down, and the table stood the entire length of the room. Everyone seemed to be talking malion, and Charlotte made herself welcome, as naturally as if she'd been one of them. Rion stayed close behind me, and I hoped he wouldn't stray far.

All the malions towered over me. Charlotte and I resembled two tweens in a room of adults. But Rion was taller than most of the others, and he kept hold of my hand, carefully urging me to the table at the centre of the crowd. When they noticed us, they parted immediately, nodding as we passed. It was excruciating to have everyone stare at me, but Rion seemed to sense it and gave my hand a little squeeze.

"Silence, everyone," Rion spoke to the crowd. "Take your places, please."

We waited a few moments for his family members to find their chairs, but no one sat down, they were waiting for Rion to speak first. Rion's place was at the head of the table and he gestured me towards the chair on his left; to his right was Rasadian, who I hadn't noticed until then. When we made eye contact, he glared at me, and I was suddenly more uncomfortable than I had been when we first arrived.

"Tonight, I have brought someone very dear to me to meet you all," Rion announced. "She will be attending dinner with us, and coming below on a regular basis. I trust you will all show her the same respect you have shown all of our trusted guests." Then he turned to me and held my hand up. "Her name is Melissa. Many of you know she has been here before, but tonight she has happily agreed to join us and introduce herself to you all."

Everyone sat down and Rion went around the table introducing all of his family and friends. I was terrible with names, but I did remember one couple that seemed to be together: Zuralina and her *sensakuru* (mate, as Charlotte translated for me), Lafe. What struck me most, and why I believe I remembered Zuralina's name so easily, was because her eyes, unlike any other malions in the room, were mauve.

As introductions came to an end, a team of malions with aprons brought in warm lemon-scented terry cloths, followed by salads and fruit platters for the females.

I looked at Rion, who nodded toward my plate, encouraging me to dig in, and began with my fruit plate—and a side of guilt for eating before him. We weren't given any cutlery, so I ate like every other female, after wiping my hands: with my fingers.

I survived the initial questions from Rion's family: where I was from, how we met, what I liked and disliked most about living above, and something I didn't expect, could I bring down some Tim Horton's doughnuts sometime. I laughed, as the question totally caught me off-guard. Jordon added his own order of six vanilla dip doughnuts with sprinkles, if I was seriously making the trip. I told them I'd make a special stop just as Rion said he would cover the cost. And with that, I began to feel much more comfortable in the presence of his family. The ice had been broken.

Servants brought out the main course dishes for the females as the salad and fruit course was brought in for the males. On each platter was the same meal: chicken, bread, asparagus and a mixture of roasted nuts. I was given a vegetable patty, and noticed that a female two seats down from me received one as well. It smelled just as heavenly as it looked, and I had just taken my first bite of an almond when I noticed a male whispering in Rion's ear. He had a look of concern on his face, and I suddenly became worried.

"What's the matter?" I asked when the malion withdrew.

Rion placed his hand on top of mine. "My father needs me."

"Okay. Will you—"

"I will not be long." He got up and followed the male out of the dining hall, and I couldn't help but hear Rasadian muttering something to himself.

"Rasadian."

His only reply was eye contact. He still had daggers for me. Conversation had resumed among the malions, so I felt confident that no one would hear us speaking. "Did I offend you or something?"

He shook his head and replied sourly, "You came back. *That* is what you did."

My eyes narrowed. "Why does that bother you?"

"Because you do not belong here, Melissa." He pushed the food around on the plate. "You are doing nothing but endangering yourself—and us—by returning here. One day, they are going to catch you."

"They won't," I disagreed, taking a sip of water. "Their persuasion doesn't work on me."

Rasadian's nostrils flared. "How could you put your family at such risk? You have no idea what they are capable of!"

"You haven't even given me a chance—"

"And another thing I do not like: you and *him*." He thumbed toward his brother's empty chair. "He has no right to go against the assembly members. Any other malion would be punished for such a senseless act, but he seems to think he is above the rest of us."

I was speechless. Rasadian had been the one I trusted from the very beginning—even before I trusted Rion. When I was lost in the tunnels, Rasadian was the one who first comforted me and assured me that Rion would take me home. I didn't recognize this side of Rasadian, and it was beginning to creep me out.

"You end this, Melissa. *Tonight*." Then he pushed his plate away, stood up, and put his finger on the table in front of me. "Because if you do not, the *vykhars* will."

"Rion will protect me."

Rasadian's eyes narrowed, and he mockingly replied through a laugh, "*Rion* will protect you? And what if he is not there? Then what are you going to do, *run*?"

"The *vykhars* don't know anything about us," I retorted. To be honest, I wasn't exactly sure. I was mostly angry at him for not trusting me like I'd trusted him.

"They know a lot more than you think." He ghosted out of the hall.

I'd officially lost my appetite. Charlotte had been busy walking around the table visiting with a few of the other females, and had failed to notice my argument with Rasadian. Jordon had his back turned to me, discussing something with a male next to him. I was about ready to walk out when Rion sat back down beside me.

"I am sorry for leaving." A plate of chicken and vegetables was placed in front of him. "My father is sick and he cannot speak very well. He needed my assistance communicating with one of the other *leighdur*s."

"I understand. Why don't you eat? You must be starving."

"Are you all right?"

I put on my best fake smile and reassured him. It wasn't necessary to bring up my concerns about Rasadian when Rion had much more important issues to deal with.

Rion took my hand under the table, and held it on his lap throughout the rest of dinner. He was silent and otherwise disconnected from me as he sat eating, so I listened to what the other malions discussed at the table, though most of it made no sense to me. It was about some of the new regulations about going above, something about the Asian malions and their new traditions about mating, and something else about Iceland—I think. Rion grumbled once or twice, adding a comment here and there, and I could feel his irritation in his tightening grip on my hand. I stole my hand back after a comment about the *vykhars* made his grasp almost unbearable.

"I am sorry! I forgot I was holding your hand."

"That's okay." I shook out my almost-demolished fingers.

He watched his family members laughing for a moment more then stood up. "Come back to my chambers. I need to talk with you in private."

I hesitated and we stared at one another for a few breaths. I didn't like the tone of his voice, but he didn't offer any explanation, so I followed anyway, saying goodnight to his family as we passed.

I walked into his room and sat on the edge of his bed, watching nervously as he pushed a pile of books and his laptop aside to clear space for both of us. I swallowed hard when he sat down next to me, looking intensely into my eyes. Inside, I prepared for the worst, like he was going to say he regretted asking to see me again. This whole situation between us had my emotions bouncing between ecstasy and worry. Or maybe it was about someone else.

"Does this have anything to do with your brother?" I immediately asked.

"No. Why? Did he say something to you?"

"I just don't think he likes me."

"I highly doubt that. He has just been unpleasant lately, because I have been making the decisions these past few months. He does not agree with some of the choices I have made, but that is not why I needed to speak with you."

When he started looking around the room, I became impatient.

"Rion, for *heaven's* sake tell me before I have a—"

"I had a dream this afternoon," he cut in, with enough dread in his voice that it scared me. "Someone had taken you."

"What?" All of my worry vanished into the musty incensed air. I almost laughed with relief.

"It was the scariest, most lucid dream I have ever experienced. I cannot get the images out of my head. I feel like I am going to lose you. It sickens me." He paused to look at the ceiling. It was like he couldn't focus, and I noticed his hands begin to shake.

I let him continue, though my stomach was suddenly taking an acidic turn.

"When I finally woke up, I had to be sure you were safe, so that is why I sent Charlotte to your house. I am sorry if it upset you."

"Not at all." I sighed, feeling slightly relieved. "She connects me to you."

"No, Melissa," he contended, taking my hand again as if he needed it for security, "*you* connect me to you…. I want to tell you something right now, and you can be upset with me if you want to. I will understand completely."

I adjusted myself on the bed, slightly away from him, and noticed his shoulders sink. My eyes surveyed his, and when he asked if he could continue, I nodded.

"I *feel* what you're feeling, Melissa."

I felt goose-bumps rise on my arms, and my heart quickened.

"Every time my hands tingle, I know that what I am sensing, emotionally, is coming from you. Like right now."

I stared at his fingers as he bent and flexed them.

"I assume you must sense me, as well."

My eyebrows closed together. "No. I've never felt anything in my hands. Why would you think something like that could happen?"

"Well, I think it has something to do with your healing. You see, I used my hands to heal you after your accident."

I tried unsuccessfully to swallow. "But I..."

"It was not just pain medications and visits from Abby that helped you recover so quickly after your accident, Melissa. I had to repair your four broken ribs, your collapsed lung, as well as your broken legs—twice." He shifted closer to me, but I didn't move away this time. "I did not have a choice, Melissa. You would not have made it to the hospital, I had to do *something*...I just did not know that it would affect us this way. Nothing has been written about using our hands to heal humans, because we have always been worried about the repercussions. Our healing hands were only meant for our mates and family members, but seeing you there in your car, I had to take that chance." He took a moment to collect himself. "I do not know how to tell you how sorry I am for forcing this connection between us...I hope that you will forgive me. I just have no information about how to reverse it—"

"I don't want it reversed!" I interjected. "You're feeling guilty for something that came from saving my life, and that is *ludicrous*. *I'm* the one who should feel crappy for burdening *you*."

He shook his head. "Melissa, you do not know—"

"No, I *do* know," I reasoned, placing my hand on his arm. "It was an amazing thing that you did, healing me and saving my life. I just might have died if you hadn't—"

He shuddered. "Melissa..."

"No." I put my hand up to speak. "If being connected to your emotions is what comes from it, I never want it to be reversed. It's actually cool to know that we reach one another on such a deep level."

He sighed. "I thought you would be upset with me."

"Think of it this way: you'll be able to sense if I'm ever in danger, because you'll pick up on my anxiety. A sympathetic nerve response is involuntary, so you feel it long before I can get a hold of you."

"You know that?"

I rolled my eyes. "Biology—*last* year."

"I never thought of it that way, but it makes perfect sense." He ran his hand through his long mane. "I just do not want anything to happen to you, Melissa."

"Well, I'm not going anywhere."

"I know you will not, because I will not allow it. You mean too much to me."

"Oh, I'm pretty strong…I'm sure I could handle myself."

"I believe *that*." He smiled. "You put up a pretty decent fight when I tried to stop you from taking out your IV."

I chuckled. "I guess I did. I hope I didn't hurt you…"

"Rasadian had to reset my jaw."

"Oh my goodness!" I gasped. "I thought it was just that cut above your eye. I'm so sorry!"

"No…I deserved it, I should not have held you down. It was my own fault." He got up and walked over to his wardrobe, grabbed something out of it, and sat back down beside me with a big smile on his face.

"What's that?" I asked when he placed a little wooden box in my hand.

"It is just a little something that I made for you. I was not sure when to give it to you, but I thought now would be a good time, since you are not mad at me. I pictured you throwing it across the room and shattering it at one point."

I raised my eyebrow. "Me or *you*?"

"Well, me, I guess." He grinned. "I am a male. I cannot help it. I throw stuff when I am mad."

"Why did you get me a gift?"

He shrugged. "Just because."

"Well, now I need to get something for you!"

"You already have."

"Huh?"

"Forgiveness—you are not pissed off at me."

I smacked him lightly on the arm and he grinned. I picked up the box, pulled the messily tied bow and opened it. Inside there was tissue paper and when I moved it away, there was a winged unicorn made from blown glass, standing on its hind legs. "You made this?"

He nodded. "You like it, I can tell."

I'd never been given a gift from a guy (besides Dad) before. It made me quiver with excitement. "I do. It's so beautiful. Thank you."

"You are more than welcome. I wanted to give you something besides my *ika—I mean*—that blue flower."

"*You* left the flower that day on the road?"

"Yeah. I couldn't think of the right thing to say to you. You were crying and...I did not know what to say...so I just dropped it in front of you and left, until I realized I had scared you. I came back because I did not want you to scream and draw the *vykhar's* attention. My methods did not quite work out the way I had hoped; we are lucky no one caught us that day."

"You know," I began, running my fingers along the wings of the glass unicorn, "that day...something happened to me..."

Rion's face hardened. "What do you mean?"

"Well, I felt like I'd been shocked or something..." I looked up at him. "Every time I got a shock, I saw an image."

His almond eyes narrowed into two thin lines, where I could no longer see his pupils. "What *kind* of image?"

185

I held his stare. "They were only for a split second, but I swear some of them were from your perspective." I put the unicorn down on the nightstand. "Did you do that to me?"

"What *exactly* did you see?" he pressed, raising his voice.

"I think you were leaning over me in one of them, another was of your chambers, in shambles. It was really bizarre how it all happened."

Rion took a deep breath, but he wasn't calming down. "I am sorry if that upset you. I was so worked up by your crying and apologizing…I just wanted to calm you, but when I touched your shoulder, I think my hands filtered my anger instead. I think what you saw were images of my own frustration. I just did not know I could do that until it happened, and then I did not know how to stop it. I had actually hoped that you had not seen anything. Rasadian had even warned me about it. Melissa, I am—"

"Don't apologize again, Rion. It's okay, it didn't hurt."

He sighed. "You are too nice to me, you know that? I have screwed up *more* than a few times, and you are *still* forgiving me."

"You deserve to be forgiven." I looked back at the unicorn.

"Do you like horses?"

"Yes, I love horses, but I've never ridden one. Why?"

He smiled at me. "Well, I was just wondering if you wanted to go riding with me one day."

"Do you have horses below?"

He laughed. "Of course not! We do not have to hide below *everywhere* in the world. We have a few places that we can be safely above for small periods of time."

"Where are those places?"

"I cannot tell you, Melissa. But I promise I will take you above with me one day, when we have more than a few hours available."

"That sounds great. I could just tell my mom that I'm staying at Charlotte's or something."

"That is what *I* was thinking." He beamed, putting his hand on my cheek, and I looked up at him. We were inches from one another, but I began to back away. I wasn't ready for anything like that.

"Are you still afraid of me?" he asked softly.

"No," I lied.

"Yes, you are. I can sense it. What are you afraid of?"

"I'm afraid of..." I didn't want to tell him about Kyle. "I'm afraid of...of water." Which was true; I couldn't swim.

He put his hand down, and raised his eyebrow. "Water?"

Metaphors came in very useful when I didn't want to talk about something, and I hoped he wouldn't figure it out, or get cheesed like Chelsea always did when I changed the subject.

"Yeah...I, um, I almost drowned once." Almost drowning was a cake walk compared to what had happened with Kyle. I shuddered and pushed those memories away.

Rion was searching my emotions. Searching, searching. "Pretty scary experience, hey? Your emotions are in overdrive right now. My hands are on fire."

"When your head gets pulled underwater by the current because *it's* so strong and *you're* so weak? I call that the most terrifying experience in the entire world, not scary."

"Come here, *m'ebesha*." He wrapped his arms around me and I fell against his chest, finally distracted by the pounding of his heart against my ear and waiting for the images to clear from my mind. "You would never have to fight against the current if you swam with me...I would never force you into the deep end...I would even sit on the shoreline beside you for the rest of my life, if that was where you were comfortable...and if you ever wanted to try treading water again, I would *always* be there to keep your head above water."

A tear trickled down my cheek, and I wondered if it was possible that he understood. I cuddled closer to him, wanting his arms around me more than ever.

I eventually laid my head down on his lap, and he stroked the hair behind my ear. Something about that gesture was so calming, and he must have sensed that I liked it. "What are *you* afraid of?"

It took him a moment, but he finally replied, "I am afraid...of not being there."

"You shouldn't be. You're too fast."

"If the time ever comes, I sure hope so."

I shifted myself onto my back and looked up at him. He seemed so content, and I realized it was because I was content, at last.

"Do you want to stay here tonight? You can sleep in my bed— alone, I mean. Or, you do not have to, I can take you home if you like."

I bit my lip. I hadn't expected the invitation, but I kind of wanted to stay. I felt safe here.

"Well, I don't know...I'd have to call my mom."

He stood up. "I will speak to Charlotte. That will give you time to call."

He left and I pulled out my cell. There were four text messages, all from Mom. Instead of texting her back, I called her at the hospital.

"Hi Mom," I replied when she answered breathlessly, "sorry I didn't get your text messages, I—"

"Liss, thank goodness! I've been trying to reach you all night, I've been worried *sick*, and I've only been able to get a hold of Katherine!"

She was still out of breath and I began to feel nervous. "What's the matter? Are you all right?"

"I'm fine Lissy, we're all fine, but the police issued a warning and it's been all over the news..."

"What?" I began to shiver. It was freaking cold down there.

"A girl went missing six blocks from our street. Her bed was found empty yesterday morning. They don't know if she was taken or ran away. Oh my Lord, I'm worried sick!"

"Who was it?"

"Dee Kojima. When I called Dad, he said Caine knew her family, her father is an employee of his. Oh it's horrible! I've been on edge all night. They have no evidence of forced entry..."

She continued and I zoned out when she went on about the details. Agents—the *vykhars*—had one enemy: malions. My heart began to race.

"Liss, are you still there?"

"Yeah, Mom, I'm here."

"Don't go home tonight, all right? I won't be there until morning, and Duke will be fine with his heated blanket outside. Can you stay at Charlotte's tonight? Do you think she would mind?"

"Um, yeah, she won't mind at all. She's just in the bathroom. I'll ask her when she gets out."

"Okay, great. Katherine is staying at Laura's. So I'll see you tomorrow morning. We're going to have to figure something out for when I'm on night shift and Dad's away from now on. I can't have you girls in the house alone if there's a psycho running around. An alarm system just doesn't cut it for me."

"Don't worry Mom. We'll figure something out."

"Just let me know, all right?"

"I will, I'll text you in a minute."

We hung up and I was rubbing my arms to try to warm myself up, when Rion came back into the room.

"Cold?"

"A little, though I'm beginning to warm up, now that you're here. That's something else I've noticed tonight. I don't know why, but I feel really warm when you're around."

"Ah, yes. I should have mentioned that. I have noticed it, too. Sorry."

"It actually feels good, I hate being cold." Which might be a total lie in summertime, but we'd cross that bridge later.

"Good." He began organizing a few things on his shelf, "Did you talk to your mother?"

"Oh. Yeah."

He sat down beside me. "Are you not allowed to stay? Because Charlotte said that she did not have a problem covering for you." When I just sat there, he got irritated. "What?"

I chewed my lip, wondering how I was going to say it without inferring it was his people, because I honestly had no idea. Without a clue of how I was going to explain, I just blurted it out. "My mom said that a *vykhar's* daughter went missing."

"Yes, that was part of the reason I had to leave from dinner," he replied. "It has been all over the news tonight. The *vykhars* think it is us, and they are searching everywhere for her, or signs we have been anywhere near the house."

"Was it you?"

"Yes—" he sighed "—and no."

I crossed my arms. "What do you mean?"

"Andrew, her brother, arranged it." He reached over and uncrossed my arms. "You must know him. He goes to your school. Tall, Asian—"

"You know him? He knows you?" I knew *exactly* who Andrew was. Mr. Creepy Creeperson was a *vykhar*? "Why would he do that?"

"He is one of our most valuable allies."

"But if he's a *vykhar*, he's your enemy!"

"No, he is a double-agent. He helped me escape when I was captured. He stumbled across my holding cell by accident. What he saw, changed something inside him. He came back a few nights later, de-activated the electrical fields, and ran off. I had Mantis contact him afterward, and we have had an unspoken trust ever since. When he asked me to help his sister, I said yes without reservation....He has also agreed to watch out for you when you are at school."

"That's why he's been showing up wherever I am."

"Exactly," Rion replied firmly. "I have never doubted he is on our side—most especially now that his sister is in our protective care."

"So what's the story with Dee? Where is she now? Below?"

"Dee's family was arranging her engagement to another *vykhar's* son, and she did not want it. She asked Andrew to help her run away. She did not know about us at the time, but Andrew explained everything, and made plans to have her brought below. I have to admit, she has been quite happy with us ever since."

"So she wasn't abducted."

"Not at all. We would never take someone below unless there was no other way to keep them safe. Right now, we are trying to find a way to get her out of the area, but she cannot handle the pressure of our deep underground tunnels for more than a few minutes. We have some malions working on eardrops with anodyne at the moment, but our tests have not been successful. The Eurafrican *leighdur* was wondering what was taking so long, because they were expecting her to arrive tonight."

"So she's going to a different third?"

"Yes. The Eurafrican *leighdur* has more places above than we do, and Dee can choose one that suits her. We gave her some options here, but she wanted to be as far away as possible."

"Poor thing," I sighed. "She'll never see her family again."

"She is not worried about that." Rion looked sad. "She told me that if she knew about us before, she would have come below much sooner."

"I'm happy for her then."

Rion shifted around. "So what about tonight? Can you stay a little longer?"

"Yeah. But what are we going to do? I'm not tired yet."

Rion's eyes widened. "Do you like cards?"

I imagined Chelsea rolling her eyes; to her, playing cards was something her grandmother forced her to do. With Rion sitting eagerly awaiting my answer, I couldn't hide my enthusiasm. "Do I ever!"

XIV

Rion and I stayed up well past midnight. He showed me how to play a few malion card games which were recognizable, but with a malion twist: Old King Jared (Old Maid), Malion's Thirds (King's Corner), and a version of Cribbage that had us counting to seventeen instead of fifteen. I showed Rion how to play Go Fish and Crazy Eights, and beat him every time, though I think he just liked to let me win.

We talked, but not about *vykhars* or the danger we all were in. Rion wanted to know more about me. At one point, he got up and started to fiddle with a stereo. I jumped at the sudden loud guitar solo coming from the speakers, and just settling in to enjoy the wicked matching drum beat when he switched it off, looking embarrassed. "Sorry."

"Don't be. I actually liked that, whoever it was."

He stopped shuffling through a small stack of CD's in his hand, and his eyes flashed up to mine. "You like *metal*?"

"That's about all I listen to lately."

He smiled. "Then I guess we have something in common; I have only ever listened to metal. I do not like any of that pansy *feshka*— I mean *reh*—" His hand covered his mouth"—I mean *crap*."

I laughed. "It's okay. It's cute when you catch yourself speaking malion in front of me. I know it's hard not to, but I'm glad you're trying."

"You know what is cuter?"

I shrugged.

"The dried sauce on the side of your lip."

"Why didn't you *tell* me!" I frantically began scratching it off. I was so embarrassed.

"I just enjoyed watching you eat dinner; I could not stop you."

I rolled my eyes.

We talked for a while longer, and when he sensed I was getting tired, he made his bed for me and chose to get comfortable at his desk chair. I felt guilty for taking his bed, but he told me he'd spent the entire weekend sleeping there after my accident, and was used to it.

"Did you really mean it when you said that you'd take me horseback riding one day?" I yawned.

"Yes," he replied quietly, sweeping my bangs away from my face with his finger. "Sleep now, you are exhausted."

I closed my eyes, and fell easily into dreamland.

What seemed like moments later, I woke up shivering. My back was turned to Rion, and I didn't want to wake him, so I tucked the blankets under my legs and curled up into a ball. I waited to get warmer, but nothing happened. I was colder than I'd ever been below, and after ten minutes, I still couldn't warm myself up. I decided to turn over, and that's when I realized Rion wasn't in his chair.

"Rion?" I whispered.

I wondered if he had slept on the floor instead, but when I looked around, he was nowhere to be seen. I wrapped the blanket tighter around myself.

"Rion?" I called out, much louder this time.

Then something clicked behind me. I spun around. Rion was there, placing his flashlight on his desk. "You are awake."

"Yeah."

"Slept well, did you?"

I nodded.

"I had to keep coming over to check on you last night. You do not make a sound when you sleep. I kept wondering if you were breathing."

"Where were you?" My body began to thaw.

"Morning prayer." He stepped closer toward me. "Cold?"

"Freezing." I was trying not to let my teeth chatter.

"Let me do something about that, okay?"

"'kay."

He came and sat beside me, took the blanket away, picked me up, put me on his lap and wrapped his arms and cloak around me. I nestled my head into his neck, and he flinched. "You were not kidding."

"It's freaking cold down here."

"I know. All of the females have been complaining since we came here."

"So it's not just me."

"Nope. I am used to it. We are just lucky there are enough males around to keep them warm when they need it. They are all so tiny, like you."

"I'm not tiny compared to most girls. Five foot ten and a half is closer to a guy's height than a girl's."

"If you were any shorter or smaller, you would look more like a *cubshen* than my...my..." He stopped himself.

"What?"

"I was about to say *wharla*. Is that okay?"

"Depends on what it means."

"It is the malion equivalent of girlfriend."

"Is that what I am now?"

"Is that what you want to be?"

I cuddled back up to him.

"Is that a yes?"

"I guess it is; just tell me *exactly* what it means." The pulse in Rion's neck quickened against my forehead and I bit my lip to keep myself from giggling. I must have excited him.

"It means petal, like from a flower, but it also means you have agreed to let a male care for you, for your beauty and delicacy. A male in a relationship is called a *dharkun*, a keeper. But it is always the *wharla* who decides if a male is worthy enough to be her *dharkun*. It is truly an honour to be accepted by a female."

"I've heard that *wharla* word before, somewhere. Maybe Jordon said it to Charlotte or something."

"Could be..." Rion cleared his throat. "Are you hungry? Is there anything I can get you?"

"Oh, um, what time is it?"

"Eight thirty."

"A few more hours of sleep then." I yawned and rolled my neck and shoulders around.

"I wish. But I have a meeting in two hours with my zone commanders in Regina, which will take me at least forty-five minutes to run to." He leaned down and gently rubbed his head against mine. "Your hair is kinked out in the back. That is adorable."

"You seriously have to stop picking on me."

"I cannot help it, I like you."

"Thanks." My stomach growled.

"Hungry, hey?"

"You heard?"

"Uh-huh." Rion stood up and took my hand. "Let us go eat. There is fresh fruit and coffee in the dining hall."

"Coffee sounds wonderful." I had become quite the coffee drinker since I started at Waves; it was hard not to be when everyone else around you was.

"Come."

We walked through a few passages, and when I was more than lost, we came to the dining hall. He pulled a chair out for me next to the head of the table and sat down beside me. There was a large fruit tray, and muffins beside it. Rion poured me a cup of coffee then one for himself.

"So when will I see you again? I don't even know how to reach you, and I hate bothering Charlotte all the time."

"Jordon will be here in a moment and he will explain. He is our technical expert. He knows all the ins and outs of the computer world, and has become an important asset over the past ten years. Before computers and the Internet we relied on messengers and re-mailing services, but that has all come to an end now."

"So we'll be able to talk *without* the *vykhars* tracing us?"

"Yes. But I will never be far if you need me, Melissa." He placed his hand on mine. "I would come above in a second to keep you safe."

I smiled, took a muffin, and nibbled on the side of it. He hadn't eaten anything yet, and seemed a little strained when he drank his coffee.

"What's the matter?"

"I am just not used to the taste of coffee."

"Don't you drink coffee?"

"No, I prefer water with melon cubes, actually."

"Oh." I took another bite of my muffin. "Why aren't you eating?"

"I do not eat muffins."

"Well, what *do* you eat then?" I chuckled.

"Malions are omnivores, but I tend to eat more meat than the average male. I have been trying to hold off in your presence. Here is Jordon."

I looked around and Jordon was standing right there. I hadn't even heard him enter the room. And instead of a cape and hood this morning, he was wearing distressed blue jeans and a thick brown hooded sweater.

"Rion," he said, nodding to him. "Melissa," he nodded to me, *"Tevanyakuman, elesandez volo sey yerduz."*

"Jordon," Rion warned.

"Another great dawn has risen," Jordon corrected, "in other words, *good morning*."

"Good morning, Jordon, thank you for my daily malion lesson."

Rion laughed. "Tell us what you have, *tarsh*."

Jordon pulled out a cell phone from his pocket. It was an old, black flip phone. "Here Melissa." He handed it to me. "This is for you."

"How did you get this?" I opened it up and turned it on.

"We have access to recycled cell phones. I found one that is able to text without Bluetooth, so you and Rion can communicate safely."

"Won't it be traced?"

"No. You cannot trace a cell phone unless it has a SIM card that belongs to a wireless network, or wireless capabilities that the *vykhars* can trace by satellite. I created my own SIM cards with the help of a friend above, so the only person who knows where the calls are coming to and from is *me*."

"That's perfect!" I exclaimed.

"The best part is the texting. I have created my own program recently, so now all of our messages will disappear just minutes after they have been read."

"And this doesn't cost you a thing?"

"Nope, it is my own wireless network. You just have to keep it hidden so that the *vykhars* do not find out you are using another phone. That would make them *really* suspicious, even though they would never be able to find anything in it."

"That won't be a problem. I'll keep it on me at all times."

"Yes. If you leave it in the house, the bugs they have placed might interfere with it, so I would keep it in your purse, or something you take everywhere."

"They do not have cameras set up." Rion looked at me. "I had Jordon take a look around your property last night. But since they are recording every conversation that goes on inside your house, texting is our best option right now."

"That's fine. I can live with that. *Anything* is better than *nothing*."

Jordon sat down across from us and leaned toward Rion. "May I change the subject?"

"Depends on what it is about. You know next month—"

"It is not about next month."

"Fire away then."

I stayed silent and sipped my coffee, allowing Rion and Jordon to converse.

"Rasadian never came home last night. I know he went above because I saw him head for the east tunnel, and he took his cloak and his *kacksuns* with him."

Rion growled. "He has been warned about going above. I will speak to him when I get back from the meeting this afternoon."

Jordon paused before continuing. "And *Farshun* sent a messenger this morning."

"*Did* he."

"The *vykhars* found one of their underground entrances. Fifteen dead. Four males and two females—one of them with three *cubshen*—managed to escape and lock the next access. The guard was not on duty."

Rion sat up. "How many females?"

Jordon swallowed as Rion's fist slammed on the table, and I jumped. "HOW MANY FEMALES, JORDON?"

"Twelve."

Rion screamed something in malion and I sank down in my chair. Jordon got up and maneuvered himself around me to take the plate off of the table, while answering more questions from Rion in malion. When the plates were cleared, Rion gave Jordon a few orders (or what sounded like orders) and whisked me home.

"I cannot hear anything, I do not think there is anyone around," he grumbled when we got to the manhole in my backyard. It was the first words he'd spoken to me since breakfast. "Quickly now, I do not want anyone to see your exit."

He wasn't looking at me, and I felt like I was wasting his time by stalling. "Who's Farshun?"

Rion looked down at me, his pupils dilated; I could sense his boiling fury. It bothered me to see him in such a state. "The Eurafrican *leighdur*."

When he wouldn't look at me, I put my hand on his arm. "Rion?"

"Yes?" We finally made eye contact. He looked so forlorn and helpless. I didn't want to make things any worse, but I had to know.

"How many malions are left in the Eurafrican Third now?"

"Twenty-one—including Farshun." He ran his hands through his thick dark mane, looking as if he was ready to start pulling out chunks.

"Oh my goodness. That's so few…"

"Their third has the smallest population. Losing twelve females is almost like a death sentence for them. It takes such a long time to build back our numbers. The females are feeling so much pressure to conceive, they are either miscarrying or their wombs are rupturing before birth—which can kill the *cubshen* and the female. It is *wrong* for them to be so stressed out about reproducing, Melissa… it is so wrong. And I cannot fix this. I cannot find a way to keep our species safe while we wait for the new haven to be built. We are going to be extinct before it is complete. *I* could have been there to defend them. If he had told me he needed more guards, *I* could have gone there and taken some of my father's guard with me." He put his hand on his forehead, leaned against the cement wall and closed his eyes.

Here was this great man, healthy and overflowing with courage, beginning to wither right in front of me. I put my arms around him. He hesitated and started to push me away, but I held on as tight as I could. I imagined that my arms were the water that he needed, and I hoped that they would sustain him before he completely wilted. A hug went a long way in my family, but then I thought: had *he* ever been comforted?

"You'll find a way." I rested my head against his chest. "I'll do anything you need done above, whatever it is."

"That is not your job, Melissa." He stood there, as stiff as the wall he was leaning on. "That is my job."

"Not any more it isn't," I argued. "I'm not going to sit around and watch you torture yourself over this, alone. So I'm going to be your partner, all right? Because that's what we do where *I* come from—*wharlas* and *dharkuns* work together."

I began to sense him relaxing ever so slightly; the next thing I knew, he was sliding his thick arms around me, too. "That is the nicest thing anyone has ever said to me…"

"Well, I meant it."

A few seconds passed and he slowly pulled away from me.

"I had better go." His sigh was almost a groan. "My day has just become much busier. I will text you tonight."

"Thanks for last night. I had a really good time."

"I did, too." He took my hand, kissed it gently, and kissed the top of my head before checking the exit and lifting me through. Before I could brush myself off, the lid was closed and Rion was gone.

XV

For the next week, Rion and I texted back and forth, and because he had so many meetings, I decided to dig into my Christmas shopping to keep myself busy. It was actually *delightful* to spend some extra time with Mom. She was back on the day shift, so we took a few nights, braved the mall, and decorated the house for the holiday season. Her arthritis always worsened in the winter weather, the cold temperatures making it much more painful to grasp and hold objects, so I was happy to carry all the bags and drive (the heated seats made a big difference to her, too). Chelsea dropped off my belongings one night while I was at work, most likely to avoid talking to me, and I began to slowly—albeit agonizingly—disconnect from our friendship. Nothing I could say was going to change her mind, and I wasn't going to start telling her my entire life story just so that she'd be my friend again. I was a private person, and if she couldn't accept that, then we couldn't be friends. Our relationship wasn't about full disclosure, and I didn't want it to be.

On Friday night, Mom and I picked Dad up at the airport, and even though it was supposed to be my Friday date with him, I insisted that Mom join us, knowing how much she'd been missing him, too (which, I think, made Dad really happy). We arrived at my favourite sushi restaurant downtown, and Dad informed us he'd had a bumper year, and had been rewarded with a weekend for two in Tofino. Of course, Mom was overjoyed. We also talked about my school graduation and about my plans to study horticulture at Kwantlen University in Langley, starting this September.

When our food arrived, I was so hungry I tuned out my parents' conversation to focus on eating, until Dad mentioned someone named Colin. I swallowed the rice noodles in my mouth before asking, "What did you say?"

"Oh, I was just telling your mother about young Colin. He's been in some trouble lately with his father, and Caine's pulled him out of school for a while. Wants to keep a closer eye on him, and has him home-schooling and working right alongside his brothers for a few months. He's hoping that'll straighten him out."

I'd stopped chewing when he said Caine. "Colin?" I stammered. "As in, Colin Mansfield from my school?"

"He's a wild one, that Colin. Always messing up his father's plans at work. Never does as he's told…Caine's been having a terrible time with that boy, ever since his mother took sick, he can't seem to get through to…"

My heart rammed into sixth gear.

"…if he were my son…" Dad was still talking but I was having trouble focusing on it. My cell phone beeped—my *other* cell. But I was busy connecting the dots between my encounters with Colin and the conversations we'd had. What *precisely* had I said to him? Had I ever hinted that I knew something? I couldn't remember, and then I couldn't breathe.

Beep-ting. Beep-ting-ting.

I shook myself back to reality, took out my phone and quickly texted:

> Imokwaitasec.

Rion texted back at once:

> ?????

Sorry. I'm fine. Hold on a second.

Text me soon as you can. I need to talk too.

"...Liss, I heard you've been spending time with him..." Dad was still talking. "But I think it's best you just stay away—"

"Liss, honey," Mom interrupted. "Was that Katherine you were texting?"

"No, it was Charlotte. She just asked if I was free tonight. Do you guys mind if I go meet her after dinner? She's got some free movie passes from a customer at the salon."

"Oh, that's nice," she answered. "I was just hoping maybe Katherine talked to you. I've been worried about her lately. She hasn't been herself. She's not moody anymore, she just seems plain lost, but she won't talk to me."

I had *zero* sympathy for Katherine after how she'd treated me. "Can I go, Mom?"

"I don't see why not, honey. You're okay with that, right, Ron? We can cab it home."

"Friends are important, Lissy," he told me. "But I don't want to see you hanging around Colin—are we clear?"

"Clear as *crystal*, Dad. He wasn't really much of a friend anyway."

"Call me when you're on your way home, all right?" Mom added. "They're still looking for that Dee girl, and until then, I want to know where you are and when you're leaving at all times."

"Don't worry, Mom. I'll keep my phone on."

Dad's cell rang, and as he talked to some associate of his, I gobbled up the rest of my dinner as fast as I could, bid my parents (well, Mom; Dad was still on his cell) goodbye and hurried to my car. I couldn't use my entrance to the underground at the house, because my parents would be there in less than half an hour; instead, I texted Rion and asked him to meet me at John Hendry Park, parking my car a few blocks away. Like before, he met me at the swing set and rushed me down the entrance where we could talk privately.

"Aren't we going to your room?" I asked him after he'd formally hugged me hello.

"Not tonight."

"Oh." I was surprised, but he didn't give me a chance to ask why.

"What happened tonight?"

"Well, Colin—this guy at school that started hanging around me right after I came home from my accident—he's Caine's son!"

"Caine has four sons. Why did you not tell me one of them was hanging around you?"

"I had no idea he was Caine's son, and then he stopped showing up at school right after Mantis was killed. I was so upset, and—oh my goodness. I can't believe I let him in the house!"

Rion eyes widened. "YOU DID *WHAT?*"

I scowled at him. "Calm *down*. Nothing happened! He just stopped by to see if I wanted to go bowling with his friends."

"I highly doubt that!"

I felt like such a naïve bimbo, easily persuaded by *the* Colin Mansfield, just like every other cornflake out there. How could I have been so stupid?

Rion instantly threw his arms around me, and lowered his voice. "Anything could have happened to you, and I would have never made it there in time. The *vykhars* are so fast, Melissa. Never *ever* do that again. Not even for a helpless stranger. We cannot trust anyone right now."

I let out a great sigh, thankful to be under Rion's careful watch. "I know. I don't think he's coming back, anyway—well, according to my dad, that is."

He kept his arms around me. "He is right. Caine has got him wrapped up tight right now. He is beside Colin twenty-four/seven trying to make him the *vykhar* he wants him to be."

"I feel like such an *idiot*," I droned. "I thought he was my friend. He was just so nice to me at the time."

"That is what they all do, Melissa. The *vykhars* are very persuasive. They know exactly how to get what they want, and they will not stop until they do, just as Caine will not stop until I am dead. That is, unless I can kill him first."

"My dad mentioned his wife is sick."

"Yes, she has terminal cancer. I heard recently that she has less than a month to live, if that. It is a tragedy, but that does not change how I feel about Caine. He is a tyrant and a coward—he will not even see his own mate anymore. He has nurses caring for her around the clock so he does not have to."

I put my hand on my hip. "How do you know all of this?"

"Andrew is one of Colin's best friends." He scratched his nails on the side of the tunnel. "He tells me everything."

I drew some circles with my shoes on the pavement as Rion adjusted his cloak and cracked his neck around. "Sore?"

"Yes. I kinked my neck in training yesterday; went at it a little too hard when I tried to squatting with a *larsen*."

"*Larsen*?"

"A boulder."

"Big one?"

"You could say that."

I nodded. "So how come we're not going back to your room tonight?"

"That is actually the reason I wanted to talk to you. And I have not much time."

"Why? What's going on?"

He stepped closer to me and took my hand. "I am leaving for a week."

"A *week*?"

"Yes."

"But then—?"

"I have assigned Jordon and Rasadian to look after you while I am away, and they will send a messenger if anything happens."

"A *messenger*? What about texting?"

"It is too far below for cell phone reception."

205

I grimaced. "How far below will you be? And if something happens, how long will it take you to get back?"

"A few hours." He leaned against the side of the tunnel. "We are going to be seven hundred feet below."

"What if I can't contact Jordon and Rasadian? How will they know if I'm in trouble?"

"They are going to text you a few times a day. Charlotte has agreed to be in the vicinity as well."

I slouched down against the tunnel across from him and frowned. "Do you have to go *away*? Can't whoever it is come *here*?"

"No. I do not have a choice this time. I must go for my father; he needs me to be with him."

"I understand," I sighed.

"I knew you would be upset." He pushed himself away from the wall and took a step toward me. "But when I get back, I thought I would take you riding…"

"Sure, yeah. Sounds great." I tried to sound excited, but it was hard because I was feeling anxious. I licked my gums and pursed my lips to try to hide my fear about him being more than an hour away. So much could happen in an hour. It could mean the difference between the *vykhars* taking me, and someone being there to defend me. Rasadian and Jordon had no intuition with my feelings, like Rion.

"*Melissa…*"

"Can't Rasadian go instead of you?"

"No," he groused. "There is a lot happening next month, and it involves me, so I must be there—in person."

"I just thought we'd get to spend Christmas together."

"Well, malions don't celebrate Christmas. Our biggest celebration is in the summertime."

"Well humans do, and I hoped to spend it with you."

He reached out for my hand. "I will make it up to you, okay?"

"'kay."

He kissed the hand he was holding. "I will be back before you know it." Though he was trying, it didn't make me feel any better—or safer. The thought of it really bothered me. He took another step toward me. "Do not make me feel worse than I already do." We stared at one another for a moment and then his cell phone chirped. He growled, dropped my hand and reached down to glance at the message.

"You're late, aren't you?"

"They are waiting for me."

I gestured him away. "I guess you'd better go then."

"I am having a hard time leaving you right now. I sense how worried you are, and I do not want to leave until you are feeling better about this."

I swallowed and looked straight in his eyes. He swept his finger down my cheek. "If I could take you with me, I would. But it is just not possible for a human to be that far below. Your body would not handle the pressure."

His cell phone beeped again. This time he answered it, hollering at whoever it was in malion.

"You know what?" I said, shrugging, when he finally got off the phone. "I'll be all right."

It was a downright fib, but I couldn't keep him any longer. His father needed him and I was holding him up. I took a deep breath and forced my mouth to grin.

"I will come back the moment we have finished our meetings." He eyed me distrustfully.

"Any chance you can come back in *between* meetings?"

He shook his head. "I have to stay with my father. I do not trust the Asian *leighdur* enough to leave him alone."

"Oh." I didn't like the sound of that. All of a sudden the so-called meetings he would be attending sounded more serious than a friendly exchange. "I—"

Rion jumped up to open the lid before I could speak. Landing back beside me, he asked, "Did you say something?"

"Yeah."

His eyes perked up. "And?"

My heart began to pick up speed, and I knew he could sense something had changed inside me. "Say this was it."

His eyes narrowed. "What do you mean? Is this some kind of female thing with an underlying meaning?"

"Say that we were never going to see each other again..."

"That is a horrible thing to say, Melissa. Why would you say such a thing?"

"I'm just being realistic. What *if*, you know?"

"I do not like *what ifs*." He shifted his weight to his other foot and his eyebrows furrowed. "Get to the point."

I took a step toward him. "What would you do if you knew you were never going to see me again? What would you say?"

He hesitated for a moment. "You really want to know?"

"Yeah. Because if we never see each other again, I don't want us to regret the way we've said goodbye." I took another step toward him, and at that point, we were inches from one another. "So what would you say?"

He raised one eyebrow and leaned back. "I do not like this game you are playing with me. I do not speak *female*. So here is my answer, in *male*: I would not say anything at all."

"Why not?" I demanded, putting my hands on my hips.

He smiled. "Because...I would have to *show* you."

His head tilted to the side; he was looking at my arm. He extended a finger toward me, and when he touched my arm, I began to tingle everywhere. Slowly, his finger made its way up to my collarbone, and he paused when I reached up and grabbed his wrist. My stomach knotted around and I gulped.

"Rion..." I protested, taking half a step back.

He stepped toward me again, leaned down and whispered in my ear, "Let me show you, *m'ebesha wharla*, please let me show you..."

I squeezed his wrist and he remained still. "Tell me what you're going to do, *first*."

The only light came from his flashlight, which was sitting on end on the ground, but I managed to catch the sparkle in his eyes as he closed them halfway. "This." He kissed the hollow space between my jaw and my ear, and I felt his hair brush my face as he inhaled deeply, taking in my scent. I began to shake.

"Is this okay?" he asked me.

I took a step back, unsure. He took another step toward me, and wrapped his arm around my waist. I was so hot at that point, I began breathing erratically. His fingers found my belt, and slowly traced around the bare skin of my lower back.

My instincts told me to push him off and start screaming, but something about how slow and tender his movements were, his waiting, his asking permission, made me feel like maybe I *could* do this. Maybe, just once, my body could allow me a moment of pleasure without panicking.

He leaned down again and his lips swept past my temple as his hands drifted up to my shoulders. "Can I keep going?"

I closed my eyes. The pine and leather fragrance made me woozy on the first inhale; I felt high with warmth and affection. Without answering, I leaned into him, and he took that as a *yes*. My hands found their way to his back, the indent of his spine, and his great shoulder blades. I wanted to do this, but I wasn't sure I was ready. He was just so strong, and...would he stop if I asked him to? Rion wrapped his cloak around us, then his giant arms pulled me closer until every line of our bodies united.

I closed my eyes as he ran his tongue over his mouth, and then...it happened.

Every nerve in my body prickled as his lips touched mine. They were soft and gentle and moist, and I began to tremble; I still wasn't sure about it, but I tried to ignore my reservations and began kissing him back. I wanted this. I wanted him. I wanted this moment. And for the love of everything divine, he tasted so sweet. Black liquorice sweet.

When I didn't pull away, he held me tighter. He made his way down my neck with his mouth then returned to my lips, with a new urgent hunger.

"*Vessen tay gee shon yew m'ebesha,*" he whispered as his hands headed south on my back once more. "*Nee neena pelansha maen...* do not fear me, *m'ebesha...*"

My knees softened, and I began to melt against him, letting him make his way to the underside of my jaw, kissing so gently. Before I knew it, my back was against the wall, my wrists above my head, held in one of his hands.

That's when I lost it.

"Rion—" I cried, pushing him away from him immediately. I was screaming NO! inside my head, and I wondered if he could hear it.

He shot back, dropping my hands, and this worried look came over his face. "What did I do?"

I shook my head. "I'm sorry, I just—"

Twitter-chirp. Rion muttered something in malion as he yanked his phone out of his pocket and texted a reply to whoever had messaged him.

"You'd better go." I took another step back when he put his phone away. Thank goodness for his phone, it was the perfect excuse. It was easier than trying to explain. I didn't want to hurt his feelings. This was *my* issue, not his, and I could sense he was bothered by the new distance between us.

"I may get angry and lose my temper sometimes..." He kissed my cheek. "But I want you to know that I am in *complete* control of *those* types of emotions, okay?"

I nodded and put my hand to my cheek; the warmth was comforting.

"I would never push you to do something you did not want me to do. I am twice your size, but when it comes to *this...you* are in the driver's seat."

"Thank you Rion, that means a lot."

"Was it at least a good kiss?"

I smiled. "It was...bang-a-rang." Then I straightened my jacket, preparing to leave.

He snorted. "I hate that word."

"Fine. It was…amazing—to say the very least."

He pulled me close once again and kissed the top of my head. "Now *that* is something I understand."

Twitter-chirp.

"I really should go," he sighed, looking down at his phone again. "If I do not leave right now, those eyes will trap me here permanently."

I glared at him. "What eyes?"

"*Those* ones." He leaned closer to me. "Those big, brown, *leikshi* eyes that I cannot seem to resist." Then he jumped up and peeked through the exit, making sure it was safe for me to return.

"So one week?" I lamented when he came back down.

He growled. "Do not remind me."

XVI

"Merry Christmas, sweetheart!"

"Merry Christmas, Mom," I said, receiving a gift bag sporting Santa and his eight reindeer with gold tissue sticking out of the top.

"And one for you, Katherine," Dad said, handing her a similar bag filled with tissue paper.

"Thank you," she said quietly.

Katherine hadn't said much to me in the last week, but our distance from one another had begun to shrink, ever so slightly. She kept looking at me strangely, and she'd been crying an awful lot. I found out that she'd broken it off with Landon from Mom, and since then, she'd been spending a lot of time in her room. It was odd that she was crying so much over something she'd brought on herself, but I didn't bother asking her about it.

"Thanks, Mom and Dad!" I exclaimed when I opened my combination shower gel and body cream. "How did you know I liked gardenia so much?"

"Call it a hunch." Mom winked at Katherine.

"Oh." I glanced over at my sulking sister.

Katherine made eye contact with me for a few seconds as one of her cheeks rose into a half smile, and looked back down at her own gift bag.

"Vanilla…" Katherine was trying her best to sound enthusiastic, but it wasn't hard to tell that she was indifferent.

"You love vanilla, right honey?" Mom asked her. "I saw that you ran out a couple weeks ago and—"

Katherine began to tear up. "Oh, Mom…I only wore it because Landon liked the smell of it…and…you know what? It's okay…"

"It most certainly is not!" Mom replied firmly. "I've got a sampler upstairs, you go ahead and try them out, and we'll exchange it."

"I actually really like the water lily one."

"Then that's what we'll get you, honey," Dad added. "Don't. You. Worry."

"Thanks…thanks so much." Katherine smiled as she swept a tear away.

"And for you, my dear," Dad said to Mom. "Our weekend away is booked."

He kissed her and she clapped her hands, cheering. "When are we leaving?"

"Next week, honey, for New Year's."

"Oh Ron, I'm so excited!" She leaned towards Katherine and I. "You girls will have a friend to stay with, won't you?"

"Oh, for sure. I was supposed to help Charlotte paint her apartment, so she won't mind me bunking with her for a couple nights." It was a fabrication of what I'd really be doing: spending time with Rion below. Charlotte always covered for me, especially since she spent quite a bit of time below herself.

"What about you, Katherine?" Mom asked.

She shrugged. "Casey invited me to go skiing with her family up at Manning Park. I just need to pay for my lift ticket."

"We'll take care of that honey," Dad reassured her. "Liss, we'll give you some spending money, too, all right?"

"Thanks, Dad, that would be great."

We opened the rest of our gifts and then Mom made a humungous breakfast for us, as always on Christmas morning. I loved the holiday, but the past few days I'd been preoccupied with Rion and the kiss we'd shared right before he left. He was going to be back this Friday, and I'd begun counting down the hours until I could see him again. Just thinking of him had me burning with excitement, something I never expected to experience. Jordon texted twice a day, and my answer was always the same: I'm okay. I hadn't heard from Rasadian at all, and truthfully, I didn't care.

Late that afternoon, I texted Charlotte about my story for the weekend, but she didn't get back to me right away, so I assumed she was below and not near her cell.

"Liss?" a soft voice spoke.

I turned to see Katherine standing there. Her hair was brushed into a ponytail, she had no makeup on (at three o'clock in the afternoon, which was very unlike her) and she was still in her bright blue Juicy terrycloth outfit.

"Yeah?" I asked impatiently. I didn't feel sorry for her and her little soap-opera tragedy.

"I wanted to tell you that you were right about Landon." She wiped her eyes as another tear trickled down her cheek.

"Yeah, so, I've always thought he was a jerk. What's your point?"

She sunk against my doorway. "He cheated on me, Liss."

"I'm not surprised."

"And—"

"Sorry Katherine, but I'm just about to get on the phone. Can this wait?"

"Chelsea wanted me to tell you she's sorry. She knows you've been hanging around with that Charlotte girl, but she hoped maybe sometime you'd call her. She wants to talk things over."

I rolled my eyes, confounded. "Why the sudden change with you two? I mean…I know you and Landon are over, but why are you talking to me now? What do you want?"

Katherine's face changed, and she looked like she was about to get upset again. "Liss…I…you know…" She sniffed and wiped her nose, and squeezed her eyes shut as her lip began to quiver.

"Liss!" Dad called from downstairs. "Door's for you!"

"Be right down!" I called back. I walked passed Katherine and she didn't say anything more. That was a surprise; usually, she'd have something to say to anyone who blew her off. I'd never seen her act so sullen before. Nevertheless, like her, I didn't want anyone diving into my personal business, so I made my way to the foyer, where Mom was hugging Charlotte.

"Hey!" I called to her from the stairs. "Merry Christmas!"

"Merry Christmas, Liss!"

"You got my text?"

"Yeah, and of course you can stay at my place. It'll be great having you over."

"Thanks!" I walked up and gave her a hug.

"Would you like to come in, Charlotte?" Mom asked her.

She bit her lip. "Actually I can't. I'm going to my *friend's* house for dinner tonight. It'll take me a little while to get there, so I'm only here for a couple minutes." Code: below. I got it when she raised her eyebrows at me.

"Well, come back for a visit soon then," Mom replied. "I just need to baste the turkey so I'll see you soon, Char. Don't be a stranger!"

"I won't, Mrs. Lawrence. Thanks!"

"Caine! How are you, buddy?"

Charlotte and I jumped. Dad was on his cell, thank goodness. Caine had phoned to wish him a Merry Christmas, and to check up on me. Dad and Caine continued their jolly conversation and I rolled my eyes as I glanced back at Charlotte, whose eyes were wider than I'd ever seen them before.

"I should get going," she said as she dove into her purse. "I just came to drop this off and say a quick Merry Christmas."

"*Charlotte*," I complained, as she handed me an envelope. "You're so sweet. The only thing I did was text you, I feel so guilty now! I really should start sending some e-cards."

Her eyes flashed up and she shook her head. "Don't feel guilty. It's not from me."

"Oh." I stepped back, almost tripping on the carpet behind me. My legs momentarily lost their sense of balance as Rion's face flickered into my mind, and I began to feel all fuzzy inside.

Charlotte smiled at my reaction, but something was off with her smile. "He wanted this to get to you as soon as it could. A messenger arrived this morning. Jordon gave it to me to give to you."

Charlotte's negative tone and stammering sliced away the hope, anticipation, and every bit of excitement about the coming weekend. I frowned and I looked down at the ground.

"He's not coming home, is he?" I whispered.

Charlotte didn't bother answering. "What time should I pick you up on Friday? I only have one parking spot at my building, and visitors can't park there over night."

"I dunno…" I was frustrated beyond belief. "Three thirty?"

"Sounds good." Then she stepped forward and hugged me. "We'll have a good time. Don't worry."

"Did he say *why*?"

"It's all in the note." Then she slung her purse back over her shoulder, and gave me another great big hug, knowing how much I needed it. "I'll see you Friday, 'kay?"

I sighed. "'kay."

I watched her leave then raced up to my room to open the envelope. Inside, was a hand-written letter, in Rion's *easily identifiable* chicken scratch, and something else I wasn't expecting: a dried *ika* flower.

Though I was disappointed I couldn't see him, I knew he'd gone to great lengths to get this message to me. He'd even written it himself.

MELISSA,

I HOPE YOU CAN FORGIVE ME. I AM NOT GOING TO BE HOME THIS WEEKEND. I KNOW I HAD PROMISED YOU ONE WEEK, BUT THE MEETINGS AND DECISIONS ARE TAKING LONGER THAN EXPECTED, SINCE SOME OF THE ZONE COMMANDERS ARRIVED LATE—AND THE ASIAN LEIGHDUR. WE ARE HOPING TO WRAP THINGS BY NEXT TUESDAY.

I WISH IT WERE SOONER, BUT RESOLUTIONS ARE SLOW WITHOUT MY FATHER. I HAD TO SEND HIM HOME WITH RASADIAN YESTERDAY.

I AM NOT GOING TO ATTEMPT TO BUY YOUR CLEMENCY WITH EXPENSIVE GIFTS. I AM GOING TO MAKE THIS UP TO YOU, IN PERSON, AS YOU DESERVE. FOR NOW, I AM RETURNING THIS FLOWER, THE ONE YOU FORGOT THAT DAY AT YOUR CAR. PUT IT IN A GLASS OF WATER AND IT WILL BLOOM AGAIN.

I THINK OF YOU EVERY SINGLE SECOND, M'EBESHA.

R.

♣

I read the note four more times. Rion knew me much better than I thought he did. Buying love and forgiveness with money and gifts was something Dad did when he felt bad for not being around. I hated it, and it drove Mom insane. Something as personal as this note meant way more than anything money could buy. I held the *ika* in my hand, and the biggest smile came across my face. I was seriously falling hard for him.

§

Chelsea texted me twice over the course of the next few days, but I didn't text her back. I wasn't ready to talk to her yet. Katherine got over her little crying spell and actually began having meaningless conversations with Mom and helping with chores. She tried talking to me once or twice, but I gave her little more than one word answers. Unlike before, I could sense it bothered her that I wasn't more forthcoming, but whatever had gotten into her and Chelsea, wherever this whole change in attitude toward me came from, was beyond me, and I couldn't just let it go the way I would have in the past. What had happened between us hurt so badly; I needed more time to think about whether I really wanted their friendship back at all.

The best part of my week was watching the little *ika* flower begin to open in its glass of water. I couldn't see the stigma yet, but I was sure the bloom would be spectacular. I was looking at it dreamily on Friday when Mom's shout from downstairs penetrated my consciousness.

She was running around the house in panic—as always before a trip—and Dad was doing his best to reassure her as he got Duke loaded into the back of the car. Mom had to quadruple check everything, which also included reminding me for the *umpteenth* time to set the alarm and lock both deadbolts. Poor Dad, it usually took at least two hours before she would calm down.

When they left, I thought I'd perk up a little at the thought of having Charlotte to hang out with for the weekend—which was better than nobody—but inside I was being hollowed out, teaspoon by painful teaspoon.

I sulked up the stairs, sluggishly made my way to my room and pulled out a bag for the weekend. It was almost three o'clock and I knew Charlotte would be arriving to pick me up shortly. I opened my drawers, shoved some stretchy pants, a pair of jeans, a few blouses and a pair of flannel pyjamas into my duffel bag, then I walked to the bathroom, grabbed my toothbrush and—

Whack

Pain came out of nowhere. A razor-sharp, invisible knife stabbed my stomach and I screamed. I keeled over and grabbed my wound, expecting to see blood, but there was none, even though it felt like I'd been ripped open. Then the slicing pain returned again with a vengeance, and I fell to the floor, gasping for breath with clenched fists, searching desperately for something to hold on to, something to help me endure the agony, but there was nothing.

The closest phone was at the end of the hall in my parents' room, but at that point I wasn't sure I could even drag myself out of the bathroom. The pain and adrenaline from the next stab jolted me right off the ground for a moment, and I balled up in defense. The room began to spin and I heaved, still writhing from the pain. It was everywhere.

218

"Somebody help me!" I cried out. "Somebody help me…" I was out of breath and the pain wouldn't cease. I struggled to keep my eyes open as the room went from dark to light to dark again, and little purple and blue stars flashed in front of my eyes. "Help… me…" My eyes closed for a moment, and I had just enough energy to reach my hand toward the figure standing illuminated in the hall. "Rion," I reached out for him. "Help me, Rion…"

The figure began running toward me, but something sucked me away from the light. I had a vague sense of noise, which slowly coalesced into my name.

"MELISSA!"

A large hand seizing my jaw and another under my neck made me aware of my body on the cold tile momentarily, but the pain in my stomach throbbed savagely, cleaving and tearing me open with each muscle movement. The voice called my name a few more times from far away then became a distant murmur.

"Get her up!" another deep voice quietly demanded, bringing me back to consciousness. "Now!"

My eyes were thumbed open, a light flashed into them, but I couldn't respond. I was too weak. Something hot and soothing pressed against the pain as a door slammed.

"Oh my God! They're here!" a high-pitched voice whispered back.

More whispers were exchanged and someone said, "Answer the door, Charlotte."

"No! What if—"

"Do as I say! Find a way to get rid of them!"

"Char…" I mumbled.

"Shhhhhhhh," a melodic voice reassured me. "*Vec che son tay meh…nee neena levekshun. Nee neena levekshun bruvo, Lissssa.*" The soothing heat returned and I opened my eyes to see Rasadian leaning over me with soft eyes.

I reached up and pushed at his chest with my flimsy hands. "Get…get away…" My voice was a muffled mewling.

Rasadian pushed my hands down and I fought him unsuccessfully, with no energy left as my vision darkened once again. He covered my mouth, and I couldn't even resist. All I could do was cry.

"Melissa, you *must* stay quiet or they are going come up here and find us."

My lip quivered and my eyes burned as he pressed a warm hand against my stomach once more. I fell back into a stupor and I couldn't catch my breath, though I was trying to maintain consciousness.

"Yes," Rasadian whispered into my ear. "That is better, is it not?"

I wanted to say no, but only a raspy gurgle came out as I picked my head up again, trying to push his hands away. I didn't want him touching me. I would have rather had the pain.

"Easy *y'ebesha*, the less you fight me the better it will be, but I cannot make it stop until I get you below."

"Rion…" My eyes began to lose focus once again.

"Shhhhhhhhhhh." He covered my mouth again and turned on the taps in the bathtub. At that point, I thought he would give me some space to breathe, but instead, he crawled right on top of me, missionary style. I was too weak to thrust him off, and though the pain was now slight, Rasadian's weight restricting me brought on a feeling of panic. Feeling completely helpless, I could only whimper beneath him.

"You must stay quiet, Melissa," he whispered. His eyes were sympathetic, and there were tears on his cheeks. "I know this makes you uncomfortable, I know this feels very wrong, but I am not as good at this as the others. To find and ease your pain, I must be in full contact with you. I am sorry. I am so sorry. Please do not fight me. I am trying to help!"

I didn't care, I wanted him off.

A knock at the door startled him, and he immediately shot up and unlocked it.

All the pain returned and I retched again, vomiting what little food was in my stomach onto the floor.

"They are gone, Rasadian," a soft voice spoke as the door opened. "Charlotte is brilliant. They believed—holy crap, Melissa!" It was Jordon. He muttered a few words I didn't understand then Rasadian kneeled down and returned his warm hand to my stomach. I clenched my teeth and grasped his wrist to try to rip it away, but it was useless, he was too strong for me. Then water dripped down my forehead, and a cold towel cleaned my face.

"We need to move her," Rasadian ordered quietly. "I cannot keep this up for much longer; she will lose consciousness if I do not do this soon. I almost did not get to her in time."

Charlotte came up the hall in a panic. "The yard's clear, let's get out of here!" My vision hazed from the exhaustion, and a blanket covered my heavy head as it fell back onto a shoulder. A pair of arms raised me off the ground and I closed my eyes, shaking uncontrollably as the pain persisted.

§

When my eyes were opened again, another light flashed into them, reviving me. Voices were shouting frantically. The one closest to me, I recognized: Rasadian.

"Everyone get out of my chambers! Clear the room; she is in shock and I am not strong enough to bring her back with you all here if she departs!" More vicious words I didn't understand were exchanged around me. "We do not have time to wait for him," Rasadian snarled. "I am going to do this—whether he approves or not!"

"We were given *specific* orders when he left, Rasadian," another voice shouted. "Wait! You are not well enough to do that, and Rion will…"

"Stop, Rasadian! Do not do this!"

"VAL CRA NEYEVEH CHE SON TAY WHARLA—NEE NEENA HACHKA!" Rasadian roared back. More voices shouted, and when

I opened my eyes again, Rasadian was leaning over me. "*Neshaviti gesanu vec y'ebesha...hortho wella neshaviti yeh,*" he whispered to me. I tried to protest, shaking my head, but it came out as a series of whines as I felt myself sinking back into sleep. Before the darkness claimed me, Rasadian crept over me, the warmth returned and the pain vanished. My restless arms went limp as something crashed in the background.

A great roar startled me and I woke immediately, and then another piercing shatter on the other side of the room made me jump. Snarls and yelps and punctuated phrases I didn't understand echoed around the room as more smashes thundered and the other voices screamed and hollered. The overwhelming chaos pounded my aching head, sledge-hammering me with each sound.

"RASADIAN! RION! THAT'S ENOUGH!" A high-pitched voice shrieked out orders, some I didn't understand, others were in English. "LAFE, JORDON, MILAN, HARKOR, STOP HIM!" Voices protested and the high-pitched voice commanded, "RASADIAN, MOVE OUT OF RION'S WAY! HE IS GOING TO KILL YOU! STOP IT!"

"STEP BACK!" another deep voice contested. "THEY NEED THIS! GET THE FEMALES OUT!"

One familiar roar caught my attention in the background. "Rion..." I moaned.

Someone growled, a breeze blew past my face, and two large, dry hands were all over me. Warm hands. Lips kissed my forehead and palms. "I'm here, *m'ebesha*. I'm here. Are you still in pain? Tell me, *m'ebesha*, and I'll make it better. Someone get me a cloth and *lemarsa* water, she is drenched in sweat!"

I took a deep breath as my *dharkun's* eyes came into focus. I reached up toward his face, but he took my hand away and kissed it once again. "I'm so tired..."

"I *know*," he replied darkly. "I got here as fast as I could." Then he turned away and shouted at someone behind him.

"Get me away from here, Rion." I put my hand on his arm. "Please just take me away from here."

"Zuralina?" Rion asked keeping his watchful eyes on mine. "Where is her—?"

"Her bag's right here, Rion," I heard Charlotte answer.

"Zura?"

"Rion."

"Tell Lafe that I will speak with him on Monday."

The female with mauve eyes, Zuralina, walked towards us. "Where are you going?"

"I am taking her above."

"You are *what*?"

"We are going to my *bornskav*. I'll be back in...a few days."

"*Rion*," Zuralina remonstrated in a motherly tone. "You know the laws of *Seconsians*. You cannot take her away from her family's mainstay—"

"I have done everything backwards so far. And *Seconsians* is the *last* thing on my mind right now. We just need some time alone, and I am not going to keep her in this *parkus* for three more days. She needs fresh air. Tell my father the same."

Zuralina put her little hand on Rion's great shoulder, nodding her approval. "Very well then, *kor tershun*. Take as much time as you need."

Rion weary eyes blazed into mine. "Come, *m'ebesha*. I am going to take you somewhere much nicer than this."

"Now?" I whispered as my eyes began to close.

"Right now." He picked me up and I burrowed my face into his velvety neck. Breathing a great sigh of relief and taking in the divine scent I'd been missing, I snuggled a little closer to my handsome *dharkun* as he began to purr.

XVII

A *clap* in the distant background startled me and I immediately reached down and grasped my stomach—there was no way I'd dreamed the excruciating episode. What I felt made me gag. Sticky, dried sweat. Yuck! But no pain. "Ahhhhhhhhh," I exhaled loudly in relief, then opened my eyes.

My mouth jerked to the side in a grimace. I'd expected to wake in Rion's dark room below, but I was in someone's log (yeah, LOG) home, in the most ginormous bedroom I'd ever seen. My clothes had not been changed, and I was lying on top of a cherry wood, king-size, four-poster bed covered in emerald sheets and matching overhead swags. A grin sprung onto my face with the overwhelming smell of pine, though it pleasantly blended with honeyed lacquer at the moment. There was only one person that smelled so divine: Rion. This was Rion's home. His home *above*.

I lifted my head off the pillow and looked around. Three of my bedrooms at home could have fit in to this one. At the other end of the room were two large French doors that lead to a balcony. We were clearly not on the first floor. And instead of a wall on my left, there were three giant floor-to-ceiling windows with a view of a great mountain range in the distance. No houses or driveways, just snow-dusted trees and nature. Paradise.

I should have bounced off the bed and started jumping up and down with excitement because I'd been waiting for this weekend for so long. But when I sat up, something deep down inside me was acidly sour, and when I inhaled, it was as if a giant hand was preventing me from filling my lungs properly. I tried numerous times, but it actually *hurt*. Short, shallow breaths were all I could manage, and my neck muscles were so tight I could scarcely turn my head. I'd been stationary for too long.

I stretched a few times and then made my way toward the French doors. The wood floor was cold on my sock feet, but I saw a mat and rested there. The sun was either coming up or going down, I wasn't sure, but a few stars twinkled in the cotton candy sky, and I had to take a moment to soak up the unbelievable panorama in front of me before I stepped out.

When I finally opened the doors, the pine smell was so concentrated I almost sneezed as it stung my nostrils. I rubbed my nose a few times, and crossed my arms to keep myself shielded from the cold breeze outside; I probably should have had a jacket, but I couldn't resist the view. I walked toward the edge of the balcony, hoping to have a few peaceful moments to collect my thoughts, and then I saw him.

Just below me, Rion was sitting shirtless and cross-legged on a rock at the edge of a cliff, surrounded by frosted grass. Even from a distance, I could see he was a block of hard muscle and perfectly defined lines, save his scars. He was resting his arms on his knees and chanting something that sounded like a prayer, but when I looked closer, I realized his fists were clenched and vibrating.

I bit my lip hard and sighed. I decided it was best just to leave him alone for a while. The sky had darkened slightly, and I gathered I was witnessing a sunset, not a sunrise. I thought I'd slept for half an hour, but it was obviously quite a bit longer, and my stomach gurgled. I turned and looked back toward the bedroom. Maybe I could find my own way to the kitchen, but I really needed to take a bath first. I wasn't going to see Rion looking and smelling like a boy's locker room after a wrestling match.

Fortunately for me, the bathroom was stocked full of fresh towels, brand-new soaps in the shape of leaves and a basket full of organic lavender-scented shampoo.

I took my time and filled the extra-large tub up to the top. I figured a giant bubble bath would probably relax me—at least for the time being.

Half an hour later, I'd located my bag, changed, and re-applied the mascara I'd thankfully packed. I was just about to see if there was a hair dryer when I saw Rion standing in the doorway. He was covered by his cloak again and examining me from top to bottom with a ruminating frown.

"Hey," I said when he just stood there.

He glanced down at my stomach and grumbled, "How are you?"

"Really good. How—"

"Hungry?"

My stomach warbled again and I shrugged. "Sure."

His protruding chin, pursed lips and expressionless glare at the floor never improved, and I could sense his complete and utter annoyance.

"I will be downstairs." He disappeared before I could answer.

I found a hair dryer in one of the cupboards and decided that maybe an extra ten minutes in the bathroom would be a good idea; even if I wasn't *really* doing anything. I hoped his mood would improve soon, or it was going to ruin the entire weekend.

When I could find nothing else amusing to smell and sample in the basket, and no more cupboards to snoop in, I walked downstairs, using every effort to keep my mouth from hanging open and my eyes from popping out of their sockets. The main floor had an open concept, and you could see right from one end of the cabin to the other. The ceiling was vaulted and there were three fat wood pillars in the center holding the main supports in place. At the back of the living room where the staircase deposited me was a giant fireplace with one large sectional leather couch surrounding it. The cabin must have been at least four times the size of my home.

"Rion?" I called out, unsure which way I should be heading.

"In *here*," he groused.

I followed his voice into a grand oak kitchen with a matching dining room table that looked as if it had been hand-carved. Rion was taking out a few things from the fridge, still refusing to make eye contact with me.

"Where are we?" I hoped changing the subject would lighten the mood.

"The Kootenays." Obviously, using more than a few words at a time was impossible for him.

I made my way to the window to get a look at the developing quilt of stars in the sky. "How do you live here if you can't be in public?"

"My housekeeper's name is on title. I just pay the bills, and George gets to live on the property for free, as long as he helps me keep this place up while I am away. His guest house is a kilometre north of here."

"A *kilometre*?" I exclaimed. "How big is this place?"

"Big enough that no one disturbs me."

"It's so beautiful out here. You must have been saving for a while."

"I have worked very hard for what I have."

That's when he placed a small plate of food at the table, took his cloak off, and gestured for me to sit down. But I couldn't. Not yet, because my legs were frozen still and I couldn't close my mouth. Since we'd met, I had never seen Rion dress in anything other than a cloak and unremarkable black clothes. Tonight, he was wearing stone-washed denim and a white t-shirt that hugged every inch of muscle on his upper body. And though his hair was still long and hanging past his shoulders, he'd pulled it back into a low ponytail, revealing just how rounded his massive shoulders were. I blushed and ran my tongue over the roof of my mouth when he looked back at me—he was hot.

He pulled a chair out for me at the table then slumped down in the one beside it.

I looked at the fruit and bread. There was only one plate. "Aren't you eating? You don't have to—"

"I am not hungry."

I sighed and picked up something I could eat quietly. I hated eating in front of anyone, especially when they were sitting right beside me. Twice I offered Rion something from my plate, and both times he just shook his head and continued to stare out of the window. After ten minutes without a word, I'd had enough. I knew what this was about. I put my cup of water down. "It's over Rion. Let it go." His fist slammed down on the table and I flinched. Then he got up and stormed into the living room, slamming a door behind him. Fantastic start.

I returned my food to the fridge and marched back upstairs to the room I'd been sleeping in. I wasn't going to spend my weekend with a moody malion who needed some serious anger management classes. I shoved my sweater into my bag and grabbed my cell.

"What are you doing?"

I whisked around to see Rion standing in the hallway. I continued zipping up my bag, and thought of the best way to get under his skin. "I'm not going to sit here and wait for you to get over your little temper tantrum, so I'm going for a walk. You can stay here and sulk, or throw boulders into the bushes for all I care. I'll see you later."

He responded just as I expected: lip curled back and canines exposed. "You are not going *anywhere* without me."

I snatched my bag off the bed and walked toward him. "Excuse me." He just stood in my way. "I *said*, excuse me!" He still refused to move. "You've got two seconds to get out of my way or I'll—"

"Or you will *what*?" he growled.

I got in his face. "Move or I'll—!"

"Then *go*!" he fired back.

I was astonished when he stepped aside and glared back at me. I'd expected him to say sorry or something decent to try to get me to stay—like most guys would have by now. But he didn't, he merely crossed his arms and let me pass with one loud growl.

I bit my lip to prevent myself from calling him a name I would likely regret, and slammed the front door as hard as I could.

I decided to take the path at the front of the cabin which looked most like the driveway. It was *freaking* cold, and I only had a thin sweater in my bag, but I didn't think it would be very long before I came to a paved road I could follow to the town, if there was one around.

Did I really care? Nope. I just wanted to get away from Rion.

What seemed like forever later, I was still waiting for the driveway to end. I began to shiver. Walking faster wasn't helping. Then I heard something snort behind me. I stopped, hearing a weird crunching noise.

"Melissa!" I heard Rion call out.

Instead of calling back, I huffed and walked faster.

"When are you going to give up?" He began to chuckle. "The town is another two hour walk at your pace!" The crunching sound resolved into loud footsteps on the gravel, coming quickly toward me, although there seemed like too many for one person alone. I kept my back turned and clenched my teeth. I'd walked all this way and he thought it was funny. Just as I began to jog, a giant horse and rider appeared out of nowhere in front of me.

I sprang back and watched as Rion dismounted. He dropped the reins and came walking toward me. That's when I turned and ran the other way, but he caught up with me half a second later and grabbed my hand. "Let go!" I demanded, pulling away from him.

"No. I want to talk to you!"

I turned around, out of breath and replied, "I'll listen when you apologize and lose the Alpha Complex."

His shoulders dropped and his eyes softened. "I am angry; is that *all right*?"

I dropped my bag and crossed my arms.

"And I promised I would take you riding, so this is my way of saying I am sorry for being mad. Please forgive me, *m'ebesha…*"

I looked around him. Standing there, as still as could be, was a black horse. And not just any black horse, but the most beautiful and enormous black horse I'd ever seen—bigger than any of the Clydesdales at the Calgary Stampede. I turned back to Rion. "You're a real stubborn jerk when you want to be, you know that?"

He broke a half-smile and held out his hand. "Come for a ride, okay? I am sorry."

I left his hand hanging there. "You couldn't have said that an hour ago?"

"Am I not allowed to be upset with myself?"

I just stared at him and raised my eyebrow.

"All right, all right," he reasoned, surrendering with his hands up. "Let us just go for a ride, okay?"

"I don't know how to ride a horse."

"I know," he replied while I took another glance at the elephant behind him. "That is why you will sit in front of me."

"Is it a nice horse?"

He cocked his head to the side and shifted his weight onto the other foot. "Do I look like the type of *dharkun* who would put you on a wild stallion?"

"Wouldn't put it past you."

Rion bent back, howling in laughter, answering, "Oh, come on. He does not bite!"

It took a bit of convincing, but I eventually got on the horse he called Sharky. We headed into the backcountry at a slow pace, and the ride was incredibly smooth. I could barely feel myself move as we trotted along.

"Where are we going?" I asked him as the forest began to thicken around us.

"You will see. Are you all right?"

"I'm fine."

"Well, then I am going to pick up the pace, but I will hold on to you— just in case." He wrapped his arm back around me, and clicked his tongue at Sharky. Seconds later, we were cantering away into the forest on a foggy, but well-worn trail lit only by the moon. The wind blew the hair in my face straight back, and every

bit of worry I had about riding on this four-legged giant disappeared as Rion pulled me closer.

Twenty minutes later, the forest opened into a large clearing
that dropped off less than half an acre in front of us. Beyond the
massive cliff was nothing but mountain range, I could hear rushing
water in the background, and a spicy-sweet scent tickled my nose.

"What's that smell?" I plugged my nose to avoid sneezing. The
smell wasn't unpleasant, just strong.

"Probably the water. In a few minutes, you will not notice
it anymore."

I rubbed my nose a few times. "It's so pretty out here, the
mountains seem to go on forever."

"This is my favourite place on earth. I love the sound of the
water." He slid down, and held his hands up to lift me off. I leaned
down to him and he grabbed my waist, but the moment he touched
me I winced. He set me down beside him quickly. "Sore?"

I rubbed my stomach. "Yeah. I don't know what happened, it
was just the most bizarre pain. It literally came out of nowhere."

Rion frowned and I could hear a very low growl within it. "Not
really, but we will talk about that. Do you want me to do something about it?"

I shook my head. "I'll be all right." Rion growled louder, so I
grabbed his hand. "Really. I'm fine."

He rolled his eyes. "I will not ask again, but knowing you are
suffering drives me mad."

We left Sharky next to a wide stream, and Rion held my hands
as we crossed via an old fallen-down log. The almost-full moon
gave the few feet of snow on the ground a fluorescent glow. When
we'd crunched our way to the edge of a cliff, the scene waiting
for us was even more amazing than I'd ever imagined: a massive
waterfall thundered into a fiercely steaming lagoon below.

"Oh Rion, this is surreal…"

"It really is."

"Is that a hot spring?"

Rion removed his cloak, laying it out so we wouldn't have to stand. "Yes."

I stared for a few minutes, mesmerized. "I don't think this place would be as spectacular in the daytime. Something about the night and the stars just makes it more...magical."

"I only come here at night." He shifted closer to me on his cloak. "It is safer that way."

"How did you find this place?"

"A lot of searching. My father said that my mother liked the outdoors and waterfalls, so I often come here..." He tore a piece of long grass from the ground and put it in his mouth. "...not just for the scenery, but to feel close to her."

"How did she pass away—if you don't mind me asking?"

Rion sighed. "She died giving birth to us. Carrying twins is... uncommon, so her chances of survival were really slim. At the time, it was either us or her, and she...well, you know."

I touched his shoulder. "I'm sorry..."

He took the grass out of his mouth and tossed it behind us. "Even though I never met her, I miss her sometimes. I know that must sound strange."

"It doesn't sound strange at all." I smiled at him and he rubbed my arms, pulling me into his chest. "How long do malions live?"

"Around one hundred and twenty-five years," he replied, resting his head on top of mine. "Provided they do not get sick." He took my hand, kissed it and inhaled its scent, and looked in my eyes. "I want to talk to you about something."

"About what?"

He glanced down at my stomach.

"Oh, that." I adjusted my sweater down. "Rasadian—"

"This isn't about my being upset with Rasadian." He took a deep breath, and I turned to give him my full attention. "Charlotte and Rasadian were suspicious of our connection from the start, and when I talked to Charlotte last night, I knew they were right."

"You've lost me."

"Melissa…while I was away, I got into a confrontation that I tried very hard to avoid. It was something I had not anticipated when I left, but unfortunately, the discussions got out of hand, and one of the other *leighdur*s and I…well, let's just put it this way: I would have killed him if no one had been there to stop me."

I put my hands up to my mouth.

"I was injured, but not as badly as him."

"Okay. Where are you going with this?"

"You felt it just the same, only you did not heal as fast."

"So you think that—"

His expression hardened as he nodded. "You are connected to me, though, for some reason, you only seem to feel physical sensations—but you do not bear the marks at all, thank the Creator for that."

"How did this happen?"

"The fight escalated to an unnecessary degree." He took another deep breath. "I am so sorry, Melissa. If I had known how it would affect you, I would have never dealt with him myself."

"That's not what I meant." I ran my hands through my hair. "I meant, why is our connection so profound? Is it because you healed me?"

He picked another piece of grass sticking out of the snow. "I assume so."

"So what happens now that *Rasadian* has healed me?" I shuddered at the memory of Rasadian on top of me.

"I truly have no idea. I lost it when I saw him on top of you. It is against our laws to heal another *dharkun's wharla* without permission…but he did the right thing. I realize that now. And the fact that it was my blooded brother gives me some comfort." He was speaking to me, but it was almost as if he was saying it aloud to try to convince himself, too.

I huffed. This changed things between us. A lot. So much more was at stake now, especially if the *vykhars* ever found out about it. It was a weakness they could use against us. "Does anyone else know about us?"

"Abby, Jordon, Rasadian and Charlotte. But they have all sworn secrecy." He said it with such fierceness that I leaned away from him; the heat radiating around us was starting to become over-whelming. "This will not happen again. I am not going to leave you next time. Everyone can haul their *yovses* here if they want to have another meeting."

I sighed. "Let's not talk about this anymore."

"Good idea. The more I think about it, the angrier I get."

"Yeah, I see that." I got up and walked to the edge of the cliff, and Rion followed me.

"What are you thinking about?" he asked when I'd been silent for a while.

"I was just looking at the water…" I titled my head to the side. "What happens when you get to the ocean, you know…when you have to go to the Eurafrican Third. Do you swim?"

"No," he replied from behind me. "We go beneath it."

"And the pressure doesn't affect you?"

"No."

"And you *never* get tired of running."

"Not so far."

I guffawed. "Is there anything you *can't* do?" He glared at me, and I regretted my question, because there *was* something he couldn't do: be above with me, without putting my life in danger. And it seemed to be a constant source of aggravation for us both. "I'm sorry, Rion. I didn't mean that."

"Whatever." He stepped back and removed his shirt, then jumped down onto a ledge just below the cliff's edge.

"Where are you going?"

He began climbing down the ledge, which really wasn't all that steep. "I am going for a swim. Are you coming?"

I shook my head. "I can't swim."

"You already told me that. So remember your water-wings next time and come in with me, now."

"I don't need *water-wings!*"

"Floatie then."

I glared at him. "Kiss my big toe!"

He laughed. "Come here and I will, *shaylanee.*"

"What does *that* mean?"

He kept descending down the cliff. "It means…beautiful."

"And now he's trying to butter me up, ladies and gentlemen!" I called up to the sky.

"Is it working?"

"Maybe." I decided to follow him down, taking the same path. When he saw I was following, he waited for me to catch up. "I didn't bring a swim suit," I told him when we got to the bottom.

"Neither did I." He kicked off his clothes until he was in only—only!—a pair of black boxer shorts. *Fitted* boxer shorts.

If I hadn't been paying attention, I would have forgotten to pick my jaw up from the ground and wipe the drool off of my chin. I swallowed the excess of saliva pooling under my tongue as my eyes wandered up and down his mid-section for the fourth time. Rion was a mass of impeccably defined, hard muscle; eight cookie-cutter ripples adorned his stomach and his legs boasted quadriceps a football player could only dream about. I didn't even see his scars.

"So go in my shirt. It is just water, it will dry."

I smiled. "Then turn around and don't watch me change." The thought of swimming in his over-sized t-shirt was much more inviting than skinny-dipping in my bra and underwear—which was *not* happening. Not now. Not ever.

His black (thank goodness he'd changed) shirt was gigantic on me. And when I told him he could turn around, he covered his mouth, trying to hide his amusement.

"What?"

"An extra-large *harpaf* would have looked prettier."

I didn't know what that was, but I still scowled at him. "You are so *not* making it easy for me to put up with you right now."

He chuckled and ran over to me. "Here, try this." Before I could even see what he was doing, it was finished. He'd made a knot in the bottom, and now his shirt resembled a fitted dress instead of a frumpy muumuu. "There. Now *that* is more like it!"

I took a step into the snow, and flinched against the cold on my bare feet. Rion picked me up without a word, set me down on the shore and took my hand. "I can't believe how warm it is. And it's so clear…you can see the bottom over there!"

"It actually drops off to about forty feet, so stay with me and you will be all right."

"Don't ever let go of me, I wasn't kidding when I told you I couldn't swim."

"I promise I will not." He gave my hand a squeeze of reassurance. "Just let me jump in first and get warmed up. Then we will go in together."

I nodded and Rion dove in, in perfect formation. When I didn't see him surface again, I got worried. I took a few more steps into the water—up to my waist—when he came up behind me and lifted me into his arms.

"Rion!" I squealed.

"Sorry, *m'ebesha*. I could not help myself." He kissed my forehead. "Ready to come a little deeper?"

I filled my lungs with as much air as possible, exhaling slowly and hoping to settle my nerves. "I guess so."

My heart was beating fast as we swam out into the center of the lagoon. When Rion assured me for the hundredth time that he'd keep me afloat and remain right beside me, I unlatched myself from his shoulders and began to relax holding only his firmly outstretched arm.

"Are you okay?"

I nodded. "This is like taking a warm bath."

"I know. It is awesome. The cold water from the falls keeps it at just the right temperature." He looked up at the sky, and I noticed something glimmer on his chest. It was a shamrock pendant on a chain, something I'd never noticed him wearing before.

"That's cool. It shines in the moonlight."

He picked it up off his chest. "It is boulder opal. It channels energy, and it is supposed to carry forth the spirit of all the past *leighdur*s who have worn it—"

"*You're* going to be *leighdur*?"

Rion nodded and shrugged as if it wasn't a big deal, turned onto his back and floated peacefully while I kept hold of his arm. "Next month, there is going to be a *geleshuvan*—a bequeathing. Then it will be official."

"Wow. That's exciting for you!"

He put his feet back under and tread water beside me. "I would really like you to be there, if you want to come. The first part is pretty serious, but the celebration after will be a lot of fun."

I smiled. "I wouldn't miss it."

His face changed and he came closer to me. "Really?"

Without thinking, I wrapped my arms around his shoulders. "Of course. If it's important to you, it's important to me." Rion froze momentarily in my grasp, shocked at my forwardness and then his free arm grabbed my waist and crushed us together. He was much warmer than the water, and his flashing eyes and strong arms made my heart pound. I knew he could sense it. His green eyes filled with rapture; he was waiting for me to allow him to make his move.

"Kiss me, Rion." I inched closer. "You don't have to ask this time."

Slowly, he leaned in and brought us together. Every nerve in my body burned as his lips slow-danced against mine. And even though he was a thousand times stronger than me, he waited patiently for me to show him that it was okay to keep going, caressing my shoulder *ever so gently*. Heaven help me. This was all *definitely* okay.

I grabbed the back of his neck, and he opened his mouth to kiss me harder. All my muscles softened, and for the first time, I didn't pull back. I was actually starting to enjoy it. And he must have sensed I was more than enjoying it, because he pulled my legs up around him. It was as if we were making up for a week of lost time.

237

And then my head plunged under the water. Rion thrust me out of the water less than a second later, but it was too late. Water had charged up my nose and I was coughing and I gasping for breath as the liquid stung my throat and sinuses. I retched twice; the disgusting taste of salt on my tongue was enough to nauseate me, and I'd swallowed a whole mouthful.

"Melissa!" He exclaimed, patting my back. "Aww *velsh!* Are you all right?" He towed me out of the water and carried me back up the hill to his jacket as I tried not to vomit. He ran off, coming back with a thermos while I continued to cough up salt water. Sharky was nearly having a fit neighing until Rion called him over to us. The next thing I knew, two watery nostrils were frenetically examining me.

"I am so sorry." Rion apologized again and again. "I cannot believe I let that happen!" I waved him off and shook my head through a few more hacking breaths. "Drink this." He handed me a cup of something that smelled like orange. "It is black tea, it will help." He helped me take a few sips, and the taste of salt in my mouth receded. "Please forgive me, *m'ebesha.* I should have never kissed you in the middle of the lagoon. I should have done it where we could both touch the ground."

I swallowed a few more sips of tea and took a deep breath. "It's okay. Don't worry about it."

"Well, I still feel horrible."

"Can we just go back to your cabin?" I began to shiver. And even though I wasn't cold, the hair was standing up on my arms.

He wrapped his cloak around me and lifted me into his arms. "Absolutely."

We arrived back at the cabin, and Rion headed into the kitchen to put together a few snacks while I changed into clean clothes. When I felt human again, I decided it was a good time to check my phone and text my parents, but there were already three messages waiting for me. One was from my parents, asking me how things were going and I texted back 'All is well, Charlotte and I are having a great time painting'. The next was from Charlotte, asking how I was feeling, so I texted her back a smiley face. The third text was from Chelsea, which said to text her back ASAP. I deleted it—I'd see her at school.

I was making my way downstairs when Rion came into the living room with a tray in hand. He'd started a fire, and the entire downstairs smelled of it.

"Snacks?" He offered, placing the tray down on the coffee table. I looked at what he had brought. The tray was filled with much more than fruit and bread this time. There was also a large bowl of pasta salad and another one filled with Cheezies—and stuff to make s'mores. "Looks like yum," I replied excitedly. My mouth was watering up something fierce.

Rion let me dive into the food, smiling at me as he made s'mores.

"Are you having a good time with me?" he asked when we'd finished eating.

My face contorted. "Of course I'm having a good time. Why would you ask that?"

"Knowing you feel safe and happy, and *full*..." he pressed his nose into my ear, "...satisfies me."

I smiled and reached for his face, but he quickly backed away. "I'm sorry!" I swiftly took my hands back. "I didn't mean to!"

He took my hands and put them down on his lap. "Just not my face, okay?" I nodded. We sat silently watching the fire crackle, until only embers remained. When the smallest trace of dawn's new light flickered at the horizon, I yawned.

Rion stood up. "Come, *m'ebesha*. I will take you to bed." I smiled and nonchalantly dragged myself behind him, hoping I wouldn't fall asleep on the way up. When Rion opened the door, I immediately collapsed on the bed and he sat down on the edge beside me. When I closed my eyes, he said, "I am going to take you home tonight."

"Really?" I protested through another yawn. "I thought I was staying until Monday..."

"Well, I have a few things that I need to finish up for next month and I do not want to leave you here alone."

239

"Oh." I frowned and rolled onto my side. "When *is* the bequeathing?"

"January twenty-sixth." He leaned back on his hands. "It is a Saturday night. Do you think you will be able to come?"

"Yeah, we're on semester break then. But even if I did have something planned, I'd miss it. You're more important."

"I do not deserve you, you know that?"

"I was thinking the same thing."

He leaned down and kissed me. It was gentle at first, but then something changed. There was a hunger—a purpose—at the base of this kiss, and all of a sudden I was frantically assessing everything about the situation: bed, me, him—*alone!* I tried to suppress my wild nerves as they plucked every petal from my budding confidence. I begged myself to relax. Rion turned and leaned toward me, but I got up on my knees to keep him from closing the space between us. He didn't seem to notice my shift in position, moving his lips down to my neck. I focused on keeping calm, and went so far as to twist my fingers in his hair as his mouth returned to mine. I swept my hands down over his arms, but just as my fingers found his shoulder blades, Kyle's face appeared in my mind, as clear as the moon shining through the window. Kyle had felt exactly the same way when I'd touched him: wide muscular arms and shoulders, impeccably defined, and *solid*. I remembered how I hadn't been able to push him away when I wanted to. As I tried anxiously to suppress that particular memory, Rion ripped off his shirt and began to work on mine, delicately manoeuvring himself on top of me all the while. Our lips were still locked, and then his tongue gently explored.

I couldn't fight it off anymore. Red lights flashed in front of my eyes, and sirens blared in my head. I immediately broke our connection and shoved at his chest. When he didn't move, I screamed at him, "GET OFF!"

"It is okay, Liss." He took my arms, attempting to put them back around him. "I do not want to have sex, we can—"

Kyle had said the exact same thing. "I MEAN IT! GET OFF ME!"

He shot away and stared at me, beside himself, with a disgruntled expression on his face. "What?"

I scurried as far across the bed from him as I could, then took the quilt and covered myself up to my shoulders. "I mean it, Rion. Please just leave."

He got off the bed and crossed his arms. Oh my goodness, was he huge! "Is there something wrong with me?"

"No."

"Then what is it?"

"Nothing. I just can't do this."

"That is not an answer, Melissa. That is an excuse. Why did you push me away?"

I just sat there.

"Does this have something to do with my not being human? Because we are the same *down there*—" He had to point to it, and make me feel like an imbecile—as if I didn't know what he was talking about. It was maddening. "—and I was not..." He trailed off and began to assess my expression. By that time, my eyes were stinging, and I could sense the sides of my heart beginning to fracture under the pressure.

It hurt like hell.

I couldn't tell him. I just couldn't. He'd never come near me again. Or worse, he'd never want to see me again and then he'd tell his entire family about it. "Please don't do this..."

"Then what is the problem? You are enjoying yourself one second, and then you *freak out* two seconds later. I am tired of getting mixed signals from you!" He snatched up his shirt and roughly forced it on, ripping his head through. "Are you not attracted to me?"

A tear streaked down my cheek.

"Is it my scars?"

"Rion..." The barrier I'd held for so long was crumbling. I knew I'd have to tell him now. I didn't want him to think for a second that it was something to do with him. My chest tightened and I could feel my hands shaking. This was it. I'd had no time to prepare.

He was beginning to turn red. "That is it, IS IT NOT?"

I stuck my finger in my mouth and bit down hard as I shook my head.

"ANSWER ME!" He turned around and raked his fingers down the back of his head, grabbing two fistfuls of hair, and I could hear his nails against his scalp. "I WANT TO HEAR YOU SAY IT, MELISSA! SAY YOU ARE NOT ATTRACTED TO ME! TELL ME I AM A HORRIBLE MESS AND YOU CANNOT STAND THE SIGHT OF ME. BECAUSE I AM NOT LEAVING UNTIL YOU TELL ME THE TRUTH!"

Something about his anger fuelled me, and I found myself ready to throttle him for hauling this out of me. With my teeth clenched together, I stood up on the bed to meet him at eye level and yelled back, "YOU WANNA KNOW RION? YOU WANNA KNOW THE *TRUTH*? ALL RIGHT THEN, I'LL *TELL* YOU THE TRUTH?"

Rion was vibrating.

I swallowed. "Why don't I start by telling you about the first time I had sex, because it was sooooo good!"

Rion's lip curled back, revealing his canines.

"Yeah…" Another tear escaped down my cheek. "And then I'll tell to you about how the guy drugged me…"

Rion's face distorted. He was finally understanding.

"Do you want to hear how long he kept me in his room while his parents were on vacation? Or do you want to hear how I told my family I'd run away because I didn't want to move to Vancouver?" I sniffed. "How about how I begged for my life—like a weak little *baby!*—when his hands were around my throat? Or how I pretended to enjoy it, because he told me he'd kill me if I didn't stop fighting him?" When he didn't answer, I opened up and let him have it. "COME ON, RION! WHAT'S IT GOING TO BE?" Now he was the one who was backing away from me, but his fists were still clenched. "How about I tell you how I couldn't walk properly for two weeks?" I shook my head when he didn't reply. "Maybe you'd like to know how he cyber-stalked me for a year, and how he still refers to me as *kitten* on Twitter? Or the part where he told me he'd come for me if I told anyone..."

Rion growled. "Who did this to you?"

"It's in the past, Rion, it doesn't matter anymore."

"Yes it does—tell me his name!" he snapped.

"And what good would *that* do, Rion? Tell me. Tell me how that's going to help me when he still haunts my dreams?"

"I will make him pay for what he did."

"That's not the point, Rion."

"Then you are going to the police."

"I already tried. You know what happened? I got a call back a few days later saying there would be insufficient evidence because too much time had passed, and that I couldn't go accusing ex-boy-friends with upstanding citizenships and no prior criminal history of sexual assault just because we broke up—if you can believe that! And besides...do you think I wanted everyone looking at me, thinking, 'Oooohhhhh there's the girl who got *raped*!'? No one would ever look at me the same again. And look at *you*, you're looking at me differently right now!"

"No, I am not."

Two more tears dripped onto my shirt. "Yes, you are. And you're probably never going to come near me again."

"You are being ridiculous, I would never—"

I sniffed and wiped my nose again. "Just don't worry about it, okay?"

Rion snarled at me and turned toward the door. The sight of his back boiled my blood. It wasn't because I was upset with myself for pushing him away. It was because I knew his opinion of me had changed, right after I'd finally gotten the courage to tell him the truth—I had dreaded it, and it had happened. "That's fine," I blub-bered through a few more tears. "Walk away. Don't say anything, because I already know. And I don't give a crap!" I scoured the room, and the first thing that came into my view was two glasses of water on the nightstand. I reached across, grabbed one of the glasses and hurled it at the wall. Water and glass shattered all over the floor and Rion whipped around, screaming something in malion, which sounded like '*Watch it*'. I wasn't feeling any better, so I picked up the next glass of water and threw it, too.

Rion muttered some other curse and left the room.

"Just GO!" I screamed at the empty doorway. "I knew you would!"

I waited for a door to slam, but there was nothing, so I assumed he'd just taken off and that someone else would be coming to take me back to my pitiful existence. When ten minutes had gone by and I could stand it no longer, I fell back on the bed, covered my head with a pillow and sobbed. Telling him didn't make me feel better. I actually felt horribly worse, repulsed, and reminded I'd always be *that girl*: filthy, damaged goods.

"Melissa?"

I didn't answer.

"Look at me, Melissa."

Rion's firm voice startled me, but I kept my head under the pillow. "I want to go home, Rion. Someone else can take me. I don't care who."

"You are not going anywhere, and despite what you think, neither am I."

I instantly pulled the pillow away and sat up. Rion was standing at the footboard with a tray full of empty glasses in one hand, and a giant mug of white hot chocolate in the other. "What are you doing with those?" I wiped my eyes. My mouth watered at the sweet smell coming from the mug.

His answer was a smile, but not just any smile. It was that big, Cheshire cat smile he wore when he was up to something. "I thought you might want to break some more glasses."

I sunk back on the bed, and even though I was laughing to the point of tears, my pain was gone.

XVIII

"Show me your best curve glass!"

Bounce, bounce. Whoosh—smash! "TAKE THAT, *MANAKACKA*!" I shouted at the green target Rion'd taped on the wall.

He laughed. "*Manakack*-O, *m'ebesha*! And harder this time. You missed his face!"

Bounce, bounce, bounce, bounce. Whing—crash!

"That is it! Now aim for his balls this time."

Bounce, bounce, bounce. Whoosh—smash!

"Oh! He is down! Two more to the head!"

Bounce. Crack!

"I want to hear your ROOOOOAR, *m'ebesha*!" His roar shook the windows.

I caught another two glasses from him in midair, the fifth and sixth straight catches in a row. I was getting *super-duper* good. "Rrrrrraaaaaaaaaarrrrrrrr!" I exclaimed through another fit of giggling and one snort. *Jump. Smash! Jump. Crash!*

Rion leaned toward me with his hand raised for another high-five. "That is my *wharla*. Nail the *qarkren* again!"

A total of forty empty mugs, glasses and Mason jars later, I was sure the springs on the bed were toast. Rion had me laughing so hard I was almost ready to pee my pants. Shards of glass covered

245

the floor like an iridescent blanket, and he could not have cared less. When we were officially out of glasses, and I couldn't jump any longer, Rion carried me downstairs and set me on the couch in front of the fireplace. My self-defence classes were never this therapeutic; somehow, Rion knew just how to reach me on a level that no one else could.

And he was staying.

I woke up in his arms sometime after one in the afternoon. He didn't question me further about the incident with Kyle, and instead of taking me home that evening, he took me for another horseback ride to a much nicer viewpoint on the other side of his property, then pushed me on a giant tire swing he'd put up for the *cubshen* last year.

We arrived back at the cabin around seven, and I discovered what an amazing cook Rion was, unlike me, who burned toast on a regular basis. He made me a vegetarian pizza and Caesar salad from scratch—he ate it, too—before we headed back to the tunnels, and from there, John Hendry Park.

Charlotte was waiting patiently in the parking lot above to take me home, but prying myself out of Rion's arms was agonizing, and he didn't seem too rushed to send me up, either.

Opening myself up to Rion this weekend and learning he accepted me—despite my plentiful flaws—gave me some relief from the entangling, helpless fear I'd been struggling with for so long. I still had moments of panic when I was alone with Rion, but I realized my fear was something that would probably never disappear. The nightmare of Kyle would always be in the back of my mind, holding a slice of my spirit prisoner; but with Rion's unconditional affection, I no longer felt I had to deal with it on my own. If it weren't for my family, I'd have run away below with him tonight and never gone back.

"You're never going to kiss me again, are you?" I said with a huge sigh when he released me and motioned to the open manhole.

He smiled. "Well, I want you to know that I meant what I said, back when I told you I would sit on the shore with you forever, whether we are swimming or...*whatever.*"

"Rion—"

He put his finger on my lips, and tilted up my chin. "Let me finish."

I pursed my lips together to keep them from interrupting, because I wanted to say, "Never, in thirty lifetimes, did I think I would find a guy who'd put his own pleasure on the back-burner for me."

He continued, "Physical intimacy is something that makes a relationship fulfilling, but that does not mean it has to be *sex.* Yes, I am sure it is a wonderful thing, but if you do not want to, neither do I. Just holding you in my arms gives me the greatest pleasure, because I sense your happiness in return."

I narrowed my eyes to theatrical slits, and glared at him with mock-disbelief. "How do I know you're not just saying that?"

He smiled. "Put it this way: your fear runs through me like venom, and it scares the hell out of me. I just did not pick up on it the first time we kissed. Because it was so new, I thought you were just nervous, but now I know better. Now I know *why.* And I do not ever want to feel that from you again." He kissed the top of my head. "I cannot feel pleasure if you cannot. So when, or *if,* the time ever comes that you want to go further, I will know because your emotions will tell me long before you do. And *that* is something you cannot hide from me."

"Have you ever gone that far before?"

He shook his head.

I looked up at him. "Really?"

He shrugged as if it was no big deal. "I have only had one *wharla.* We maybe kissed—once, I think—but I told her to find another *dharkun* just before I was captured by the *vykhars.* We were set together as *cubshens* by our fathers, but I could not go through with it. It just did not feel right to pretend I felt something for her."

247

"Was she upset?"

"*Oh* yes, and her father is still mad at me, but there is nothing I can do about it." He kissed my forehead. "And besides, there are probably fifty other males in the Asian Third that would fight *Netka Rhamos* for the chance to be her *dharkun*. I am just glad I did not have to fight anyone to be yours."

"I don't think you ever will."

His eyes narrowed. "Not unless you have changed your mind and want to tell me that *packa*'s name."

"Not a chance."

"Then I guess you are right."

"Promise me you'll never tell anyone my secret."

He shook his head and brought me against him one last time. "You are lucky that you can hide your past deep down inside. I see mine every time I look in the mirror."

I held his eyes with mine. Yes, I was lucky. In many ways. "Just promise me."

"I swear, *m'ebesha,* on every ounce of blood that flows in my primitive veins that it will never leave my lips." He grumbled a little saying it. "So long as *you* promise to talk to me when something bothers you in the future. I do not want you holding anything in anymore." Then he took my hand and kissed it gently before raising it above his head.

§

When I returned to school, Chelsea's car wasn't in the parking lot. She usually arrived early on Mondays to check the fields for divots after weekend soccer, but she was nowhere to be seen. When I got to my locker, I discovered why: hers had been abandoned. Resentment washed over me; she must have switched lockers to get away from me. I still hadn't gotten used to the fact we weren't friends. I didn't notice Katherine walk up beside me until she spoke, her words stiff.

"She moved away." Katherine was wearing pastel pink jeggings, Keds and a white hoodie. Her hair was up in a clip and she had no makeup on again. I wanted to say, 'Boo-freaking-hoo for you!' but it wasn't worth my breath. I was beyond the pettiness now. So I took the high road—so unlike her, with her verbal diarrhea.

"Where did she go?"

"North Carolina." She played with the loose sole on her shoe. "A scout offered her a full-ride scholarship starting in September, so she's finishing up school down there so she can start practicing with the team."

I just stood there in shock. A move out of the country wasn't what I'd expected. I knew she'd been texting because she wanted to apologize, but I didn't want to pretend everything was hunky-dory between us after the way she'd acted, so I'd ignored them. I wasn't sure how I felt about Chelsea; there was just me, her, and this big black hole between us.

"She tried texting you..." Katherine added. "She still wants you to text her or call her or something. We've—she's got a lot to say, and—"

I glowered at her. "What's *with* you two? One minute, you're doing everything you can to make my life a living hell; the next minute, you're both anxious to be my friends again." I shook my head. "You have no idea how..." I couldn't even think of the words to describe how crappy I'd felt. "You're my sister for crying out loud! Freaking *family!*"

Katherine's eyes began to water. "Liss, please...I'm...I'm *so* sorry...I *totally* deserved that punch in the face."

"Why are you saying this? Because you have no friends now?" She flushed, and I actually felt bad for a moment, but she needed to hear the truth. "I don't have the faintest clue what you're up to, being all nice to me now, and I don't care why. It's not going to change the past. Our relationship has been ruined ever since you got all hung up over some loser that decided to prey on *me* instead of *you!*"

I closed my mouth hard, but it was too late. I'd already said too much. Katherine was gaping at me, as if I'd confirmed some suspicion she'd been brooding over. But she didn't press the issue like she would have in the past; instead, she just gazed at me sadly, waiting.

I kept quiet.

"Maybe—"

The warning bell rang, and I slammed my locker before she could finish her sentence. "I don't have time for this, Katherine, I've gotta get to class. Please leave me alone." I was going to be firmly polite with her from now on, because that's the way that I would have wanted to be treated by someone who despised me.

Her shoulders dropped. "Will you just text Chelsea at least?"

I began to walk in the other direction. I wanted to say "forget it," but my resolve to take the high-road made me reply with a quick sign-language "K" over my shoulder, instead.

§

I kept mostly to myself for the next ten days. Rion's hectic schedule of meetings meant we couldn't see one another; however, the time apart was easier than usual due to the fact that Katherine actually respected my request and stayed out of my hair. Andrew checked in with me every day, and once he took me out for my favourite White Spot veggie burger and yam fries because he knew I'd been a little bummed out (though I think Rion may have put him up to it). Dad came home for a few nights on the weekend, but by the following Tuesday he was back to work, and Mom was back on nightshift, as miserable as ever that Dad was gone. By Thursday afternoon, I'd officially exhausted my efforts to stay busy. I slumped down on the couch to see what kind of gossip magazines were hanging around (my absolute *last* resort) after a lengthy walk with Duke, when my cell phone chirped—my *other* cell phone. It was Charlotte.

Watcha doin?

I texted back:

        Readn smut.

        Plans on Sat?

        Negatory.

        Well u do now.

        Whats happenin?

        Girls night below!!!!!

After a week of dog walks and books, Charlotte's idea for Saturday was just what I needed. Rion's last meetings were scheduled for Saturday anyway, so I was definitely available. And even if he finished early and wanted to hang out, a few more hours wouldn't make much difference (in other words, he'd have to wait until girl's night was done, thank you very much!). According to Rion, malion guys knew how to have a good time, but I was curious to find out what the girls did for fun.

When I arrived at Charlotte's apartment and saw what she was holding, I knew I was in for a real treat. She had two shopping bags stuffed with promising detritus. I could make out an iPad, nail polish, sundries, popcorn and a box of Timbits. She opened an identical phone to mine and started texting as soon as we were out the door.

"Jordon?" I asked.

"Yup. We're meeting him and Lafe in three minutes." Then she nodded her head, gesturing I should follow her. "They don't have to be at the meeting tonight, so they're going to bring us in."

"Right." I clicked my imaginary finger gun in her direction.

We walked to a dark corner of the hall, and entered the stairwell. At the bottom was a janitorial door that Charlotte opened with her own key. Inside the small closet were a few mops, brooms, one large plastic bucket and a bunch of cleaning supplies.

"Why are we—"

"It's just a cover for my entrance." She winked at me. "The janitors use it, but they don't know that *I* do, too." She lifted the mat from the floor, pried her fingers between the tiles and lifted, revealing an entrance. She held out her hand. "After you."

I made my way down the ladder and she closed the door, meeting me at the bottom with her flashlight. "This way."

We walked through the darkness for a few moments with only the occasional drain above letting in light, before we came to a brightly lit area. "When will—"

"Shhhhh!" She pointed up toward the city. I buttoned my lips. Moments later, Lafe appeared in front of us.

"Hi, Lafe," Charlotte whispered.

I almost said "Hi" too, but Charlotte signalled me to keep silent. Lafe looked exactly like Jordon, only his hair was much longer. He had a tattoo on his neck and this strong orangey-cloves smell. Charlotte jogged off into the darkness, and Lafe stepped toward me with his arms outstretched. "May I?"

"Oh...um...sure." It was really awkward to be in someone else's arms, and for a moment I wondered what Rion would think of this.

Lafe took off running and caught up to Jordon, who was carrying Charlotte. It was near pitch black in the tunnels and I began to worry about colliding with something because we were going really fast. I shut my eyes tight.

"Are you all right?" Lafe asked me.

"How can you see down here?"

"Night vision. All malions can see perfectly in the dark."

When we made eye contact, I realized that his eyes were glowing, something I'd never noticed before in Rion.

"Well, Rion usually brings a flashlight for me, and I'm just not used to not seeing."

Lafe hesitated, and Jordon asked where we were headed. "My chambers," Lafe answered, speeding past him to take the lead.

"Who is with Zuralina right now?" Jordon asked him.

"*Ka'a li sarven.*" Then Lafe glanced at me and corrected, "Her sister, I mean."

After a quick and easy visit with the guards (one of them actually remembered my first name), we arrived at Lafe and Zuralina's chambers.

Zuralina's mauve eyes opened wide, and she clapped her hands excitedly the moment we opened the door. "Hey guys—and Melissa, you came, too!"

"Charlotte insisted." I smiled back.

"I am glad she did."

Lafe walked over to Zuralina, kissed her hand and raised it above his head. "Have a wonderful time, tonight *m'ebesha*." Then he turned to us. "Take care of my *kuru*—and my *cubshen*. Feed them well. And call us when you are ready to go above."

"We've got it covered," Charlotte answered him over a chuckle, with her thumb gesturing to the bag of treats she brought. "Now *out*—you, too, Jordon! *Nesfaras* only, tonight."

"I am going, I am going!" Jordon replied, winking back at her before shoving two Timbits in his mouth.

Lafe and Zuralina exchanged a few melodic phrases in malion, they touched foreheads and he kissed her hand once more, whispering, "*Li havash nathe, velehandra*" before heading out reluctantly. The last phrase was definitely something endearing, because Lafe had made a clear effort to ensure she was looking right at him when he'd said it. And she'd said it back. I wondered if it was something similar to "I love you."

When he left, I looked around the room. It was much bigger than Rion's, and definitely homier than his, with bits of knitting, a sewing machine and piles of material in the far corner.

"You sew?" I asked Zuralina.

"I make all of the cloaks, and most of the clothes for the males who do not fit in human sizes—which basically means Rion."

"And soon to be Lafe if he doesn't quit growing soon," Charlotte added.

"I knew he had another spurt in there," Zuralina replied. "You should see him and Rion eat lately. They just cannot get enough food this past month. Though I think it must be their new training regime; they have really been going at it."

"Who's hungry?" Charlotte asked, setting the bags on the floor beside us. She turned to Zuralina, "Well, you're a given, but what about you, Melissa?"

"Sure."

"I really need something with sugar," Zuralina begged. "The *cubshen* really wants something sweet today."

She sat up, and I could see the hint of a little baby bump under her cotton blouse.

"Your eyes are looking a lot more mauve than last month," Charlotte said. "This one must be a keeper."

"I do not know," Zuralina answered. "It has only been just over a month."

"How long will it be before the baby is born?" I asked her.

"I have a forty-seven weeks to go, provided I make it that far. Malion gestation is quite a bit slower than a human's—especially the males. But when *cubshen* are born, they grow quite a bit faster."

"You must be really excited."

"I just hope we make it to the end—or at least one of us does," she replied buoyantly.

"Don't talk like that!" Charlotte snapped at her. "Everything is going to be fine."

Zuralina smiled. "Leave it to Charlotte to erase the negativity in any room. Now let us eat!" Charlotte pulled out her iPad and started the first movie, and Zuralina dove into the Timbits. We made fun of her after she ate all but three of the thirty-eight left in the box, and insisted she eat the rest. Halfway through the movie, Charlotte took out her nail polishes and painted Zuralina's toes, then manicured her hands. Apparently I was next, so I began to search through the colours, laughing at the O.P.I. titles: *I'm Not*

Really a Waitress, Changing of the Garnet, Paint your Toron-toes red, Aphrodite's Pink Nightie, Purple with a Purpose, Teal the Cows Come Home, Peel Here...

"So this bequeathing is pretty big stuff, eh?" I asked Zuralina.

"Yes," she answered with a full mouth, accidentally. She covered her mouth immediately after, and swallowed. "Ramses has been *leighdur* for the past forty years. Having a new *leighdur* is going to be a huge deal, but I could not think of anyone better than Rion."

"How old is Ramses?"

"Seventy-one."

"He had Rion and Ramses after he turned fifty?"

"Well, my *maymus' tarsh* just had two more *cubshen*, and he is over a hundred—it is not unusual. It is almost impossible to tell the age of a malion; once we are fully mature, we stay the same until the day we pass into the afterlife."

"Then why is Ramses so sick, if he's so young still?"

Charlotte had obviously known all about this, because she was busy working on Zuralina's nails, filing away.

"He became really sick after Rosensha, Rion and Rasadian's *maymus*, passed away. He has refused medications, refused to be healed, and he barely eats at all. It has taken a toll on him, but he does not seem to care."

"That's terrible."

"I know." She swallowed the last big gulp of water from her glass. "I have never met a malion who refused to be healed before. He is so stubborn, but there is nothing anyone can do to change his mind."

"I think I know someone else just as stubborn," I quipped.

"Isn't *that* the truth!" Charlotte piped up.

We all laughed, and Zuralina added, "Yes, but he listens to you!"

"Usually."

"It is because he is your *dharkun*," Zuralina said to me. "A *dharkun* may argue with his *wharla*, but he would *never* disobey her."

"So what's a *kuru*?" I asked her. "Isn't that what Lafe called you?"

She nodded. "It is short for *sensakuru*. It means 'The one who completes me'. It is the equivalent of husband or wife, where you come from."

"That's cool." I began to look around her room in more detail, and noticed an *ika* flower sitting in a glass of water. It looked exactly like mine, only in full bloom, with its sky blue petals surrounding hot-pink anthers and green stigma. I pointed at it. "Hey, Zuralina, you've got one, too!"

Her smile shone bright, and her eyes widened. "Did Rion give you one?"

"Yeah, he did."

Charlotte joined in her astonishment, and Zuralina came back with, "Oh, dear *revanahtha* Creator…"

My eyebrows pulled together. "I'm missing something…"

Zuralina's eyes sparkled. "To receive an *ika* flower from a male…well, that is the most genuine promise of commitment a *dharkun* can offer his *wharla*. Each male is given just one from the great *ika* vine when they reach full maturity. He did not even give one to Gyn—" Charlotte shook her head furiously at Zuralina, as I watched nonplussed.

"Huh?"

"Keep it safe, Melissa," Charlotte said, smiling and winking at me. "It means he really cares about you."

I nodded and bit my lip to keep myself from blushing. I had known he was serious about me—his acceptance of my past and his willingness to put himself in danger made that clear—but I hadn't realized how permanent of a commitment he'd made 'til that moment. I was taken aback.

"Melissa, could I ask huge favour?" When I nodded, Zuralina said, "Could I have some more water?"

"For sure," I reached for the glass pitcher on the desk. "Oh, it's empty. I can get us some more."

"Do you know how to get to the dining hall? There is a kettle there that should still have warm water."

"I'm sure I can find it, if you tell me how to get there."

"Outside, second left and down to the end of the passage."

"Got it," I said, after repeating it back to her. "Charlotte, do you need anything?"

"I'm good. I'm working on the Cheetos over here."

"Right on," I laughed. "Save some for me!"

I left the room and found the dining hall. The passages were lit by torches, so I had no problem navigating my way through. I refilled the glass pitcher, and was about to go back when I heard voices coming up the passage. I couldn't make out what they were saying at first, though it sounded like they were arguing. As the voices came closer, I realized they were speaking English. One voice I didn't recognize, the other was Rasadian; no one spoke as slowly and precisely as Rasadian.

"Where have you been?" the unknown voice queried. "Jordon has been trying to reach you for days!"

"That is not your concern," Rasadian answered firmly. "And I do not have to answer to *Jordon*." The voices came closer, and I didn't want them to know I'd overheard their conversation, so I hid around the corner as they made their way into the hall.

"Has he told her yet?" Rasadian asked. "No?"

"The assembly cannot interfere with personal matters, you know that."

"This is not a personal matter, Benjamin. This is a matter of doing what is right, and protecting our species. She needs to know the truth. And he cannot keep going above to protect her. All the strength in the world does not help you when you cannot see—"

"Keep your mouth shut. This is not the time, or the place."

Rasadian muttered something as their footsteps receded.

It didn't take a genius to figure out who they were discussing; Charlotte didn't need protecting. They'd been talking about *me*. Rion was hiding something from me. We needed to have a serious talk. I spun around, deciding to head back to Charlotte and

257

Zuralina with the water, before I went *dharkun* hunting, but a flash of light appeared in front of me before I took my first step.

I knew it was Rion. There was no mistaking the smell of pine and the soaring temperature of my body. He flicked off his flashlight and snarled at me. "I HAVE BEEN LOOKING ALL OVER FOR YOU! WHY HAVE YOU NOT ANSWERED YOUR PHONE?"

Oh. No. He. Didn't.

"Chill out!" I hissed back. "Don't you ever start with hello? I haven't even *seen* you this week!"

He grabbed my hand. "WHAT ARE YOU DOING DOWN HERE WITHOUT ME? AND WHAT MALE CARRIED YOU?"

Obviously, a discussion was not possible. I snatched my hand back and leaned toward him. He had no right to yell after keeping secrets from me, so I let him have it. "I don't have to ask you if I can leave the house. I came here with Charlotte, and if you don't mind, I'll head back now because Zuralina needs some water. When you're ready to lower your voice and purchase a set of patience, you and I need to talk. *Excuse me!*" To be honest, as angry as I was that he was hiding something from me, I was more pissed off that he was scolding me like a child.

I shouldered around him, but didn't get far; he stopped me with an outstretched arm and pulled me close.

"Please…just wait…" His tone was much softer, and he buried his face in my hair and breathed in deep. Something changed inside him as he cradled me to his chest, wrapping his cloak tightly around me like a security blanket. The hairs on my neck stood up and my skin began to prickle everywhere. I felt myself shuddering, and he pulled back. The junction of tunnels was dimly lit, but I could still distinguish how his terrified eyes searched mine. Something was very wrong. He was trying to stop his lip from quivering. I secured the warm pitcher against my hip. "Rion… what's wrong?"

"I was so worried about you," he began. "I went to the entrance near your house. I texted Andrew—who had no idea where you were—you never answered my calls. I thought something had happened to you!"

I shook my head. "My battery was low this afternoon, and I forgot to charge it..."

He took a deep, shaky breath. "I am sorry for yelling, I just...I just panicked when I could not find you. And then I picked up your scent in Zuralina's chamber when I ran past. I think I scared the *pakar* out of them when I busted through the door, and then she told me that you were getting water...I was so angry, but I was just so *worried*."

"Rion, tell me what's going on. I've never seen you like this before."

He closed his glassy eyes and looked down. He couldn't even look at me.

"Rion?"

A moment passed before he finally said, "Abby is dead."

The pitcher of water dropped from my hand, as my legs fell out from underneath me.

XIX

It was all over the Internet. News of Abby's apparent suicide and images of her SUV being pulled out of Howe Sound were pasted all over the local news sites. Allegedly, the reporters stated, she had driven her vehicle into the ocean of her own accord, as there were no signs of impact on her vehicle, and no evidence of homicide. There were also no witnesses to the incident, which RCMP believed happened in the early hours of the morning.

I sat on Rion's lap as he navigated the articles, my stomach twisting into a knot, because my worst fear had come true. And I had to say it out loud. "This is all my fault."

Rion snorted and flashed me a dirty look, as his other knee shook fiercely. "Do not be ridiculous, *m'ebesha*. This has absolutely *nothing* to do with you."

He could say anything he wanted to, but it wouldn't stop my conscience screaming, "You should never have gone to that party! You should never have returned home!" A picture of Abby floundering in panic inside her submerged SUV, desperate for oxygen and a way out, entered my mind. I squeezed my eyes shut to see if I could evict it. It wasn't easy.

I kept quiet as he continued to search, though something had begun to change inside of me: the part that supposed this whole thing could work between Rion and me. Was it really worth it?

Who would the *vykhars* go after next? I couldn't even fathom the thought.

Maybe it was best to just break it off.

I squeezed my stinging eyes at the thought; my heart throbbed.

"It is the *vykhars*," Rion blurted out, too distracted by the articles to pick up on my change of emotion. "They got to her. And if I ever get my *shapps* on that *fenyeka* Caine—"

I put my hand on his; I didn't want to say anything about *us* just yet. "How do you know for sure?"

"They have been quiet for some time, because they were working on something. She told me that she would take her own life before she gave them any information, so she must have known they were coming for her."

I rubbed my forehead. "So, what now?"

"When was the last time Caine was at your house, or telephoned?"

"Uh..." I tried to think back. "Dad talks to him all the time. He sent over a basket of food and wine at Christmas. I'm sure he's phoned when I'm not there."

"But he has not been at your house, because you would have told me, right?"

I nodded quickly.

"Have they driven by lately?"

"Not that I know of."

He slammed his fist on the desk. "I knew it. I was right."

I shook my head. "I'm not following you."

"They had another lead, *m'ebesha. That* is why they have left you alone for the past month." He smacked his fist against his other hand. "I *knew* something else was up, especially when they ignored the fact that I disconnected the bug on your car."

I sat up and took in a deep breath. I couldn't stay any longer. "I've gotta go home."

"No," he answered firmly, grasping my hips and pulling me back on to his lap. "You are staying right here."

261

"Rion…" I twisted around to face him. "My mom is going to be super upset about this, and my dad's not home until Tuesday." It was the truth, but I also needed some time to think rationally about this whole situation.

He put his arms around my waist. "This is not up for negotiation."

"I didn't say it was." I pushed his hands away. "I'm going, whether you take me or not."

Rion growled. "Then I am coming up to your room tonight."

"No." He'd never been inside my house, and I didn't want him there—particularly now, when I needed some time alone. I pulled another few reasons out of my head. "You're way too big to hide in my closet, and if anyone catches you, Caine will take my whole family hostage." I grabbed my purse. "I'll be fine. I'll text you if I have any troubles."

"You are acting strangely." He searched my eyes for answers. "Is something else bothering you?"

"I just feel sick about this whole thing. I don't know…I just need to go home and make sure my mom is okay."

Rion raised a suspicious eyebrow at me, then shook his head and grinned. "I just had an idea."

"What?"

"Give me a few minutes. I am going to make a quick phone call, and—" Rion's phoned chirped, and he answered it before the second ring. The caller was speaking malion, but Rion answered in English.

"Where did he go now? He just got back! I do not give a *pechka*, Lafe. Get his *tavan* to the hall—*shekrayvan vet nee neena quay*!" Fuming, he slammed the phone shut.

"What was that about?"

Rion huffed. "Rasadian just took off again!"

"Where did he go?"

Rion shrugged and rolled his eyes. "Hopefully somewhere I can call him this time. He has a terrible habit of shutting everyone out—even his own *krighven!*" He fumed for a moment, but pulled himself together, finished his phone calls, and then we burned home.

"So what's your idea?" Rion was lifting the lid to the exit at John Hendry Park, which we used when someone was home at my house. "You were going to tell me right before your phone rang."

"Well...come here first." His eyes were soft.

Since the weekend at the cabin, he'd only pecked the top of my head. He was probably scared that I'd freak out again, and as he stepped toward me, I did contemplate stepping back; I couldn't just kiss him and act like everything was all right. That was wrong. But deep in the pit of my soul, I wanted him. Badly. I was desperate for the feel of his warm chest against mine, and for two giant hands that knew exactly how to make me tingle in places they'd never been. I tried to will my feet to move backward, but they wouldn't. And he must have sensed my longing, because he immediately wrapped me in his cloak and scooped me up.

My reception unleashed him from his stronghold. He let out a low growl and was all over me. Without a thought, I wrapped my legs around him as he backed me up into the wall, and I squealed in pleasure. His lips seized mine and then he made his way down to the little space between my ear and my jaw.

"Say the word and I will stop," he whispered in my ear, before gently kissing it.

"No." I meant it to come out as a protest, but it ended up as more of a moan. It felt so wickedly selfish, and my heart craved him. I just *wanted* him, even if this was, perhaps, the last time.

Rion purred, and he kissed my lips again, opening his mouth wider. His tongue rolled ravenously around mine, and I found myself putting my hands in the back pockets of his midnight jeans as he ground his hips against me. His sultry hands crept up my back, roaming in circles; it made me shiver. I breathed the pine scent of his skin as I swept my fingers under his shirt and down his washboard abs. He kissed me harder, holding me tighter. I loved how safe I felt with him, and the excitement; it was something I'd never experienced with a guy, in my entire life. Before I knew it, emotion overtook me and my eyes filled with water.

"I am about to break my promise..." he said all of a sudden, sucking gently on my neck.

For a moment I wasn't sure what he meant, but then I realized I'd aroused him. Well, that made two of us.

He started extricating himself from me. "...and this is not the time—or the place."

I swiftly pushed him back. His words reminded me of something *else* that had happened tonight, which had been set aside in the last hour with the news of Abby's death, and our little *practice* session.

"I did not mean that I was not in *control*, I just wanted to—" his face contorted when I glared at him "—what is that look for?"

"I overheard Rasadian talking to someone named Benjamin tonight."

His eyes narrowed. "Okay..."

"I think they may have been talking about us."

Rion's eyes filled with rage as his chest expanded and his fists balled. "What did you hear?"

My eyes narrowed as an intense wave of heat washed over me. He was definitely guilty of something. "Are you hiding something from me?"

His lip curled back, baring his teeth, and he hissed, "There are certain things I do not discuss with you, because you do not need to be frightened any more than you already are and—"

"I don't like secrets." I crossed my arms.

"Really? You are one to talk. You kept secrets from me!"

"But I still told you!"

"And that was your choice." He stepped closer to me, but I stepped back, shook my head and locked my teeth together. "If there comes a time when I feel it is necessary to tell you about it, I will. For now, forget about it. You do not need to concern yourself with things that involve my physical wellbeing."

I scowled at him. "That's not fair, Rion!"

"Yes, it is. You are the one not being fair to me by prying." He jumped up to open the exit.

Our conversation was over. I hated secrets, and I didn't agree with him, but I let it go because I was keeping something from him, too; how *I* felt at the moment. I forced a smile. I didn't want to end tonight on a bad note.

"Are we done with this conversation?"

I sighed. "Done."

He kissed the top of my head and lifted me toward the exit. "Thank you."

"I'll text you when I get in the door."

Rion kissed my hand then the corner of his mouth pulled up into a smirk. "You could have your new *above* escort do that."

I gave him a rotten look. "My *what*?"

"Remember my *idea*?" He gestured toward the exit. "Meet my *idea*."

"Hey, Liss!" Andrew poked his head down from the exit.

I beamed. "Andrew!"

A few minutes later I was walking up the front path to my house, as Andrew ran a quick perimeter inspection of the yard—which took him all of four seconds—before I entered the house.

Mom was on the couch when I opened the door, and to my surprise, she was in Katherine's arms. I wanted to say, "Since when...!" but I didn't. Katherine was really turning over a new leaf since her break up with Landon, and I wondered if it was possible that my old sister was on her way back.

"Liss..." Mom sniffed and wiped her eyes as Katherine handed her another tissue. "I'm so glad you're home. How was your girl's night with Charlotte?"

"It was really great. Until I heard," I lied, turning toward the television that was updating the situation with Abby.

Mom sniffed and wiped her eyes again, then rolled her neck and shoulders around. "I still can't believe it. She must have been feeling so overwhelmed for so long...." She got up. "I just need to take a nice hot shower and get some sleep. If you girls hear about the funeral anywhere, let me know because *I'd* like to go—whether or not your *father* decides to come home and go with me or not."

Katherine and I exchanged looks, and Katherine rolled her eyes. I didn't need to ask, because it was obvious: Mom and Dad were scrapping. Again.

"We'll go with you. Right, Liss?" Katherine finally answered.

"Absolutely. I'd like to. I wouldn't be here if it weren't for her." I shuddered as I spoke, because I couldn't help thinking that she just might be alive if it weren't for me.

When Mom disappeared upstairs, I began to walk toward the kitchen. Tea. I needed a strong cup of tea.

"Liss?" It was Katherine.

"Yeah?"

She came into the kitchen and sat down on a chair at the table, intertwining her fingers. "I really need to talk to you."

"Then talk." I filled the kettle with water.

"I can't right now, because Mom's here and I don't want her to hear."

I rolled my eyes, shut off the water and spun around. "Is this about Chelsea, again? Because if it is, I'd rather it waited. I can't handle any more drama tonight."

"No, it's not. But Chelsea was the one who found out about it, and that's part of the reason she's been trying to get a hold of you—besides the fact that she was going to North Carolina."

I put my hand on my hip. "Just say it, Katherine. I can call her tomorrow, and—"

Her eyes glassed over. "Liss...we can't talk about this *right now*. Could we please just find a time to go for a walk? Or a have dinner in a private restaurant where no one can hear us?"

I huffed. "You can't just tell me whatever the heck is bothering you right now?"

A tear escaped her eye and fell onto the table.

I scowled at her. "Are you pregnant?"

She furiously shook her head. "It's not about me. It's about you."

Ten seconds must have gone by that we just stared at one another. I wondered if she knew about my going below. About Rion. About everything.

"You tell me right now, Katherine. I'm not leaving this room until you tell me what this is all about."

Her lip began to quiver. "It's about Kyle Peterson."

I inwardly exhaled a huge sigh of relief. My double life had not come unwound. "Then it can wait until after finals. I've got too much on my plate right now to think about that jerk-off."

"I don't know if it can wait until then, Liss," she begged, sniffing and wiping another tear away. "The—"

"It's going to have to," I replied firmly. "I've already wasted more than enough time in my life with him—time that I'll *never* get back!" I stormed out of the kitchen.

"Liss! Liss, *please!*"

I sprinted up to my room and shut my door, shoved my iPod buds into my ears and blared Daniel Wesley until the images of Kyle's face vanished from my mind. Just hearing his name was enough to bring back the phantom pain between my thighs and the burn of his cigarettes on my stomach and back, following the r—.

I swallowed hard; I couldn't even think the *word* without wincing. Katherine had just made an already confusing evening worse. And I found I couldn't sleep. At all. Not with his face in my head.

My other phone beeped just before ten. It was Rion.

```
Are you all right? I sensed something.
```

I texted back:

```
Nothing. Just thinking about
     Abby. Had a good cry.
```

It wasn't exactly a lie, but it was easier to say that then bring it up again.

He texted back:

```
Come back to me. Right now.
```

```
No
```

```
Kel fandra deh nee neena jimbre
tonn quesce prevyntos!!!!
```

He knew how much I hated when he talked malion to me. I replied:

```
Not helping. Good night!
```

Before he could get another text in, I shut the phone off, put it on the charger, and slumped back down on my bed. It drove me nuts that we had to sneak around like this. It would be so much easier if...but no, wishing that he was someone different was wrong on so many levels.

And so unfair. I didn't want him to be different. I wanted him. Just him. And I was tired of hiding and hoping nothing would happen to him. We couldn't help who we were.

We couldn't help falling in love.

I stared at the phone for a few moments, and then I knew what I had to do: I had to end this. I would never be able to introduce Rion to my family, the same way I knew I'd never be entirely safe. And, let's face it, I wasn't wholly accepted by his family, either. Rion and I had gotten off to a rocky start, but with Mantis—and now Abby—dead, and the risk of the *vykhars* catching us increasing (I needed an *escort now*, for crying out loud!), it wasn't worth it. Sooner or later, one of us was going to end up dead, too. We both had enough on our plates to deal with right now—my finals and his bequeathing preparations—so I made a promise to myself that I would break things off immediately after the ceremony. Another two weeks wouldn't make much difference, and I wanted some time to think about how the hell I was going to do it.

And how the hell I would make him accept it.

Before I fell asleep that night, I took a long, hot bath, and even though I tried very hard not to, I bawled my eyes out.

For Mantis.

For Abby.

For Rion.

And everyone else I'd sucked into this abyss.

My only saving grace was the trickling water from that tap that disguised my heaving sobs.

XX

Andrew became my personal chauffeur to and from school, and rumors began to spread that we were an item; anything was better than the *vykhars* suspecting I was dating a malion, and it didn't bother Rion when I told him (obviously, it was his idea). Katherine smiled when she saw us together, and even offered to drive me to work when Andrew had an unavoidable after-school commitment with his family. I refused, preferring to call in sick, because her new dramatic outbursts were making me crazy, and because Rion had made it clear that I was not to leave the house without Andrew; only Andrew had the strength to protect me when I was not in close proximity to a malion entrance—at least until Rion showed up, that is. I hated the restrictions and freedom it robbed from me sometimes, but Andrew was a gentleman. He went out of his way to please me every day, and I knew it made Rion feel better knowing that I wasn't alone.

I also snubbed Chelsea's emails and text messages. I didn't want to hear about Kyle; it was probably just some stupid thing about his dad's oil company hitting the big time (everyone knew he was going to strike it rich), anyway. I just wanted to focus on finals and getting my life straightened out. I did, however, attend the service for Abby with Mom and Katherine. At one point, though, I ended up walking out; surrounded by everyone who loved and respected her, my grief became too overwhelming.

After my last final was complete (chemistry, which I hope I passed), I should have been feeling relieved, but I couldn't even muster a smile. I'd been waffling around how to break up with Rion, and it was eating me alive. I wasn't sure I could wait until after Saturday anymore, it just felt terribly wrong for me to keep pretending things were fine. I'd been leading him on for a while, and I felt horrible about it.

Andrew was waiting for me in the parking lot, as usual, and when he leaned over to open the passenger door for me, he didn't look as cheery as he did on most days.

"Physics didn't go so well?"

He shook his head. "Do you need to go home right away?"

My eyebrows pulled together. Something about Andrew's grim face frightened me. "Actually, I—" My phone beeped. "Just a sec."

I pulled out my phone. Rion. He must have sensed something, but he was disguising his over-protective wonts with a—albeit genuine—simple inquiry:

```
How was your chemistry exam?
```

I didn't want him worrying for nothing, so I texted back:

```
So glad to be done.
```

He came back with:

```
Ready for Saturday?
```

I sighed—*NO!* The text conversation continued from there, even though Andrew seemed to be getting impatient.

```
I guess so. What are you wearing?
```

```
Leighdur goes commando, so does his wharla.
```

He wanted to play, and though I was miserable, I tried not to be.

Shut the front door.

????

Seriously?

Oh I am serious.

Well, Charlotte's going to dye my hair
bright blue and green tonight. Hope
your family likes a girl with colour.

Tell me you are joking.

Are you?

Yeah. But it was worth a try.

Me too.

Miss you, m'ebesha.

I gulped as my chest tightened. I couldn't say it back. I had to do this. Now. I texted back:

Are you free tonight?

Not tonight. Prayer and soli-
tude before bequeathing is manda-
tory for the next leighdur.

You're so full of it.

> You got me. I am just very
> tired. Rain check?

I bit my lip. It was strange that Rion didn't want me to come below, now that his meetings were out of the way. I groaned; talking to him would just have to wait until after the weekend. I texted back:

> Okay.

> I will make it up to you. Promise.
> I will text you again tonight.

I tucked my phone back into my purse as Andrew and I sped out of the parking lot. "So what's up?" He seemed to be travelling at a higher speed than normal. I gripped the armrest, trying to remain calm, or Rion would notice immediately and think something was really wrong.

"We need to talk, Liss."

"Can you just slow down a little? We're still in a school zone."

He huffed. "Sorry. I've just got so much on my mind." He was going the opposite direction of my house.

"Uh...where're we going?"

"To the mall."

"What's at the mall?"

"Somewhere *no one* can overhear us."

Which meant not my house. I wondered if Jordon had already tapped his own microphone into the wiring, just for my safety's sake. "Oh. Okaaaaay."

We parked on Robson and walked to the food court in Pacific Center. Andrew bought us Orange Juliuses, and we picked the most crowded area to sit. That afternoon, he was genuinely apprehensive—I'd never seen him that way before. He started to speak, but stopped himself and scoured the area around us first. When he finally turned back to me, his normally black eyes were more hazel-brown, and there wasn't a hint of oscillation in them them—no persuasion. I relaxed, a little.

"Liss..." He took a deep breath.

"Andrew..."

"You can't go on Saturday."

I shook my head. "I have to go. It's the most important day of Rion's life, and he'll be heartbroken if I don't show up."

He pressed his lips together. "I mean it, Liss. You *can't* go."

I swallowed, and then I suddenly understood. "What's going on?"

It was so wild in the food court, no one was paying attention when Andrew opened his shirt. "No wires, okay?"

I nodded.

"Rion and I had an argument last night."

I leaned closer to him. It made perfect sense now; Rion hadn't wanted me to come below because Andrew was most likely with him at the time.

"Something is up, Liss. Someone's been giving the *vykhars* information. I have no idea *how* they know, but they've found out that something big is happening on Saturday. Thirty-seven *vykhars* from Mexico flew in this morning, and they're all heading east of Vancouver to some smaller town, but I couldn't catch the name."

"Why Mexico?"

"The largest and strongest *vykhars* are born and raised there. You've never seen anyone so big and...*resilient* in your life."

"Oh my...Andrew—!"

"They're preparing for a fight, I swear it, and they're going to use the outcasts on the front lines, with the Mexicans to back them up."

"What do you mean, *outcasts*?"

"The *vykhars* that cause the most trouble for them. They put them on the front lines of a battle or investigation to do away with them. They've always done it that way—Caine also leaves the area beforehand, and takes his family."

My hand flew to my mouth. "Oh. Crap."

"Do you know where the ceremony is?"

Even though I was shocked, his question caught me totally off guard. It was strange that he'd come right out and ask me such a question; I became a little suspicious of him at that point. Even if I did know, I wouldn't feel comfortable telling him.

"Rion hasn't said a thing to me."

"I know a lot of his *family* will be coming in from out of town, but I've told him specifically that my sister is not to attend—and I don't think you should, either. I think the *vykhars* are up to something. I told him to call it off, and have it some other weekend, but with his father so sick, he said it's too late to change the date."

"How do you know all of this?"

"I overheard my dad talking to Caine early this morning from a phone number I traced back to somewhere in the Bahamas, and then I hacked into my dad's email and it was all there—everything about Saturday."

My stomach began to twist itself around, but I took a few deep breaths. "Do any of Rion's allies above know about Saturday?"

"Only Charlotte and me, according to Rion." He shuffled around in his chair, then leaned even closer to me; so much that his spicy chai breath and peppery cologne began to nauseate me. "He's confident the *vykhars* will never get through the entrances because he's got extra guards coming in from Europe, so he's going through with it."

"He would never put me in danger, Andrew."

"That's exactly my point, Liss. It's not the *vykhars* I'm worried about coming in from the outside. I think there's a mole within the malions. I think a malion has been feeding the *vykhars* information."

I sat back and gaped at him.

"I think Abby's death had something to do with it, and I think Caine's obsession with hunting Rion has come down to a bribe. I think they've got a malion informant and they're paying him off."

I rubbed my hand along my perspiring forehead.

"You can't go, Liss. I feel as if something is going to happen, and I don't think Rion introducing you to all of his family is a good idea. You being seen with him and then coming above after? As soon as the *vykhars* find out that you're with Rion, they're going to use you against him—and your whole family."

"Does Rion know you're telling me this?"

He shook his head.

"What do I do, Andrew? I can't just tell him that I can't go. He'll know…"

"*Please* think of something, Liss. Just don't go."

When I got back to the house, I paced around my room like a caged animal, regretting what I was about to do: break up with Rion before the ceremony. I believed Andrew, and it was the only way to get out of being introduced as his *wharla*, which would only serve to embarrass him afterward, as well. It was bad enough I'd let things go on *this* long. But it had to be face-to-face. Not in a text message—I owed him that respect.

My head began to pound. I was so frustrated I grabbed my sweat-filled hair tightly in my hands. I wanted to pull it all out.

Rion texted me twice to see if I was all right, and I lied to him both times saying that I was just nervous about meeting his family. I crawled into bed that night and just stared at the ceiling, listening to the raindrops *pitter-patter* against my window. Duke whined and licked my face, sensing something was off when I kept hugging him—there was just no way I could relax with the bazillion thoughts besieging my brain.

Rion's extended family knew about my relationship with him, and if any of them were going to rat me out to the *vykhars*, they would have done it already. The informant had to be someone who had never met me before.

Who could possibly want Rion captured, and cared less about how many other malions were hurt or killed in the process? The only malion I knew with a beef against Rion was the Asian *leighdur*. They'd fought, and apparently their issues were still unresolved, or so I'd heard. Rion would have killed him, he'd said, for reasons unknown to me. That was some serious hate. Could the Asian *leighdur* be willing to risk annihilating an entire colony because he despised Rion so much? I wondered how many malions from the Asian Third would be at the bequeathing. How convenient would it be if they all just happened to pull a no-show?

So very convenient. And it would have guilt written all over it.

XXI

My pursuer's raspy, slurring voice had stopped, but I knew he was gaining ground: I could hear the pounding and scraping of his feet on the gravel as he came after me. I wasn't moving fast enough. All of a sudden, I stumbled and fell; my knees burned, the pain familiar. I was going to have to speed up if I wanted to survive, if I wanted to make it out a second time. I struggled to stand up, but two hands gripped my shoulders. I screamed. It was too late. He'd caught me.

But the hands that turned me around were not Kyle's, they were Abby's. Her glowing, cloudy, iris-less eyes were vacant. She was soaking wet, and seaweed and blood drizzled out of her caved-in temple. I tried desperately to free myself from her grip, but her eyes widened and her fingernails dug into my shoulders. She was shouting at me, pleading and terrified, yet no noise came from her mouth. I wanted to know what she was saying, but the sight of her frightened me and I had to turn away.

She put her cold hand on my cheek. I flinched at her touch, but I realized I could finally hear her, her voice was faint and faraway. "I'm sorry Melissa…I'm so sorry!" She released me and repeated her apology over and over again as her ghostly form began to vanish.

"Abby! Wait!" Only it was useless; she was already gone. Then the voice changed. It was one that I recognized, but I couldn't make out the words. A hand smacked my cheek, extracting me from the dark night, and back into the safety of my bedroom.

"Liss!" Katherine's voice hissed.

I shot up from my bed, gasping for air in the darkness. I smelled her water lily and violet body lotion before I could make her out next to me, and for the very first time, I wished I could wrap my arms around her for some sort of comfort. I was in utter shambles.

"Liss! Wake up!"

I rubbed my eyes and her face came into focus. Duke had long since left my side, but the bed was still warm—very warm. "What are you doing in here?" I whispered to her between pants, combing my hand through my hair, which was now slick with perspiration.

"Your phone's been going off for the last half an hour, and when I came in to turn it off, you were thrashing around. I didn't mean to startle you....Are you okay?"

I rubbed my forehead. "What time is it?"

"Three in the morning."

My phone chirped again, and my eyes shot over to it vibrating on my nightstand. There was only one person that could be texting me right now, and only one reason I was overheating.

I grabbed my phone and quickly texted Rion a reply:

```
Ok—dream. Call u in the morning.
```

When I put the phone down, I glanced out the window wondering just how near *he* was, because I was exceedingly feverish.

"Who was that?"

"Uh...just a reminder alarm," I stumbled. "I set it for AM instead of PM." I looked back at the window, waiting for Rion's face to appear, but there was nothing.

Katherine leaned around to see what I'd been focussing on. "Liss?"

"Yeah. I'm fine. Real—"

279

She took my face in her hands. I wasn't the only one with clammy hands, although hers were chilly. "No. You're not. Look at you. I know you're not...and neither am I anymore..." She trailed off as our eyes searched one another for the right words. "I haven't been able to sleep Liss." She sat in front of me on my bed and crossed her legs. "I can't wait any longer. We need to talk about this—right now!"

My shoulders dropped and I unstuck my shirt from my sopping back. "Katherine..."

"Please, Liss..."

I sighed, and she took that as a *yes*.

"Kyle Peterson was arrested three weeks ago," she spit out.

I sucked in a breath and shuddered as my body began to prickle; my dream resurfaced, instantly refreshed, vividly nauseating. I could taste his garbage breath in my mouth again.

A tear left her eye. "He's been accused of rape, unlawful confinement and extortion." Then she reached out and hugged me hard. "The police are investigating, but they've released him on bail because he's got a clean background. The girl who's accusing him has been moved to a safe house out-of-province until they can gather more information. There's a hearing scheduled next month, but they are hoping more victims will come forward before then."

I began to shake in her arms.

"He drugged you didn't he? Just like he drugged that other girl."

"The worst part..." I tried to pull myself together enough to talk about it. "...was that I don't even remember taking anything from him. Just all of a sudden, I didn't have any control."

"It's okay, Liss." She stroked my hair and hugged me tighter. "What's important is you got away." As strange as it sounds, I was glad to have my sister back; I'd missed her. Really.

"I'm so sorry Liss...all those times you clung to Duke and locked yourself in your room when Mom and Dad left the house... you were scared, weren't you?"

I sniffed. "When he was chasing me, he told me he'd come for me if I told anyone. He said that he'd know it was me."

"You *have* to go to the police again. I'll come with you if you want me to."

I pulled back and looked in her eyes. "You didn't tell anyone did you?"

She shook her head vigorously. "And I won't, if you don't want me to."

"Not Mom and Dad?"

She shook her head again. "I couldn't tell them something like that, not without talking to you first. Dad would *flip*."

"Do you *promise* not to tell them?" She nodded, but her eyebrows furrowed, so I explained, "I just don't want anyone looking at me differently. People who know stuff like that look at you like you've got a disease, and think if they touch you, you'll shatter into a million pieces. I don't want anyone's pity. I'm the one who followed him out of the corn maze!"

Katherine leaned closer to me, and her eyes widened. "That's not your fault, Liss! Chelsea—"

"You told *Chelsea*?"

"No, Liss. Chelsea was the one who found out about it on Facebook. One of her soccer friend-of-a-friend's put it on her wall. When she saw it, she asked me if it was the same Kyle Peterson, and that's when I figured it out…"

My eyes bugged out.

"…I told Chelsea not to say anything to anyone. I knew there was a reason you'd kept it secret. We both just feel so awful about how we've treated you. You've been holding this in for so long."

"I'm better now, Katherine."

"Is Andrew helping you? You know, now that you're together…"

"Andrew and I are not together."

"Then what about that Ryan guy?"

My eyes narrowed. "How do you know about him?"

"Chelsea mentioned him." She tucked a few stray strands of my hair behind my ear. "Charlotte said he was a good friend when I asked her if she knew who he was. I didn't mean to go behind your back, Liss. I just thought maybe Ryan was the one who had hurt you, but she said he'd slaughter anyone who harmed a woman."

I smiled. Wasn't *that* the truth. No one would ever get past 250 pounds of malion muscle and severely over-protective instinct.

"Ryan must be a pretty big guy, eh?"

I nodded. "Yeah, I guess you could say that."

"Will I ever get to meet him?"

"He's just a friend, Katherine. And he's super busy with his new job right now, so I don't know. We're not—"

Her mouth dropped. "You mean he's not in school? How old is he?"

"Nineteen."

"Nineteen!"

"We're just friends, Katherine."

"Where did you guys meet?"

I smiled. "We actually met…by accident."

She bit her lip. "Really?"

"Yeah." I ran my hands through my greasy hair again, keeping mindful of the bugs in my walls which could be recording this conversation. "I spilled a drink on him one day at work…he was on his way to an interview, too. It was super funny—had to be there."

"So you guys are seeing each other then?"

"No…not even close…" I choked up for a moment. It was so hard to speak those words, but very shortly, that would be the reality.

Katherine put her hand on my shoulder. "You don't have to say anything…I know what it's like to love someone who doesn't love you back…it hurts bad."

Oh no. It would do more than just hurt him. It was going to destroy him.

She hugged me one last time before she got off the bed. "Do you think we can start over, Lissy?"

I nodded. "I'd like that."

"Do you promise to go to the police?"

"Next week, on semester break—and only if you promise to *never* tell Mom and Dad."

"I promise I won't. I'll tell Chelsea as well, but you still should call her."

"Next week, on semester break," I repeated. "Deal?"

"Deal."

When Katherine left, I began to wonder what the protocol for bail release was, and if Kyle would come looking for me, on the off chance he thought I might testify against him. Google was a wonderful resource when it came to these things. I grabbed my laptop and it wasn't hard to find.

Under Canadian Law:

Following arrest, a person also may be released on entering an undertaking with one or more of the following terms:

- *Remain within a certain area (city, country or province).*
- *Deposit the person's passport.*
- *Notify police of any change in address or employment.*
- *Abstain from communicating with any person or from going to any place.*
- *Abstain from possessing a firearm and surrender any firearm.*
- *Report to police at specified times.*
- *Abstain from consuming alcohol or other intoxicating substance.*
- *Abstain from taking drugs except in accordance with a medical prescription.*

I bit my finger. Since when did Kyle Peterson ever follow the rules? I was going to have to stay in the house as much as possible after seeing Rion tomorrow, and keep the doors locked at all times. Duke was going to love his new and improved job as my hip attachment—though I would have preferred Rion.

All I ever wanted was Rion. No one made me feel as special and safe as he did. How different my life would be if he could just live above like everyone else. How different my life would be if I'd just agreed to stay with him in the beginning. But, neither option would have been viable; of that, I was absolutely positive. And if we stayed together, we'd continue in a vicious cycle, always returning to the same realization: he didn't belong in my world, and I didn't belong in his.

XXII

I lay awake for the rest of the morning, waiting for the sun to light the sky and warm my room, but the dawn only brought a storm of hail and thunder. In the past, I'd always been soothed by the drumming beat of drops against the siding of my house, but not that day. The rain only added to the gloom of what I knew would be the second-worst day of my life.

My eyes focussed hard on the blue *ika* bud floating lifelessly on its side in the glass of penny water I'd placed it in. It hadn't bloomed like Rion said it would; it just drifted there, swathed up tightly, and was beginning to lose its vibrant blue hue. It almost seemed water-logged. So much for my green thumb.

I still wasn't exactly sure how I was going to tell him, but I knew it had to be soon—and definitely *before* the bequeathing. I closed my eyes and wondered if I could keep my emotions inside; I didn't want anyone to recognize that I, too, was drowning.

When the clock read 10:07, I dragged myself out of bed, and into the shower (*yeowch*...my skin was still so sensitive). I tried desperately to remove the mascara smudges under my eyes, only to realize they were actually dark circles. When I got out, I noticed my phone was still turned off. I picked it up to turn it on, but changed my mind. Rion must have been texting me like crazy, but it was time I got used to not communicating with him on a regular basis.

At noon, I couldn't even bring myself to eat, so I just sat and stared at the silver and pink flecks on the kitchen table, sulking. Mom was working the day shift, Dad was away again, and Katherine was still in bed (or out, I hadn't even heard from her). I was alone with my empty feelings of regret: regret I'd agreed to see Rion again after our first meeting, regret I'd lead him on, regret I'd placed his family in jeopardy by allowing myself to become his *wharla*.

Regret I'd completely fallen for him in every way imaginable.

I picked up my cell and called Charlotte at three thirty, unable to contain myself any longer. It rang seven times before she finally answered. "You could have just texted me," she chuckled. "And since when do you call? I'm not *late*. I'm not doing your hair until four!"

"Charlotte..." I droned, combing my fingers furiously over my scalp.

"Hey now—what's up, buttercup?"

I swallowed and closed my eyes. "I need Jordon to take me to Rion—right away."

"Is everything all right?"

I could feel a tear balling up in my eye, but I quickly wiped it away. "I can't do this, Charlotte."

"What do you mean?"

"Rion. I just can't do it anymore."

Charlotte knew exactly what I meant and didn't say anything into the phone for a while, but I could hear her breathing. "I know you're scared," she finally said. "I was, too. But it'll all be okay—I promise! Pretty soon, the *vykhars* will leave you alone, and they'll start bugging someone else."

"I just can't..." My chest felt so tight, I almost broke down right there, but I had to be strong if I was going to face Rion and have him take me seriously.

I heard Charlotte sigh. I knew what she was thinking: she was disappointed in me. But I was glad she didn't press me with questions or try to persuade me to change my mind, because at the moment, I wasn't in the mood to be cross-examined.

"How long until you're ready?"

"I'm ready right now."

"I'll tell Jordon. Be at the entrance in five."

I wrote Mom a note saying I'd be back soon (I wasn't sure how long it would take) and grabbed my purse, but Katherine was standing in the kitchen, arms crossed, toe tapping, with her eyebrow raised.

"Where are you going?"

"Out...for a coffee." I began chewing on my lip. "I need to get out of the house."

"You can't leave, Liss."

I glared at her. "Why not?"

"Because Andrew paid me two hundred dollars this morning to keep you in the house for the rest of the day and tonight, for some reason he can't tell me about. So you can't leave, or I have to give it back, and I've already spent half of it on pedicure supplies, magazines and pizza."

"I appreciate the gesture, Katherine, but I really need to go. I'll only be an hour—I promise."

"Are you going to see that Ryan guy?"

"No," I lied. "I'm really craving a latte, and I need to get some new underwear. La Senza's having a sale." I was getting good at this fibbing business.

Her face lightened. "Okay, if you *promise* to be back in less than an hour..."

"I will."

"Well, I'm running up to shave my legs." She took off toward the stairs, tying up her hair on the way. "*One hour*, Liss!"

"*One hour*! I've got my cell—I'm taking the Sky Train!"

My mind cycled as I made my way to my entrance. It had been horrible being separated from Rion after my accident; it nearly

drowned the life out of me. But those feelings had been com-
pounded by my confusion about Rion and my fear of the *vykhars*. I
could handle it better this time. I needed to hurry before I changed
my mind—again. My conscience was becoming quite the revolv-
ing door, but it was time to stop going in circles.

Jordon was peeking at me from under the manhole lid as I
approached. He ran me back to Rion's door, and I thanked him
profusely for going out of his way on such a busy day. Heavy
metal blared from the inside of Rion's room, as I hesitated outside
the door with the shriveled *ika* flower bud in my hand. The out-of-
control drum beat mimicked my heartbeat.

"I do not want to witness this. Good luck, *farvenala*." Jordon
whispered, and was gone.

I scowled at him as he tore off into the tunnels, and then I
closed my hand around the flower bud and put it behind my
back. Whatever name he just called me, I hoped it was a bad one.
I deserved it. And though I felt like there was a hundred pound
block of cement surrounding my feet, I mustered the energy to
walk through the door.

Rion was sitting cross-legged with his back to me while
Volbeat's lead belted out the lyrics to *A Warrior's Call*. I shut the
door as quietly as I could, and watched Rion peacefully breathe in
and out. It only lasted a moment before he realized I was there and
twisted around. He had the music turned off and his arms around
me less than a second later. "How did you get here? I thought I was
meeting you at five?" When I refused to participate in the embrace
and looked down at the floor, he knew that something was really
amiss. "What is wrong?"

He bent down to kiss my forehead, but I leaned away. It was so
hard not to rest against his chest and hug him back. Inside, I longed
to hear the beat of his heart. I wanted to put my hands on his shoulders and caress the lines of the sharp blades with my fingers, but I
willed myself against it.

"Melissa?" He sounded nervous. "I do not understand what
I am sensing from you. Please say something...you have been

distant lately and hardly talking to me!" My eyes glazed over, but Rion forced me to look into his beautiful, avocado eyes. "Say something, *m'ebesha!*"

I was terrified for more reasons than just the *vykhars*, but he didn't need to know about Kyle's arrest and release; it didn't concern him. I needed to focus on one thing tonight: breaking up. My vision became fuzzy as liquid built up in my eyes, but I ignored it and blurted, "I'm not coming tonight, Rion."

His eyebrows pulled together. "Of course you are. You are here now—you are coming!"

I shook my head again. "I have something to say and then I want Jordon to take me back home."

Rion's face contorted and he inhaled. "What is that *smell?*" Then he leaned down and sniffed me again. "My *tarvas, m'ebesha.* What did you spray on yourself?"

"It was a gift from my parents. I got some body spray and lotion for Christmas."

"It is so strong—and it smells awful!" His face twisted up again.

I pulled out of his arms. "Stop trying to change the subject, Rion. I'm serious."

He chuckled. "All right, all right." He made to snatch me back into his arms, but I stepped away. And even though I knew it offended him, I stood my ground.

"*M'ebesha—*"

I stared at him, burning with an unfathomable need for his body against mine as he spoke that beautiful word, ready to throw in the towel and forget about everything I'd come to say, but my conscience trampled on my indecision, compelling me to answer, "Please don't call me that anymore."

"Why?" He was becoming cross, folding his arms over one another.

I took the hand holding the *ika* flower, opened it and held it out to him. When he saw it, I could hear a low growl coming from his chest. "I'm not coming below anymore, Rion. I just think we need to end this. This is never going to work."

He glared at me.

"I'm sorry. I—"

"Andrew talked to you, did he not?"

I nodded, and his growl became louder. "But that's not the only reason. This isn't something I just decided today…"

"Do you not think I can keep you safe?"

"It's not that," I cried as a tear left my cheek.

"Have you found another male?"

"No."

"Then why are you saying this? You know you do not mean it!"

The sting in my eyes became overwhelming at that point. I blinked a bunch of times, hoping I could stay strong for just a few more moments, but I was struggling. "I just can't live this double life anymore. I can't keep pretending this is going to work, when I know it won't. I'm not going to leave my family to be with you, and the more I come below, the more risk we—"

He threw his hands in the air. "Have I *ever* asked you to make a choice?"

"No, Rion…" I wiped another tear away. "But I know one day it's going to come down to that! The *vykhars* are going to—"

"*KARK* THE *VYKHARS*!"

"Rion, please!" I cried. "This isn't how I want to end things with you!"

"YOU ARE LETTING THEM CONTROL YOUR LIFE, MELISSA. DO YOU NOT SEE? YOU ARE LETTING THEM GET TO YOU…YOU TOLD ME YOU WOULD *NEVER* LET THAT HAPPEN!" He stormed toward me. I was about to turn and make a run for it, worried that he was going to lock me in with him, but he stopped abruptly, the anger gone from his face, and he began to search my eyes with a brand new tenderness. All air left my lungs as I stood there, numb from shock. He reached out toward me: with one hand, he closed my hand around the *ika* flower, with the other he stole the lone tear from my cheek and kissed it. "I know you do not want this to end, *m'ebesha*, I can sense it…"

Another tear rushed from my eye, and my lip quivered as I began to yield. "You're right. I don't." I wiped my cheek, blathering, "I want this so badly...I want *you*, so badly.... But it's just never going to work...and I'm just so scared that something terrible is going to happen to us...I can't even fathom what I would do if something happened to you, because of me. I'm already going crazy after what happened to Abby—and I don't care what you say, if I hadn't gotten in my car that night, none of this would have happened!"

I couldn't form another word, and I didn't have to, because he'd already seized me in his arms, crushing us together. The beat of his heart against my cheek was so soothing, I found myself grabbing hold of his shirt, straining to bring myself as close to him as humanly possible. Sensing my need, he held me tighter and kissed the top of my head. "Stop blaming yourself for everything, *m'ebesha*...everything happens for a reason...do you not think I am scared, too?"

I sniffed. "Andrew said that the *vykhars* know that something is happening tonight."

"I know. I've got Charlotte and four other allies of mine keeping watch in a few different locations above. The Eurafrican *leighdur* has also brought his entire guard to assist ours."

"Charlotte's not coming tonight?"

"No." Rion smiled and raised his eyebrows. "She is keeping an eye on *your* house. Six of the largest guards we have will be stationed right at your entrance, should she need to call backup tonight."

I stared at him. I didn't want to hear that my family could be in danger.

"Do you honestly think I would miss even *one* detail when it came to protecting the one I love and her family? What kind of *leighdur* and *dharkun* do you think I am?"

"Listen to yourself, Rion." I stepped away and grabbed my hair. "Guards at my *house*?"

"Is there something wrong with my ensuring their safety?"

"YES!"

"You are not making any sense."

I sat down on his bed. "This is exactly what I'm talking about. This is why I can't be with you anymore. It's never going to stop with the *vykhars,* despite what you think. And we seeing one another is only going to become more risky as time moves on."

He sat down at the edge of the bed and held my hand. "I will not stop seeing you, *m'ebesha.*"

"No, Rion." Thick tears were forming in the corners of my eyes again. "This is the hardest decision I've ever had to make, but I know it's the right one, despite what my heart is telling me." I stood up, and placed the wilting *ika* flower on his desk. My hands were shaking so badly, I had to clench them into fists to hide it from him.

He walked over and put the flower back in my hand, closing my fingers around it. "This is yours. I gave it to you. I do not want it back." I reached up to touch his face and thank him, but he backed away when he realized what I was doing. "If this is truly what you want, I have some things to say to you before I take you home… but I need more time than what we have right now."

"Just say it, Rion. I'm not coming back after tonight."

"No." He took a deep breath. "You have to come to the ceremony *first.*"

I wanted to shut down his request immediately, but there was a sullen look about his face that made me wonder. "Tell me why."

He tried reaching for one of my hands, but I hid them in my arms.

He took a deep breath. "A *male* needs to have his hands on you during the ceremony."

"What—*why?*"

Rion took a deep breath. "Believe me…the thought of another male's *anything* touching you is enough to send me off *Carvath Shays*…but when I become *leighdur,* they are going to make a couple of little marks on my back, and"—he stole my hand— "*knowing what we know now,* I do not want you to suffer from it."

292

I shook my head, but I kept my hand in his. "You don't need to do anything. I can handle it. I'll just stay in my room tonight. I'll be fine."

Rion's humble eyes hardened. "I would just feel much better if I knew you were not feeling *anything*—it is going to be more than a scratch, to say the least."

I suddenly recalled the pain I'd experienced when Rion had left me and fought with the other malion. I hated pain, and when I looked back up at his eyes, they were smouldering. He was dead serious. "How much more than a scratch?"

"About an inch deep. Three times."

I gulped and shuddered. Clearly, I had no choice. "Okay. I'll go."

He gave a great sigh. "Thank you."

"I'll go, as long as you promise to let me go home *immediately* afterwards."

He squeezed my hand. "*I* will take you home. Right after I finish what—"

I clenched my fists together, balling up inside. "You're not going to change my mind, Rion. It's...it's killing me already, just having to stay here."

He grabbed me as I began to sob again. "Why are you doing this? You know I am doing everything in my power to make this work, you just have not given me a chance...*please m'ebesha...*"

I was about to gripe at him, but a knock at his chamber door interrupted us. Rasadian walked in, and I scowled at him. He had terrible timing.

"The items you requested," he mumbled at Rion. He glanced down at me and nodded. "Melissa."

"Thank you, brother. Just set them on the desk."

"One and a half hours." Rasadian set down the items.

"Indeed. We will be ready in thirty minutes. Leave us, please, until then."

He glanced at me then back to his brother. "Is she coming?"

"Yes." Rasadian just stood there, sizing me up, until Rion asked, "*Brother*?"

Rasadian shuddered out of his trance. "As you wish." He quickly ducked out the door, and I realized I was still in Rion's arms.

"I have something for you." He gently returned my arms to my sides.

"Oh no...no gifts. I—"

"I had them made for you. You *must* accept them now."

I huffed, wondering if he was trying to butter me up. But that wasn't his style—and not mine, either. He walked over to the table and picked up two items. One was a heap of velvety material; the other was a book with a scintillating, milky gemstone on the front.

"These are for you," he said despondently.

I swallowed and took the book from his hand, sweeping my finger over the jewel. "What is this?"

"It is a copy of the original *Moonstone, Mae and Malion Tales*." He opened the cover, and there it was, in Old English font, freshly typewritten. "I had the stories translated into English, and then I took the first edition cover from my own copy and had it rebound and set with a moonstone. I *had* hoped to read it to you, but I know you are..." He swallowed and paused for a moment. "...you are very capable of reading them yourself."

I almost started crying again. I *wanted* him to read to me. I would have loved nothing more. This whole breaking up thing was proving to be totally agonizing. "Oh my goodness...I don't know how to thank you..."

Rion put his hand on my chin, tilting my face up until I looked into his magnificent green eyes. "Do not thank me, just read them and know you are seeing the truth."

"You never did tell me what happened to Ranion after Queen Alysia died."

He frowned. "He became the greatest *leighdur* that ever walked the earth. And for his grand leadership, the Creator promised him that he would meet his beloved Alysia again."

"You mean, like, reincarnation?"

He shrugged and looked down at the floor. "Malions have always believed in reincarnation. Just read it—there are more stories than just *The King and the Malion Healer* in there. The others are just as good."

I bit my lip to prevent myself from sobbing. "I will."

"Oh…and do not forget this one, too."

"A-a-a-another one?"

He brought over the bundle of velvet, and with one motion, shook it free from its satin fastening. "This is for…uh…just *tonight*, I guess."

He held a deep crimson cloak, and I gasped. "My own *cloak*?"

He nodded. "I had hoped for you to use it more than once…I still hope that you will."

He'd totally gone overboard, and now I felt absolutely horrible. "Did Zuralina make it?"

He nodded. "I asked her to make it when you told me you would be my *wharla*. All the females wear crimson in this Third."

I placed the *ika* flower bud I still held in my hand into the cup of water on his nightstand, as he draped the cloak over me. It was much heavier than it looked, but the layers of fabric underneath were silky smooth and it smelled like citrus—just like Zuralina.

"It fits perfectly. Do you like it?"

"I love it. It's so soft…" We stared at one another for a moment. A week ago, we would have made-out ravenously, but now, there was just this vacant, awkward distance between us. The new ache in my heart stung so hard, I winced.

"We should go," he finally said. "I would like to arrive early, and I may have to help my father."

"Right. Let's go."

XXIII

I texted Charlotte, asking her to leave a message at the house for Katherine that I'd be home tomorrow, and then shoved the phone into my back pocket. Katherine was going to be right choked with me, but there was absolutely nothing I could do about it.

Rion and I joined up with ten other malions to make the hour-long trek to where the bequeathing would take place. I'd hoped to avoid any more physical contact with Rion—Heaven knows what an effect he has on me—but it was unavoidable. I didn't want a stranger to carry me, and the only other malion male I recognized was Lafe, who had Zuralina. Rion lifted me gingerly, and held me slightly away from his chest, for which I was grateful and slightly disappointed. Rion, Lafe, Zuralina and I were surrounded by guards, and one of them held onto Rion's shoulder as we ran. Normally, Rion informed me, it would only have taken twenty minutes at full-speed, but with Zuralina's pregnancy, we travelled at a more moderate pace. My ears popped four times over the course of the trip, and when we finally stopped, Rion seemed astonished that the pressure didn't bother me.

We were standing among a crowd of twenty guards in almost complete darkness, on an extravagant stone vestibule in front of a fat metal doorway through which light flickered among the shadows. A waft of burning oil caught my nose as the one particularly overweight guard ushered us through before slamming the door shut behind us. Something about the *bang-clunk* made the hairs on the back of my neck stand straight up.

"Are you sure you are all right?" Rion asked me.

I nodded, rubbing my perspiring forehead. It was almost impossible not to think about how far below we were, and the weight of the rock above us. He put his hands over mine and I could sense the healing warmth radiating from them. "Is that better, *m'ebesha*?"

"It's not my head, I'm just…this room is just…I think I just need to step away from the crowd."

"Come here for a minute."

I was about to step back, but he pulled me against him and shushed me until my heart stopped racing, calling out orders to the guards between amorous whispers to the top of my head. Seconds later, I was at ease, and I decided to stay there as long as I could, soaking him up for what might be the last time.

I was so going to miss him.

"You have to go in now," he whispered at last, separating us. "I will be there in a few moments."

"Congratulations," I whispered back, as he pulled my hood over my head. He stepped back and kissed my hand, raising it above his head before motioning to leave; yet for some reason, I couldn't let go. In the chilly depths of this unfamiliar cavity, so far below, I just wanted to stay in his arms.

He sensed it immediately when I didn't release his hand, and his expression softened.

"You will be right beside me in the first row, okay? Do not worry. Rasadian will take care of you."

"Rasadian?" I exclaimed as softly as I could. "He—" I couldn't voice my opinion of him in front of everyone, so instead, I said, "He can't stand me!"

Rion's eyes flashed. "He is the only one I trust!"

"But—"

"I have to get ready, Melissa." He was getting impatient, and a few malions were beginning to gather around. "Go with him, you will be fine."

I sighed and rolled my eyes as he walked away, turning around to find Rasadian standing right behind me. He'd heard what I'd said, and he was scowling at me.

"Is that what you think?" he growled. "That I cannot *stand* you?"

I crossed my arms. "It's obvious by the way you've been acting toward me lately. And every time I'm below, you're either giving me a dirty look, or you're gone above somewhere—" My hand shot to my mouth the moment I said it. Rasadian had been gone a lot, and not even Rion knew where he was half the time. Was *he* was the mole? I hadn't even thought about Rasadian as a possibility. He was glaring at me, and when he saw Rion was far enough away, he answered, "I know *exactly* what you are thinking, and I want you to know that you are wrong."

I had no idea how could he read me so well. I tried to hide my suspicions with a flat denial. "What are you even talking about?"

He leaned down and whispered, "You are scared of me, Melissa. I can sense it. You think I am the one who is passing information to the *vykhars*, do you not?"

"...I *thought* it was the Asian *leighdur*, but—"

"Well you are wrong on both accounts then, because he is here tonight, and so are his *harlenday* and *sensakuru*."

I searched his eyes for any hint of a lie, but his gaze didn't waver, so I pressed him further. "Then tell me the truth, Rasadian. Tell me where you've been for the last few days, and why it's such a big secret."

Immediately, Rasadian's eyes glinted a much brighter green; it reminded me of a jack-o-lantern on Halloween night. It scared the crap out of me. I leaned back, preparing for something fierce to arise from him, but he just stared at me. I couldn't tell if it was anger or sadness, but whatever was, it was seriously intense. "If you..." He paused, and turned away from me to collect himself. When he looked back at me again, the glow in his eyes had disappeared.

I raised my eyebrow.

"Melissa..." He let out a snort, and pressed his middle finger into his forehead.

I don't know if it was my intuition, but my stomach began to curdle in that moment and I had to take a deep breath, because I almost felt like I was going to be sick. Rasadian hunched over and covered his eyes.

I swallowed and leaned toward him. "What's going on with you, Rasadian?"

"You are not the only human female who has been loved by a malion, Melissa." He uncovered his glowing-again, freaky eyes and glowered at me. "And every time I see you with Rion, I am reminded of what happened with my Twila."

My mouth involuntarily unhinged.

"I go, twice a year, to visit the place where we always met, the place where I delivered her unto the Afterlife. It takes me two days to get there, because I am not as fast as the other males."

I kept eye-contact with him, and I could feel my heart beginning to race. Everyone filing into the nave seemed to disappear around us, but I was focused only on Rasadian's words.

"When my brother brought you below, my nightmares about her resurfaced. I could not get them out of my head. I felt as if I was going mad. I had to get away. And since then, I have done everything in my power to convince Rion to leave you alone, to convince *you* to leave *us* alone. You have no idea what it is like to lose someone close to you....The pain never disappears, Melissa—ever!"

"Oh Rasadian...I'm...I'm so sorry..." I reached out for his arm, which he swiftly snatched back.

"You do not belong with us, Melissa..." He rubbed his eyes and put on his hood. "Not because you are not malion...but because you cannot keep dawdling above and below. You need to make a choice, because as long as you keep this up, either you or Rion will end up dead—I promise you that!"

"I know, Rasadian..."

"No, Melissa, you do not." He bared his teeth and growled. "Because if you did, you would not have come here tonight. You would have stayed above with your sister like you were supposed to!"

All of a sudden, it was all *very* clear. "You put Andrew up to that, didn't you?"

"It obviously did not work." He curled his lip. I crossed my arms as he ended with, "I do not give a *leck's hushqua* about the money. I was trying keep you from coming below!"

I leaned closer to him. "You don't run my life, Rasadian!"

"No, I do not." His face softened, but his eyes were still glowing under his hood. "But I do not want to see it come to an end, either."

Before I could reply, Zuralina seized my hand, startling me. "It is about to start!" She drew me away, giggling as she walked, holding her little belly next to Lafe, and then all I could see was Rasadian's thick navy hood covering his face. Beneath that hood, I realized, was not emptiness, but something much more magnificent: benevolence. It looked like I had just acquired a big brother. He was looking out for me. He was on my side, just like that first night when I ran into him in the tunnels. But in a Rasadian way: an enigmatic and laudable way.

Much different from Rion's way.

Rasadian followed closely behind us, as we were the last to enter the hall. When the door thudded close behind us, I looked up, and my mouth dropped open. The entranceway, which Rasadian called the narthex, was tiled to the ceiling in beige and brown marble, cut and shaped into ocean waves. Zuralina kept poking my back to keep me walking as we proceeded into the atrium, and thank goodness she did, because I would have stopped the second we stepped onto the forest green velvet runner. The entire nave was marble and granite, smoothed to perfection, unlike the tunnels, where sharp edges were plentiful. An arcade of twenty white marble piers, each at least fifty feet high, made a canopy over us as we strode past the glossy pews toward the altar. Attached to the wall, at the end of each pew, was a flaming torch, providing the only light. Above us, paintings of malions in battle and families with their *cubshen* frolicked from one side of the stone ceiling to the other in a remarkable collage. I wondered how long it took for them to create such a sacred masterpiece.

The pews were filled to the outright maximum. I saw females with long hair and hazel eyes; others had cropped or undercut bobs and green eyes. A few of the males had mohawks; there were also some males who wore a tight braid down the back of their heads with shaved sides. Many had tattoos on their necks and arms, and some had deep battle scars or missing limbs.

Every one of them stared at us as we walked past. At one point, I pulled my hood farther over my head to hide my face; I didn't want them to see how pale their stares made me. I grew light-headed, unable to slow my shallow breathing. I hated being at the center of all their attention, and I hated that everyone knew I was human: they didn't know whether or not they could trust me. It was almost impossible not to meet their incredulous stares, but I tried to ignore their arbitrating eyes, feeling like an imposter.

Though a spot in the back close to the exit would have sufficed for me, I knew I'd have to sit in the front. I tried to assure myself that being close to Rion during the ceremony was a good thing, and it would all be over in a short amount of time, but I wasn't sure of the former or the latter. Two hours before, I hadn't even planned on coming.

When we got to the first pew, I kept my hood on—as did most everyone else—and sat next to Zuralina. She put her hand on my leg and flashed me a smile before returning her focus to the front. Someone tapped me on the shoulder, and I looked behind me to see Jordon winking. His levity didn't help. I wanted to bolt. Everyone was piling in so close. Too close.

"Hold my hand if you need to, okay?" Zuralina whispered to me when everyone became quiet. My eyebrows pulled together, but there was no time to ask, so I nodded, feeling immensely nauseated again. When everyone stood, I followed suit, looking up at the altar. Green velvet swags and curtains lined with gold made it look like a theatre stage, save for the few marble stairs and the large black wooden case in the center. An older malion limped onto the altar with the help of two other males, un-hooding himself when he reached the center.

"That is Ramses," Zuralina uttered in my ear.

He looked exactly like Rion, only much older, and even though I was only fifteen or so feet away, I could smell this intolerably sweet, bubble-gum scent coming from him. His eyes seemed weary, and large dark puffy circles sagged beneath them, but when he spotted me and smiled, I saw a familiar face. When he spoke, his voice was husky, and he hunched over, wincing as he shifted his weight to the other foot, trying to get comfortable; I got the sense this introduction wouldn't be long. I also didn't have the first clue as to what he said. I just stood and politely listened.

Zuralina began to say something to me, but Rasadian hushed her with a solid glare. I'd almost forgotten that Rasadian was standing next to me, I'd been so preoccupied by my surroundings, but now, I was suddenly more uncomfortable than ever.

"He said a prayer, and thanked the Creator for bringing everyone safely to the Great Hall for this bequeathing tonight," Zuralina told me when the males raised their fists and cried out in what seemed like strong agreement.

"Where's Rion?" I asked her.

She quickly pointed to the aisle. "Right there."

Rion stood at least one head's length above everyone else. I hadn't realized how tall he was compared to the other malions; however, seeing him surrounded by so many made it blatantly obvious. His standard navy cloak had been replaced by one of forest green, and when he un-hooded himself and knelt in front of the black box, I felt my hands begin to shake. All I could think about was what would be making those marks on his back.

Ramses spoke again when Rion bowed his head and Zuralina translated for me what she could without being too disruptive. All in all, it was a beautiful address to the crowd, especially when Ramses touched his son's shoulders and grinned proudly.

"Is that it?" I asked Zuralina, with manufactured hope.

"Almost." She snatched my hand as Ramses opened the black wooden box, and I saw a large metal anvil inside it. My eyes began furiously scanning the room when a buzz of rapture rose from the crowd; I knew something else was coming, but I didn't anticipate it would be some*one*. Someone who was also covered in a green cloak.

"That is Farshun, the Eurafrican *leighdur*," Zuralina whispered to me. "He's doing the honours tonight."

I saw what he was holding in his hand, and my stomach lurched. I momentarily lost my ability to stand straight. Rasadian grabbed my waist when he saw I was about to lose it, and Zuralina pulled my face around hissing, "It is going to be fine, okay? This will be over in just a moment. It will not hurt him—he is incredibly strong, Melissa. Honour him, do not fear for him." But it was too late. The metal chain whip Farshun held in his hand sparkled across the room and he shook it out with two crisp *snaps*. Rion was already uncloaked when I looked back to the front. I started to cover my eyes, but Zuralina whipped my hands away. "It is disrespectful to hide your eyes." Less than a second later, two large warm hands clutched my shoulder blades.

"Be still and be *quiet*," Rasadian warned me when I jerked forward, troubled by his weighty grasp.

"He is not holding the *xorth*!" Zuralina hissed to Rasadian.

"He has had much worse," Rasadian whispered firmly, staring at the spectacle of his brother. I flashed a look up at Rasadian, and he glared back, adding, "Do not move an *inch*. We must not let anyone know…"

The first crack of the chain-whip hit Rion square in the back, and the tiniest huff came from his mouth. My attention was suddenly, completely focussed on Rion as I leaned forward, gasping for breath. Rion flinched and growled ever so slightly under his breath as dark amethyst blood poured from the vertical wound. Zuralina put her other arm around me as I clutched my stomach, which was contracting and readying for release. The heat from Rasadian's hand amplified, and Farshun struck Rion twice more.

CRACK!

SWACK!

Each time, Rion shifted less than an inch; even his hands, unrestrained, rested calmly on the anvil.

By that time, malions from all around the crowd were crooning, and I was struggling to keep myself composed and on my feet. I couldn't handle the fact that Rion was being beaten; it brought back those horrid photographs Caine had shown me. For a split second, I didn't see the new *Leighdur* Rion, I saw an underweight juvenile…confined…helpless.

Prolonged applause ringing throughout the nave brought me back to the present, but all I could see were fresh wounds needing some serious pressure and bandages.

"Why'd they do that?" I cried to Zuralina, but she was in Lafe's arms.

"The *leighdur*s must endure three initiation scars," Jordon answered me from behind, as Rasadian kept silent with his warm hands cemented to my back. "They symbolize the power each new *leighdur* inherits from the spirit of *Lorkon*—we try to envision that He has come and struck Rion with his mighty paw. It is a blessing, for past, present and future."

"It's freaking torture!" I hissed.

Right on cue, Rion turned around and winked at me. I was stunned.

"See!" Jordon nudged me in the arm. "He is fine!"

"Yeah, well I'm not!" I held my stomach tight. Rion kept steady eye contact with me, shaking his head at my frightened face, mocking my weak stature with a half grin. Ramses then stepped forward and placed his hand upon Rion's back, stopping the bleeding, and replaced his cloak before gesturing him to stand. Rion rose to his feet, proudly calling out to his people in malion, and everyone returned with roars and applause. I hoped that was all. I couldn't handle any more gore, but Rion did seem genuinely proud to publicly display his resilience and masculinity. Men.

Malions lined up to greet and congratulate Rion as the new *leighdur*, and I stood back trying my best to smile; I didn't want to intrude on his exultant parade, though it hardly seemed necessary as his eyes constantly sought mine. Zuralina and Lafe left to talk to their families, and before I knew it, everyone was up and visiting casually at the altar. Jordon was joking and trading cheap shots with a few males sporting mohawks, but I didn't have the nerve to venture out of my alone-zone; I just wanted to stay close to Rion—and Rasadian. With so many malions present, it could have been difficult to track Rasadian, but like Rion, he towered over everyone.

"You did well," a quiet, gravelly voice spoke. I spun around, and there was Ramses, making a full-fledged effort to smile, but only half of his face managed. I looked into his dull, pale green eyes, and watched as one of his hands shook uncontrollably while the other tried to settle it. He shuffled toward the pew behind me, slumped down and nodded, inviting me to sit next to him. Something about his expression reminded me of my grandfather, the retired workaholic entrepreneur, delighted with my company and desperate for conversation that didn't involve business when I visited him.

"I almost had to look away." Out of respect for his dignity, I made eye contact when I spoke to him, ignoring his shaking hand, which he was clearly self-conscious about.

"But you did not." He winked at me. "My Rose ran out the moment they chinked the *wornstoff*. I remember how angry I was with her afterwards, which was...*vakar dontest*—entirely out of line, on my part. She was such a delicate little petal; I did not think she would be so upset by it."

I smiled at the recollection of his late *sensakuru*. No one was perfect. Not Rose. Not Ramses. Not Rion or Rasadian.

Not even me.

305

"What is troubling you tonight, Melissa? Because I sense it is not the ceremony. Something else is on your mind. Tell me..." he trailed off, coughing a few times over his shoulder. I couldn't believe he'd picked up on it. I didn't answer, I just shook my head.

"I understand the challenges a relationship with Rion presents to you," he continued. "I know you feel as though you must live two different lives."

I nodded.

"That is exactly how my Rose felt when we first met—I was not exactly the type of male her father envisioned for her at first. I was a foolish young *nesfaru*. We loved in secret for a long while... until she became *pey cubshen* with Rasadian and Rion." He was trying his best to keep a smile. "Being my son's *wharla* is not without incredible risks. I fear for you, just as Rion does, when you are above." Then he leaned toward me, and the sweet bubble gum scent filled my nose once again, only much stronger this time, because it was coming from his breath. "But with Rose, I never regretted listening to my heart. I dismissed everyone's opinions and went after my *wharla* like a selkie on a warpath."

I chuckled. He was once a strapping young male, madly in love, just like Rion.

"Obey your heart, Melissa, whatever it may be saying to you."

"My conscience doesn't agree with my heart, Ramses." Rion had my heart wrapped around his finger, while Rasadian fought to keep my feet on the ground. Like a tug-of-war, at some point, I would get pulled completely to one side or the other. More weight rested on Rion's side, but Team Rasadian was a potent force, with the threat of the *vykhars* on its side. And though Rion had never asked me to make a choice, I knew I would have to, this night.

"By the Creator, Melissa—fight it. Your conscience will regain strength in time, but a broken heart will never heal. Of that, I am certain."

I closed my eyes and swallowed hard. He was so right.

"He has changed, my *charkon*." I caught him staring at Rion, who briefly looked over at us and beamed when he noticed we were sitting together.

"He has?"

He raised his brow. "He is talking. He has come out of his chambers of his own accord."

"Did he not before?"

Ramses sighed. "I honestly did not know what I was going to do with him after he returned to us from the *vykhars*..."

I shuddered.

"...The Rion I knew no longer existed, it was as if another soul had claimed him—we all feared the very worst. I hated myself for sending him to the Asian Third, but at the time, I had no other choice. I could not handle him anymore. His anger was...consuming him." He coughed a deep raspy cough and gasped to sustain his breath. I began to reach around his back to comfort him, but he kindly waved me away and continued. "He does not deal well with failure, as I am sure you know. And it was not until he met you that he started to come around." Ramses sat up and cleared his throat. "It was a divine encounter, my dear, and just in time. We were certain we had lost him for all eternity when he went above that cold, October night. No one could stop him...but you...you stopped him."

"I didn't do anything special. I'm just glad he was there."

Ramses eyes flashed up at me for the slightest instant, then he coughed once more before adding, "He is looking at life in a new light now, and you lit the spark I could not. You brought back the son I used to know, and I want to thank you."

"I think he's the one who lit the spark in me."

"Meeting the *one* can definitely have that affect." He smirked at me, reminding me precisely of a look I frequently saw from Rion. Then he sighed, and said, "As did my Rose within me."

I could feel my heart beginning to tear. Another malion came up to us, one I didn't recognize, wearing a navy cloak. "The *marvon* is about to start, Ramses. We need to make our way now, or the food will be cold when we arrive."

"*Fenyecka* formalities," he barked back. "I do not care about the food. I do not want any!"

"How can I assist you?" the malion asked him. Apparently he'd become accustomed to Ramses' outpourings.

"You can assist me by leaving me *alone*," Ramses answered gruffly.

I pursed my lips together to stop myself from laughing at the crotchety old man, who reminded me more of my grandfather with each moment.

The malion said something in their language, and helped Ramses to stand. Right before they walked away, Ramses turned back and said, "You have my blessing, Melissa, wherever your heart may lead you."

I smiled as he pulled his hood over his head and tottered away. It's remarkable how someone can reach into your soul and iron out some of the creases in only a few short moments. I knew what my heart wanted, but, like he said, I was going to have a ruthless fight on my hands.

Maybe the fight was worthwhile. Maybe Rion was right: we could find a way to make it work. It was just so much to think about right now. I needed time. Much more time than the night afforded. It was time to find Rion. I was ready to go home. We would just have to talk about everything tomorrow, or the next day, when all the formalities had come to an end; I didn't want to be a party-pooper, but I also didn't want my ruminations to ruin his night (Katherine was also expecting me ASAP).

I didn't get more than a few steps into the aisle before a thunderous rumbling shook the underground, like a massive earthquake. My first instinct was to run toward the vestibule, in case something dropped from the ceiling, but there were so many malions crowded around me yelling and screaming from the clamour, I couldn't get through. I saw Rion, standing on top of a pew with his hands outstretched. "Stay right where you are," he mouthed to me, just as chunks of marble suddenly crumbled down around us.

XXIV

"RION!" I screamed.

I was in his arms less than a second later. He'd leapt over the crowd.

"What's happening?" I shouted over the cries and bellows.

"I do not know, it is coming from above..." he shouted back. "I must get you and the rest of the females out of here in case this collapses!"

"Is it the *vykhars*?"

"IT BETTER NOT BE!"

The great rumbling continued, shaking the floor around us, and an ear-piercing crackle made us both jump. The ceiling began to rain dust and small rocks. Everyone was trying to get out, but the exit was so small. Rion bolted to the doors of the vestibule and began shouting orders. "*TES CARTA NESFARAS—JEM TILATH HARKON VAH*!" Rion roared above everyone. "*RASADIAN! LAFE! LES NESFARAS H'AVAB HARKON VAH—YAVAN NAH!*" Rasadian raced to Rion's side and stole me from his arms.

"What are you doing?"

Rion took my face in his hands and his eyes opened wide. "Go with Rasadian. He will take you and the rest of the females to my cabin. Wait for me there."

310

I shook my head, and grabbed his arms. "No! I want to stay with you!"

"We do not have time for this!" Rion snarled. "GO NOW...PLEASE!"

He forced my shoulders back into Rasadian's clutches, kissed my forehead and whispered, *"Li havash nathe, m'ebesha wharla. Li havash nathe."*

Rasadian drew me away before I had a chance to reply, I'd taken too long. "NO!" I turned to face Rion, but I could only see his back. "RION!" I kept screaming his name and fighting Rasadian's grasp as three other males raced towards us with their females. More arrived seconds later.

Everything after that happened so fast.

More than two dozen females in the arms of males followed us as we began to make our way out of the vestibule. I insisted that the other females go first, and Rasadian counted them all as they passed us: forty-nine and six *cubshen*. The rumbling increased, and a few more large stones fell to the floor behind us. Malions everywhere were screaming orders and females were yelping for loved ones left behind; I lost track of Rion when he plunged back through the crowd toward the altar, and then I saw Zuralina, who was three females ahead of me, in Lafe's arms. She reached out for me, her mauve eyes, brighter and wider than I'd ever seen them. We rushed out of the nave, into complete darkness. But...I could see. I could see just fine.

Up ahead was a very steep staircase, and all the males ahead of us seemed to take them without the slightest exertion. Rasadian, however, was panting. "How long will it be before we get to the exit?" I asked him.

"It is not far. We need to cover more vertical than horizontal distance, then we will go through the mountains toward Rion's cabin."

When I looked into his eyes, his pupils were dilated. "But what if the *vykhars* are up there? Maybe everyone should head to another third, rather than above! What if someone sees us?"

"Absolutely not!" Rasadian shot back. "My orders from Rion were to take the females *above*."

Above seemed like the wrong way to me. We could never defend ourselves against the *vykhars* if they were up there waiting for us; they'd finish us in seconds, and the malions would never be able to recover their numbers. More than one hundred dead malions would be a colossal blow. It made way more sense for everyone to go further away from the danger *below*, but I knew that I'd never get the males to turn around. There was only one way to ensure that it was safe above: I had to be first. No one would question a human walking around above.

"Rasadian, tell the males to stop!"

"What? Why?"

"Just do it! I want to go through the exit first. If the *vykhars* are up there, you can all stay below and run to safety."

"NO. I—"

"STOP EVERYONE!" I screamed when Rasadian wouldn't. "STOP!"

The entire group halted and scrutinized me as I wrestled out of Rasadian's grip.

"Melissa, WHAT ARE YOU *DOING*?" Zuralina shouted at me.

I was too busy trying to get away from my leech of an escort. "Let GO!"

"Do not do this," Rasadian begged me. "Let a male go through the exit first."

"And THEN what?" I fired back. "Lose another male?" Rasadian freed me. "News flash, Rasadian: *males* are just as important as *females*, despite what you think. And I'm sorry, but I don't care what you say, I'm going *first*!"

"WAIT!" Lafe shouted to me. "NO, MELISSA!"

I ignored him and ran to the front of the line. An exceptionally large male was holding a female with long brown hair and a violet cloak.

"If I'm not back in three minutes, I want you to get as far away from here as you can. *Below*. Okay?"

312

The female nodded. The male gaped at me like I'd lost my marbles. Maybe I had. But it was for a good cause. Before I reached the speck of moonlight up ahead, I turned back, adding, "Even if it's to the Eurafrican Third—just do it!"

I heard Lafe call out for me again, but I pressed on. I hoped that I'd made the right decision, and when I heard another thundering blast, I knew I couldn't turn back. The malions were running out of time.

I crept toward the exit, stopping to listen carefully. The tunnel opened up to the surface at the edge of a hill, hidden by a boulder and some overhanging rock. There were all sorts of clamours and bangs, so I poked my head out to look around before venturing out. At first, the return of fresh air was welcoming, and I shivered for the first time, sucking in the icy cold, January air. But the freshness was short-lived, when I caught the scent of what I thought was gun powder. It was the same scent I smelled at the fireworks in summertime.

There was just enough room between the earth and the rock for me to squeeze my torso through to get a better look, but I still couldn't see far. I started to pull myself through, when something seized my cloak. I gasped, before realizing it was Rasadian. His eyes were glowing again, and a little whimper fled his throat.

"Rasadian…"

"I promised Rion that I would not leave you, Melissa." He pulled me back toward him. "Do not make me break my promise!" He'd also smelt the gun powder.

I gently pried Rasadian's hand away, though I knew it would shame him. "So help me, Rasadian, you have to stay below with the rest of the females….They need you."

He swallowed. "What am I going to tell Rion when you do not come back?"

I sighed. *When.* There was no *if.* Somehow, we both knew this was a one-way trip. "I owe this to all of you, Rasadian. I'm the one who insisted on returning home after my accident. I'm the one who put everyone at a tremendous risk because of it. I'm the one who's fallen in love with someone who can never be a part of my world. I'm the one who agreed to be his *wharla*. And *I'm* the reason the *vykhars* haven't stopped looking for you all!"

Rasadian shook his head furiously. "We have *all* let this go on, Melissa. It was not just you—we are all to blame!"

"Believe whatever you want, Rasadian…" I began to shove my body back between the earth and the boulder. "I'm going. And I'm going to make things safe for you again—even if it kills me."

His eyes widened and he stole my hand back quickly, gave it a kiss, and raised it above his head. "*Seen taylee va leivemont, y'ebesha…* until the next lifetime."

I nodded and smiled my best smile.

"Now go," he ordered, "before I change my mind!"

Rasadian whisked back to the group, and I closed my eyes until I could no longer hear his footsteps.

The forest was thick with brush, and I could hear a humming drumbeat commotion coming from somewhere in the distance. Unsure of what exactly was out there, I began to creep toward the noise. I found a small path to tread, where branches were few and far between, and even though the night was calm, my skin crawled with the expectation of horror waiting for me in the clearing. I prayed that my notion of *vykhars* lurking above was just my imagination taking over; that in a few moments, I could run back and tell the group that our journey to Rion's cabin would be secure. But as I got closer to the clearing, the moon gave off more than enough light for me to see exactly what had come to shake us tonight.

It also confirmed my worst fear: the *vykhars* were invading.

I waited and watched as sixty or so *vykhars* crowded around a gigantic hole in the ground. Someone in the group kept shouting orders, and firing his gun into the sky at regular intervals.

They'd been trying to access the Great Hall. Somehow they'd managed to pinpoint the exact location on the surface, and they were blasting their way below.

I wasn't going to let them get any further. I needed to redirect them.

And I knew just how I was going to do it.

XXV

It takes me less than five minutes to light a fire without a match, thanks to Girl Guides and my love of the outdoors. I hoped my adrenaline level would cut that time in half, but first, I needed to find somewhere to start the fire, away from the tunnel's exit. I wanted to give the malions a fighting chance to get away, not give the *vykhars* the entrance they needed. Thank goodness for all the yelling going on, they didn't notice the *crack!* when I stepped on some branches as I ran from the hill.

I glanced over my shoulder as I ran, keeping an eye on the dark silhouettes around the blast zone. When they were only indistinct blurs in the distance and the rattle of gunfire and occasional concussions from the blasts were slightly muted, I stopped and surveyed my location. I was on the edge of a small clearing, and I could hear cars pass, which meant I was close to a road. Satisfied, I grabbed a few dry leaves and twigs, two good sized rocks, and went to work. A few minutes later, I could smell smoke, but the spark burned out. The ground was too wet. Stupid rain.

I tore off a sleeve from my sweater, placed it on the ground and tried again. When the fire finally lit, I crouched in front of it and turned my back to the *vykhars* to block it from view and give it time to grow. I added leaves and brush, whatever I could find that wasn't mushy—including the other arm of my sweater. The last thing I added was my bra, but I left my undershirt on. It worked; the fire was ready to turn some heads.

That's when I called out to them.

Bodies started rushing toward me, bellowing for others to follow. I waited a few moments and then started to run. I wanted them to see me at first. I kept my cloak on, though I knew it would slow me down; I didn't want the *vykhars* to know they were pursuing a human. I surged forward, running along the road, veiled from drivers by the forest and brush. I wasn't ready to reveal my humanity; we were still too close to the entrance.

I was passing trees faster than I'd thought possible, and with much less effort than I'd expected. When I looked back, the fire was just a flicker in the distance, but there were still footfalls behind me. Before long, I was at the edge of the forest altogether, crossing the road into open farmland.

Open farmland was bad. I didn't want to be seen, and looking around me, I realized I had no familiarity for the area. It was time to flag down a car and get away, if I could shake the *vykhars* chasing me.

I ran through an intersection on a barely lit road and headed in the direction of streetlights. The *vykhars* were still behind me, but their shouting became less and less audible with each passing second. I remembered the night Mantis was killed and how I'd run for miles without tiring. What the heck had happened to my body after Rion healed me? Whatever it was, it had worked to my advantage; I couldn't see or hear the *vykhars* any longer. I felt I'd salvaged enough time to stop running and hitchhike a ride home. In the morning, I would send Rion a message, and if I was lucky, he might actually reply.

Or yell at me—in person—if I was *really* lucky.

I ran to the next stop sign. There were two gas stations and an IGA supermarket that had closed for the night, but no traffic coming in either direction. I didn't know how long I had before the *vykhars* caught up. My only chance was a pub named the Artful

317

Dodger on my right. The lights were on, but the door was locked when I tried it.

I was about to walk away when the door to the pub opened. A middle-aged woman, who looked like she'd just finished her shift, strode out.

"Excuse me, I'm sorry to bother you, but my boyfriend just kicked me out of his car and left me here. Do you think you could give me a ride home?" I scoured the area for signs of *vykhars* as I spoke.

"Sure, darlin'." Her voice was deep, reminding me of the real estate agent Dad hired when we were looking for a house in Vancouver. "Where 'bouts do ya live?"

"In East Van."

Her eyes popped out. "East *Vancouver*!"

"Yeah. Is that far?"

"Honey, this is the Township of *Langley*. That's a whole hour's drive for me, and it's past midnight. I gotta work again at six in the morning. Sorry, but I just don't think I can do that." She took forty dollars out of her purse and handed it to me. "Take this and grab a bus or a cab—or whatever you need to get you home. Just do me a favour and don't let a man treat you that way again. It ain't worth it, believe me!"

I shook my head and tried to give it back to her. "I'm sorry, I can't accept that. I—"

"THERE IT IS!"

I wrenched around to see three *vykhars* standing on the other side of the parking lot, staring at me. I dropped the money and ran.

Hidden by my cloak, I ran toward the trees on the side of the road to disguise myself once again. I found myself cutting through yards and jumping fences, and before I knew it, I was back into thick forest. Stopping to listen, I could hear them calling out for me in the distance, so I took my phone out of my back pocket and turned it on, thinking I had at least enough time to text Charlotte. But I couldn't get any reception. Jordon must have disabled his

318

network. I dropped the phone and fled. Maybe knocking on some-one's door and calling the police was a better idea.

I shed my cloak, kept my head down, and continued soundlessly in the forest. When the trees thinned, I stopped before stepping out into another section of open farmland where an old elementary school and a corner store resided. The half-full moon lit the area very well, but now the night was *way* too silent. There weren't any crickets singing or frogs croaking. The bitterly cold air was still and there were no houses near.

Not what I needed.

If I ventured out into the field, someone would hear me. Someone would see me. And I would look like a fugitive. I took in a deep breath, closed my eyes and dropped to my knees to listen.

Nothing.

The next thicket was a few acres away across the exposed field, and there might be a house hidden on the other side of the trees. Someone had to own this field. I took one last look around, and ran straight across the clearing.

In baseball, when I was younger, I loved stealing bases. It was such a rush. As I ran for the thicket, I welcomed that old familiar urgency. I ran faster than I ever had. My hands became clammy midway across the field, and I looked back, but I was still alone. I smiled. No one had seen me. I was going to make it! I had lost them altogether!

"Oh, *Kitten*! It *is* you!"

The words from that familiar deep voice struck me so hard, I tripped over my own feet and fell flat on my face onto the frozen ground. Blood dripped from my lip, and the metallic nastiness made me gag. I wondered for a moment if I'd imagined his voice. It was something I'd heard many times in my head, especially the way he emphasized *Kitten*. But when I looked up, I saw that I wasn't dreaming at all. Kyle Peterson was standing over me in a black suit, flexing his fingers and having a good, long look. Flanking him were two more *vykhars*.

One of them was holding my cloak. The other was holding my phone.

XXVI

"What a *pleasant* surprise," Kyle chirped, rubbing his hands together. "I planned to kill a few malions before I came for you, but I won't even need a whole weekend now. It's all going to happen tonight!"

I stared back at him in horror as he knelt beside me, laughing his revolting hoarse laugh that made my skin crawl. The memory of him sweating and breathless on top of me flashed through my head.

"We had fun, didn't we, *Kitten*?"

He leaned down and put his finger on my cheek, but I pushed myself up onto my knees and hit it away. "Don't touch me."

"Oh, she's feisty now!" he teased, as his wing-men hooted in the background. "A lot more than I remember, hey *Kitty Cat*?"

When he looked up for approval from his comrades, I swiftly punched him in the balls, which gave me just enough time to stand up and run. I looked over my shoulder to see if he was following me, and he wasn't. He was holding his groin and addressing his partners.

"Go back to the park and see what's happening with the malions. I'll take care of *her*."

I faced forward again and ran as fast as I could, but I was light-headed from my fall, and the faster I ran, the dizzier I became. I could hear Kyle gaining ground behind me. I turned to face him, choosing to save my energy to fight. It was something I hadn't done back in Alberta. No, I'd just let him have his way with me, because I was too scared of what he'd do if I retaliated. Tonight, that wasn't the case. If I was going to die, I wasn't going down easily.

He flew at me when I turned around, driving me headfirst into the ground. I grabbed his right arm to stop him from seizing my hair, and plunged the heel of my palm into his jaw, blocking his other hand with my forearm. My hand came around faster the second and third time, and the blows stunned him for a moment, which was just enough time for me to stand up and kick him in the stomach. I hoped he'd had enough, but he was up less than a second later. There was no stopping him. Just like before, he was a machine. A *vykhar* machine.

I dodged a few of his kicks and jabs, but his fists became too fast for me to avoid. They were coming at me so quickly, they started to blur in my vision; I did the best I could to step out of the way, block, and strike back when I could, but suddenly his left hand came out of nowhere and connected with my nose.

Crunch.

My head snapped back and my body went limp. Kyle used the opportunity to put me in a full-nelson headlock, holding me tight to his chest.

"Gotcha, *Kitten*," he whispered in my ear. "Now we're *really* going to have some fun…"

Even with a broken nose bleeding down my shirt, the smell of his rancid, sweet cologne made me want to puke. "If you're going to kill me, you'd better do it now. Because if I get away from you, I'm going to tell everyone what you did to me—I'm not scared of you anymore!"

"Noooo, no no no no," he sang sweetly. "First, you're going to tell me how you found the malions, how you get below to see them, and *then* we'll discuss what I'm going to do with you."

"I'm not telling you anything!" I shot back, struggling within his grasp.

"I don't want to have to do this the hard way, Kitten, but I may just have to." His grip tightened around my neck as more blood dripped down into my mouth, which was opening and closing mechanically as I tried to draw breath. I was beginning to feel faint.

Then he bit my ear. He'd done that before.

"Stop it!" I tried to yell, but it came out as a gurgle.

"Talk, *Kitten*. This is your last chance."

My arms and legs were going numb. I could feel my body heating up as the trees in the distance began fading into bright light.

"We want the scarred one, *Kitten*. ANSWER ME!"

I shook my head weakly. He could do whatever he wanted to me. I'd never tell him a thing. Never. I relaxed into the warmth of approaching unconsciousness, ready to close my eyes, vacate my body and flutter away. In my mind, I had already won.

"THEN COME AND GET ME, *MANAKACKO*!"

Kyle gasped. He loosened his grip on my neck, and wheeled me around to face the deep, heavenly voice of my *dharkun*. I hacked and tried to catch my breath as sweat trickled down my back.

"Rion, no!" I cried out through another cough. "Get away!"

"Shut the hell up!" Kyle barked at me, taking a fist of my hair in his hand.

Rion yelled something back in malion, and belted out a thunderous roar that made the hair on the back of my neck stand up.

"Show your face, malion!" Kyle yelled back. "Show your face or I'll snap her neck right now."

"Snap her neck and I will tear each of your limbs out, one by one. Just like my people did to your comrades tonight!" Rion's magnificent figure emerged from the forest a hundred yards from us. He was striding confidently towards us, un-hooded, with his arms moving coolly at his sides. "You are the last one, *shesthef*. And you are not going to live through this. Especially not now, since you have just threatened my *wharla's* life."

"Don't come any closer, malion! I mean it. I'll *break her neck*— right now!"

Rion continued to walk towards us, calm and collected, and made solid eye contact with me, though he was speaking to Kyle. "My blood flows in her veins, *vykhar*. You cannot kill her. No matter what you do, she will come back to life and curse your family for centuries to come."

I didn't have time to process his words. Kyle's hands were still at my throat. I wanted to scream for Rion to stop, because Kyle would kill me no matter what. I could only shake my head furiously.

"LIAR!" Kyle shouted.

Rion's eyes widened and he clenched his fists; I thought he was going to spring at us, but instead, he stopped twenty feet from where we were standing. "Come and fight me, *vykhar*."

I pulled on Kyle's arm, and his grip loosened slightly as Rion stared anxiously at us. For a moment I thought Kyle would let me go, but then he did something I didn't expect: he licked the side of my face.

That was the wrong thing to do.

"You BASTARD!" I exclaimed. I turned, eager to hit him wherever I could, but Rion was much faster. He leaped, knocking us both over, separating us on impact. I rolled away from them, leaning over to catch my breath, just in time to see Kyle boot Rion away and reach for me. I shot my elbow toward his face, but I was too late, everything went starry and white as his arms wrapped around my neck again.

The last thing I heard was Rion's howl in the distance.

XXVII

I'd never had a near-death experience before. I always figured spirits float around peacefully for a while before slipping through the gates of Heaven.

I couldn't have been more wrong.

My spirit didn't depart. It stayed right inside my body, ensuring I remained for each and every insufferable moment as I lay paralyzed. I couldn't move as Rion fought desperately to breathe life back into me. The most excruciating part was that I felt nothing. I watched him pumping my chest, feeling absolutely nothing, and panicked, because I realized I wasn't near death.

I was already dead.

Frantically, I tried to call out to him, "I'm here! I'm here!" But he couldn't hear me. My arms wouldn't move, my toes wouldn't twitch. It was torture. And why? Kyle was nowhere in sight, Rion must have won the fight.

"How many times have you tried?" Rasadian's anxious voice startled me. My head happened to be tilted up enough to spot him standing next to Rion. His pupils were dilated as he inspected me.

I tried harder to move, reaching out for him. All of a sudden I felt my arm lift, and a ghostly hand slipped into my vision, passing right through his face. The realization made me scream, but no one heard me.

"THREE TIMES!" Rion continued to press on my chest. "Come on, Melissa—FIGHT!" I watched Rion's lips touch mine again, before he continued his attempt to resuscitate me. "Move your lips *m'ebesha*, blink at me, roll your eyes, for the *Lorkon's* sake, GIVE ME A SIGN!"

I was still unable to respond with my physical body. Each time he pressed down on my heart, I could hear the cracking of my broken ribs as the bones scraped along one another, but I still felt nothing. The trees above us began to turn white. Like someone had dribbled frosting over them, whiteness oozed over the branches and trunks and toward me until white was all I could see.

"They are waiting, Rion," Rasadian said. "If we do not go now, they are going to leave without us."

"I AM NOT LEAVING HER, RASADIAN!" Rion threw his hands in the air, bent back and bellowed the most ear-piercing wail. He cried out to the Creator, beseeching Him and the stars for my life. Rasadian yelled at him, and Rion screamed at me, something with my name in it. Whatever it was, I didn't understand.

And then I saw…it.

The ghost of a malion came into my view, opposite Rion. His body glowed a silvery-blue. He didn't have eyes, just hollow almond-shaped sockets. The malion peered deep into my eyes, sweeping his frigid spectre hands over and through me, again and again, and around my face. It calmed me, instantly. He began to coax me away from my body, but I fought hard, hauling myself back.

"NO! I want to stay!"

Taken aback, he hesitated and tried again, but I persisted. I wasn't going anywhere. I wanted to find a way back into my body.

"Stop! Don't take me! I won't leave him!" I pulled as hard as I could, but the malion was so strong, I soon realized I was no match. I tried to persuade him, but he pulled me away inexorably. Either I wasn't getting through to him, or he didn't care. In desperation, I tried a few malion words that I knew. "*Nee neena!*"

He stopped and looked back at me, puzzled. I shook my head and quickly pointed to myself. "Rion's *ebesha wharla*! Please! *Pers*—oh what's the word, dammit—*pershavi*!"

He finally understood and stepped back, raising my hand above his head and grinning as his form slowly darkened before vanishing completely.

Rasadian took my hand just then, his touch drawing me back to the darkness of the field and surrounding forest, but what caught my attention, was that I actually *felt* it. I very much wanted to squeeze his hand back, but my fingers still wouldn't budge. "It is no use, Rion...she is dead. Let us get her below before the sun rises."

"I am not giving up, Rasadian!" Rion argued back, still performing chest compressions, which I sensed as a slight pressure. I was feeling much heavier now. "She is going to come back. I am going to try once more!"

"You cannot, Rion. She is human. You will scorch her insides. Do not do this. *Please*..." Rasadian attempted to pull Rion away, but Rion shoved back, thrusting his arm out. "Leave us then!"

Rasadian grabbed his hair and growled, as Rion straightened my clothing and brushed my hair away from my face. I could feel his warm hands on my skin, fond and gentle. "Return to me... *please* return to me..." With his hands on my cheeks, he pressed his lips to my forehead and placed his head next to mine. "I know you are not ready, Melissa. I can still feel you...so come back to me, my precious *wharla*...I love you...I love you!"

He wrapped his arms around me, and all of a sudden, my body was on fire.

327

XXVIII

I opened my eyes, to find myself lying in bed at home. It was daytime, and my alarm clock read 10:02. I was wearing flannel pajamas for the first time since my accident, but for some reason, I wasn't stifling hot. I had to pull the covers up around me because I was shivering. My first instinct was to get up and see if Rion was hiding in my closet or underneath my bed, but he couldn't have been, because I would have been warm. I tried to sit up, but my neck and back prevented me. Ugh...what a night.

After a few tries, I stretched and managed to get myself upright. I felt stiff, and a little sore, but not so much that I couldn't move properly. I wanted to get up and see who was home, and I wanted to call Charlotte, because I needed to talk to Rion.

I made my way downstairs, plunging into the smell of coffee and cinnamon buns. Someone had been cooking, so I ran into the kitchen, but it was vacant. The warm breakfast rolls were still sitting in the pan, and the oven was still warm.

"Mom?" I called out.

"Nope, just us." Katherine voice came from the living room. "I'm in here."

I marched into the room and she was cuddled up on the couch, reading a magazine with her cell phone to her ear. "How—"

I jumped back when she threw her phone at me. "Here, Liss, talk to Chelsea."

I sighed and answered the phone, knowing now wasn't exactly the right time, but I couldn't avoid it any longer.

"Liss, oh my goodness…it's so great to *finally* hear your voice!"

I smiled. "It's nice to hear your voice, too."

Katherine gave me the *Ya see? It's not so bad, right?* look.

Chelsea and I talked for a few minutes, apologizing to one another; I could tell she was upset, and I did my best to comfort her. I wasn't mad anymore. Life was too short, as I told her. She made me promise to fly down with Katherine and see her; her mom would pay for the tickets with the points she'd accumulated on her credit card. Chelsea also mentioned that she'd met someone special, someone who liked art and was interested in astronomy, like her, and I was glad. Even so, I was thankful when, a few minutes later, Katherine's low battery warning chimed, and we had to cut our conversation short. I wanted to figure out where Rion was, so I promised to call her next week to make arrangements to visit.

When I hung up the phone, Katherine sneered at me. It was her way of saying "Told you so!" Yeah, I guess talking to Chelsea wasn't that hard after all, but I still needed to know about the previous night: I hadn't been home, and Katherine didn't seem to have noticed. Normally, she would have been royally pissed if I stood her up. I had told her I'd be gone an hour, but obviously I'd been gone longer. Much, much longer.

"Geez, you sure slept in," she said past a mouth full of cinnamon bun. She licked her fingers. "We didn't even stay up that late."

I looked down at my manicured toes and finger nails; both had been painted the exact same colour of aquamarine blue—the same colour as my *ika* flower. Was that a coincidence?

"That's a good colour on you. *I* would have done something purple or light pink on you…blue is so…I don't know…sad. But don't get me wrong, it looks good—for someone who doesn't normally paint her own nails."

I didn't remember painting my nails the night before. I remembered a very different version of the previous night. Whoever had painted them had done an okay job. I couldn't even do that, especially when I had to paint my right hand with my left. Something was wrong.

"Where're Mom and Dad?"

"Out for the day—but not together." She turned the page in her magazine. "I'm surprised you didn't hear them arguing this morning. Mom broke one of her good China plates on the wall. Woke me up. Now she's over at Judy's, I think, and Dad's...well, Dad's out—*somewhere*." She said *somewhere* as if she didn't care.

"Did anyone call for me this morning?"

"Nope."

"No one?" I thought for sure that Rion or Rasadian or Andrew or Charlotte might have tried to send me a message or something. Anything.

"Well..." Katherine bit her lip and looked up with her eyebrows furrowed. "Colin Mansfield stopped by, sporting two black eyes. I think he got in a fight or something, and he looks like he's lost about twenty pounds."

I sucked in a little breath. He'd been there last night. Had to have been. And now, he was checking up on me.

"What did he want?"

Katherine kept her eyes focussed on her magazine, answering, "His dad kicked him out. He's going to text you with his new number. He's living downtown now with a buddy." She flipped a page. "I asked him what happened, but he just changed the subject. What a loser—he probably got in a fight and lost, that's all. Good thing we weren't out last night, apparently there was a riot outside one of the clubs downtown, too."

"Oh. Yeah."

She shuddered and rolled her shoulders. "I can't stand it when he looks at me. He's so weird."

I wish I could second that, only he'd never been anything but nice to me. Untrustworthy? Yes. Sneaky? Quite possibly. But weird? No.

Katherine dove back into another cinnamon bun and continued reading her magazine.

I didn't understand why Katherine had a different memory of last night. Why had she not given me trouble for *not* coming home within an hour? Why wasn't I grounded? And how was my nose perfectly intact. Had Kyle not broken it?

"Did you grab a cinnamon bun? I made them—not from scratch, but I..." Katherine kept talking, but I wasn't paying attention. I couldn't stand here and talk any longer. I needed to go over to Charlotte's apartment and find out what the heck was going on. It would have been much easier to text her, but there was way too much to discuss.

"I'm going to take a shower."

"Okay. But I want you to try one before you go. If you don't, I'll just end up eating them all!"

I hesitated for a moment. Katherine's appreciation for fatty foods was new, yet another odd thing. It wasn't *Wacky Wednesday*, but if I got up to my room and saw shoes on the wall, I was going straight back to bed.

I took a quick shower and washed my hair. I couldn't find my jeans and torn sweater from the night before. As I grabbed some clean clothes from my closet, I wondered why Rion hadn't left me a note, or phone number, or some other way of reaching him. It frustrated the hell out of me, but then I thought that maybe he was just mad at me for taking matters into my own hands, and leaving the group of females last night. Before the ceremony, he'd promised me that we'd get a chance to talk; that we'd have time to discuss everything he'd wanted to tell me—what we hadn't had time for. I was ready for it now, but not because I was ready to officially break things off with him, like I thought I'd wanted to. I realized last night, in the midst of the craziness down below, that Ramses was right: I needed to follow my heart.

When Rasadian tore me away from Rion, it was like he had taken the most significant part of my existence away. The separation, and not knowing if I'd ever see him again, was excruciating.

I never wanted to feel that way again. My heart had led me to Rion. I knew now, I belonged with Rion.

He saved my life, and respected my wishes to return home— risking his own exposure by doing so, and then welcomed me back. He put up with my stubbornness. He found out about my past, and instead of judging me, he helped me cope and move on. He was there when I needed him the most, protecting me, caring for me, and giving me the kind of love I didn't think existed, except in fairy tales. The truth was, I couldn't imagine my life without him; I'd waded into the shallows, and now there was no going back to the shore. I was ready to be with him, no matter what risks we had to endure. Together, we were stronger. Together, we would fight to keep our love alive.

Rion was right, all along: together, we'd find a way. A way I could live above, and see him below, whenever we could spare a free moment. And it would only have to be until school ended. In June, I could move out, and see him more frequently. Yes, it could work *smashingly*—in the wonderful words of my grandfather.

I pulled my jeans on, dried my hair and brushed my teeth, and straightened my bed. That's when I saw it: a cream envelope with my name, written in Rion's chicken-scratch. I gasped and dove over my bed to grab it before it slipped between the wall and mattress, and I tore it open. Struggling to unfold it without giving myself a paper cut, my heart sped up and my hands began to shake. I'd never been so anxious and excited about something as silly as a note, but as I began to read, there was much more than anticipation running through my body.

I began to panic.

MELISSA,

WHEN YOU READ THIS NOTE, I KNOW YOU WILL BE SORE AND NOT RESTED, BUT MY TIME HERE IS RUNNING SHORT. ANDREW HAS USED PERSUASION ON YOUR SISTER;

SHE KNOWS NOTHING OF MY BRINGING YOU HOME LAST NIGHT, AND ANDREW HAS CONTRIVED A STORY OF NAIL PAINTING AND MOVIES, AS HE INFORMS ME. I HAVE SO MUCH THAT I WANT TO SAY TO YOU, BUT I DO NOT HAVE MUCH TIME TO BE ABOVE, SO I MUST MAKE THIS QUICK.

I CAN NO LONGER KEEP MY SECRET, MELISSA. I HAVE STRUGGLED WITH EXACTLY HOW I WAS GOING TO TELL YOU, BUT MY MIND HAS BEEN AT A LOSS FOR WORDS. NO MATTER HOW I GO ABOUT IT, I KNOW IT WILL CHANGE HOW YOU FEEL ABOUT ME. SO HERE IT IS: I DID IT, MELISSA. I WAS THE ONE WHO CAUSED YOUR ACCIDENT THAT FIRST NIGHT, AND I CANNOT BEGIN TO TELL YOU HOW VERY SORRY I AM: FOR NOT TELLING YOU, FOR PLACING YOU IN THE MIDDLE OF A DISASTER THAT I CAUSED, AND FOR PUTTING YOU AND YOUR FAMILY AT RISK.

YOU HAVE BEEN HONEST ABOUT YOUR PAST WITH ME, AND NOW I MUST BE HONEST WITH YOU.

I dropped the note, and fell to my knees. It was a whole page and a half longer; part of me wanted to keep reading, but I was in such shock, I needed a minute to catch my breath.

That very first night, when I flipped into the ravine, it was because of Rion. I didn't know what to think. Inside, I was angry. I wanted to tear the note up. But I also needed to understand why. Was it out of anger? Did he mistake me for someone else and toss my car off the edge on purpose?

A minute passed before I was able to pick up the note and begin reading again.

I DO NOT KNOW IF YOU HAVE NOTICED, BUT I AM THE ONLY MALION WHO CANNOT SEE IN THE DARK. I HAVE ABSOLUTELY NO NIGHT VISION. MY EYES DO NOT GLOW LIKE THE OTHERS'. I CARRY A FLASHLIGHT TO SEE IN THE TUNNELS, AND EVEN THEN, THE CONTRAST IS TOO MUCH FOR MY SENSITIVE EYES AT TIMES. I WAS RUNNING WITHOUT MY FLASHLIGHT THAT NIGHT, AND I DID NOT EVEN SEE OR HEAR YOUR CAR, BECAUSE YOU WERE ON

MY DEAF SIDE. I WAS RUNNING TOO FAST, AND THEN BEFORE I KNEW IT, WE COLLIDED.

I DID NOT TELL YOU AT FIRST BECAUSE I WAS EMBAR-RASSED, AND THEN, LATER ON, BECAUSE I DID NOT WANT YOU TO THINK THAT I WAS WEAK. THAT I COULD NOT PROTECT YOU WHEN YOU NEEDED ME. THAT I COULD NOT BE EVERYTHING YOU WANTED IN A DHARKUN, AND MORE.

My eyes began to sting, but I kept reading.

I DID EVERYTHING IN MY POWER TO HEAL YOU WHEN I PULLED YOU FROM YOUR CAR, BECAUSE YOUR HEART WAS NOT BEATING. I HAD NEVER HEALED A HUMAN BEFORE. THE FIRST TIME, ON THE SIDE OF THE ROAD, I SHAT-TERED YOUR LEGS BECAUSE I USED TOO MUCH FORCE, BUT YOU WERE ALIVE. I WAS SCARED TO TOUCH YOU AGAIN, UNTIL RASADIAN URGED ME TO TRY ONCE MORE. I WAS WORRIED THAT YOU WOULD NEVER WALK ANOTHER STEP. THAT I HAD DONE EVEN MORE DAMAGE TO THE MOST EXQUISITE HUMAN FEMALE I HAD EVER ENCOUNTERED. WHEN ABBY SAID YOU NEEDED BLOOD, I GAVE YOU MINE; I WOULD HAVE DONE JUST ABOUT ANYTHING FOR YOU THAT NIGHT. WE HAD NO IDEA IF OUR FLUIDS WOULD BE COMPATIBLE, BUT I HAD TO TRY, BECAUSE YOU HAD LOST TOO MUCH ALREADY, AND WOULD NOT HAVE SURVIVED THE FIRST NIGHT. I KNOW THIS SOUNDS CRAZY, BUT IN THAT SHORT AMOUNT OF TIME WE SPENT TOGETHER THAT WEEKEND, I FELL IN LOVE WITH YOU. SO MUCH, I FOUND IT IMPOSSIBLE TO LIVE WITHOUT YOU. EVEN IN THIS MOMENT, WATCHING YOU SLEEP SOUNDLY, KNOWING I HAVE TO LEAVE IS KILLING ME. AND NO MATTER HOW ANGRY I WAS WHEN I HEARD FROM RASADIAN THAT YOU TOOK OFF TO MISLEAD THE VYKHARS, I WAS STILL IN LOVE WITH YOU—MORE THAN I EVER HAVE BEEN, AND PROUD (AND PISSED) BECAUSE YOU WERE SO BRAVE TO TAKE THEM ON BY YOURSELF.

IF YOU NEVER WANT TO SEE ME AGAIN, BECAUSE OF WHAT I HAVE DONE, I WILL STILL, ALWAYS, BE IN LOVE WITH YOU.

I HAVE ASKED ANDREW TO HAVE YOUR SISTER WAKE YOU EARLY, BECAUSE I AM ONLY GOING TO BE HERE FOR THE MORNING. I AM LEAVING AFTER THAT, TO ESCORT THE LAST FEW OF US AWAY FROM THIS THIRD. WE ARE GOING TO JOIN THE REST OF MY FAMILY IN THE EURAFRICAN THIRD; THE ONES WHO, THANKS TO YOU, ALL SURVIVED THE INVASION BECAUSE THEY WERE GIVEN THE TIME TO ESCAPE. I CANNOT BEGIN TO TELL YOU HOW MUCH YOU MEAN TO ME AND THE REST OF THE MALION COMMUNITY. YOU SAVED US. YOU GAVE ME THE TIME THAT I NEEDED TO GATHER THE GUARD AND LAUNCH AN ATTACK ON THE VYKHARS ABOVE. FOR THAT, THE MALIONS AND I ARE FOREVER IN YOUR DEBT. THIS WAS SOMETHING THAT NONE OF US COULD HAVE EVER DONE WITHOUT YOU.

THERE IS SO MUCH MORE I WANT TO SAY, BUT THAT WILL DEPEND ON YOU. WHETHER YOU WANT TO SEE ME AGAIN IS YOUR CHOICE. I WILL BE AT JOHN HENDRY PARK UNTIL THE SUN RISES AT APPROXIMATELY SEVEN FORTY-FIVE. AT EIGHT, IF YOU ARE NOT AT THE ENTRANCE, POSSIBLE EXPOSURE BECOMES TOO MUCH OF A RISK FOR ME, AND I WILL ASSUME

I didn't read the rest. I looked at the clock.

It was almost eleven.

"KATHERINE!" I ran downstairs toward the door, shoving the note into my pocket. "WHY DIDN'T YOU WAKE ME UP THIS MORNING!"

A look of sheer horror came over Katherine's face. "Oh no, Liss! I'm so sorry. Your appointment with Dr. Hendry. I *knew* I was forgetting something! Andrew was here, and then Colin showed up—"

"I'm sorry, Katherine," I interjected, grabbing my car keys. "I don't have time. Whatever. I have to go—I'm more than two hours late!"

As I wriggled into my Keds, Katherine added, "Andrew said he's really good! Easy to talk to! Good luck!"

I rolled my eyes, tore open the door and sprinted to my car, but when I got in, I saw that she was out of gas. "CRAP!" I jumped out and ran as fast as I could to John Hendry Park, though I couldn't seem to run as fast as I did the night before. In no time at all, I was out of breath.

Fifteen minutes later, I was dizzy, and my chest was aching from the cold, but I'd finally arrived at the manhole cover. I combed the parking lot for signs of life before beating on the cover incessantly with my fist.

Nothing.

I checked my watch. It was just past eleven. I was three hours late. "DAMMIT!"

One hundred knocks later, I knew he'd left for good. I could see his face in my mind, as clear as the spikes of frost glistening on the weeping willows in front of me. And I knew how utterly heartbroken and devastated he must have been when I didn't show up. He was probably halfway to the Eurafrican Third already.

"I forgive you," I whispered with my forehead against the manhole, closing my eyes as tears trickled down my face. "Please come back...I forgive you...I forgive you!"

I must have sobbed for an hour, because when I looked at my watch again, it was after twelve. I should have gone home, but I couldn't peel myself away from the manhole. I kept tracing the waffled squares with my fingers, holding on to the memory of what we shared at this place: my first voluntary trip below, the first jump (I was so terrified at that moment, not knowing if I could trust him—how silly I'd been!), and oh...our first kiss. I wanted so badly to feel his arms around me once again, to get drunk on the piney, leather and musty scent of him.

I fell asleep after a while, and eventually cuddled myself up next to the building's heat vent for warmth. When I woke again, my stomach was growling and the sun had begun to set. Grey clouds were forming in the sky, and it smelled of snow—that sweet icy scent that tells you flakes are on the way. Mom and Dad were probably going to be home soon, so I picked myself up off the ground and rubbed my arms to get the circulation going.

As much as I wanted to stay just a little longer, it wasn't worth worrying anyone, or drawing attention—not to mention the fact that I was freezing my freaking butt off. My eyes still ached from crying, and as I began to walk away, I hoped that no one at home would notice the red blotchiness around them before I had the chance to whisk up to my room. I decided to walk slowly, to give my heart a chance to adjust to this new dull reality. I passed the swing-set, and stopped to stare at it. It was the same swing I'd chosen the night I'd agreed to meet him. I sat down and let my legs pump a little as the frosty air irritated my nose, when I heard a crunch behind me.

I stood up and spun around. My knees almost gave out at the sight of him. I blinked a few times, but yes, it was definitely him. He was standing under the willow tree, hidden by the umbrella of hanging branches, un-hooded, staring at me. I unsteadily walked towards him. When I got closer, I saw his eyes were brighter and more dilated than I'd ever seen them. I wondered if he was waiting for me to make the first move.

He was. And I did.

I ran at him, full tilt, right up into his arms.

"I thought I'd never see you again," I said as I held on tight.

Rion rubbed his head against mine. "That makes two of us."

XXIX

"I didn't know you were there," I said. "I didn't feel warm."

"I know," he said, warily. "You got my note?"

"Yes." I nuzzled back into his neck. "And I'm not mad, Rion... I'm not mad at all. I forgive you."

He squeezed me, lifting me off my feet for a moment before setting me down, but he kept hold of my hands. "I have a lot more that I want to say."

"Sure."

He shook his head. "Not here. Can you stay out for a few hours?"

"I'll need to have a good excuse."

"Just use Charlotte. Jordon is screening her calls right now, so you will be covered."

"Where is she?"

"On a plane."

My eyebrows furrowed. "To where?"

Rion swallowed hard. "I cannot tell you, Melissa. Not until we have had a chance to discuss a few things."

"Okaaaaayy..."

He put his phone in my hand. "This number cannot be traced. Call whoever you need to. I'll be waiting at the entrance when you are ready."

He left, and after a lengthy conversation with Katherine about taking a cab to meet up with Charlotte to talk about my appointment with "Dr. Hendry" (whom she was "also a patient of"), I was free for the night.

When I got to the manhole, Rion was already below, waiting for me. Unable to hide my enthusiasm, I nuzzled up to his neck the moment he caught me in his arms.

"You *are* cold." He wrapped his cloak around me, placing me next to his chest for warmth, which helped the cold abate but not my craving for him. It actually made things much worse.

"Why don't I feel warm around you anymore?"

He shrugged. "I noticed it when I brought you home, but I do not have an answer. Maybe it is for the best. If I get hurt again, maybe you will not feel it, either."

"I could do without *that* part...but I think I'll miss the warmth."

He smiled.

I lifted my head off his shoulder. "So where're we going?"

"To my cabin." He raised one eyebrow. "It is not safe here in the city anymore, and I do not have much time. Is that all right?"

"Oh, sure." I didn't like the tone he was using. I thought everything was good between us, but maybe it wasn't.

He was silent the entire way, other than checking with me once or twice to see if he was running too fast. I told him both times that he could go as fast as he wanted, because his lack of conversation drove me nuts. He was very distant, and I just wanted to get there and find out what the heck was happening between us.

When we arrived, he didn't stop at the cabin, he took me right to the lagoon and waterfall, where we'd taken a sunset horseback ride and swim not so long ago. The sulphurous scent from the hot spring still made me recoil, but I was much more concerned with what Rion had to say, and I soon forgot about it. He laid his cloak out on the frosty ground for us to sit on, and after a few moments of star gazing, he took my hand.

"I do not even know where to start, Melissa."

"First tell me how you found me last night."

Rion's ears perked up, and he chuckled. "It was that body spray you had been wearing. I could smell you a kilometre away. I would have found you anyway, eventually, but that scent made it so much easier…and I am glad, because I might have been too late."

I gulped. "Is he dead?"

Rion nodded. "When he…I lost it. I am sorry. I could not help myself."

I didn't want to know how it happened. The whole ordeal was something I just wanted to forget, so I stared down at the ground and pulled a piece of grass.

"Are you upset with me?"

"No. I just don't know how to feel about it." I turned the grass spear in my fingers. "I guess I'm just glad that I don't have to worry about him coming after me anymore."

"Me, too." We made eye contact then. "I did not realize who he was until I sensed your anger toward him. And it was more than just anger that radiated from you. Your fury was so profound, I knew there was something more besides the fact that he was a *vykhar*. When I looked into your panicking eyes, I swore that your heart whispered to me: "It is *him*.""

I smiled and nudged him. "Maybe it did."

He smiled back. "How is your neck?"

I moved my head around. "A little stiff, but good. Thanks."

"I am glad."

"Did anyone else get injured?"

"No," Rion answered quietly, "but my father had a heart attack shortly after the third explosion."

"Oh my. Is he—"

"He is not doing well," Rion interrupted. "I do not know if he will make it through this calendar year. He has been sick for such a long time."

"I'm so sorry to hear that." I looked out at the water. The rushing falls in the background gave off a mist that chilled me and I shivered. Rion noticed and put his arm around me, and I didn't pass up the opportunity to snuggle a little closer. "Did you really kill all the other *vykhars*?"

"No, that was a lie." Rion pulled up his own piece of grass and put it in his mouth. "When we launched our attack, I insisted that no lives be taken. Instead, we captured them. We are not the monsters the stories make us out to be, Melissa."

"So what did you do with them?"

"The guards took them to the new passages we have been creating in the Eurafrican Third. They are doing manual labour now—lots of it."

I laughed. "That sounds like a first."

He sighed. "It is. I had a hard time restraining myself, but I did. I just did not want all the bloodshed—I have already seen enough for one lifetime."

I took the grass from his mouth and threw it aside when I noticed he was grinding his teeth again. "How do you think they found us?"

He sighed and put his hand on my knee to pull me closer to him. "Andrew found Abby's notebook in the field where they were letting off grenades."

I gasped. I remembered seeing it in her car.

"I told her not to keep that notebook. I wanted her to remember everything. But I realize now, that was asking too much. She was a very busy physician with a more hectic schedule...I should not have put so much pressure on her. It was wrong."

I glared at him. "Not everything is your fault, Rion. You have to stop blaming yourself for everything all the time."

Rion shook his head. "It is my responsibility, Melissa. I am *Leighdur* now. When something goes wrong, it is all on me. I just have to figure out how to deal with it. Sometimes, it keeps me up all night."

I could totally relate. "So what happens now? Is Caine going to know all the entrances? Are we even going to be able to see one another?"

Rion frowned. "That was the whole reason I asked you to come here tonight. We need to talk about *us*."

My heart suddenly jumped into overdrive. "Did you bring me here to break up with me? Is that what this is all about?"

Rion turned himself toward me, and took both of my hands, squeezing tight. I closed my eyes, preparing for the absolute worst.

"I cannot protect you anymore, Melissa…not if you are going to live above."

I didn't like where this was going.

"I have been dismissing what you have said about the danger of us being together, what my brother has been saying, and what my assembly has been saying…" He leaned forward and put his forehead against mine, whispering. "I know I told you that I would never ask you to make a choice, but now things are different. Too many lives have been lost already. We cannot take any more, Melissa. And I will not put my people and allies in jeopardy to pursue my own personal interests."

A tear trickled from his eye, and I could feel his grip on my hands tightening.

"I cannot take you against your will, so what I am trying to say, is I am not going to see you again, after tonight."

This whole day had been such a rollercoaster, and I was conjuring my last bit of strength to speak. I could feel myself beginning to shake. "Rion…"

"I am sorry, Melissa. But you have been right all along. This is just too dangerous." He pulled back and looked at me, as two more tears trickled from his eyes. "If I could get to Caine, I would deal with him, and then the rest of the *vykhars* would have no choice but to surrender. But I cannot get to him. He is too protected. I cannot even get close to his house…"

I sat and listened as his words trampled over my heart.

"…The night of your accident, we had tracked his position to a place not far from where you and I collided, and I was on my way there. I wanted to give myself to him and end the bounty hunt he had created, so my family could be free from danger. That night, no one could stop me, but you did. And...I am glad you did, because you are the best thing that has ever happened to me. My family is thankful for you every day, for keeping me alive and returning my happiness." Rion squeezed his eyes shut. "I feel so blessed, having been given the chance to be your *dharkun*. But I cannot be that anymore. Not if you need to be above, too."

In the heat of the moment, knowing very well he would not like it, I took his face in my hands. I wanted him to look at me. He was shocked, but he stayed very still. And then, without warning, he slowly placed his hands on top of mine; they had permission to stay, for the very first time. His cheeks were soft and fuzzy, like a peach, and I was careful not to move my fingers too much; I didn't know how sensitive the scars would be, even after all this time. I gazed into his eyes as two more tears trickled down his cheeks, over and under my fingertips, and I leaned in and kissed them off. I delicately pressed my lips to all the deep, yet healed, wounds, and whispered, "Take me with you."

Rion's eyes flashed, and he grabbed my wrists and pulled my hands down. "Melissa—you do not know what you are asking."

"I mean it, Rion. Wherever you're going, I want to come. I love my parents, and I love my family and friends, but I can't live without you. It's taken me a few months to come to that realization, but I'm sure now."

"*M'ebesha*—" Rion grabbed my waist and pulled me toward him. Our lips met and I welcomed his mouth against mine. I grabbed his neck and ran my hands down his shoulders, begging him to hold me tighter. When he opened his mouth, I rolled my tongue around his and before I knew it, I was straddling him. He stroked my spine, but when I inched toward him, he held me in place for a moment before gently pushing me away.

"If this is what you want," he said, looking deep into my hopeful eyes, "I would be honoured to take you with me. I would love nothing more than to give you everything you have ever wanted. And after what you have done for my people, you will be welcomed not only as my *wharla*, but with the status of a *leigh-dur's wharla*. A queen."

I kissed him again. "I want you, Rion. I don't need anything else but you."

"You have no idea how much this means to me...." He beamed. "I love you, Melissa. I love you so much."

"I love you, too, Rion. *Li havash nathe*."

His eyes widened and he grinned. "You have no idea how badly I want you when you say that to me."

I bit the knuckle on my first finger, blushing from his comment. "Was it the malion, or the way I said it?"

"Both." He raised his eyebrows a few times. "I think I am going to have to practice controlling myself when you learn to speak malion. For some reason, hearing it from you really does something to me."

"Something good?" I teased.

"Something *really* good."

I laughed as he pulled me close and kissed me once again. It felt so good to be there. I had the sudden urge to be even closer, though it was much too soon to think about that. I ran my hands over his chest as he pulled at my thighs. Things were heating up, and he stopped and licked my upper lip.

"So how soon can you come below with me? Would tomorrow be too soon?" He proceeded to kiss and suck the underside of my jaw.

"Well, I guess that's the one thing that I *am* going to need."

Rion pulled back and raised one eyebrow.

"Time," I elaborated. "I've got so much to do if I'm leaving for good. And I have to make sure that my sister will be around for my mom, because my dad doesn't work from home."

He shook his head. "You cannot tell anyone you are leaving, Melissa. It has to be unannounced—that is the only way. The safest way. You will only put your family in danger by mentioning it."

I sighed.

"It will not be easy, but if you truly want to leave, that is how it has to be done."

I rubbed my temples. "Then what's the maximum amount of time I can have? How long can you wait?"

Rion leaned back on his hands and stared at the ground. "One month. Max. By that time, I will have everything moved to the Eurafrican Third, and then I can come back for you."

I swallowed. It was so soon. "How about three months?"

He shook his head again. "The longer I wait around, the more risk I take. It has to be sooner than three months. I am sorry."

"Two months."

"*One* month."

"Come on, Rion. You've got to give me more time than that."

He smiled. "Thirty days."

I smacked his shoulder and glared at him, though it was hard, because I was trying not to smile. "What next, four weeks?"

"Yes, that was next," he chuckled, snatching my wrists to prevent me from smacking him again.

I bit my lip and huffed. "All right. Let go. One month. I'll figure something out. Just don't leave without me, okay?" He laughed again as I stood up and brushed myself off. "I can't talk about this anymore. I need to go for a swim or something. I'm starting to have anxiety overload. I need an hour off before I implode!"

"Well, before we do that, I have something for you..." He peered into a pocket in his cloak. "...and...yes, that is about right." Rion stood up, towering above me, and reached in. "This belongs to you, my precious *wharla*."

He held out my *ika* flower. But it wasn't a bud anymore, it was in full bloom. Its glowing, hot pink anthers and green stigma shone brightly under the moonlit sky, surrounded by pointed, sparkling aquamarine petals. The saccharine scent of it immediately caught my nostrils.

I took it from his hands. "Oh, Rion, it's so beautiful."

He smiled. "I know. I never thought I would live to see ours in full bloom."

"Well, don't put it back in your pocket. I don't want it to get crushed."

"Do not worry, it will not." He placed it in my palm. "It looks delicate, but it is actually very resilient. You could step on it, and it would spring back to its natural form in seconds."

I felt the petals in my hand. True, they were very rigid, but also soft between my fingers. It was hard to tear my eyes away from the glittering glow it emitted, which illuminated the area around us like a night light. I set it down on his cloak and looked out onto the water. I was still chilly, and the thought of dip in warm water was inviting.

"Wanna go for a swim?" I swiftly ripped off my shirt. I only had a bra underneath, but that didn't matter to me anymore.

"Uh…sure. Yes." He sat there wide-eyed while I stripped down.

"Then what are you waiting for?" I whisked off my pants—yes, I was in just a bra and underwear, but I could've cared less—and fled towards the warm water, eager for him to follow.

"Hey! Wait up!"

The water was hot, but I didn't waste any time before jumping right in. It was freaking cold outside. "Hurry up then, because I need my floatie!"

Rion raised his first finger. "One floatie, coming right up!" He undressed to his boxer shorts, and was beside me seconds later. I wrapped myself around him as he treaded water for us, but hovering in the water together didn't last long, because we were soon making out. Seconds later, I was trying to wriggle out of my bra, keeping as close to him as possible to prevent submerging my head.

Rion put a stop to that instantly. "No, *Melissa*. Wait."

"What? I thought you'd want to have a little skinny dip."

"Save it, *m'ebesha*."

"Do you want me to speak malion again?" I kidded. "'Cause I've picked up a few phrases, you know."

"No!" he said through an almost-snort. "Save it for a more special night. Tonight is going to be magical, but *that* is something

346

I do not want to rush into. And we are going to have forever, so let us wait."

I never thought I'd be so dissatisfied to hear those words come out of his mouth—he was looking so very delicious right now. I smiled and pecked his mouth. "Okay. So what do you want to do?"

He raised his eyebrows a few times, with that Cheshire cat smile on his face again. Then he took my hand and looked closely at my nails. "Do you like how I painted your nails?"

My eyes widened and I smiled. "*You* did them?"

He kissed my fingers and smiled back at me. "I actually enjoyed it, though it would have been more fun if you were awake to see it."

"I love the colour."

"I thought you would. I had to send Charlotte out to get the right shade of blue."

"Just like my *ika* flower, right?"

"I wanted you to think of it when you woke up." He kissed my neck again. "At least I hoped that you would."

"I did...okay, stop!" I said through a giggle when he tickled my collarbone with his nose, even though I really didn't want him to stop.

"Can I show you something?"

"Like what?"

"Like how to swim underwater."

I leaned away. "Not a chance. Last time, I choked."

He chuckled. "The idea is to breathe out, not in, *Melissa*."

I rolled my eyes. "Not funny. At all."

"When you need air, I will give it to you. That is, if you need any air at all, because we will not be down for too long."

I tried not to panic. "I don't know..."

"Come on, *m'ebesha*." He grabbed my waist, bundled me against him, and wiped my hair away from my eyes. "You trust me, right?"

"Yes!" I exclaimed.

"Then hold your breath, and close your eyes. I will do the work, just hold on to me, and do not let go."

347

"Don't worry." I wrapped my legs around him. "I won't. Ever."

Rion's eyes softened, and he smiled wide. "Ready?"

I nodded quickly.

"One…"

I closed my eyes.

"Two…"

I took a deep breath.

"Three…"

Rion pressed his lips to mine, and I held on to him for dear life, as we disappeared beneath the surface.

Acknowledgments

I want to send a tremendous thank you to those who joined me on this journey. Without their support, their expertise, their guidance and reassurance, I may never have had the self-confidence to publish:

my editor, Jessica Lowdon, for taking on this new author, teaching me her secrets about craft, ensuring every question had an answer, and then polishing *Beneath the Surface* until it sparkled like a diamond;

my copy editor from Purple Pen Editing, Micheline Brodeur, for her time, superior vigilance, and for bringing attention to the smallest yet crucial details of my manuscript—you and Jessica made a brilliant editing team;

my marvellous Auntie Necey, for her thrice-over, hush-hush's kept to herself, and time spent making sure every word counted—hugs and cheek kisses;

my best friends, first readers and cheering squad, Kim,
Tash, Leigh, Kristina, Brooke, Leslee, my second family
at Wave and my sister Leanne—you guys ROCK;

fellow authors Nora Snowdon, Eileen Cook, Kate Austin,
R.G. Hart, T. Rae Mitchell, Susan Lyons, Charlene Groome,
Roxanne Snowpek, Carolyn Jursa and Lisa Hatton for
lending their knowledge, a helping hand, a listening ear
and reply to my inbox within seconds of my questions;

my wonderful writing friends at RWA-GVC and the
Murrayville Writer's Group, for their ongoing support, their
honest opinions, and for being my sounding board when I
was ready to throw in the towel on a bazillion occasions;

Carmen Sum, Paula Duncan, Mathieu Robitaille
and everyone at Friesen Press for making my
pathway to publication a smooth one;

Kim Killion and her magnificent team at The Killion
Group, for bringing the book cover I'd dreamed
of to screen with impeccable precision;

my cousin Jo, for her two cents—which
made perfect sense—love ya, girl;

Vice Principal Doris Sandri and the staff and stu-
dents of Gladstone Secondary, for making me feel
welcome, answering numerous questions, and showing
me what makes your school extraordinary;

Mom and Dad for your unwavering love and support,
for being my number one fans from day one, and for

assuring me that I hadn't gone off the deep end when
I told you what was going on inside my head;

my husband Chad, who soon realized he was going to have
to share me with my friends below (I know you like to have
me all to yourself), thank you for understanding and support-
ing my dream. I love you to the furthest star…and back;

my two beautiful children, Charlotte and Nathan, for making
me laugh hysterically everyday, and for playing so nicely
together when mommy needed a malion moment;

Jessita Reyes, Paul Cantelon, Carter Burwell, Amy Lee, Ben
Moody, David Hodges, Alecia 'Pink' Moore and Billy Mann
for writing the most beautiful music and lyrics I've ever heard,
including *Moon on the Water, The Execution, This is Your World,
Anywhere* and *Glitter in the Air*, the songs which I took me away
to my storyland below and abetted many blocks along the way;

the courageous and astonishing auburn, a champion and
survivor in my eyes, who shared with me her teenage story of
abuse and assault through shed tears over cups of her favourite
white hot chocolate, and then trusted me enough to keep her
secret safe, while ensuring the facts and fine points of this story
rang true—thank you, little brave one, with all of my heart;

and finally…my remarkable and beloved hero, Rion, for
sticking around more than decade (haunting my dreams
and scaring the hell out of me at first, mind you), long
enough for me to realize you had a story to tell, and then
long enough for me to find the courage to start typing it.

Un havankarogard…li havash nathe.

Every two and a half minutes, somewhere in North America, someone is sexually assaulted. One in three are female, one in six are male.

If you have been a victim of a sexual crime, please reach out for help. You are worth it. There are people out there who love and care about you, and they want to help. They are ready to listen. They are ready to support you.

They believe you.

Please pick up the phone. Right now.

Kids Help Phone: 1-800-668-6868

RAINN (Rape, Abuse & Incest National Network) 1-800-656-HOPE

National Domestic Violence Hotline 1-800-799-SAFE

Call your local hospital or police detachment

Or just dial 9-1-1

Think of how many minutes have passed since you started reading this book.

YOU ARE NOT ALONE.

Biography

Miranda Rae Carter has lived in British Columbia her whole life, and is a self-proclaimed home-bug. She spends most of her time doing what she loves, and that is being a mom and wife—and trying to master the art of cooking. The rest of her time is divided between looking in mouths and writing. For more information on Miranda and her malion series, visit her at www.mirandarae-carter.com, Facebook and Twitter @themaliongirl.

CPSIA information can be obtained at www.ICGtesting.com
Printed in the USA
LVOW08s2344271013

358649LV00003B/11/P